Edge of Darkness

Also in J.T. Geissinger's Night Prowler series

Shadow's Edge

Edge of Oblivion

Rapture's Edge

J.T. GEISSINGER

EDGE of DARKNESS

A NIGHT PROWLER NOVEL

 Montlake
Romance

Text copyright © 2013 J.T. Geissinger, Inc.

Printed in the United States of America

Published by Montlake Romance, Seattle

www.apub.com

ISBN-13: 9781477848944

ISBN-10: 1477848940

Library of Congress Control Number: 2013910956

Printed in the United States of America

To Jay,
for making me laugh and having my back.

Think not you can direct the course of love,
for love, if it finds you worthy, directs your course.

Khalil Gibran, *The Prophet*

PROLOGUE

March 31, 20—
Easter Sunday

Hello, human.

I know your kind normally address you as President or Prime Minister, Chancellor or Chairman, or even that most amusing title Supreme Leader—as if you, mere Man, could ever be supreme over us—but I have no use for your silly titles. They are as meaningless to me as your names, nearly as distasteful as your very existence. To me you are one thing and one thing only: human.

Enemy.

I acknowledge there are those among us who disagree with that label, fond as they are of your foibles and farces, foolishly tolerant of your small, petty lives. I imagine they find you charming and adorable in the way of newborn kittens: bumbling about on unsteady legs, blind and weak and helpless. You are all of those things, to be sure, but I admit your charm escapes me, the same way the charm of a virus escapes me. In fact, of all the living things on this planet you resemble a virus the most closely. You infiltrate where you are not wanted. You consume far more than you produce. You proliferate with the mindless speed of a bacterium. You take and you take and you take, until all that is left is diseased and ruined, and then you move on and begin the process all over again.

You have ruled this planet far too long. I will remedy that.

Beginning today.

In our eagerness to be left alone, we have allowed your sickness to spread. We have turned a blind eye to the evil of your ways. We have lived in secrecy and in silence for millennia, learning to live alongside you, learning to dress and eat and speak like you, learning to hide.

Who are we, you ask?

We are Vapor and predator and quick, slinking death, relics of an age when Nature ruled and beauty abounded and magic still lived and breathed. Born in equatorial Africa where all of life originated, we are the firstborn children of Mother Earth, and her most splendid creation.

We have many Gifts you can only dream of.

We can smell a bird on the wing miles away in the winter sky and know if it is hawk or pigeon or starling. We can hear the heartbeats of all the small, unseen creatures, foraging under fragrant beds of leaves or burrowing tunnels into damp earth or clinging to the boughs of trees. We can hunt in the dark and outrun a gazelle and rip out your throat with sharp fangs before you even know you're in danger. We hold the power of transformation from thought, and I've heard it said that to look upon even the least beautiful of us is to see the face of an angel.

We are Ikati. We are your superiors in every way.

You'll understand that much more clearly in a moment.

You're about to make history, you see. Undoubtedly you think you already have, with your wealth and your title and your "power," but all of that is nothing in comparison to the everlasting fame I will bestow upon you.

The kind of fame one can only achieve with a spectacular, unforgettable death.

So be quick now, look up from these words—do you see him, the lithe creature approaching on silent feet? Never mind how he stole past your guards and your pathetic security systems—do you see his cunning smile, the bloodlust in his eyes? Does your pulse quicken, realizing these breaths you draw will be your last?

Mine does. I'm with you even now, here in your final moments, living it all in my imagination just as you are living it in the flesh. I've waited a lifetime for this, and I am willing to admit I owe you some thanks.

Because you, by your death, and the deaths of all the other human leaders like you who are at this very moment also reading a copy of this letter, are going to help me rule the world.

Ciao, enemy mine.

I hope you rot in hell.

Caesar Cardinalis
King of the Ikati

ONE

Beautiful Stranger

The first time Ember laid eyes on the man who would destroy her life, she knew with a sharp, blood-curdling certainty, like a knife shoved between her ribs, that he was—in a word—dangerous.

It wouldn't be until much later that she found out just how dangerous he really was, but on that particular evening, amidst the chill of a February thunderstorm, she was standing where she stood six days a week, from ten in the morning until six at night, behind the polished oak counter of Antiquarian Books, the snug little bookstore in the old Gothic quarter of the city. It was near closing time, and through the tall windows that flanked the door she saw the rain sheeting down in a black, sideways slant, bouncing high enough off the uneven cobblestones of the narrow street outside to indicate it wasn't letting up anytime soon.

Ember was sick of rain. Sick of winter.

Sick of pretty much everything.

It had been a bad day in a worse month in an even worse few years, and she was tired to her bones. Though only twenty-four, she felt decades older, having already survived things that might have sent other people less stubborn straight to their graves. She never indulged in luxuries like self-pity, but she couldn't escape the bone deep fatigue that would creep up on her on nights like this.

Rain held bad memories for her. So did that melancholy hour just after sunset, when the last happy rays of daylight are devoured by the hungry, spreading gloom of night. So the moment the shop door opened and the little welcoming silver bell sang its merry jingle, all she wanted to do was go home, take a hot bath, and crawl into bed.

She looked up to see who'd come in, and it was as if an invisible hand reached out and seized her heart.

A man stood inside the doorway, shaking the rain from a large black umbrella. He closed it, lowered it into the antique iron stand nearby, smoothed the collar of his beautifully tailored suit jacket, and slowly, deliberately, gazed around the store. Tall and dark-haired, broad-shouldered and substantial yet somehow simultaneously lean and dancer-lithe, he was both forbidding and fascinating.

Assassin, she thought, and a little chill ran down her spine.

It wasn't his clothing—a tailored charcoal suit that screamed bespoke, black Ferragamo loafers polished to a mirror gleam, a platinum and diamond Patek Phillipe watch she knew from her stepmother's rotating stable of

wealthy boyfriends cost more than she'd earn in a decade—
or his quiet confidence, or the way he glided noiselessly as
he moved away from the door, those gleaming loafers silent
against the floor as if they never touched the ground. It
wasn't even his general mien of elegant, menacing mystery,
or the way the air seemed to gather around him, tense and
expectant like a held breath.

It was his eyes.

Electric, smoldering, *unearthly* green, rimmed in the
kohl of thick lashes and heavy-lidded as if he'd very recently found his satisfaction in some lusty woman's bed, his
eyes held promises of sin and carnal pleasures. They also
held a distinct, ominous, unspoken warning—*Danger*—
which offered an irresistible opposition to their seductive
invitation.

His eyes were, simply, stunning.

So was the rest of him, and she wasn't the only one who
thought so. The swath of gaping women he left in his wake
as he slowly threaded his way through the clusters of low
tables and book displays toward the counter where she
stood was ample evidence of that.

Because Ember was the kind of girl who despised the
kind of man who reduced otherwise intelligent women to
gelatinous puddles of blathering goo, she hated him on
sight.

Why should he be prettier than the prettiest woman in
the room? And possibly the world? Really, it was indecent.
Unless he made his living as a model or an escort, no self-
respecting man should pay so much attention to his wardrobe. Or his grooming. His hair, jet-black and glossy,
trimmed short on the sides and in back but with a studied
bit of tousle up top, was as perfect as the rest of him.

Maybe he's an actor, she thought, watching him approach, his stride liquid and leisurely. He did have a definite Pierce Brosnan/Daniel Craig kind of thing going on, though he was younger, and infinitely prettier than either. She pictured him jumping from a helicopter to the roof of a speeding train to engage in a fistfight with a knife-wielding psychopath, emerging after it was done without a speck of grime or a single wrinkle on that beautiful suit.

Or maybe he was gay? It was so hard to tell; these Spanish men were much more sophisticated and better groomed than the boys she'd known back home in the States. Ember wished her friend Asher was here to rule definitively on the matter. His gaydar was far better calibrated than her own.

Green Eyes stopped in front of the counter. He looked at her. In a commanding, masculine tenor refined by a cultured British accent, perfectly suited for ordering terrified servants to do his bidding, he said, "*Casino Royale.*"

Ember almost laughed. Instead she blurted, "You've got to be kidding me."

Casino Royale? The book that launched James Bond into pop icon status? The coincidence that she'd been imagining him as exactly that was, in itself, incredible. She wondered if Green Eyes was a mind reader. In addition to being a beauty queen.

King. Whatever.

The corners of his full lips lifted, the faintest chagrin. "As it happens, I'm not. I'm looking for a first edition, hardcover, 1953. I was informed this is the best rare bookstore in the city." He paused, let his gaze drift over her plain brown cable-knit sweater, her baggy jeans, her scuffed running shoes, long faded from their original white to a dingy, dusty gray. When his gaze rested again on her face, he murmured, "Or perhaps I was misinformed."

Wondering if this was some kind of joke, Ember studied him. Depending on the condition of the book and the dust jacket, a first edition copy of *Casino Royale* would cost somewhere between fifty thousand and one hundred fifty thousand euro. With the economy the way it was, she hadn't had a sale like that in . . . well, too long. She decided to call his bluff.

"No. you weren't misinformed. It'll have to be tomorrow, though."

His brows lifted.

"Storage," she replied, by way of explanation. Antiquarian Books didn't keep the rarest and most valuable books on the shelves for the general public to paw over. They were kept in acid-free book boxes, on rust-resistant metal shelves, in a temperature and humidity-controlled storage facility on the outskirts of the city. She was tempted to add a churlish, "Duh," but held her tongue. "What condition are you interested in?"

"Perfect," he replied instantly, as if it should have been obvious.

Of course he'd want perfect. From the looks of him, she assumed perfect was all he'd been accustomed to, all his life.

In swift assessment, his blazing green eyes narrowed. "Irritating you, am I?"

That startled her. Ember was certain she hadn't curled her lip, snickered, or otherwise given physical proof of what she'd been thinking. Though she wasn't the superstitious type, the vague notion that maybe this pretty, pampered stranger could read minds deepened into something nearer certainty.

"Um, no. Of course not." She cleared her throat and tried on her best "interested professional" face. He was still a customer after all, and she had to be polite. The bookstore and rare book dealing business her father started had been teetering on the verge of bankruptcy since he died three years ago. Well, technically since he opened it, five years ago. Her late father, an artist and daydreamer who had a fetish for collecting books, wasn't a very good businessman. And if she was being honest, she wasn't really up to the task either. She'd inherited both his artistic ability and his lack of business acumen. Music had always been her thing.

Until it wasn't.

So if Mr. Bedroom Eyes Assassin wanted to spend his money, she'd better be nicer to him. She thought she'd have to warn him, however, just to be fair. "You're looking at a substantial investment, though. A first edition in perfect condition is likely to run you—"

"I understand. Shall I leave a deposit?"

He hadn't even waited for her to say the price. He didn't seem the least bit interested in the price. Ember didn't know if he was being arrogant, or if he actually was one of those people who never had to ask the cost of anything. Fascinated in spite of herself, she wondered what that would be like. Awesome, no doubt. Completely awesome.

And she could barely pay the rent.

Her dislike took a sharp turn toward envy. Then she was irritated with herself for being so petty, and even more annoyed with him for making her mad at herself.

Before she could even open her mouth to answer him, his eyes had narrowed again. But he didn't seem angry, only bemused. "Whatever it is I'm doing to annoy you, I sincerely apologize. It's not intentional."

Her "interested professional" expression vanished, replaced, she was sure, by one of obvious shock. Face flaming, she stammered, "No . . . it's . . . I'm not . . . I'm the one who should apologize. I'm being rude."

Inside, she was being rude. But how the hell did *he* know that?

Bedroom Eyes Assassin had officially creeped her out.

He reached out a hand toward her, but then seemed to think better of it as he abruptly lifted it to his head and ran it through his hair, rumpling the artfully arranged dark strands. He sighed, let his hand drop back to his side. "I'll just leave my information then, yes?" Without waiting for an answer, he reached for the cup of pens on the counter beside the register. On the white notepad next to the collection of pens, he wrote something in swift, precise strokes. "Call me when it arrives. I'm leaving my credit card information as well; charge whatever deposit you feel is fair."

He straightened and held out the paper. Ember took it between her fingers.

Christian McLoughlin, it read, followed by a series of numbers, credit card and telephone.

Christian. She wondered if his friends called him Chris for short, then immediately dismissed it. No nicknames, she was sure of it. No informalities. His own mother probably called him Mr. McLoughlin. Or possibly sir.

She wiped the thought away, worried he might guess it again, and tucked the paper into the back pocket of her jeans. "A deposit isn't necessary."

He waited silently, watching her with those preternatural eyes. A passing car's headlights slanted through the front windows and reflected off the long mirror behind the counter, and a sliver of light caught his eyes. She imagined for a moment that something in those green depths changed. Something tangible went aqueous and ephemeral, as if she were looking at the surface of the sea.

A tingle of fear raised the hair on the back of her neck.

"You should see what you're paying for," she explained, lifting her hand to the delicate chain she always wore around her neck.

It was an unconscious habit, something she did when preoccupied or upset, and one his sharp eyes didn't miss. He watched her twist the two gold rings on the chain between her fingers and his face softened. He nodded, as if he'd made up his mind about something.

"I'm not the kind of man who has to see things to believe in them," he said, still watching her twist the necklace.

This flew in the face of the opinion she'd formed of him in the few short moments since he'd approached the counter. He looked like a man who wouldn't believe anything that wasn't written in a contract, visible to the naked eye, or otherwise provable beyond a shadow of a doubt.

His gaze found its way back to hers. Keen and penetrating, it fixed her in place, made her forget her wariness her dislike, her distrust of strangers. She said impulsively, "The only things worth believing in are things you can see. Anything else is just self-delusion."

He seemed to take that as some kind of challenge, because his eyes flashed, then a slow smile spread across his face. "Hold out your hand and close your eyes."

"What?" Startled, Ember took a step back.

He chuckled, then said, "I don't bite. Unless, that is, you want me to."

That brought the blood back to her cheeks. Was he *flirting* with her?

No, men like him didn't flirt with girls like her. Plain girls. Ruined girls. Girls with one good hand and two left feet and a lifetime of could-have-beens choking their throats until they wanted to scream.

"Just hold out your hand," he insisted, his voice low and persuasive. "Trust me."

He said those last two words as if they were a dare, and he looked at her that way, too.

Trust you? Ha. As if.

However, because he was in possession of what was apparently a bottomless bank account and she needed the sale, Ember silently proffered her right hand, palm up.

His smile grew mocking. "Halfway there. Close your eyes."

It was her turn to narrow her eyes at him. She glanced around the store. There were a dozen people within eyesight; the women's book club that met every Wednesday sat at a table near the back of the store—all six of them still gaping at Christian—a few more customers were browsing the aisles. She was probably safe.

When her gaze fell back on Christian, his lips were pressed together but his eyes were bright and amused, as if he was trying to hold back a laugh.

Let him laugh. She knew from experience that you were never safe, even in the most familiar of places. Life had a way of knocking you down and spitting in your face when you least expected it, then cutting off your legs at the knee when you tried to stand back up.

Think of the sale, Ember. Think of your rent. Indulge him and get a payday or piss him off and get evicted.

She huffed a short, impatient breath, then closed her eyes.

She didn't really know what to expect, but what she definitely *wasn't* expecting was a slow, sliding stroke of his finger, feather-light, from her inner wrist down the center of her palm.

His touch jolted through her like a bolt of lightning.

She gasped. He warned softly, "Eyes shut." So she kept them shut and let the feeling of his finger languidly sliding against her skin sizzle through her, snapping her nerves alight like a thousand switches had been flipped to "on" inside her body. She became exquisitely aware of her breathing, the warmth in her cheeks, the smell of old books and the sweet musk of the cone of incense burning in a far corner of the shop, the low murmurs of the book club ladies and the rain drumming outside on the cobblestones. Every sensation was heightened because her eyes were closed, blocking out the room and all its color, light, and distractions.

In a dark, soft voice, Bedroom Eyes said, "You can't see me touching you, correct?"

Breathless, Ember nodded.

"So how do you know I am?"

Because I feel it in places in my body I barely remember having.

She shoved that thought aside and aloud said, "Because I can feel it."

His finger withdrew. The electric tingle abruptly ceased. When she opened her eyes Christian was staring at her. As she stared back at him, some unknown emotion fleetingly crossed his face, hardening those perfect features, darkening his eyes. A muscle twitched in his square jaw.

"That's how you know something's real. It doesn't matter if you can see it. Your eyes can and will play tricks on you. But if you can *feel* it, it's real."

There was a lesson here, but Ember wasn't sure if it was in any way related to what he'd just said. It seemed more likely her body had just tried to tell her something, the same thing his eyes had told her when she first saw him. *Come closer* and S*tay away.*

She swallowed, embarrassed by her heated cheeks, disturbed by her fluttering heartbeat. She straightened and looked him in the eye. "And this relates to your first edition *Casino Royale . . .* how?"

The smile returned, dazzling in its dark, knowing perfection. "Because I can trust you not to swindle me. I can *feel* it."

She laughed a little disbelieving laugh, unsure if he was toying with her or being serious. Either way, it probably didn't matter. She was going to give him his book and never see him again.

And good riddance. She didn't need a beauty queen—king—panty-melter like him hanging around her bookstore. There'd be so much ogling going on, no one would ever buy a damn book again.

"Okay, then, Mr. McLoughlin. I'll call you tomorrow."

From the corner of her eye, Ember saw Sofia approach. One of the book club ladies, she was sixtyish and matronly, with a stout build and an alarming, tall gray bouffant coiffure. Her lack of a youthful figure didn't seem to be standing in the way of her determination to get an introduction. She sauntered forward like a paunchy lioness looking at an easy meal, her eyes roving all over Christian as if she was deciding which part to sink her teeth into first.

Ember turned her back on him, strode resolutely to the end of the counter, and reached Sofia before she could do something embarrassing. She'd been widowed more than ten years, and never missed the opportunity to stalk a young, good-looking man. Ember had seen it end badly too many times before, and was determined to spare her from another humiliation.

"Do you ladies need a refill on your tea?"

Ember tried to communicate with her eyes that Sofia should go back to her table. But, as luck would have it, Sofia took a wrong step and twisted her ankle on an uneven floorboard Ember had been meaning to fix as soon as she had the money. Eyes wide, hands outflung, Sofia pitched forward with a small, surprised cry. It happened so fast Ember didn't have time to react.

Christian, however, did.

Somehow, from all the way down at the end of the long counter, he was there in time to catch Sofia before she fell. With a hand under one arm, he steadied her and brought her back to her feet with a murmured, "Watch your step, madam. These old floorboards can be treacherous."

Sofia, wide-eyed, hand fluttering around her neck like a big, pale moth looking for a place to land, breathed, "Oh, yes, they can. How silly of me. Thank you, Mr . . . ?"

He didn't take the bait. He simply smiled down at her— incredibly, she simpered and blushed—then released her arm and turned his keen gaze to Ember.

"Tomorrow, then."

She nodded, slowly, calculating the time and steps it would take to appear where he had, seconds ago. She didn't think it could be done. But . . . it had.

"Tomorrow," Ember repeated. It almost sounded like a threat.

But Christian's smile grew wider and his eyes crinkled, as if he were enjoying a private joke. "See you then, September."

He turned and, with a dozen pairs of eyes watching, made his way to the door. He collected his umbrella and went outside, pausing for a moment on the sidewalk to open it. Then he took a few steps forward and melted like a phantom into the rainy night.

Beside her, Sofia exhaled her breath in a gust. Fanning herself with one hand, she said in Spanish, "My God, sweetheart! Who was *that*?"

"James Bond," replied Ember with frown.

Sofia blinked at her, confused.

"Never mind. Are you all right?"

Sofia nodded, still distracted. She looked back at the door Christian had disappeared through. "So how do you know this James Bond?"

"I don't. He was just looking for a book. I never met him before tonight."

Sofia turned toward Ember. Her brown eyes were full of questions. She pointed a finger at the small gold nameplate pinned to Ember's sweater and said, "Then how did he know your full name?"

With a sinking feeling in the pit of her stomach, Ember glanced down at the nameplate.

Ember, it read, in clear bold type. Of course it did, because Ember never went by her given name. But Christian, the beautiful stranger disgorged and swallowed again by the night, had somehow known it.

How?

She glanced up at the door of the shop, looked out the windows into the sideways slanting rain, and thought that was a very, very good question.

TWO

Quicksand

Ember awoke early the next morning with no foreboding premonitions about the day. The rain had tapered off during the night—thank God—and through the windows of her apartment the sky loomed a perfect, cloudless blue. In the distance the round mosaics that topped the spires of Gaudí's Sagrada Família cathedral glinted red and yellow and green in the morning sun like enormous bowls of fruit, and all of Barcelona—labyrinth streets, medieval churches, plazas and palm trees and the shimmering azure strip of the Mediterranean sea in the distance—was laid out like a sumptuous feast.

The view from her bedroom was the absolute best thing about her apartment. That and the rooftop terrace, where she took her coffee every morning and tried not to think about the past.

"*Americana!*" a male voice shouted from the street below. "*Hermosa Americana! Estas despierto?*"

The worst thing about her apartment lived downstairs.

"No, Dante, I am not awake," Ember muttered, eyeing the window. She carefully edged away from it, imagining her elderly landlord standing with arms akimbo in his white undershirt, paisley silk robe, black dress socks, and white slippers in the middle of the plaza, neck craned back as he stared up at her window and called to her. He was totally unconcerned with disturbing anyone else in the vicinity, or with how he might look, black toupee askew and hairy shins on display. One of the reasons her rent was so cheap was because she gave Dante English lessons, but said rent was several days past due—again—and judging by the sound of it, and the way he'd called her gorgeous as he did whenever he was going to ask for money, the subject was about to come up.

Again.

She crossed to the secondhand wood console table near the front door and picked up the piece of paper from where she'd left it last night when she arrived home.

Christian McLoughlin. Even his handwriting looked rich.

"Okay Mr. Moneybags," she said sourly, staring down at it. "Time to put up or shut up."

A sharp knock on the front door startled her so much she jumped.

"Hey, delinquent. You in there?" a voice whispered through the wood.

Ember heaved a sigh of relief and shoved the paper in her pocket. She wore jeans again today, though different ones from yesterday. She wasn't going to have Moneybags thinking she dressed any differently for him than she did every other day. Even if he was rich and sexy and . . . irritating. Let all the other females fall at his feet, her dignity was about the only thing she had left. And it wasn't for sale.

Well, it *mostly* wasn't for sale. She'd risen early so she could get to the storage facility and retrieve a certain expensive tome for a certain odd, otherworldly, over-confident customer. But that hardly counted.

At least that's what she was telling herself, anyway.

Quickly and quietly, trying to make as little noise as possible, Ember cracked the door ajar and peeked out into the hallway.

"Need a quick getaway?" Asher whispered.

Her neighbor from across the hall peered in, brown eyes sparkling merrily behind a pair of trendy glasses, a crooked, mischievous smile on his face. An expat like herself—originally from Boston—he worked as a sportswriter for the local paper. He was tall, athletic, and deeply fabulous, and also one of the smartest, funniest and most interesting people she'd ever met. He knew about books, art, politics, music, how to make you laugh just when you needed it, and how to stay quiet when words could only make things worse. Asher was the kind of person who made you feel smarter and more interesting just by association.

An added bonus: his apartment had a staircase leading down to the back alley. She'd made good use of it to escape from Dante on more than one occasion.

"You heard, huh?"

He snickered. "Honey, everyone within a five-block radius heard. Dante's got a voice that could wake the dead.

C'mon, hurry before he gets tired of yelling in the street and comes up for a little one-on-one."

He dashed back across the hallway and held open the door to his apartment, gesturing for her to follow.

Ember grabbed her house keys and her handbag from the console table, scanned the hallway left and right, pulled the door shut, locked it behind her, and darted across the corridor into Asher's apartment. His door slid shut behind her with a near-silent *snick*.

"You're a lifesaver, Ash," she breathed, leaning against the closed door.

He made a wry face and drawled, "Well, if you're going to compare me to candy, I'd rather be a lollipop if you know what I mean."

On the television hung above the fireplace, a newscaster was saying something about a reward of one million euros for information leading to the capture of a terrorist. Asher clicked the power off with the remote control on the coffee table, then crossed to the kitchen. He poured a shot of vodka into a highball glass and added tomato juice, Worcestershire sauce, and lemon juice. After swallowing a long draught of the concoction and sighing in pleasure, he lifted the glass in her direction. "Bloody Mary?"

"Ash, it's eight o'clock in the morning. On a Thursday."

He rolled his eyes. "Which is why I'm not having wine, darling. Don't be a pill. I know you don't like to drink but a little sip here and there won't kill you."

An old wound, scabbed but never scarred, still raw and bloody just beneath the surface, peeled open. The first wave of panic left her breathless as it tightened around her chest like a vise. She felt alternately hot then cold, and struggled to keep her face straight, her knees from buckling and sending her sliding down to the floor.

"Sweetie, you look pale. Are you feeling all right?"

Asher had lowered his drink to the counter and was staring at her with wide eyes, his expression concerned. She wanted to say, *All right is something I will never be again,* but instead she forced a shaky smile and nodded.

"I'm fine. I just forgot to eat breakfast. Low blood sugar." She pushed away from the door and walked across his living room, toward the little back patio with its narrow metal staircase, twisting down to the yard below.

"Let me get you something to eat before you go—"

"No, it's okay." Ember yanked open the glass sliding door. "Thanks for saving me. I'll see you later."

She slammed the door shut behind her and turned to the stairs, but not before she saw the look of surprise on Asher's face.

And hurt.

He wouldn't understand, though. He couldn't. It wasn't as if she would ever tell him what happened, because she didn't speak about it with anyone anymore. After a dozen different therapists over the years, she'd learned long ago that airing your sad stories didn't help you heal. Nothing helped. There were things that just couldn't be fixed.

Some bridges, once burned, were burned down forever.

Ember took the stairs three at a time and set off down the alley at a run.

The call came at precisely ten o'clock, just as Christian was reaching for the phone. He pulled the cell from his coat pocket and stared at it a moment, looking at the number on the screen.

It was September. Having not five minutes ago looked up the phone number to the book store, *he'd* just been about to call *her*.

It was nothing, it was less than nothing, but Christian very firmly believed coincidences were anything but, so he stared at the phone for a few moments longer before finally answering. He held the phone to his ear, listening.

"Um . . . hello?"

Her voice on the other end of the line was tentative. She was, no doubt, wondering why he hadn't said the same thing himself.

"Good morning, Ember," he said, watching a russet falcon far off in the distance soar over a stand of Aleppo pines. His new home was situated deep in the Parc de Colleserola, a vast, forested, natural preserve in the mountain range that rose above the city of Barcelona. On any given day he saw wild boar, genets, stone martens, rabbits, and an extensive array of birds.

All the creatures of the forest skittered away from him in terror, of course, even the huge and vicious wild boars, but the place reminded him of his real home. Of the wild, ancient woods at Sommerley that he knew as intimately as his own face in the mirror, and missed with an ache in his chest that felt carnivorous.

"I have your book," Ember said in her straightforward American way, and Christian smiled. The accent he found so charming lent every vowel a blunt vigor, nothing at all like his own *Downton Abbey* languor he thought made him sound like an overbred plonker in comparison.

But it wasn't her accent that had his thoughts returning to her again and again last night after he'd left the store.

She wasn't the prettiest girl Christian had ever seen—in fact she seemed determined to be plain. Her modest way of dressing, her unstyled hair, and her lack of makeup or jewelry all screamed *I'm invisible!* But there was something different about her, something indefinable, which caught and held his attention. Something about the eyes, perhaps—wide and brown and piercingly intelligent—or maybe it was the way her dark eyebrows, operating independently, seemed able to indicate disbelief, amusement, or, as they did frequently as she looked at him, deep disdain, all with a single swift arch.

Even her eyebrows were intelligent. Christian had the vague, discomforting feeling this girl with the clever eyebrows might be the kind of girl who knew people's secrets.

She might even know *his* secrets. What a goddamn disaster *that* would be.

"Good. I'll be in today to collect it." On impulse, he asked, "Where are you from, originally?"

"Originally? My mother's womb," she replied a little tartly, and his smile grew deeper. He found her inexplicable dislike of him intriguing. It had radiated from her in waves yesterday at the store, little *zing*s of irritation that felt like nettles against his skin. He didn't normally have that particular effect on women, and it surprised him. It made him want to change her mind.

"How interesting. We have that in common."

Through the phone came a very unladylike snort. "Really? You're from my mother's womb, too? We must've had different fathers because you sure don't look like you're from his side of the family."

He tipped his head back and laughed. Crossing through the study, his valet Corbin paused mid-stride, blinked at him in surprise, then continued on his way.

Christian was known for many things, but laughing was not one of them. Especially over the past few years.

"I meant what part of the States."

She paused before answering. Christian sensed her irritation through the line, and wondered again why she didn't like him. And why she didn't like answering personal questions.

"New Mexico. Taos."

He waited for more, but when no further details were forthcoming, said, "Beautiful country there, I understand. Big art scene."

On the other end of the phone, her silence was deafening.

He cleared his throat. "There's a famous music school there, too, if I'm not mis—"

"I've got two copies of *Casino Royale* for you to look at," she said, her voice terse and unhappy. "We're open until six."

Then the phone went dead in his hand. Christian, staring down at it, wondered if there was something more to her dislike of him. Something to do with her avoidance of personal questions.

Because he loved solving mysteries as much as he loved a challenge, he became determined to find out.

With a muttered oath that made the elderly gentleman in the bowler hat browsing through a folio of antique maps turn around to give her a disapproving stare, Ember slammed the phone back in its cradle on the wall.

"*Lo siento, señor,*" she said apologetically. "*Mi suegra.*"

My mother-in-law. The international word for misery, it had its intended effect. The gentleman smiled wryly and nodded, turning back to the sheets of yellowed parchment.

Ember passed her left hand over her face, noting it was trembling.

Damn.

She flexed the hand open and pulled it back the way the physical therapist had shown her all those years ago, painfully stretching the shortened tendons in her wrist and garnering a loud crack as they slid over the metal pins that secured her bones together. There were twenty-one pins in her left hand and wrist, and three metal plates in the bones of her arm, all permanent. The nerve damage and scars were permanent, too, as was the anger that had settled between the ruined byways of her healing flesh, cleaving itself to her body like dark matter, an unseen and undetectable anomaly that only made itself known at moments like this.

Moments when memory would come flooding back. Choking her, filling her with an old, familiar enemy: despair.

She'd done battle with despair since she was eighteen years old. Knowing the worst of it would pass in a moment, Ember closed her eyes and let it slice through her like a thousand sharpened knives. She breathed through it, trying to block out all the images his words had evoked. All the pain.

Big art scene. There's a famous music school there, I understand.

"Sleeping on the job? Even for you that's indolent."

Another old, familiar enemy: her stepmother, Marguerite. Just hearing her icy voice made Ember's skin crawl.

She turned and gazed into Marguerite's cold gray eyes, and kept her voice light as she said, "Oh, good morning, Marguerite. I didn't realize your kind could come out during the daytime."

"And I didn't realize bag lady chic was all the rage this season," Marguerite replied in exactly the same offhand tone, letting her disdainful gaze travel over Ember's usual ensemble of jeans, shapeless sweater, old running shoes. Her upper lip curled as if she smelled something rotting.

A walking advertisement for the finest haute couture houses, Marguerite was nothing if not perfectly put together. She was tall, blade thin, and bone pale, with dark hair scraped severely off her forehead and gathered into a low bun at the nape of her elegant neck. At the age where a woman had to decide to embrace growing older gracefully or wage a losing battle against time with fillers and needles and surgical blades, Marguerite had gone with the latter. Her poreless skin was pulled just slightly too tight over her cheeks, her brows were just slightly too arched. Combined with an almost entirely black wardrobe and lips that were a cheerless slash of vermilion, she held more than a passing resemblance to certain bloodsucking creatures of the night.

Without a hint of warmth, the two women smiled at one another.

"Where're the Tweedies?" Ember asked sweetly.

Marguerite's smile vanished. She loathed Ember's nicknames for her twin stepsisters. Analia and Allegra were Tweedledee and Tweedledum, respectively, and the bane of Ember's existence. Two of the banes, anyway. Pie-faced and rotund, they were spoiled to within an inch of their lives by their doting mother, and never missed an opportunity to make Ember's life hell.

They had far fewer opportunities since Ember moved out of the house three years ago, after her father died, but that didn't stop them from trying.

Marguerite crossed her arms over her bony chest and gazed down her hawk-like nose at Ember. "I've had a call from Señor Alvarez."

Ember's heart sank. Señor Alvarez was the family accountant. This wouldn't be good.

"And I'm sure you can guess what he told me."

"You've won the lottery? Congratulations."

Before answering, Marguerite pressed her lips together so hard there was nothing left of them but a downward-turned red sliver. She leaned forward and hissed, "Thanks to your total lack of business sense, Antiquarian Books is on the verge of *bankruptcy!*" Now enveloped in the cloud of heavy perfume emanating from Marguerite like the evil mist preceding the arrival of a monster in a horror movie, Ember took a step back. "If something isn't done immediately, we'll owe the creditors more than it's worth. Your father would be appalled to find it in such a state—"

Ember's temper, volatile under the best of circumstances, snapped.

"My father would be appalled by a *lot* of things, Marguerite! Including the way you've spent what was supposed to be *my* inheritance on your own daughters—"

"How *dare* you!" Marguerite exclaimed, her bony frame stiffening. Several customers glanced over, but neither Ember nor her stepmother cared. They were sucked suddenly into the ancient morass of animosity that existed between them like quicksand, thick, deep, and suffocating.

"—And what you've done with his *work!* I'm sure gifting it to your revolving door of *boyfriends* isn't exactly what he had in mind!"

Marguerite gasped. Her face, never flush with a healthy glow in the best of circumstances, paled to a blotchy, unnatural white. She sputtered, "Why you little—"

"Excuse me," interrupted a cheerful, familiar voice. Ember looked across the counter to see Asher, thumbs hooked in the belt loops of his jeans, clearly amused at the spectacle she and her stepmother made. "I'm looking for a very rare, very *expensive* book. Which of you lovely ladies can assist me?" He wiggled his eyebrows at Ember, who, instead of clawing her stepmother's eyes out, released her breath in a hard exhalation.

Like a snake furling its coils, Marguerite slowly withdrew. She hated men to catch her with her fangs exposed, and so she tried on a chilly smile, which looked out of place on her livid face. If she didn't know better, Ember would have sworn the woman was hiding a forked tongue in that venomous mouth.

"Ember would be happy to assist you, sir," Marguerite said smoothly, still with a frigid smile. Then she turned and hissed under her breath, "We'll finish this discussion later!" She stalked away and vanished through the swinging door that led to the back of the store.

"Oh, my God," said Asher with a shudder as soon as she disappeared. "That woman is *frightening!*"

"Just wait til you see her head spin completely around," Ember muttered. "You're lucky she doesn't know you're a friend of mine or she might have taken you back to her web to feed to her offspring."

He grimaced. "And I thought *my* mother was bad."

"Stepmother," Ember corrected. "And don't even start, your mother is amazing."

Ember had met Asher's mother twice when she'd come to visit from Boston. Valeria was zaftig, noisy, and hugged everyone in sight. She wore a rosary of freshwater pearls that was swallowed by her voluminous cleavage, regularly made the sign of the cross over her chest, and cooked authentic northern Italian food so delicious Ember thought she'd died and gone to heaven. Asher was her youngest, the "baby" of six, and her favorite. He complained about her in that way favorite sons do, all grumbling and grousing with nothing substantial behind it, secure in the knowledge he was loved.

That's how it is for people who know they're loved. They have the luxury of being dismissive of love, of taking it for granted. But for the unlucky ones who live day after day with no one who cares whether they live or die, they know exactly what it is they're missing. And unlike the lucky ones, they ache for love so badly the emptiness inside becomes a thing that pounds and burns, a need so vast and deep there is no end to it, and no bottom.

"Well, at least she lives three thousand miles away. If I had to see her every day, I'd kill myself."

"Yeah," said Ember sourly. "I know the feeling."

He smiled sympathetically at her. "Bet you can't guess why I'm here."

With a rueful twist of her lips, Ember said, "I thought you were going to buy a *very expensive* book and save the shop from ruin."

"You wish, lady. Actually I brought you something." He bent and retrieved a small brown paper bag from the floor by his feet. He dangled it in front of her like a cat toy. "Lunch. You said you didn't eat this morning, so . . . "

Ember's eyes misted. He brought her lunch after she ran out on him like that? Damn. This was turning out to be one hell of a morning. She took the bag and peered inside. Sandwich, fruit, a cup of plain yogurt. "Is it poisoned?" she asked, to hide how touched she was by the gesture.

Asher smiled and his eyes twinkled through his glasses. He saw right through her tough act, but never called her out on it. He was a good friend for many reasons, but primarily because he let her have her secrets and didn't press too hard when she shut down. He knew that was the surest way to make her run away.

"No. You're not getting off that easily."

He blew her an air kiss and turned to go, but Ember said, "Wait," and he looked back at her, brought up short by the emotion in her voice.

She rounded the counter, wrapped her arms around his broad shoulders, and hugged him. "Thank you, Ash," she whispered. "I really appreciate it."

He chuckled and gave her a squeeze. "Don't get hysterical on me, sweetie. I only know how to handle hysterical *boys*." He pulled back, still holding her around the waist, and smiled down at her, his brown eyes soft. "You creatures with ovaries really terrify me. You're so unpredictable. Creatures with penises are much more straightforward."

"I think you mean *simple*."

He shrugged. "You say potato, I say potahto . . . "

She smiled back at him, her first true smile in days, and gave him a kiss on the cheek.

At exactly that moment, Christian McLoughlin sauntered through the front door.

THREE

All Animals Are Equal

Ember knew it was him without looking because the air in the shop suddenly became charged.

That and *Asher* became charged.

He turned his head toward the door as he heard the jingle of the bell, and the smile on his face faded, replaced by a look of wide-eyed, gaping shock. His fingers tightened on her waist. From his mouth came a little, wordless noise, and his eyes, fixed on some target, travelled up, down, and back again. He exhaled a slow, whistling breath.

Ember sighed, released him and turned to look at Christian.

As elegant, regal and, well, *gorgeous*, as the first time she'd seen him, he looked back and forth between her and

Asher with a quizzical lift to his brows. *Good,* she thought peevishly. *Let him think Asher is my boyfriend. Even though he's looking at Christian as if he'd like to lick every part of his body.*

"Helllooo, beautiful," Asher purred. Ember elbowed him. So much for the boyfriend cover.

"That was fast. Did you fly here?" she said to Christian, not particularly warmly. *The rent, Ember,* she reminded herself. *The rent.* She forced herself to smile at him.

The corners of Christian's lips lifted and he walked forward, his stride languid, posture cocksure. He wore dove gray trousers and a perfectly cut shirt of indigo blue, which made his eyes appear even more vivid green than they did yesterday. The hair was perfect again, too, and Ember childishly wanted to run her fingers through it just to ruffle those perfect strands and mess it up.

Or did she just want to run her fingers through it?

She mentally slapped herself. There was a line a mile long of females wanting to run their fingers through this man's hair, she was sure—and she was equally sure she would *not* be standing at the end of it.

Not that he'd want her to, anyway. He looked like he only dated lingerie models and starlets. Women with perfect hair and gym-taut bodies and long, manicured fingernails who'd leave scratches when they clawed at his back while they arched and moaned in ecstasy beneath him—

"I'll get the books!" This was said much louder than necessary, loud enough to startle Asher who was still standing inches away. He jumped and put a hand to his throat.

"Jesus, Ember! Tell the neighborhood, why don't you?"

"And a good morning to you, too," said Christian, watching her with an amused look on his face, as if he knew exactly what she'd been thinking. Really, the man had an unnerving habit of looking at her like that. Was he always this intuitive?

"Oh. Yes, good morning." Ember cleared her throat. "Sorry, I'm just really busy at the moment," she added lamely. Christian and Asher glanced around the store. The customers who'd been browsing a few moments earlier had left, and there wasn't a soul in sight aside from the three of them. Asher cocked an eyebrow and looked at her as if she were insane, then turned to Christian with a wide smile.

"It's nice to hear someone other than me and my girl here speak English." His voice dropped, and he batted his eyelashes. He actually *batted* them. "Though of course I've always said a British accent makes everything sound so much more refined."

Oh, God, she thought, cringing. *He's really going to make a meal of it.*

"I've always preferred American accents, myself," Christian replied, returning Asher's smile. His gaze, electric green, flickered to Ember. "They're so . . . invigorating."

She'd never seen anyone appear so at ease in his own skin. He didn't cross his arms or fiddle with car keys—he wasn't holding car keys—or do any of the other little things people did when having a standing conversation. He simply *stood*, with his legs slightly apart and his arms hanging loose at his sides, taking up more space than he should have with the simple fact of his presence. There was a strange magnetism about him, a pull, something that made her want to reach out and touch him, something that surrounded him like an energy field, forceful and electric.

As he looked at her, Ember felt again the weird tingle of fear that had raised the hair on the back of her neck yester-

EDGE OF DARKNESS

day. But now the fear slid closer to a dark kind of excitement, a hum in her blood, like the threatening rumble of thunderclouds just before they discharged a bolt of lightning. He was so beautiful . . . she wondered absently what he might look like without clothes.

Then she stiffened, aghast. *Oh, no. I do not like him. I DO NOT!*

Unbelievably, horribly, Christian's eyes went wolfishly bright and narrowed on her face. His nostrils flared with a tiny inhalation and the smile faltered, replaced by a look of . . . what?

Hunger?

No, it must be anger, or something else—she didn't know what—but she sure as hell wasn't going to ask. This man was proving to be a little too sharp for comfort. She had the eeriest feeling he could read her like a book.

Time to move him along.

"I'll just be a sec," she said to Christian without introducing him to Asher.

He seemed to take it as a personal affront to his manhood because he put his hands on his hips and muttered to her with a glare, "Rude." He then turned to Christian with his hand out and introduced himself. They shook hands—Asher glowing, Christian bemused—while Ember made her way around the counter. She silently willed Asher not to say anything too embarrassing, or to kiss Christian on the lips and try to pass it off as the regular greeting of people from Boston when meeting those from another country.

When she came back from retrieving the two copies of *Casino Royale* a minute or two later, she found Christian and Asher engrossed in a serious discussion about the merits of Ian Fleming versus Ernest Hemingway.

"*The Sun Also Rises!*" Asher insisted vehemently. "*For Whom the Bell Tolls! A Farewell to Arms!*"

Clearly unimpressed with the litany, Christian returned, "*The Old Man and the Sea?*"

"Well," Asher replied after a pause. "You've got me there. That one was a little . . . astringent."

"Astringent?" Christian laughed, while Asher watched in slack-jawed admiration. In spite of herself, Ember had to agree; laughter on Christian was like gilding a lily. You didn't think it could get any more perfect, but then . . . *voila.*

Stunning.

Asher regained his composure enough to offer a faint, "But still, Ian Fleming. *Ian Fleming?*"

"You can't seriously think Ian Fleming was a better writer than Ernest Hemingway," Ember cut in, siding with Asher, who smugly pointed a finger at her as if to say, *See? Proof!*

Christian turned his attention to her and it felt as warm, focused, and bedazzling as a shaft of sunlight through clouds. He tilted his head and sent her a small, intimate smile that managed to bring a flush of blood to her cheeks and unsettle her in a way she definitely did not like. God, he was starting to get under her skin.

He said, "I have three words for you, Ember."

Ignoring the traitorous little butterflies dancing in her stomach, she cocked a brow and waited.

"Double. O. Seven."

The way he was looking at her—hot and half-lidded— was intimate, too, and she sternly reminded herself that this man was in all likelihood very, very practiced at giving women intimate looks.

Remembering how he'd looked at her when he first came in the store yesterday, how his keen gaze had travelled over her plain clothes, her unkempt hair, she decided it was much safer having him look at her *that* way, than this new, disquieting, butterfly-stirring way.

Time to remind him he couldn't melt the panties of *every* woman on planet Earth, even if her stupid butterflies wished he would melt hers.

In a light, mocking tone Ember said, "I hate to break it to you, but those are three *numbers*." She crossed her arms over her chest and looked him up and down. "All beauty and no brains, hmm? Well, it's not exactly a shocker. With that face, you probably haven't needed to think too much."

Seemingly not insulted at all, Christian drawled in a sensual purr, "Why, Miss Jones, was that a compliment? Did you just call me beautiful?"

He knew her last name. He knew her real first name. What else did he know about her?

Intrigued, in spite of the voice screaming in her head that she was an idiot, she replied a little too quickly, "Actually, I just called you dumb."

He smiled at her, lips twitching as if he might break out into laughter again, but the look Asher gave her was so horrified, so full of wide-eyed, open-mouthed disbelief, she couldn't help but smile too. It was a big one, a real one, teeth and all, and it felt absolutely fantastic.

And when he saw it, Christian did the strangest thing.

He froze. His own smile faltered. His face contorted with a fleeting, unidentified emotion, before he looked away, jaw tight, and swallowed. He cleared his throat and murmured, "It seems you've got me pegged."

When he looked back at her, it was like watching a door slam shut. There was a coldness there, a new, flat hardness, which began in his eyes and went everywhere at once. It was even in his voice when he spoke again.

"May I see them?" His flinty gaze dropped to the two paper-wrapped books she cradled in her arms.

"Oh. Yes. Of course."

The voice in her head was satisfied with his new coldness. Unfortunately the stupid butterflies were not, and began to mope, drifting down to the pit of her belly where they lay heavy and silent, staring up at her with accusing eyes.

Asher looked back and forth between the two of them several times, then politely excused himself and began to browse through a nearby shelf of mid-century cookbooks, picking out Julia Child's *Mastering the Art of French Cooking.* Considering he thought ordering takeout was the equivalent of cooking a meal, Ember realized he wasn't really browsing. He was eavesdropping.

Okay, Ember, pull yourself together! Be nice so you don't lose the most important sale the store has seen in years!

"Please, follow me," she said more forcefully, adopting an all-business attitude. She walked to the round table where Sofia's book club usually met. Christian silently followed her. She indicated he should take a seat, which he did—after waiting for her to sit first—and then she carefully unwrapped both editions of *Casino Royale* from their black, acid-free paper.

She turned them toward him without a word and sat back in her chair.

It was a moment before he moved. He stared down at them, looking at first one, then the other, taking in the condition of the dust jackets, examining the curl of the bottom edge on the less expensive edition. He dismissed that one and opened the cover of the pristine edition, the one worth twice as much.

"It's in perfect condition, as you can see," said Ember, watching him reverently touch the cover page. He ran his fingers slowly along the edges of the stacked pages, lifted the dust jacket and traced the gold lettering on the spine. The hard look on his face from before was being replaced, inch by inch, with something softer, an expression of affectionate melancholy she recognized as sentimentality.

Unable to stifle her curiosity, she asked, "Is it a gift for someone, or . . . ?"

Without looking up, he quietly answered, "This was my father's favorite book. He owned a first edition like this one, signed by the author. He used to read it to me every night before bed when I was a boy. I'm sure I could quote whole pages from it. I haven't been in Spain long, and I thought . . . maybe if I could find a copy just like the one my father had . . . it might make me feel more at home . . . "

He trailed off into silence while Ember sat there feeling like a first-class idiot for making fun of it before. She'd never have guessed someone like him could be so sentimental. Or homesick. On impulse she said, "My father used to read me *Animal Farm*."

Christian looked up at her then, and another expression replaced the quiet melancholy, a look of such pure, crackling intensity it took her breath away. His eyes glowed vivid, burning green. The air between them went electric.

"'Whatever goes upon two legs is an enemy,'" he recited in a voice low and infinitely dark.

"'Whatever goes upon four legs, or has wings, is a friend,'" Ember replied breathlessly. She didn't know why she was whispering, but something in his manner elicited it, his menacing, urgent look that spoke of secrets and mysteries. Of danger.

He said, "'No animal shall wear clothes. No animal shall sleep in a bed. No animal shall drink alcohol. No animal shall kill another animal—'"

"'All animals are equal,'" Ember finished, her voice barely audible. She and Christian stared at one another in tense silence. Goosebumps broke out all over her body.

The seven commandments the rebellious animals of *Animal Farm* made to unite themselves against the cruel rule of humans and prevent them falling into humans' evil habits sat there between them like the proverbial elephant. She didn't know why his manner was so changed, but Ember knew one thing for absolutely certain.

She *wanted* to know.

Dammit!

"Do you believe that? That all animals are equal?"

His question was asked with such searching earnestness, Ember felt the sudden, irrational urge to reveal something of herself, something she never felt, with anyone. "My father always said man and animal are interdependent. What we do to them, we do to ourselves. And I think that's true. I think . . . we're not better than animals. Humans *are* animals. Just a different kind."

He sat slowly back in his chair, his gaze never wavering from hers. "Smarter, though, than all the others. You have to admit that gives humans a distinct advantage. You don't think that's enough to make humans 'better' than the other animals? You don't think that gives them the right to rule over all the other animals as they see fit?"

"Absolutely not," she said instantly. "Am I 'better' than a five-year-old child because I'm smarter? No. Am I 'better' than someone who's mentally handicapped because I'm smarter? No. Are men 'better' than women because they're—usually—physically stronger? No. There're just differences that should be respected, not degrees of superiority."

"There are many who'd disagree with you," he said flatly.

"Just because they disagree doesn't make them right. There was a time when it was generally accepted that white people were 'better' than black people. And there was a time when a failed German painter convinced a lot of people that Jews should be wiped off the face of the earth because they were 'inferior.' And thousands of years of history have shown us what a bunch of frightened, cowardly mice people really are. General consensus doesn't equal incontrovertible truth. As a matter of fact, I think you're safe going *against* whatever the popular ideology happens to be. If there's anything I know for sure it's that people are easily led, and don't like to think for themselves."

She didn't know why she spoke so passionately; it just came out that way. She was sitting forward in her chair, gripping the edge of the table hard enough to turn her knuckles white, staring at him in unblinking intensity.

"Well," he said after a time, his voice tinged with new warmth, "it doesn't appear you have that particular problem."

She released the edge of the table and sat back in her chair. Heat rose in her cheeks, spread throbbing hot to her ears, down her neck.

"That's another thing my father always said," she muttered. "I'm way too opinionated for my own good. Sorry."

She dropped her gaze to the table, ashamed by her inappropriate outburst. The man must think her crazy. Or at the very least overbearing.

But why should she care what he thought? She didn't— she just wanted the sale . . . right?

He sat forward suddenly and grasped her hand. The contact shocked her, and she looked up at him, startled, as the butterflies sat up en masse and looked at him, too.

"Don't ever apologize for being yourself." His voice was urgent, his gaze scorched hers. "That kind of self-confidence, especially for someone so young, is amazing."

His hand was warm and big and she wanted to look down at it, to see it touching her own, but she was held in place by the sheer force of his gaze. He was so . . . *fierce*. Why?

"It's not self-confidence," she whispered, staring into his eyes. "It's more like misanthropy."

He slowly shook his head. "You don't hate people. You're too kind to hate anything."

"You don't know that. You don't know me."

"No. I don't." His voice dropped. His grip on her hand tightened. "I'd like to, though."

Everything ground to a halt. The sun slanting through the front windows of the shop, the sound of traffic on the street outside, the familiar, musky scent of old books—all of it vanished. In its place came white-hot, encompassing heat.

No one had ever looked at her the way he was looking at her now. He, the perfect, mysterious, beautiful stranger.

She couldn't move. She couldn't speak. She sat there bombarded by unfamiliar sensations, lightness and warmth and a dizzying, stupid kind of wonder. Wonder that someone like him could have actually said those words to someone like her.

For the first time in a very long time, Ember felt alive. The butterflies were soaring and screaming in glee.

And then his cell phone rang, shattering the moment.

There were several more rings before he finally released her hand—almost begrudgingly, it seemed, almost reluctantly. Without taking his gaze from her, he reached into the pocket of his shirt and answered it with a curt, "Yes."

Whoever it was on the other end spoke a few, short sentences, and Christian's entire demeanor shifted from impassioned intensity to stiff, jaw-clenched strain. Suddenly, he radiated violence.

"How many?" he hissed into the phone. He listened for a beat, then, "And you're certain they're headed *here*?"

Another beat of silence, then Christian, in a move that was shocking in its speed, shot to his feet. "Send me everything you've got. I'll be back at the house in ten minutes."

Then without another word or glance in her direction, he turned, ran to the door, then set off at a flat-out sprint down the street.

Ember sat at the table in stunned disbelief, her eyes trained on the front windows, staring at the view of the street beyond, of the pedestrians and the traffic, until Asher darted over, still clutching *Mastering the Art of French Cooking* in his hands.

"What the hell have you done to Christian? He ran out of here like he was being chased!"

Ember shook her head slowly from side to side. "I have . . . absolutely . . . no idea."

He sighed. "Well, there goes your big sale. Looks like I'll be needing to hide you from Dante for the rest of the month."

She looked down at the copies of *Casino Royale* on the table, sitting as he'd left them, and had the sudden, uncomfortable realization she didn't really care about the sale at all.

Even though she absolutely hated to admit it, what she cared about had just run out the door, and possibly out of her life forever.

FOUR
Carnaval

"Faster, Corbin," Christian barked from the back seat of the Audi. At his command, Corbin pressed his foot to the gas pedal and the car lurched forward. The powerful engine propelled them through the winding, cobblestoned streets of Barcelona so fast the scenery became a painted blur of color flashing through the windows.

His mind was a blur as well.

All animals are equal. People are easily led. General consensus doesn't equal incontrovertible truth.

Ember might be surprised to discover exactly how much he agreed with each of those sentiments. She would definitely be surprised to discover the effect her words had had on him. And the effect her smile had on him.

Jesus, that smile.

He'd thought her plain, but now realized his mistake. She was plain in the same way the ocean was plain before dawn, before the sun illuminated the unembellished dark surface of the water, bringing all its color and motion and beauty into brilliant focus as the light reflected off the waves. When she smiled it was like watching sunlight play over water. Her entire face was illuminated. It was transformed.

It took his breath away.

In a quiet, natural, earthy way, Ember was lovely.

She was also human. And, therefore, as much of a danger to him as he was to her. He should stay away. He knew he should.

And yet . . .

All animals are equal.

If there ever was to be a chance for his kind, if there was to be a future for them, it would hinge on people like her. Like the modest and lovely September Jones, she of the piercing dark eyes and passionate convictions, of the wary glances and spectacular smiles. Of the slightly trembling left hand and arm filled with metal she tried to disguise with long sleeves.

What is your mystery, human girl? Christian mused, watching the sprawl and chaos of the city give way to the green expanse of the rolling foothills as they sped nearer to home. *And why, why do I care?*

He had no answer for either one. By the time the car pulled up to the scrolled iron gates that marked the beginning of his property, Christian had managed to convince himself it didn't matter. He wouldn't be seeing her again. The quest for an original copy of *Casino Royale* was a sentimental one, entirely ridiculous. It had no place in the stark reality of the reasons he'd come to Spain in the first place, and the phone call he'd received had only reinforced that.

He couldn't afford to get distracted now. He couldn't afford curiosity. Or flirtations, no matter how innocent they seemed.

As the gates swung slowly open, his cell phone chirped with an incoming text message. He lifted it from his shirt pocket, gazed down at it, and felt his heart twist in his chest.

Hope everything is OK. If I don't see you again, it was . . . interesting . . . to meet you.

He muttered an oath and Corbin's gaze flickered to his in the rearview mirror.

"Nothing," he said to Corbin. "It's nothing."

Corbin nodded wordlessly and Christian turned his face to the window, wondering if he'd ever uttered such a colossal lie in his life.

Ember passed the rest of the day in a haze.

Asher left and she ate the lunch he'd brought her, standing behind the counter, leaning against the wall. She couldn't concentrate and she couldn't banish the thought of Christian and his strange visit from her memory, either. She'd re-wrapped both copies of *Casino Royale* in the tissue-thin sheets of black paper, carefully set them back into the transport box and put them on a shelf in the store room. She sent him the text, but her own phone remained silent; he hadn't responded.

She didn't try to fool herself that her reasons for wanting to hear from him were entirely financial.

By six o'clock, when she locked the front door and flipped the square white sign that hung in the window from *abierto* to *cerrado*, she was exhausted.

Mentally exhausted, that is. Physically, she felt as if she might crawl right out of her skin.

In chilly twilight with her coat buttoned up and her scarf wrapped tight around her neck, she walked the few blocks from the bookstore to her apartment building in the *Plaça Sant Jaume*, blind for once to the lighted fountains, carved marble statues, and vendors with food carts hawking *helado*, *chorizo*, and *chopitos*, her least favorite: crispy fried baby squid. It was only a few days before Carnaval, and preparations were being made all over the city. Already the bars were full to bursting, breathing crowds of people in and out into the streets, laughing revelers dressed in bright colors who were determined to stuff themselves with food and alcohol before the fasting period of Lent began next week.

A block over on *La Rambla*, the main thoroughfare, the Carnaval King parade that signaled the kickoff of the week-long festivities was already in full swing. Music and singing filled the air, drums beat, a rash of azure and crimson and gold fireworks flared in the dark sky then began a slow, dying float back to earth, teased apart by the salt-laden breeze from the Mediterranean. There would be floats and masked dancers and costumes aplenty, and though she couldn't see it, she could imagine it well, as she'd attended every year since she'd moved here at eighteen.

But not this year. She just wasn't in the mood.

When she arrived at her apartment, Asher was just leaving. Dressed in black military boots and a hot pink

mini skirt with orange ruffles, he wore two bandoliers with
fake ammo slung across his bare chest, had a plastic rifle
strapped to his back and a variety of fake knives and other
weapons on a belt around his waist. Atop his head perched
a towering hat of colorful feathers and fruit. It appeared as
if he'd oiled himself; his muscular arms, chest and legs
glistened in the fluorescent hallway lights with an irides-
cent sheen.

His skin was tanned and hairless. She resisted the urge
to ask him if he shaved or waxed his entire body, because
that would be a little too much information, and also because he probably did.

He sent her a roguish smile and made elaborate spokes-
model hands at his outfit.

"Whaddya think?"

"I think you have bipolar disorder," said Ember, eyeing him.

"Puh! You're just jealous I come up with all the creative
ideas for costumes. Isn't it genius?"

"You look like the love child of a Navy Seal and a vege-
tarian *cancan* dancer."

"Exactly!" he shrieked, clapping. It was alarming to see
an oiled, half-naked man in a fruit hat and bandoliers
shrieking and clapping, but it definitely wasn't the strangest
thing she'd ever seen, so she just shook her head, laughing.

"Okay, I give. What's her name?"

Because there was always a name when Asher donned a
costume. At his Halloween bash last year when he'd dressed
as a nun from the Order of the Sisters of Perpetual Indul-
gence, his name had been Helen Bed. Hell-in-bed. Where
he came up with these little gems, Ember had no idea.

He grinned. "Carmen MiRambo."

Ember blinked at him. "You're right. That *is* genius."
Looking him over again, she said, "Where are you hiding
your wallet in that getup?"

He blinked demurely, but his rogue's grin grew wider.
"You *don't* want to know."

"No. You're right. I really don't." She smiled and gave
him a kiss on one ruddy cheek, then unlocked her apartment door and turned back to him. "Be safe tonight. I'll see
you tomorrow."

He looked crestfallen. "You're not coming out? But it's
tradition! And I wanted you to meet Rafael!"

Interested, Ember leaned her shoulder against the
doorjamb. Since Asher's long-term partner Sebastian had
died last year, he'd developed an ironclad rule never to get
serious with anyone again. He claimed he needed to make
up for being with just one man for so long, and so was going
to dedicate himself to sampling every young thing Barcelona offered up, but Ember knew better. It was really his way
of staying detached, because no one could ever measure up
to Sebastian. And Asher didn't want anyone to. Bas had
been the love of Asher's life. Deep down, he didn't think he
could bear that kind of loss again.

*There are only so many times a heart can break, Ember, before
it's broken for good.*

He'd said that the first week she met him. And she knew
from personal experience it was true.

"Rafael? Is this your new flavor-of-the-week?"

Asher playfully batted her on the arm with his plastic
gun and did a happy dance in the hallway, which included a
twirl that dangerously flared the mini skirt. She quickly
averted her eyes—Asher was infamous for going commando.

"Flavor-of-the-month if I play my cards right, honey. Please come. Please? *Pretty* please?"

Each entreaty grew progressively louder . . . and ultimately proved disastrous. From downstairs came a hollered, "*Septiembre! Es que se?*"

Ember hissed a curse, Asher gasped an apology, and they both scuttled into her apartment just as the sound of shuffling, slipper-clad footsteps began to travel up the stairs.

"Dante!" Asher said in a stage whisper as they stood with their ears pressed to the back of the door in her dark apartment.

"You've officially woken the beast," Ember muttered. "Thanks a million, Carmen."

Even in the dark she saw him cringe. "God, that man has hearing like a bat! I'll make it up to you, I promise. Come out with me tonight and I'll buy you as many—"

Her glare stopped him before he could say "drinks as you want." It was force of habit, all his friends drank like fish, Asher included, but Ember never touched a drop. He amended it to, "—*chopitos* as you can eat."

She sighed. "You know I hate *chopitos*, Ash."

"Honey, they're so good. Don't discriminate based on how they look—"

"They look like fried alien afterbirth. I am not putting fried alien afterbirth in my mouth."

"They're chewy, and salty, and entirely delicious. Close your eyes if you have to, it works for me."

"Ugh. Gross. Forget it. I'd rather eat toe jam."

Asher snickered. "There's a whole underground fetish movement in this city devoted to exactly that, you know."

"Double gross! Stop talking before I barf on your shiny combat boots."

The two of them were whispering, listening to the slow, shuffling footsteps draw inexorably nearer as Dante climbed the staircase. The apartment building was old, and lacked an elevator, a fact she was now grateful for. The reprieve would be short—though Dante moved slowly, once he decided on a course an act of God couldn't deter him—but any reprieve was better than none.

"Okay," Asher said, brightening, "here's the plan. You go put on that fabulous costume you wore to my Halloween party, and I'll go tell Dante you're staying the weekend with your boyfriend in Terrassa."

Ember stared at him. "*What* boyfriend in Terrassa?"

"The pretend one, knucklehead! Do you want me to buy you a weekend so you can put together the rent money or what?"

The footsteps moved closer. Through the windows of her apartment, the rising moon hung heavy and languid in the sapphire sky. Ghostly pale moonlight sketched shadows along the floor and walls, creeping over to where they were huddled by the door. "Fine," she relented. "But I get to choose the name of this pretend boyfriend. I don't want you saddling me with a Xalbadoro or an Innocencio."

Asher sent her a sly, sideways smile. "How about a . . . Christian?"

"Funny. Very funny, Mr. MiRambo. You're lucky I don't give you some authentic knife scars on your stomach to go with that costume."

As she turned and tiptoed toward her bedroom, Asher chuckled quietly. "Kitty doesn't like to get her tail pulled, does she?"

She waved a hand and disappeared into the darkness of her bedroom, while Asher slipped out into the hallway to break the news to Dante that he'd just missed her. She'd left with her boyfriend Christian for a leisurely weekend touring the Romanesque monasteries of Terrassa.

Six hours, four bars, two discotheques and one hellish taxi journey that rivaled Mr. Toad's Wild Ride, Ember was ready to drop.

"I'm calling it a night, Ash!" she hollered over the pounding of the music. Though Asher's ear was inches away, he gave her an *I can't hear you* shrug, and went right back to grinding against the very pretty Rafael, who was dressed as the Black Swan, complete with tutu and red contacts.

Ember made hand motions toward the exit. Asher gave her a giddy thumb's up, which she interpreted as, *knock yourself out, there's no way I'm leaving, sister.* She sent him an air kiss, along with one to a pirouetting Rafael, and pushed her way slowly through the gyrating crowd on the dance floor until finally she stood outside on the pavement, breathing in lungfuls of fresh night air.

She wasn't cold because her costume was composed entirely of latex. She was encased head to foot in a thick, shiny layer of black material. She'd have to peel herself out of it later, but for the moment it was doing a fine job of protecting her from the chill of the February air.

A half-naked woman with her entire body painted gold shoved past her with a laugh, dripping red feathers from an elaborate headdress. A man in a yellow dragonfly outfit followed her, weaving drunkenly, his green wings listing dangerously to one side, perilously close to sliding off his back. The scents of perfume, wine, and smoke from the fireworks hung heavy in the air; even at midnight the crowds had not thinned. The streets were a riot of noise, color, and motion, and Ember felt pleasantly invisible among the chaos, able to drift through and just watch. The smaller side streets of the neighborhood were closed to everything but foot traffic, so she made her way through the throngs toward one of the main thoroughfares, still open to cars. She hoped to catch a taxi to take her back home; her feet, clad in four-inch heels, were killing her.

She rounded the corner of the *Rambla de Catalunya* and spied a taxi stand next to a little French restaurant. She began to walk toward it with a sigh, anxious to get off her feet, but as soon as she stepped off the curb and into the street, she jolted to an abrupt stop.

Because there, just emerging from the restaurant and striding down the red-carpeted steps toward a sleek black sedan waiting at the curb, was one Christian McLoughlin.

FIVE

Pretending

Their eyes met at the exact same moment. Christian felt it in his body like the weightlessness that accompanies the start of a free fall on a rollercoaster, just before the hot rush of euphoria, terror, and heart-pounding glee seizes you and as you tip over the edge you raise both hands in the air, a scream of exhilaration ripping from your throat.

His stomach dropped. His heart clenched. He froze just as she had, and stared at her.

Corbin walked around the rear of the Audi and opened the passenger door for him. When Christian didn't move, he turned his head to stare in the same direction as his employer, and his whole body jerked.

"Good Lord in heaven. Is this a joke?" Corbin whispered, stunned as Christian was.

But it was no joke. Fate had decided to once again put September Jones directly in Christian's path. Only this time, Fate had a trick up her sleeve.

Fate was being sly.

Ember, frozen on the street with one stiletto-booted foot in front of the other, her hand stopped halfway to her face, was clad in the most astonishing outfit, something he never would have believed possible had he not seen it with his own eyes.

A cat. She was dressed as a cat.

Complete with a little headband from which sprang two pointed cat's ears, and a long, curving tail that trailed behind her, tufted at the end. The costume was tight and black and entirely revealing and had it not been for the nature of the costume itself he would have been devouring the sight of slim curves that her usual ensemble of baggy jeans and even baggier sweaters managed to hide completely.

But—a cat? A goddamned *cat*?

He'd never been so shocked in his entire life.

She recovered first. She took a few tentative steps forward, then a few more, more confidently. By the time she reached his side of the street and stood looking up at him—*she even drew silver whiskers on her cheeks and blackened the tip of her nose, Jesus Christ*—Christian was in slightly better control of himself, and managed to greet her with a semblance of civility.

"Ember. How nice to see you."

"Um, you too," she responded, sounding a little unsure if that were actually true.

Her brown gaze flickered over him, uncomfortably keen, and he hoped she overlooked the pulse throbbing in his temple. He wanted to press his fingers against it, but restrained himself.

"Having dinner?"

"Oh . . ." Christian glanced back at the restaurant, still feeling as if he'd been hit by something large and heavy. "Yes. It's my favorite place in the city. Have you ever eaten here?"

Ember wrinkled her nose. Her whiskers twitched with the movement, and he stared at them in utter fascination. "Nope. This is more my stepmother's speed."

There was faint distaste in her voice, and he wondered whether it was directed at him or her stepmother.

After a moment's pause he said, looking over her outfit, "So . . . been out on the town I see."

She looked down at herself and blushed. Crossing her arms over her chest, she muttered, "Asher—you met him earlier—we always do Carnaval together. It's a tradition."

A smile tugged at his lips. "It's a nice tradition. Especially when you get to dress up."

She glanced up at him, saw him smiling, and gave him a tentative smile in return. "It's my thing. Cats. I volunteer at the shelter on my day off. Asher's always telling me I'm going to wind up one of those crazy old cat ladies with like two hundred of them in her apartment and no friends so that when I die, it'll take weeks before someone discovers my dead body and by then the cats will have eaten half of it away."

Good God. The thought made the veal fricando he'd had at dinner turn over in his stomach.

Seeing the look on his face, Ember quickly said, "I mean, I don't have any cats now—my landlord won't allow pets in the building—I didn't mean to make it sound like I'm some weird collector or something . . . "

She trailed off, color rising in her cheeks, and Christian felt a sudden, violent urge to touch her face, feel the heat of that pale, almost translucent skin. He stifled it by biting down hard on the inside of his lip and shoving his hands into his pockets.

"Well, anyway, it was nice to see you," she said, stepping back. "If you still want the copy of *Casino Royale*, you know where to find me. Have a good night."

She turned away but he stopped her with a blurted, "Do you need a ride home?"

Corbin looked at him over her head with raised brows. Yes, he knew it wasn't a good idea for a million different reasons, but he didn't like the thought of her wandering around in the dark alone. Wearing *that*.

"Um . . . well . . . sure. I guess." Dubiously, Ember looked at the car. "This is yours?"

He inclined his head and didn't look at Corbin, whose mouth had pinched to a tight line. He wouldn't dare contradict Christian aloud, but his expression was proof enough of what he thought of this plan.

"That would be great. If it's not out of your way. I live in the *Plaça Sant Jaume*."

"By City Hall, I know the place. It's not too far." He gestured to the open door. "After you."

She hesitated for a moment, sending a surreptitious glance toward Corbin, then shrugged, capitulating but still with that slight uncertainty. She climbed in the back of the Audi and he tried very hard to keep his eyes averted from the incredibly alluring sight of her latex-clad bottom, embellished with that sinuous tail, disappearing into the car.

He followed her in and settled himself but then lifted his backside from the seat when he realized he'd sat on her tail.

"Sorry." He held the fuzzy tail aloft between his fingers. "This is yours, I believe."

"Well, it sure isn't yours," she quipped and lightly removed it from his hand.

Buckling his safety belt in the driver's seat, Corbin sputtered a horrified cough that Christian tried to cover by leaning forward and pounding him on his wide shoulder.

"That cold still bothering you, Corbin?" His voice was stern, his gaze full of warning. Their eyes met in the rearview mirror, and Corbin acknowledged the warning with a small, curt nod of his head.

"These things sneak up on you when you're least expecting them, sir," he replied. "I'm sure I'll be fine, though. Thank you for asking." Then he started the car and concentrated on steering them out into traffic. He didn't look in the mirror again.

"So . . . do you always eat so late? It's past midnight," Ember said softly from beside him, pulling his thoughts back from a precipice. He turned to look at her, admiring the way light from the passing streetlamps wove strands of bright color into her dark hair, gold and bronze and mahogany glints that flared and faded as the car picked up speed. They were seated close together but not *too* close; the sedan had a spacious interior and the back seat would easily fit three adults. He noticed she'd chosen to sit as close to her door as possible, while he'd taken a spot almost in the middle. He hadn't done it consciously, but as he looked at her, he was glad he had.

He smelled the clean, warm scent of her skin, the citrusy shampoo she'd used earlier to wash her hair, the chemical smell of her latex costume, the liner she'd used to draw on her whiskers, and the paint she'd used to blacken the tip of her nose. Still she wore no other cosmetics, no lipstick or mascara, and he was glad she didn't. It made her seem more real to him.

More . . . bare.

"Usually, yes. I'm a bit of a night person."

He willed Corbin not to cough. It must have worked, because the man didn't even flinch.

"Really? I'm a morning person myself. When I first came to live here I couldn't believe how different it was from home. Breakfast at ten in the morning, lunch at two in the afternoon, a two hour siesta then back to work until eight, dinner practically in the middle of the night." She shook her head. "I still can't sleep past six."

A personal revelation. Her first. Intrigued, he said, "You're originally from New Mexico, you said. What brought you to Spain?"

She looked down at the tail she still held in one hand and her fingers tightened around it. She swallowed, said in a lowered voice, "Life." She sat quietly a moment, then glanced up at him. "You? You're originally from England, correct?' He inclined his head. "So what brought you to Spain?"

"Life." Their gazes held. Outside, the night sped by in a blur of color. He watched her face, watched her eyes, large and dark. "It seems to have a way of derailing even the most carefully laid plans, doesn't it?"

Her face grew somber, a little furrow appeared between her brows. She drew her bottom lip between her teeth and turned to look out the window, as if she couldn't meet his eyes. Her hand rose to touch the gold rings that hung on the delicate chain around her neck, and she twisted them between her fingers, round and round. Staring out into the passing night, she said quietly, "Life is cruel in the same way people are. Casually. Randomly. Indifferently. Sometimes I wonder how anyone survives it at all."

"Ultimately, we don't."

She turned back to look at him just as the car went over a bump in the road, an unseen pothole or crumbled, unrepaired piece of curb that had Corbin cursing and swerving to correct. They were jolted, kicked out of their seats, a nanosecond of weightlessness and then settled again, but they'd both put their hands on the seat between them to steady themselves and realized at exactly the same moment that they were, just barely, touching. Pinky to wrist, their hands met against the leather, and neither one moved away.

They pretended they weren't touching. They both looked forward, silent, gazing out the windshield, but neither one withdrew. As the blocks passed by it became an almost unbearable agony, the slightest pressure from her hand, the warmth of her skin grazing his, the urge to lean into her, or say something, or do anything, anything at all. But Christian held himself still and felt thankful for the darkness, because he was sure if she looked at him now she would see what was written plainly on his face, and she'd open the door and run.

Hunger. Hunger unfurled inside him, dark, savage, and selfish. And all from a touch of her hand.

Bloody hell. This had epic disaster written all over it in blinking neon letters.

"Just a few blocks more."

Ember's voice sounded a little breathless. He tried to block out the sound of her blood rushing through her veins, of her heart pounding in her chest. Her breathing had increased, too, and all the little signs of her reaction to him made the animal inside him hiss in pleasure. He closed his eyes and tried to calm himself, breathing steadily through his nose.

Then someone darted out into the street directly in front of them, a man in a blue parrot costume waving a neon glow stick and cackling drunkenly. Corbin slammed on the brakes to avoid him. Neither he nor Ember wore seat belts, and he saw her begin to fly forward as if in slow motion, her eyes wide, lips parted in horror.

His reaction was instantaneous. Unthinking. He reached out, grabbed her with both hands, and flung her back against the seat. He landed half on and half off her body, blocking her with his own, one leg braced against the back of the driver's seat and one thrown over hers, his hands gripping her shoulders, his face inches from hers.

It was awful. It was amazing. It was terribly intimate and awkward and inappropriate, their bodies pressed hard against one another, their legs entangled, but they stayed like that for long, breathless moments, staring at each other with pounding hearts and unblinking eyes, frozen, until the line of cars behind them began to honk, their drivers leaning out the windows to curse in Spanish.

"Sorry, sir," Corbin huffed, fingers white around the steering wheel. The drunken parrot doddered off, leaving a trail of listing blue feathers in the street behind him. "Everyone all right?"

"Yes," he whispered, staring into Ember's eyes, his voice hoarse. He said it again and for some reason it didn't feel like he was answering Corbin's question this time. It felt more like an invitation. The answer to a question his body screamed for him to ask.

Yes, say yes, please say yes to me.

The car began to pull forward and Christian was jerked out of his reverie. Suddenly aware of the indecorum of his position and what an ass she must think him for throwing himself on top of her in the most crude, blundering way, he abruptly sat up, released her arms, and retreated to his side of the car.

She let out her breath in a soft expulsion, lifted a shaking hand to her chest.

"Forgive me. I hope I didn't hurt—"

"No," she interrupted, still shaking, refusing to look at him. "Please. I'm not hurt. I might have been though, if you hadn't stopped me. You have . . . amazing . . . reflexes." A tiny little laugh escaped her throat, tinged with what sounded like impending hysteria. He looked over at her sharply. If he didn't know better, he'd have guessed her in shock. The hand on her chest—her left hand—shook so badly now she curled it to a fist, placed her right hand over it and pressed it against her stomach.

"Where shall I stop, miss?" said Corbin, slowing as he pulled around the corner and onto the one-way street that ran behind the plaza. Like many plazas in Barcelona, the large cobblestone square was for pedestrians only, off-limits to all but delivery vehicles or the police.

"There," Ember said, her voice trembling. With her right hand she indicated the back of a building half a block up. Her left remained curled to a fist in her lap, and Christian impulsively reached out and placed his own on top of it. Beneath his fingers, her hand was ice cold. It felt very fragile and small.

She turned, startled at the contact, and looked at him. Reflected in the moonlight streaming through the windows, her face was wan and pale. She was frightened, deeply frightened, and he sensed her reaction was about far more than what had just happened. He felt an unexpected, almost overwhelming urge to take her in his arms and comfort her.

"You're all right," he reassured her softly, holding her gaze. "You're safe."

"I'm safe . . . with you."

It was a whisper, nearly inaudible, and Christian wasn't sure if it was a question or a statement. Either way, it was a minefield, one he didn't want to explore.

She could never be safe with him. Not really. Temporarily, maybe, and in instances like this where he could save her from little accidents, prevent her from coming to harm in one of the million ways a human could be harmed going about their everyday lives.

But in the big ways, the ways that really mattered, she'd never be safe with him. Quite the opposite, in fact.

Unfortunately, his body didn't care. His heart didn't care. *He* didn't care, in spite of all the reasons he should.

"Let me walk you up," he said.

She shook her head. "I'm fine."

No, she wasn't. And he wasn't taking no for an answer. "I'm walking you up." He opened his door before Corbin could get out of the car, and had her door open before she could protest. He held out his hand and she stared up at him, seeming very small and fragile in the back seat of his car, her little cat's ears pricked forward as if listening for something.

"Really, Christian, I'm fine."

"So you've said. Now get out of the car or I'll throw you over my shoulder and carry you up."

Her face went a shade paler and he had to smile. "That was a joke. A bad one. I apologize. I promise to behave."

Her lips twisted, a rueful little smile that had him dying to know what she was thinking. Without commenting, she accepted his outstretched hand and climbed out of the car. Once standing, she immediately withdrew her hand from his. "It's just over here," she said, and turned, leaving him to follow behind her.

He nodded to Corbin, who watched them through the windshield, and turned away before the sight of Corbin's worried face could distract him.

When they reached her apartment building—a five-story walk-up of creamy stone, with a tiny café and a news-stand on the ground floor and stone gargoyles leering down from the balustrades of the terrace on top—she hesitated, looking up. "Um, I think this is good. My landlord lives on the second floor and . . . " She hesitated, chewing her lip. "He sort of thinks I'm out of town. I don't want to wake him up."

His brows rose. "How will he know it's you? And why does he think you're out of town?"

She crossed her arms over her chest and sent a nervous glance at the dark windows on the second floor. "He always knows it's me, he's got Spidey senses. And . . . I'm a little behind on the rent. Asher covered for me and said I was out of town so I could buy a few more days. It's been really slow at the bookstore lately, and I just," she cleared her throat, "I just needed a little more time to get it together."

She looked pained as she spoke the words, scuffing the toe of her boot against the ground and lowering her lashes, and it was obvious it galled her to admit she was short on her rent. Especially to someone like him, he realized with an unhappy clench in his stomach, a man who dined at the finest restaurants in the city, owned a car that cost upward of six figures, and had a driver to boot. He'd never given much thought to his own wealth because he'd always had it, as had his father, and his father before him. As the son of an Earl, Christian had never wanted for anything.

Anything material, that is. He'd wanted plenty of things that had nothing to do with money. Those things— freedom, autonomy, the choice of where to live—were far more important than all his wealth and privilege combined. Ember had those things, and though she probably wouldn't believe him if he told her, he'd trade places with her in a minute.

He sometimes thought people had no idea how good they really had it. They seemed always to focus on the bad things, the little inconveniences or discontents, when in reality most people had far, far more valuable things than he did. He was Gifted, as were all of his kind, but most humans had the greatest gift of all: choice.

He shook all those thoughts off and to Ember he said, "So we're sneaking you in, then." He grinned at her. "Cool."

He wanted to laugh at the look on her face. Startled, horrified, relieved, her expression went through a dozen transformations in the five seconds it took for her to compose herself and answer.

"Oh, so we're inviting ourselves up, are we?"

"I'd love an espresso, if you've got it. And I did promise to behave," he said, very seriously, with his best "I'm trustworthy" face.

"No, Mr. Fancypants, I do *not* have espresso."

Her voice was cool, she'd arched one dark eyebrow, which clearly telegraphed disdain, and she was looking at him as if he were an insect she'd like to smash beneath her boot.

Insanely, he was crushed. She didn't want him to come up. She wanted him to leave—

"But I do have tea, if your snobby palate can handle that."

She broke into a smile, wide and unguarded, and he felt the same punch to the gut he'd felt the first time she smiled at him. Her smile was nothing short of breathtaking.

"Well, I am British. We perfected the bloody stuff. I think my palate will survive."

She rolled her eyes—cheeky girl—and said, "All right, but you have to be quiet. Like, *really* quiet. Dante can hear mice going up those stairs and I live on the top floor."

"Ah. Spidey senses." Christian's grin grew wider. "In that case, you better leave this to me."

She cocked her head, brows drawn together quizzically, and before she could utter another word, feeling a strange, dark exhilaration heating his blood, he leaned in close to her ear and whispered, "You're going to want to hang on for this."

Then, surprising himself with his boldness and the strength of the sudden, fierce glee that seized him, he picked Ember up in his arms and began to run.

SIX

Off Balance

It all happened so fast. Faster than she could react, faster than she could draw even a single breath. One second he was leaning down with a mischievous glint in his eye, whispering in her ear, the next second she was aloft, held tight in his arms, flying through the air as if propelled by a jet engine.

He was running with her. In his arms. *Fast.* And it was utterly, completely silent.

There wasn't even the sound of his shoes striking the worn cobblestones of the plaza, or the hollow echo of the wood as they hit the stairs. There was only the slightly nauseating sense of rapid motion, the wind cool on her face, the plaza and stairwell a passing smear of color. And when they arrived at the top of five flights of stairs in less time than it would take to count from one to ten and Christian stood looking down at her, smiling at what must have been the sheer, obvious shock on her face, she felt a lurching in her stomach completely unrelated to the speed at which they'd just travelled.

"What—how—"

She couldn't get it out. She was breathless, stunned, stiff as a board in his arms. Her arms were wrapped tightly around his neck, and her fingers were sunk into the hard, bunched muscles of his shoulders. It was a good thing she didn't have long nails, because he would definitely have been bleeding.

His smile grew wider. Those green, green eyes twinkling with a seductive dark glow, he said, "Your landlord's not the only one with Spidey senses."

Ember made a noise that was neither a word nor a gasp, but something in between, a little sound that was the perfect description for everything she felt.

Carefully, he eased her to the ground, making sure she was able to support herself on her own two feet before releasing her. She wobbled unsteadily in her high-heeled boots and had to lean against her apartment door for support.

"How did you do that?" she finally managed, trying to catch her breath.

He shrugged, slid his hands into his pockets, smiled, and said nothing.

"Okay . . . secrets. Great. I can deal with secrets." She'd had her own for years.

His smile faltered, replaced by a look of intensity, a look she was beginning to recognize too well. "I'll show you mine if you show me yours."

"Tell, I think you mean."

He gazed at her, his expression contemplative and somehow severe. A current of electricity crackled between them, bright as danger. "Do I?"

Trying to feign indifference to cover her pounding heart and the heat flooding her cheeks, Ember swallowed and said lightly, "You promised to behave, Fancypants."

A muscle in his jaw worked. "Believe me, Ember, this *is* me behaving."

Her heart fluttered, a direct response to the glowing dark burn in his eyes. "How bout we just get you that tea, then you can go back to training for the Olympic sprint?"

Before he could answer she turned to the door, hiding her face from his ignited look, eager to get inside and avoid any more sudden, weightless travel in his arms.

What on earth had just happened?

She'd hidden the house key in the saucer of the drooping, potted pothos beside her front door, and quickly retrieved it. She unlocked the door and entered the apartment, with Christian following silently on her heels.

She didn't turn on any lights, because she wasn't even supposed to be there. But that presented a problem. The two of them couldn't wander around in the dark . . . and how was she going to make his damn tea if she couldn't see the stove?

And did she really want to be alone with Mr. Spidey Senses in the dark?

Her body said one thing, her good sense another. She stood undecided for several moments, then muttered, "Oh, screw it." Kicking off her boots, she padded to the kitchen and turned on the little light above the stove, which gave her enough illumination to work with but left the rest of the flat in semi-darkness.

"Make yourself comfortable." She waved a hand toward the living room and set about retrieving a mug from the cupboard in the kitchen, filling the kettle with water and setting it to boil on the stove. Which tea to serve him, she wondered, hesitating over the collection of small, colorful boxes in the spice cabinet. Ceylon? Oolong? Chamomile?

She went with Earl Grey. It just seemed to fit.

"I like your place," he said from behind her.

She imagined him gazing around the flat, taking in the low gleam of the polished terra cotta floors, the gilt and claret velvet antique divan her father had bought for her and restored to its pre-flea-market glamour, the exposed dark wood beams that bisected the whitewashed ceiling and lent the room a stately, rustic air. And of course, the books. Acres of books lined one entire wall, and though he couldn't see it, the bedroom sported its own wall of books, all of them snug in the custom floor-to-ceiling shelves she'd built and stained herself.

Ember acquired her artistic bent from her father, but from her mother—a woman who'd milked her own cows, made her own clothes, and knew the name of every plant, tree, and wildflower—she inherited a practical talent for making things with her hands. And a love of the natural world, and all the things in it.

"You don't have a television." He sounded surprised, and no wonder; what kind of weirdo didn't have a television?

The September Jones kind, that's what.

"I hate television. The only thing more depressing than a reality show is the news. And besides, if I had a TV, that would leave less room for my books. I'm a bit obsessed, as you can see."

"You don't say." There was wry humor in his voice. She imagined that dazzling smile of his, those sculpted lips curving upward, and she had to smile, too. "There's this new-fangled technology that might help you out with your book fetish. Maybe you've heard of it . . . a *Kindle?*"

She shrugged. "I like the smell of books, especially old ones, and the way a book feels in my hands. And sometimes I write in the margins or underline things. It's more . . . interactive. More real, in a way. I did try a Kindle once, though. Honestly I thought it was kind of freaky, all those tiny books trapped inside. Just looking at all those half-inch book covers crowded together on an eight-inch screen made me feel claustrophobic."

"Ember, the words 'seek therapy' come to mind," he said dryly.

Been there, done that. Didn't work. She shrugged again, and he began to slowly walk through the room, his footsteps nearly inaudible.

"That's a beautiful cello."

Ember stilled, teabag in hand. She'd been just about to put it into the mug, but then he'd spoken. *That's a beautiful cello.*

It was. Old and burnished and haunted by the ghost of her former self, it rested on a stand in one corner of the room, where she could always see it. Because she needed the daily reminder.

Nothing lasts. Impermanence is the only permanence there is.

Once you fully realize you can die at any moment, tomorrow is nothing more than wishful thinking. Today is the only reality that exists. Right now. Past and future are just figments of your imagination.

When she didn't comment, Christian asked, "Do you play?"

She released her breath in a long, silent exhalation. "No. Not at all."

There was a pause, but he didn't press it, and the tension in her shoulders eased.

But when she turned back to him, the tension seized her again, only now it was in every muscle in her body. He was standing beside the low console table that flanked the divan, studying a framed picture he held in his hand. A picture he'd lifted from the table. He looked up at her and said, "Is this your family?"

Ember swallowed around the flame of agony that rose in her throat. It still hurt, after all these years, those four simple words that should have started with *was* instead of *is*.

Fighting back the sudden, horrible onslaught of tears, she swallowed and said, "Yes. That's my mom and dad, Keely and Carter. And my . . . my little brother. August."

Auggie. We called him Auggie, she thought, and bit the inside of her mouth.

"Your parents named you and your brother after months of the year?" He seemed interested, not at all critical or mocking the way the kids at school had been.

"My mom was a bit of a hippie. She grew up in a commune in Oregon and had strange ideas about a lot of things."

That was a gross understatement. Her mother had strange ideas about everything. She was into astrology, numerology, and the Tarot, and often said she was just biding her time on Earth until the mother ship arrived to take her home. An Aquarian, the free-thinking, oddball, idealistic sign of the zodiac, Keely Carter was a natural force unto herself. She was a passionate, challenging, unconventional person, and Ember missed her, every single day.

Her mother had devoured life. She'd inhaled it. To this day, Ember had still never met another person so unafraid.

"My brother was born in August, hence the name, and I—"

"You were born in September," Christian correctly guessed.

Ember sighed. "A few more days and my name would've been October. Scary thought, right?"

He was looking at her sharply, his green gaze piercing. "And they live in Spain, too?"

Her stomach dropped. She turned back to the stove, and the kettle began to waver from the moisture suddenly welling in her eyes. "Tea's ready. Do you take milk? Sugar?"

There was a pause that seemed pregnant, then he came up behind her. He was still in stealth mode, his steps silent over the floor. She knew he was there anyway because she was so attuned to his movement, to his presence, his warmth, his very breath, she could pinpoint his exact location in the room. He leaned with his hips against the counter next to the stove and watched her pour the boiling water from the kettle into the waiting mug.

In a quiet voice, he said, "My parents were killed in a car accident six years ago. It was the worst day of my life. But, in a way . . . I'm glad they went together."

Stricken, unable to speak, Ember looked over at him. Tears burned her eyes.

A car accident. Killed in a car accident.

She had to fight to breathe, and slowly, very carefully, set the kettle back on the stove.

"They were married thirty-five years. In all that time, they never once spent a night apart. They still held hands. It used to make me cringe when I was young, seeing how they looked at each other. I thought it was so embarrassing. But now I realize how lucky they were. How lucky my brother and sister and I were to have them as parents."

Ember felt her lower lip tremble, and bit down on it, hard, to make it stop. His gaze dropped to her mouth then jumped back up to her eyes. He waited, silently, for her to speak.

"My father died three years ago. Just a year after we moved here," she whispered.

"It was sudden?" Christian's voice was lowered to match her own. The intimacy of the moment was excruciating, standing in her kitchen with a total stranger, serving him tea and speaking aloud words she had promised herself she'd never speak again.

Ember nodded. "Heart attack."

Christian watched her, still waiting, his eyes vivid with empathy.

She took a breath, tried to blink the moisture away. It didn't work. "He was at his easel, painting. I'd come up to the studio to bring him lunch and he was fine, everything was fine. Then after we ate he went back to work and I was just sitting there, reading a book, and I heard him make the oddest noise."

Ember closed her eyes and saw it all again, just as clear as if it had happened yesterday. The relentless summer heat, the smell of oil paint and acetone, her father at the easel, both handsome and haggard. The Beethoven he always played drifting through hidden speakers in the walls.

"He looked out the window—there was a wall of windows in his studio, he needed the light—and he had this expression on his face, as if he . . . as if he'd seen something. Or someone. But there was no one there, just the trees, the clouds, and the sunshine. And he said, 'Oh.' Just that. 'Oh.' Then he fell off the stool onto the floor. He didn't suffer, he was gone instantly. When the ambulance came to take him away the medic said he'd never seen anyone look so peaceful."

But that wasn't what the medic had really said. The medic had said *happy*. He'd never seen a dead person look so happy. And Ember knew he was right. Her father had technically died of a heart attack, but it had been brought on by a broken heart and he had been glad to finally be rid of life.

On the worst of the nights afterward when she couldn't sleep, she'd stare up at the dark ceiling while memories crowded in, cold and frightening like hovering ghosts. As pain crawled over her body like a thousand writhing snakes, she'd wonder what it was her father had seen outside the window. She'd wonder what it was that had startled him, what had made him meet his maker with that look of relieved euphoria on his face.

Or who.

"And your mother?"

Ember's left hand stuttered—that awful, telling tremble she hated with every fiber of her being—and she curled it to a fist at her side. With her right hand she picked up the mug of tea and handed it over without looking at him.

He took it from her, cupped it between his palms, looked down at it. He drew in a breath and exhaled it in a rush. "I'm sorry. I'm being rude. This is none of my business."

In a barely audible voice, Ember said, "Thank you for saying that. You're not being rude, though, I am. It's just . . . It's just that I can't talk about it. It only makes it worse."

He nodded, still gazing into the mug. "I know exactly what you mean. Consider the subject closed." He downed the scalding tea in one long swallow and set the mug back on the countertop. "So," he said brusquely, shoving away from the counter and looking at her with a pleasant smile, "I'm still interested in that copy of *Casino Royale*. You never did quote me a price."

Equal parts relieved and grateful he hadn't pressed her and had made an elegant segue into another topic, Ember made an attempt at lighthearted normalcy. "Well, a certain someone ran out on another certain someone before a price could be negotiated, but I'll let that go. On second thought," she cocked her head, eyeing his shiny platinum watch, encrusted with tiny diamonds. "Maybe I'll add a nuisance fee into the price. Say . . . twenty percent?"

"Twenty percent?" he echoed, smiling widely now. "That's highway robbery! I should report you to the authorities! Do they have a Trading Standards Institute or a Better Business Bureau in this country?"

"If they do, Antiquarian Books isn't a member of either," she scoffed. "With me running it, there's definitely nothing 'Better' about it. It's practically bankrupt." The minute the words left her mouth, she regretted them, but too late—Christian had already latched onto them like a dog on a bone.

"The store isn't doing well? What's wrong? How bad is it?" He straightened, suddenly imposing with his height, breadth of shoulders, and the electric intensity that came and went with dizzying speed, like a light switch being flipped. At the moment, the switch had been turned to *on*.

"Oh, please," she said, trying to laugh it off, "forget it. I'm just joking." Avoiding his intent gaze, she brushed passed him and went into the living room. She looked around the darkened room a moment, unsure whether to stand or sit . . . Was he staying? What exactly *was* he doing here?

But Christian decided for her when he said, "A joke. Of course. I understand."

She turned and watched him walk closer, searching his expression suspiciously, on the lookout for any hint of emotion to indicate what he was thinking. But his face was smooth and composed, entirely unreadable.

Damn. She didn't want him thinking she was desperate for money. The two most unattractive things to men were women who were one: desperate for money, or two: desperate for love. She was neither. Or if she was, she definitely didn't want to seem like she was. For the money, that is. Love was the last thing her mangled heart would ever be able to feel.

"Well," he said, pausing a few feet away, "it's late. I've imposed on you long enough. Thank you for the tea."

"Sure. Anytime."

He smiled at that—*anytime*—and something in her chest softened, a peculiar sort of melting. The man was so handsome it made her head hurt. That face. That body. Those *eyes.* Jesus. She had to get him out before she lost her mind and threw herself on him.

She ground her teeth together. *Not desperate. NOT desperate. And,* she reminded herself, *I hate him. He's too pretty for his own good.*

"What is that look you're giving me? Are you by chance plotting my death?" Christian asked, bemused. Her cheeks flamed—caught again.

"I've just really got to get out of this costume," she said, careful to keep her face blank. She crossed the small living room quickly, put her hand on the doorknob. "I think I'm suffocating my poor skin, latex doesn't exactly breathe. Plus, I'm beat."

She turned the knob and cracked the door open, as clear a signal as she could give that she agreed with him—it was time for him to go.

He watched her with those preternatural eyes, his gaze taking in her bare feet, the cat's costume, the tail dangling behind her like a dare. Her expression, so carefully neutral. A slight upward lift curled his lips as if he found something amusing. Leisurely, with his hands in his pockets and his gaze never leaving hers, he crossed to the door and stood looking down at her, mere inches away.

"I'll see you at the store tomorrow."

It sounded like a threat. She peered up at him, lips pursed, hating the way his proximity sent her blood into a frenzy. Her heart pounded so hard in her chest she wondered if he could hear it. "Okay." She shrugged, feigning nonchalance. "Whatever."

His smile deepened. "Doesn't really matter either way, hmm?"

She moistened her lips and shrugged again, looking away.

Then he did the most astonishing thing, something that turned her to stone and stole all the breath from her lungs.

He reached out, touched two fingers to the pulse throbbing wildly in her neck and held them there with the softest pressure, subtly dominant. She glanced back at his face, speechless, and he was looking down at her as if he knew all about her, as if he could read every single thought that crossed her mind.

He murmured, "Secrets are okay. Secrets I understand. But don't lie to me, Ember. You want to see me tomorrow as much as I want to see you."

She was pinned in the raw force of his eyes, magnetic, overpowering. Very slowly, oh-so-lightly, he slid his fingers down the length of her throat, skimming the surface of her skin, dipping his thumb into the hollow at the base of her neck, until his hand came to rest in the center of her chest, directly over her heart. He opened his palm over the rings on her necklace and pressed against her breastbone.

Boom, boom, boom, throbbed her heart. Her traitorous, telltale heart.

"Admit it."

She bit her tongue. He leaned slightly forward when he spoke and she felt his warm breath brush her cheek. "Ember. Admit it."

There was fire in his eyes, fire in her blood, fire in the air all around them. She breathed fire into her lungs with each breath, and with each breath felt it scorch through her body, consuming. Dangerous.

She whispered, "I'm not looking for any complications in my life, Christian. And that's not a lie. It's taken me a long time to get to this point, where I'm . . . " She faltered, because he was watching her lips as she spoke, looking at her mouth in total concentration. And somehow he'd moved closer. "Where I'm safe."

The word *safe* affected him, made him hesitate. She felt it in the tension in his body, the slight twitch in the hand he'd pressed over her heart. He closed his eyes for just longer than a blink, then withdrew his hand. The sudden loss of heat against her skin was jarring.

"Of course," he murmured. He exhaled. "You're right."

He didn't say *I understand.* He said *you're right.* The difference struck her as important, but she couldn't pinpoint why.

He stepped back, turned to the door and gave her a small, apologetic smile over his shoulder. "I'll have to ask you to forgive me again. It seems I'm always off-balance around you." He exhaled again, ran a hand through his thick black hair. Then with a quiet, "Good night, Ember," he slipped through the open door and silently, swiftly, disappeared down the stairs.

Ember closed the door and stood in the darkness for long minutes, unseeing, her blood and nerves and thoughts frenzied, her hands shaking at her sides.

I'm always off-balance around you.

Well, that definitely made two of them. And despite feeling very clearly he was somehow dangerous, despite her resolve to dislike him and keep it all business, she was equally certain there was something going on between them. Something her body recognized and to which it responded. Something her mind—always so careful, always so calculating—was doing little to counteract.

"Christian McLoughlin," she whispered to the dark, empty room, "who are you? And what the hell have you done with my brain?"

The room had no answer.

SEVEN

Alphas, Betas & Others

In spite of his promise, Christian didn't come into the bookstore the next day.

Ember arrived to work early—successfully avoiding Dante—and spent the day in a state of suspended animation, both hoping he'd walk through the door and dreading it.

Because what exactly was going on here? In the clear light of day she determined it was nothing, that's what. He was toying with her, he was indulging in some kind of macho ego-trip, the knight in shining armor winking at the poor, mud-splattered village girl before riding up to the castle on his steed to ask for the hand of the princess in marriage. She was a diversion, that was all. A momentary blip on his radar.

At least, she'd convinced herself of that until precisely five minutes to six, when the door to the shop opened and a man walked in carrying the most enormous bouquet of roses she'd ever seen in her life.

Ember couldn't even see his upper body behind the mass of foliage and flowers spilling voluptuously from the vase. The thick, etched crystal vase, no less. The man took half a dozen careful steps into the shop before halting in the middle of the floor and announcing loudly in Spanish, "Flower delivery!"

Certainly he'd been hired for his acute grasp of the obvious.

"Yes, over here!" Ember called, waving from behind the counter though he couldn't see her. After several unsuccessful attempts to determine her location by peeking over and around the voluminous spray, he finally turned sideways and addressed her, his face strained with the effort of balancing the enormous arrangement in his arms.

"Roses for a Miss Jones."

"That's me."

His expression registered gratitude. "Where you want it?"

"Uh . . . " She looked around for a space large enough and spied the round table where Sofia's book club met each week. "Over there. That would be great, thanks."

He made his way slowly to the table, going sideways like a crab, until finally he'd deposited his burden to the wood tabletop with a relieved sigh. He turned to look at her, a canny smile on his face. "Somebody is in love, eh?"

Ember blushed to the roots of her hair. "No! No, nothing like that. These are from, er, my, uh, um—"

"Boyfriend?" he supplied helpfully.

Ember's blush spread down her neck. "NO! He's a customer! Just a customer!"

His brows rose. His gaze moved around the shop and he saw the handwritten sign Asher had taped to the side of the one of the rare book displays near the register as a joke. It read, "Don't touch yourself. Ask the staff for help." The delivery man's gaze settled back on her and his knowing smile grew wider. Ember had the sudden horrible thought he might be wondering exactly what type of customer she'd been entertaining behind the shelves.

"Thanks again. We're closing now. Good-bye." She ushered him to the door, all the while avoiding his sideways glances and cocky grin, and locked it behind him. Once alone she crossed slowly back to the table that housed the ridiculous display of roses and stood staring at it in stupefied wonder.

Lavender roses—dozens and dozens—so silvery pale and silky they glimmered beneath the lights.

There was no card, no enclosure note saying *Hi* or *Thinking of you* or *Sorry I blew you off,* but as Ember stared at the massive display, she remembered something that made her heart first skip one beat, then two, then stop altogether.

Well-versed in the language of flowers, her mother had often recited to her all the meanings for the different colors of roses they'd grown in their garden at home. She'd had to coax them, of course, the heat and altitude of Taos was an unforgiving place to grow roses, but under her mother's patient, intuitive care, they'd flourished. Their front yard was a riot of color and all kinds of plants, but the roses that lined the brick walkway to the front door were the *piece de resistance,* and not one bush was the same.

Red meant love, white meant purity, pink was grace and appreciation, yellow was friendship. Orange was desire. Peach was sincerity.

And lavender roses, rare and royal, the most beautiful of them all, meant love at first sight.

"Oh, boy," whispered Ember, staring at the luscious blooms. "This is gonna get messy."

"What *happened* to you last night?" Asher shrieked down the phone line. Ember winced and held it away from her ear. "You *disappeared!* I was worried *sick!*"

She'd been back in her flat just long enough to change from jeans to sweats before her cell phone rang. She pretended she wasn't disappointed when she saw the number on the readout, but when he started yelling at her, Ember didn't have to manufacture the anger that had her yelling right back.

"I told you I was leaving! You didn't want to go!"

"What? You never said you were leaving!"

"I pointed to the exit!"

"I thought you had to go to the *bathroom!* I'd never let you wander around the city in the middle of the night by yourself, knucklehead! Do you have any idea how worried I was?"

That took the wind out of her sails. "Oh," she said, much calmer. "Sorry. I thought I was being clear that I was leaving."

Asher huffed indignantly. "No, *I'm* sorry! Your vague hand signals were anything but clear, a friggin' mime would be more obvious! I thought I'd have a heart attack when you didn't come back! I spent an hour trying to find you at the club until I finally gave up and came home. And lo and behold, there she was! Sleeping like Goldilocks—"

"Wait, I wasn't in *your* bed. What are you talking about?"

There was a short silence. "I used the spare key you gave me to get into your apartment. I just needed to check and see if you were home. And yes, you were—snoring in blissful ignorance, I might add—so I didn't have to take that extra Xanax—"

"Asher!" Ember stomped her foot, and immediately felt so ridiculous she was grateful there was no one there to see it. "You can't just sneak in to my bedroom and watch me sleep! This isn't *Twilight*, for God's sake! Do we need to have a talk about boundaries?"

"I wasn't watching you sleep, I was just checking on you! I just peeked in and then left! Sorry for *caring!*"

Uh-oh. She knew Seriously Cranky Asher when she heard him. This was a precursor to Arctic Cold Shoulder Asher, who could last an indefinite period of time, in which case she'd only have Dante, her stepmother, and the customers at the store to talk to. Keeping to yourself really had its drawbacks sometimes.

Reining in her temper, she blew out an exasperated breath. "Ash," she said, in a soft, cajoling voice.

"No," he said firmly, but she still detected the pout.

"C'mon, don't be mad at me. I'm sorry I scared you. And I'm glad you care. You know you're my only friend. Who else will put up with my crap? You said it yourself, you're my fairy godmother, so you can't stay pissed. I might need you to turn a pumpkin into a coach one of these days."

There was a low, disgruntled, *hmmpf,* but nothing more.

"I'll make it up to you. How about . . . " Inspiration hit. "How about if we watch *Reservoir Dogs* together tonight?" His favorite movies always involved a lot of macho gun-slinging, bromancing, and blood, so he adored anything involving Clint Eastwood, Charles Bronson, or Quentin Tarantino.

His response to her movie invitation was silence.

"And I can order *tapas* from that place you like down the block."

More silence. He still wasn't taking the bait. Ember knew she had to get serious, or risk a pout-fest that could last well into next month. "And . . . I'll tell you all about what happened with Christian last night after I left you at the club."

There was a loud, high-pitched inhalation on the other end of the phone that sounded very much like the noise a vacuum cleaner makes when turned on. She thought her brain might get sucked out through her ear and disappear through the line.

"Christian! Not *the* Christian?"

At her sound of affirmation, Asher said, "I'm on my way," and hung up.

It couldn't have been fifteen seconds before he knocked on the front door. Ember opened it to find him in a pea-cock blue kimono and bare feet, his face slathered in a thick layer of pale green cream.

"Is that moisturizer?" she asked, stepping back to let him in.

He breezed past trailing the scent of cucumbers and lavender. "Pore-reducing mask. It's wonderful for the skin tone. You should try it."

"Is that your way of telling me I have a problem with my pores?"

He swung around and his kimono billowed in a bell around his ankles. Arms akimbo, he looked her up and down. "Honey, your pores are the least of your problems. When are you going to let me take you shopping?"

"Hmm." She looked at the ceiling, pretending to decide. "How about the Tuesday after never?"

"You are *no* fun. Seriously, what's a fairy godmother good for if she can't buy you a dress for the ball?"

"*Ball?* There will be no balls, thank you very much. The only thing worse than wearing a dress is hearing the howls of laughter as I do my version of dancing, which looks uncannily like a reanimated corpse during an epileptic fit. So not going to happen."

"So *that's* why you never dance when we go out! Well you just need the right teacher, honey! I can teach anyone to dance! Here, follow me."

Before Ember could protest, Asher had gathered her up in his arms and begun trilling "I Could Have Danced All Night" from *My Fair Lady*, swinging her around like laundry on a clothesline. It didn't last long because Ember trod on his bare feet so many times he finally released her and limped away, gasping in pain.

"Christ, you weren't kidding!" He hobbled to the couch and threw himself on it, collapsing with a theatrical sigh to rub his bruised toes. "Were those feet of yours donated from the morgue?"

"I tried to warn you." Ember flopped down on the couch beside him. "You should have seen the carnage when my mother tried to put me in ballet when I was fourteen. Those poor, poor boys."

Asher sighed. "Ballet boys. In *tights*. God was good when She thought of that one." He turned to her with twinkling eyes. "And *speaking* of ballet boys . . . spill it, sister. Spill it all. And don't leave a single dirty detail out. You need to make up for damaging my arches."

Ember blew out a breath, trying to decide where to begin, and then started with when she first saw Christian at the store and ended with the delivery of roses.

When she finished, Asher was sitting with his shoulders hunched up around his ears, clutching the neck of his blue silk kimono, gaping at her through his pore-reducing mask.

"Oh. My. *God*. I knew he was hot, but lavender roses? 'You want to see me as much as I want to see you?'" He fanned himself with one hand. "Scorching, honey. Seriously scorching. I need to go take a cold shower with my George Clooney blow up doll."

Ember said, "You are a very, very disturbed person."

He shrugged. "Of course I am. All the best people are. What, you want to hang out with *normal* people?" He shuddered and drew his robe tighter around his neck.

"No, I suppose not. Normal people aren't nearly as interesting as you."

They shared a grin. "So what are you going to do?"

Ember's smile faded. She looked down at her hands, inspected her nails—in dire need of a manicure—and sighed. "Nothing, obviously. It's your classic *Beauty and the Beast* tale, except he's Beauty and I'm the Beast. Honestly, I'm sure he's just in-between lingerie models or something. I can't figure out why he's giving someone like me the time of day."

Asher reached out and brushed a stray lock of hair off Ember's shoulder. He rested his hand there for a moment, then softly said, "You don't always have to do that, you know."

She glanced at him, confused. "Do what?"

He was looking at her carefully, his brows drawn together, his mouth—surrounded by green cream—downturned. "Put yourself down."

"Look at me, Ash. I'm the poster girl for 'Average.' There's nothing about me that would tempt a man like him."

"Except there *is*. *You*. You're a lot cuter than you give yourself credit for, even if you are hiding it behind all those baggy clothes and unplucked eyebrows and scowls. You're smart, and you're funny, and you're not full of bubblegum and bullshit like a lingerie model. Trust me, I've known a few. Plus, you've got a tight little figure and a very perky set of headlights," he added, glancing down at her T-shirt clad chest. "If I were into that kind of thing, I would totally do you."

Ember pulled a face, a combination of *gee, thanks,* and *gross, stop.*

"Granted, that attitude of yours is a little beastly, but if he can see past that, he might be a keeper."

"Uh, let's not get ahead of ourselves here, Ash. I've known him a few days. He could be a serial killer, for all I know. Or—worse—an accountant."

Her mother had once told her never to marry an accountant because even while he was making love to her, he'd be counting all the ways he could be saving money instead. It might have been unfair, but it was an unattractive image that had stuck.

Asher scoffed and rolled his eyes. "If that man is an accountant, I'm the King of Spain. Seriously, honey, Christian is one thing and one thing only."

Ember lifted her brows.

"Hot, hard Alpha male."

Ember's nose wrinkled. "You make him sound like a horny wolf or something. Alpha male?"

"There are only three types of men, honey. Alphas, Betas and Assholes. The last two come in varying degrees, but an Alpha . . . well, they only come in one size. A smart woman's job is to find out what kind of male she's dealing with, *before* she falls in love with him. Because once your heart gets involved, you're toast."

Smiling, Ember settled back against the cushions of the couch and tucked her feet up under her legs. "This should be educational."

"Okay, we'll start at the bottom. Assholes, well that speaks for itself. The tricky thing with an Asshole, though, is that they can manage to convince you—sometimes well enough so you'll marry them—that they're not really an Asshole. They're generally charming, intelligent, and magnetic, and it's easy to mistake that magnetism for maturity, for authentic masculinity. They're fun and dynamic, they're exciting. But their true nature eventually reveals itself. These are the guys who walk slightly ahead of you, just a little bit faster so you have to hurry to keep up. They always forget how you take your coffee, they flirt with other women right in front of you, they drive like madmen and tell you— not very nicely—to lighten up when you remark that you'd rather not die in the passenger seat of their car.

"They commit all kinds of minor, seemingly forgivable trespasses against your self-esteem, they make you feel slightly off-kilter and convince you it's your problem, not theirs. They are masters of manipulation, utterly narcissistic, and very, very seductive. At first. You will never feel so desired as when an Asshole has you in his sights. But as soon as the conquest is made, he's off to greener pastures and you're left feeling like a baby duckling who's had a nuclear bomb dropped on her head."

Ember laughed. "Duly noted. No Assholes. What about Betas? Isn't that a fish?"

He chuckled, nodding. "Close. Betas are much more sensitive and nurturing and seem like ideal husband material compared to the Asshole. Again, at first. They won't stray, they won't lie, they're usually solid as a rock. And twice as dull. They're the mama's boys, the wimps, the conformists who don't have the spine to stand up for themselves, let alone anyone else. Ultimately, they bring out the worst in a woman because of their failure to take charge in the relationship, the way a man secure in himself and what he has to offer would take charge. Betas let you have your way in everything and you end up feeling overworked and underappreciated. You end up feeling like their mommy because they're too scared to make the hard decisions for themselves. If the words, 'Yes, dear,' ever leave a man's mouth, you know you're dealing with a Beta. There are a lot of women who've had enough of Assholes and settle down with a stable, passive Beta, only to regret it for the rest of their lives."

Okay, that was a lot to take in from a man with a face covered in green beauty cream.

"And the Alphas?"

Asher sighed. "Ah, the elusive Alpha. The cream of the crop, so to speak. He is masculine in the purest form of the word; confident, capable, fiercely protective of those he cares about, a good father to his children, and a good lover to his woman. He won't always go along with what you want because he's got his own ideas of how things should be done, but when it really matters, he'll listen to your opinion.

And your feelings. Though he doesn't often talk about them, he's not afraid of feelings—yours or his own—and he's not afraid of commitment like an Asshole is.

"The flip side of that coin is that he's not afraid of confrontation, either. He'll call you out on your bullshit. He'll stand his ground when you fight but forgive you as soon as the fight is over. He says what he means, he means what he says, and he's someone you can lean on when times are tough. He's assertive, self-determined, and everything a real man should be. You might not always agree with him, but you will always *admire* him, and feel cherished by him. That's how you know you're dealing with an Alpha male."

There was a long silence after this speech, in which the two friends stared at one another and the only sound was the clock ticking on the wall.

"Forget about writing about sports, you should write a romance novel! How do you know so much about men and women's relationships anyway? I mean, seeing as how you only date *men*?"

Asher cocked his head and smiled at her, slightly sad, and very knowing. "I've been around a long time, honey, and I've seen a lot of things. I was thirty years old before I came out of the closet, and I dated my share of women before then, let me tell you. Being gay wasn't accepted back in the day the way it is now, especially in the States. There was a time a man could be arrested just for dancing with another man in public, and I lived through that. I lived in the Village when the police raided Stonewall and sparked the riots. I grew up in a time before Gay Pride, activism, and tolerance, back when the FBI kept records of openly out gays and the Post Office kept track of addresses where materials they labeled 'homosexual' were sent. I served in the Marines for eight years and every single day of that time I was scared shitless someone would find out I was gay and deem me unfit to serve my country."

Ember looked at Asher's full head of dark hair, the smooth, unlined skin around his eyes, his baby soft hands and muscular limbs. "Ash, I know you once bit my head off for asking this question, but exactly how old *are* you? I thought you were like, I don't know, fifteen years older than me?"

He beamed. "Oh, honey, that is so sweet! I'm telling you, if you take care of your skin you can look young forever. Sunscreen is your friend. And . . . I may have had a little maintenance nip and tuck here and there."

When she raised her brows, Asher said defensively, "If the roof of your house collapses you don't just leave it there and say it's aging gracefully, right? No, you fix that sucker up! Also, remember these two very important words: Bo. Tox."

He waved a hand, indicating this part of the conversation was over. "Anyway, after thirty years of living a lie, do you know who the first person I told the truth to was?"

Ember shook her head.

"My mother. God bless her, she acted as if I'd just told her I passed the Bar. She said, 'Finally!' gave me a hug and a kiss, and that was that. And then I called all the girls I'd dated in college and afterward and told them, too. *Every single one of them*—except Mary Catherine Campbell, she was always an uptight little priss—told me they were happy for me and wished me well. There were a few tears, a few mutters of 'I thought something was odd,' but on the whole they were amazing. So I have experience in relationships on both sides of the aisle, but women have always been my best friends. Just like gay men, they understand what it's like to be marginalized. They know what it's like to have to keep their mouths shut and their heads down and their true hearts locked up tight. They know how it feels to smile so hard their cheeks hurt while inside they're dying."

He closed his eyes and let out a long, heavy sigh. "Or maybe it's just because they dress so much better than most men." He glanced over Ember's outfit of sweats and a T-shirt and sent her an affectionate smile. "Present company excluded, of course."

Ember felt a sudden, warm tenderness for him, this comrade-in-arms who'd learned all about pain and shame and loss. It pierced her heart like a spear and she had to make a joke in order to lighten the mood and hold back the tears. "I don't know, Ash, that outfit of yours isn't going to win any fashion awards."

He pretended outrage. "This kimono is *Gaultier*, honey!"

She smiled. "I should've guessed."

"And don't think I've forgotten your promise of movies and *tapas*, baby girl. Get on it." He shooed her off the couch and lay down with his bare feet up on the arm at one end while Ember went to the kitchen and dug around in the junk drawer for the takeout menu.

Just as she was about to dial the number to the restaurant, the phone in her hand rang. She looked down at it, saw who was calling, and the folded paper menu slipped between her fingers and drifted unnoticed to the floor.

EIGHT
How to Live

"Hello?"

Her voice was low and a little breathy, as if she'd run across the room to pick up the phone.

"Did you get the flowers?" Christian said, smiling. He'd wanted a bigger display, but the flower shop only had a vase large enough to hold one hundred of the beautiful lavender roses, and he thought sending another vase of a hundred might have been overkill. Especially since she seemed determined to keep him at arm's length. He was determined to keep it that way, too, but still—a few flowers couldn't hurt.

"I did." Ember cleared her throat. "They're beautiful, thank you. That wasn't necessary."

She sounded lukewarm about the roses, a little businesslike, and it made his smile turn to a frown. Did she think he had some ulterior motive for sending them, perhaps to get a better price on the copy of *Casino Royale*? That was a disturbing thought, and couldn't be farther from the truth. He'd simply been driving down *Las Ramblas*, spotted the little floral boutique, and given in to the strong impulse to buy her something that might put that spectacular smile back on her face.

"I didn't get a chance to ask you what your favorite flower was, so I sent mine."

There was a loaded pause. "Oh. Lavender roses are your favorite."

Now she sounded disappointed for some reason. His frown grew deeper.

"Actually, I love all colors of roses. My mother was an incredible gardener; we had what seemed like acres of roses covering the grounds of our property when I was growing up."

There was another pause, this one longer. Christian imagined her thinking on the other end of the line, worrying her bottom lip like she did when preoccupied. He wished he could see her face, be near her so he could judge her reactions. He wished he could press his fingers to her throat again and feel that swift, hot throbbing against his skin.

"By the way you say, 'grounds', I'm guessing we're not talking about a little country cottage here."

Her voice had now turned from disappointed to wry, faintly acidic. He'd never thought he could irritate someone so much in three short sentences. "I'm sorry, this conversation doesn't seem to be going the way I'd hoped. Have I said something to offend you?"

She exhaled, a pretty, feminine sound that was heavy with some unnamed emotion. "No, of course not. Ignore me. I shouldn't be allowed to speak to normal people, my bad manners are practically contagious. The roses were beautiful. Really, thank you again."

Christian's voice came very low. "You think I'm *normal?* Let me assure you, September, that couldn't be farther from the truth."

"Well, your distractingly pretty looks aside—"

"Distractingly pretty?" Christian felt vaguely insulted. She'd called him pretty before too—did she mean she thought he looked effeminate? Jesus, this conversation was getting entirely derailed.

She didn't even have the decency to sound apologetic. "You are the prettiest man I've ever seen, and that's the ugly truth, Fancypants. You must be aware of how you look by now, you've been living with that face for . . . "

"Thirty-one years," he said between gritted teeth. "And how long have you been cultivating that devastating charm of yours, Miss Jones?"

She chuckled. "Twenty-four years. Perfected it, haven't I?"

"To a science."

She chuckled again, then sighed. "Okay, truce. I promise not to call you pretty anymore if you promise not to send flowers again."

"You don't like flowers? Are you allergic?"

"Yes, and no. I love flowers, especially roses. My mother was an amazing gardener, too." Her tone grew light, suspiciously offhand. "She taught me all the meanings of different flowers. The meanings of their different colors, too."

A slow, spreading grin took over Christian's face. *Now we're getting to the bottom of it,* he thought. "That's very interesting. We seem to have much in common, Ember. My own mother taught me the exact same thing."

The silence from the other end of the phone actually burned. He had to bite his tongue to keep from laughing.

"So—is this—is this a business call, or—to what do I owe the pleasure of your call?"

Stammering her way through it, she sounded equal parts horrified, shocked and utterly confused. God, she was adorable. He knew her face was aflame with heat right now and he wanted to reach through the phone and caress her red cheeks. "Both business and pleasure I think. I'd like to invite you to dinner so we can finalize the deal on *Casino Royale.*"

"We don't . . . we don't need to have dinner to do that. I can quote you a price over the phone and have it delivered—"

"But then I won't get to see you," he said abruptly, his voice very low. He'd gone back and forth over it in his head a hundred times, and hadn't been able to talk himself out of seeing her again. Just one last time, and then he'd be done with this nonsense for good.

He let it hang there for a moment, giving her space, giving her a chance to say no, though it was all he could do not to find some way to force her to say yes. Ignoring that faint, ringing alarm in the back of his mind that whispered *stupid, danger, stay away,* he waited.

Finally after a long, tense silence, Ember said, "All right then. When?"

"Tonight," he said instantly. "I'll pick you up in an hour—"

"No, I can't tonight. I'm busy. I have a date."

That brought him up short. "A date," he repeated, surprised how much it angered him.

"With Asher," she said innocently, and he heard her smile through the line.

Oh, the little minx.

"Tomorrow then. Unless you have another date."

"No, tomorrow's perfect. It's my day off."

"Seven o'clock?" Christian felt the anticipation start to rise within him, dark and electric like the precursor of a storm.

"Seven o'clock," Ember agreed softly. Before he could say another word, she disconnected the call.

Ember stood staring at the phone silently for several moments, her mind a tangle of unanswered questions, her body a riot of emotions. She raised her gaze to Asher in the living room. When he had realized who she was talking to, he'd sat up ramrod straight on the couch and listened breathlessly to every word she spoke.

"So?" His voice was hushed, his eyes, wide. The green mask had dried in irregular patches on his skin and was beginning to flake off around his nose.

"So . . . it appears you're going to get to buy me that dress after all. My knight in shining denim is coming to pick me up tomorrow night at seven o'clock. For dinner."

After a low, thrilled gasp, Asher whispered, "You have a date with him, Ember. *A. Date. With. Him!*" He emphasized each word, his hands clutching the edge of the sofa as if he was afraid he might fall off if he didn't hang on.

It occurred to her that this might be the worst idea she'd had in a long time.

"Don't freak out," Asher warned, reading the look on her face that must have telegraphed the sheer terror by which she was suddenly frozen. "It's just dinner, Ember. Even you can make it through one dinner."

"It's not the dinner I'm worried about, Ash. It's . . . everything else."

Asher stood, crossed to her in a billowing cloud of blue silk, took her shoulders in his hands, and gave her a hard little shake. "Repeat after me: one day at a time."

"One day at a time. Right. And how exactly does the motto of Alcoholics Anonymous apply to this situation?"

"Oh my God, is that the motto of AA? How the hell would I know that? Do you think that's a sign?" He looked nauseated for about half a second, then shrugged it off. Asher was very good at shrugging off inconvenient thoughts, a talent of which Ember, plagued by not only inconvenient but agonizing and often immobilizing thoughts, was insanely jealous. "Anyway, it's universal, honey. Life happens one day at a time. We're just going to apply that to your relationship with Christian."

Her eyes bulged. "*Relationship?*"

Asher rolled his eyes at her horrified expression. "Okay. Friendship, acquaintance, business association, whatever. We're just going to take it one day at a time, one dinner at a time. We're not going to worry about the future, we're just going to enjoy the ride. Even *you* can do that. Right?"

Ember blew out a breath. The not-worrying-about-the-future part she had down pat. It was the enjoying the ride part that was going to give her trouble.

But Asher was looking at her with such . . . hope. He really was the only one in the entire world who gave a damn about her. She could probably manage one dinner for his sake.

"I suppose," she relented. Then when his raised brows and pursed lips indicated he wasn't quite satisfied with this answer, she said, "Okay, fine! Yes! I can do that!"

He beamed, and a little shower of green flakes from his dried mask drifted down like snowfall from his crinkling cheeks. "Good. One dinner at a time, starting with tomorrow night. And then after you've had a few dinners and basked in all his Alpha male glory, you're going to answer me one question."

"Which is?"

Asher's smile slowly faded. He studied her face, and even through the thick layer of crusted pore-reducing mask she saw how concerned he was about her. How much he worried.

"The question is this: how alive do you want to be?" His voice was soft and tender. "Because you, honey, are barely breathing."

Barely breathing. That sounded just about right. To compensate for the sudden flood of emotion she felt, the rush of sorrow and weariness and longing that squeezed her heart, she said, "You're a real pain in my ass, you know that?"

He leaned in and gave her a swift, hard hug. "And that's exactly why you love me," he whispered into her ear.

When he pulled away Tender Asher was gone and he was in full Bossy Asher mode, complete with lifted chin, arch demeanor and a dismissive hand wave that would have been at home on the Queen of England. "Food first, then we're going to talk about where I'm taking you shopping tomorrow morning."

"What about the movie?"

"Screw the movie, sister, we've got plans to make! My boy Quentin can wait."

Ember spent her Sunday morning—and most of the afternoon—being dragged from fancy boutique to fancier boutique by an over-caffeinated, almost manic Asher, who insisted they had to find the exact perfect thing for this momentous occasion. Knowing she'd become a project, Ember allowed herself to be manhandled and clucked over by a host of vaguely disgruntled shopgirls who stared at her as if she were a lab animal on which vaginal deodorant sprays had been tested.

She didn't understand how other women loved shopping so much. It was exhausting. And more than a bit depressing; the clothes always looked much better on the mannequins than on her.

By the time three o'clock rolled around, she'd had enough.

"Enough!" she said to Asher just as he was about to wrap a tissue-thin silk Hermes scarf around her neck. It was the color of the Mediterranean, an enameled azure blue, and floated like a cloud between his hands. She spied the price tag and nearly gagged.

"Don't even start with me, *chica*, you're getting this scarf whether you like it or not. You need color against that pasty skin of yours." He eyed her complexion and clucked in disapproval. "When you're that pale, you need something slightly darker yet brighter than your skin tone to complement it. This is definitely your color." He held it up to his face and examined himself in the nearby full-length mirror, smiled at his reflection, and blew himself a kiss. "And mine."

"Asher, you know I can't afford—"

"Tch! Quiet! Not another word, ingrate! I told you this is on me!"

He'd already bought her a dress, shoes, and a matching handbag, and had snuck in some lacy black underwear while she wasn't looking—a matching bra and panty set that looked decadent enough to eat. She wouldn't wear them. If she wore them, she'd be exquisitely aware of them all during dinner. She'd know they were there, lurking beneath her clothing, all fancy and feminine and demanding to be ogled.

Too dangerous. No elaborate underwear. She wasn't even sure she was going to shave her legs.

By the time they made it back to the apartment, Ember was so exhausted she forgot to be quiet on the way in. Four steps past Dante's apartment door and he burst through it as if he'd been coughed out.

"*Americana!*" He held his arms out wide, beaming at her as if she were a long-lost relative. His black toupee was askew atop his balding head, as always, but at least he was dressed: trousers and a dark blue cardigan that looked a little moth-eaten around the edges. "So good to see you! How was the weekend in Terrassa with your *amor?*"

Asher and Ember glanced at one another. Asher made a jerking little head motion toward Dante: *play along!*

"Um, it was, um . . . short."

There. That wasn't exactly a lie. It was so short it actually hadn't happened at all.

"Ah! Young love! So . . . " He muttered to himself in Spanish, searching for the right word, then, finding it, brightened. "Sweet!"

Love? Ember's face reddened. With a sour glance at Asher, she said sarcastically, "It really is, isn't it? Love is like oxygen. Love is a many splendored thing. Love lifts us up where we belong—"

"Dante, your English is getting so good," Asher interrupted smoothly, ignoring her. "Ember's lessons have been working!"

"*Muchas gracias!*" Dante made a low, sweeping bow that would have done the king proud, and when he rose someone stood in the open door behind him. A girl of about ten, pale and willowy, with dark hair and eyes the exact color of the summer sky in Taos—a deep, fathomless blue.

"Hi! I'm Clare. What's your name?" The girl skipped forward to stand near Ember. She looked up at her with an open, curious expression, very direct for such a young person. At her age, Ember had avoided adults like the plague.

"My granddaughter," explained Dante, turning to the girl with an expression of such obvious pride and tenderness Ember had to look away.

"I'm Ember."

Clare stuck out her hand and Ember, bemused, took it. They shook hands as if they'd just sealed a very important deal and Clare began to chatter in perfect English.

"Cool name! What does it mean? I was named after my grandma who died. You're pale like me. Roberto says I need to get out in the sun more, but I like to read and watch TV and play with Bieber and he doesn't like to go outside very much so neither do I. Do you like video games?"

Clare was looking at her expectantly. Some kind of reply was obviously in order but she wasn't sure where to start after that dizzying intro.

"Who's Roberto? And Bieber?"

"Roberto is my son, her father," Dante said, ruffling Clare's hair affectionately. "And this little monkey knows she's not supposed to call her father by his first name, but 'not supposed to' never stopped her from anything, did it, Clare?"

Clare beamed. "Nope." She turned back to Ember. "Bieber's my dog. He's a Yorkie. I named him after my favorite singer. Do you like Justin Bieber? Roberto says little dogs are for gays but I love him." Now she turned her direct gaze to Asher and smiled at him. After looking him up and down—taking in his gym-perfect physique, skinny jeans, the designer glasses, and the fuchsia socks that peeked out above the patent leather Pradas—she said with innocent curiosity, "Do you have a little dog?"

Asher answered with great sincerity, "No. But according to Roberto, I definitely should."

"Cool!" Clare beamed again, glad that was settled.

"Go back inside, *gordita*, it's too cold out here for you and you're not wearing your jacket," Dante scolded gently.

Though there was a slight chill in the air, the sun was shining brightly, and neither Ember nor Asher had bothered with jackets today. She wondered if Clare caught cold easily, if that was the reason for her pale skin, those faint purple bruises beneath her eyes. And she was so *thin*. Maybe she was recovering from the flu that was going around?

Looking up at him, Clare smiled at her grandfather and patted him on the arm with motherly fondness, as if she were the adult and Dante the child. "Don't worry so much, *abuelito*. It's bad for your old man heart."

"Old man! Ah, I'll give you that spanking, little monkey!"

Dante was obviously teasing, trying to suppress a smile and failing. This seemed an old threat between them, a game they played, because when Dante made a menacing move for her, Clare squealed with delight and skipped away. She darted inside the apartment, swift as a hare, then popped her head back around the door a second later.

" 'Bye Ember! 'Bye Ember's friend!"

Ember and Asher waved goodbye, and Clare disappeared for good.

"How old is she?" Ember asked, and Dante's smile began slowly to fade.

"*Diez.*" Ten. "But only outside. In here," he pointed to his chest, indicating the heart, "she's older than those mountains." He lifted his gaze to the jutting dark line of the Collserola range rising above the city, and closed his eyes just longer than a blink.

Sensing more to this than simple metaphor, Ember asked, "Is she okay?"

Dante, with a quick glance inside to make sure Clare wasn't standing near the door to the apartment, slowly drew it closed. He sighed and shoved his hands into the pockets of his trousers. "For now, yes. She's been out of the hospital for three months, which, for my little *gordita*, is good. Usually the good times don't last this long."

Asher said, "What's wrong with her?"

"Cystic fibrosis." Dante spat the words as if it burned his tongue to say them. "God's curse on innocent little children. Their lungs fill up with mucous, their bodies don't grow, they can't digest food or sleep without pain or run without gasping for breath." He put a hand to his forehead and Ember noticed it was, very slightly, trembling.

Ember knew nothing about cystic fibrosis, except it was bad. Exactly how bad, she had no idea. "Is there a cure?

Can they do surgery? I mean, don't they have drugs for that now?"

Dante looked at her, his eyes suddenly fierce with unshed tears. "There is nothing to be done. When it gets bad, she goes to the hospital and they can make her a little more comfortable. They have some things they can do to help, some medicine to reduce infection, oxygen to help her breathe. But there is no cure. Children with this disease usually don't live to become adults."

His voice grew bitter with grief. "In her case, the doctors don't think she'll make it another few years."

Horrified, Ember and Asher gasped in unison.

"That's awful, Dante! That must be so hard for you and her parents!"

Asher's words were met with a surprising reaction. At the mention of the word *parents*, Dante practically growled. "Ah, my good-for-nothing son drops her off here when he can't take the pressure of caring for his own child anymore. And that woman who is her mother"—he spat a curse in Spanish, a terrible word for any woman to be called—"I hope she rots in hell! She's a junkie and a worthless waste of human life. She deserted her daughter and my son, left them both when Clare was just a baby. My poor *gordita*, God tests her courage every day."

Tears threatening, Ember covered her mouth with her hand. "Oh, Dante. I'm so, so sorry."

He suddenly looked older. His toupee drooped, his skin was sallow, the light that normally shone from his merry dark eyes grew dim. He shook his head slowly back and forth. When he spoke again, his voice had lost all the anger it held when he spoke of her parents, and now had only sadness, and a quiet sort of wonder.

"Clare has faced death every day since she was a baby. Nothing scares her anymore, not people, not dying. She is kind and happy and open, she is fully present in every moment, every hour for her is big and round. Death is just another door that will soon open for her. Because that's how she sees it: the start of a new adventure. With rainbows and unicorns and the cat she had when she was five that got hit by a car." His voice grew even quieter. "I have raged against God for the unfairness of this, I have prayed and cursed and cried. But now . . . now I believe there is a reason behind her suffering. She is teaching me and everyone who comes in contact with her something priceless, I think. Something holy."

"What's that?" Asher asked in a hushed whisper when Dante faltered.

He lifted his gaze straight to Ember's. "She is teaching us all how to live."

The three of them stood there in silence for a moment, a silence that seemed almost reverent in its depth. Ember felt a little shell-shocked, a little unsteady on her feet. With new appreciation, she remembered what Asher had said to her only hours before.

How alive do you want to be?

Dante, recovering his smile and looking as if it cost him to straighten and throw back his shoulders, said, "Enough of this sad talk! Don't let me keep you two! Enjoy the rest of your day!" He turned and was just about to close his door before Ember—now overwhelmed with guilt that she'd been hiding from her obligation—stopped him.

"Dante, about the rent—"

"No worry, no worry, *hermosa!* We'll talk about that some other time. Go on and enjoy the rest of your Sunday."

Just like that, he disappeared into his apartment and closed his door, leaving Ember and Asher staring at one another on the stairs.

"That just happened, right?"

Asher looked from her to Dante's door, then back again. "I think so. Did we have any hallucinogens with lunch? Or maybe Dante was taken by a body snatcher. Because for him to not care about the rent is very . . . "

"Strange," Ember finished quietly. Of course it had to do with Clare; the poor man didn't want to waste any time with Ember discussing what a delinquent she was when he had so little time left to spend with his dying granddaughter. Another wave of guilt hit her, and Ember couldn't remember feeling so ashamed in a long, long time.

Asher said, "Well, don't look a gift horse in the mouth, as my mother says. If he's not worried about it, at least you're off the hook until you can get it together. And look on the bright side; you don't have to sneak into your own apartment anymore! C'mon, let's get you ready for tonight. I only have a few hours to work on you and I'm going to need every minute." He turned and began the four-story climb up the stairs.

Ember followed him silently, thinking about love and loss, thinking about courage and suffering, thinking about a pale little girl with a wide open spirit, and eyes like the desert sky.

Thinking about another pair of eyes, burning green and endless, eyes she would be gazing into in less than four hours' time.

NINE

Firecracker

By the time the knock came on her front door at precisely seven o'clock, Ember had been pacing the living room floor so long she thought she must have worn visible grooves in it.

She'd been painted and polished and buffed to a shine by a deadly serious Asher who wouldn't even let her speak during the process, such was his concentration. And when it was all over and he'd gone and she stood admiring his handiwork in the full-length mirror in her bedroom, she had to admit he'd done an amazing job.

In a pretty dress the color of apricots, high-heeled strappy sandals, and a thick, decadent cashmere wrap wound around her shoulders, with her hair washed and curled, and an expert makeup application that included smoky eyes and lips stained berry, she looked—well, pretty good.

In other words, she looked nothing like herself.

At the sound of the knock she froze, looked at the door, and released the thumb she'd been chewing from her mouth. Asher had painted her nails a delicate shell pink and he'd be horrified to see she'd already eaten a chip out of one of them.

"Maintain," she whispered to herself, still staring at the door. "Maintain, maintain, maintain."

The knock came again, a little louder, and propelled Ember out of her state of suspended animation. With sweating palms and a pounding heart, she crossed the room, turned the door handle, and swung the door open. She looked up with breathless anticipation—

Into the stern, unsmiling face of Christian's driver.

"Good evening, miss." He tipped his hat with one gloved hand. "Lord McLoughlin has been detained, but he desires for you to accompany me to the restaurant where you will await his arrival."

For a split second there was confusion—*Lord* McLoughlin?— but then Ember's fraught anticipation morphed to crackling anger. He sent his driver! He couldn't be bothered to get here on time! She'd wasted her entire day getting beautified for this jerk and he was basically standing her up! And he actually expected her to sit alone in a restaurant waiting for him like some idiotic Disney heroine, pining for her hero to show up so her life could begin?

No. Not going to happen. Damn you, Fancypants!

Ember moved Christian from the category of Alpha where Asher had so erroneously placed him, straight into another category, the other one that began with the letter A.

"*No*, I will *not* accompany you, and I will not wait anywhere for his arrival! If he's too busy to come himself, that's all I really need to know!"

Because she was so mad, this was said a lot louder than Ember anticipated. The driver's face paled. His eyes—vivid green like Christian's, strange she hadn't noticed that sooner—popped wide.

"Miss! Please, you don't understand! If I don't take you to the restaurant I'll be in serious trouble! You must come with me, I implore you!"

He was so obviously taken aback at her reaction, and even more obviously terrified of what would happen if she refused him, it gave her a moment's pause. She crossed her arms over her chest and stared at him, unblinking, the heat in her face matching the ire in her heart.

"What exactly is he doing that is so important he has to send someone else on his date?"

His face grew another shade paler. His voice trembled when he spoke, and had dropped an octave, sounding suspiciously near fear. "Working, miss."

"Working." Ember repeated it acidly. "He's working."

When the driver offered nothing more, Ember said, "Okay, I'll bite. What kind of work does he do?"

Now the driver began to sweat. Light beads of perspiration broke out on his forehead and upper lip, and he removed his hat and began to twist it around and around in his hands. "I'm so sorry, miss, I don't believe I'm allowed to disclose that."

She pursed her lips. The man really seemed afraid. Curiosity got the better of her and she asked, "And what exactly will he do to you if I don't come with you?"

The driver swallowed, his Adam's apple bobbing up and down in his throat. Unbelievably, his face went white. But no answer was forthcoming.

"Oh, forget it!" Ember threw her hands in the air. "Listen, I feel sorry for you that you work for such a dick, I really do, but I am not going to sit alone in some restaurant waiting on some rude, arrogant, inconsiderate man. You can tell Christian for me that I'd rather eat a hundred pounds of *chupitos* than ever lay eyes on him again!"

His brow twisted. He stared at her, utterly confused, the hat now clutched so hard between his fingers it had crumpled in the middle.

"*Chupitos* are fried octopus."

His blank look told her she wasn't making any progress.

"They're disgusting. I *hate* them. Understand? Oh, never mind." When he didn't show any sign of comprehension, Ember began to close the door and the driver began to plead with her as it swung shut.

"Please, miss! Please, you don't understand, you *must* come—"

But then she spied the copy of *Casino Royale* on the console table and had an idea. She held the door open again.

"On second thought, I'll make you a deal . . . " She was going to say his name, but realized she didn't know it. "I'm sorry, what's your name?"

"Corbin, miss."

"Well, Corbin, I really need to sell this book. *Some of us* can't afford chauffeurs. Also there's a few choice things I'd like to say to your employer. And apparently you really need to drive me somewhere, or you'll get into trouble. So I'll make you a deal. I'll go with you . . . "

His face instantly brightened. When she finished her sentence, however, it fell again.

"If you take me to wherever Christian is right now so I can tell him off to his face."

Corbin gaped at her like a suffocating fish. "That is not possible miss! If I were to disobey a direct order from Lord McLoughlin—"

"Take it or leave it, Corbin. And if it's any help, you can tell him I forced you."

There was a moment's silence as Corbin, twisting the hat to death in his hands and chewing the inside of his cheek, debated with himself. Finally he muttered, "As you will, miss. After you." He stepped away from the door and held a gloved hand out toward the staircase.

Feeling vindicated, imagining every vile thing she would say to Christian after they'd agreed on a price for the stupid book, Ember picked up said stupid book, locked her apartment and followed Corbin down the stairs to the waiting car.

Fifteen minutes later Ember had forgotten her anger because she was too awed by the view.

"I've never been up here," she said to Corbin from the back seat of the Audi, watching through the windows as the first of the rolling foothills gave way to the steeper, more densely forested slopes of the Collserola mountain range. A full moon blazed white fire in the night sky above, crowning the trees in opal and pearl, and the stars were clearly visible without all the city lights to muffle them. They sparkled in the deep sapphire bowl of the sky like newly minted coins at the bottom of a wishing well. The winding road snaked away in front of the car, disappearing beyond the reach of the headlights, and the trees crowded closer and closer to the road as they drove, thick and dark and towering, their gnarled roots wreathed in ghostly gray coils of fog.

"Yes, it's beautiful."

Corbin's less-than-enthusiastic response prompted Ember to ask, "What did Christian say when you told him I was coming?"

There had been a discreet phone conversation when they'd first set out. Corbin called Christian to report the change of plans, then replied with hushed, monotone answers to whatever Christian was saying on the other end of the line. She would've given anything to know the particulars of that conversation, but unfortunately hadn't been able to hear anything beyond Corbin's tense "Yes, sir," and "No, sir," and "I understand, sir."

"After his initial surprise, he . . . laughed, miss."

Laughed? That son of a—

"Why would he *laugh*? What's so funny about this situation?" she demanded, getting angry again. The nerve of this man!

"If you knew Lord McLoughlin better, miss, you would know what an uncommon thing it is for him to laugh." Corbin looked at her in the rearview mirror. "I believe it to be a true compliment."

A compliment. That he was laughing at her. The British were very strange.

"So you're not in trouble then?"

A ghost of a smile flickered across Corbin's face. "He, ah, he didn't seem to think it quite out of character for you, miss, that you waylaid me. The word 'firecracker' may have been used."

Firecracker. She hated herself for being so pleased by that. The word filled her with satisfaction, buttery and thick, and she felt like a cat who'd just gorged itself on cream.

"Here we are," Corbin said. Ember looked through the windshield just as they pulled to a stop in front of a massive scrolled iron gate. Corbin rolled down the window, pushed a code into a security box on a pedestal, and the gates began slowly to swing open.

That's when the real adventure began.

Ember expected a house—this definitely wasn't the industrial side of town—but what she saw instead in the distance was a mansion, massive and sprawling, nestled in the hollow of a low hill surrounded by dense forest. It was dark and brooding, this place, with an elaborate French roof, iron finials on arches, and lightless windows over three stories that reflected back the moonlight like row after row of sightless eyes. It looked more like a fortress than a country home. Ember felt the fortress metaphor even more apt when she spied the low stone bridge that they would have to cross in order to arrive at the circular drive in front of the house.

There was a bridge because there was a *moat.*

It was beautiful in a forbidding sort of way, and for some reason Ember felt an odd sort of recognition, almost déjà vu, as if she'd been here before, or somehow knew this place.

"It looks very . . . secure."

Corbin's only response was a noncommittal noise of agreement.

Once over the bridge and parked in the lamp lined circular drive, Corbin helped her from the car and accompanied her silently over the groomed gravel to the massive front doors that swung open on silent hinges. He ushered her through and bid her to wait in a room just off the main hall, a room with a fire crackling merrily in the hearth, a huge mahogany desk with two high-backed crimson leather chairs in front of it, and three walls lined to the ceiling with books.

After a deep bow in her direction, Corbin retreated, and Ember was left alone in the library.

And what a library it was. There were more first edition classics than Antiquarian Books had ever owned, books the value of which she could not even guess. Henry James and Virginia Woolf and Samuel Johnson, a section of works in beveled glass cases that included a sheaf of stained vellum from the Elizabethan era. It was an original hand written manuscript by Christopher Marlowe that was, by itself, worth a fortune.

Because there *were* no surviving original works by Christopher Marlowe.

Ember drew close to the case, mesmerized, staring in open-mouthed awe at the papers. Staring at the inkblots and ragged edges, at the irregular brown stain in one corner she imagined was a centuries-old drop of spilled wine.

"Magnificent, isn't it?" came the low voice from right behind her. With a startled yelp, Ember jumped and turned to find Christian standing not two feet away, gazing down at her with hooded eyes and a faint smile on his lips.

Her first instinct was simply to stare at him, because in his own home, surrounded by all this finery, he was somehow even better-looking than ever before. He was dressed in a suit, as he'd been the first time she'd seen him, this one a deep, midnight blue with a pewter pocket square and a matching pewter dress shirt, open at the throat. No tie.

Skin, face, hair: perfect. Square jaw, full lips, straight nose: check.

Beautiful. Why did he have to be so beautiful?

The faint smile grew wider as she took him in, and her mouth went dry.

"I think you're rude," she pronounced, to manage the heat he conjured in her blood.

"So I've been told," he replied, holding her gaze. "I believe the word 'dick' was mentioned?"

Oh, you traitor, Corbin!

"Hey, if the shoe fits . . . " Ember shrugged and crossed her arms over her chest, a small sort of safety measure, because suddenly it seemed he was standing much too close.

He ignored that. His gaze leisurely travelled over her hair, her dress, the dainty sandals, and her painted toes. When he looked back into her eyes there was an edge to his own, a dark burn that made her want to take a step back. She didn't.

"You look edible," he murmured, staring straight into her eyes.

If she hadn't already been so angry with him, that would have really pissed her off.

"I came here to tell you to your face that I think you're an egotistical, entitled, spoiled, bad-mannered, inconsiderate—"

"Don't forget *dick*," he cut in, his eyes bright with laughter.

"—oaf!" she finished, fighting the urge to stamp her foot.

His brows rose. "Oaf? Hmm, this *is* dire. I don't mind being called all those other names, but an oaf, now, that really hurts."

"You're laughing at me," she said, astonished. "*Again!* After you stood me up—"

His face darkened. "I would *never* stand you up, September. I merely had a pressing issue to attend to and could not get away on time—"

"Yes, so *I* was told! And are you going to tell me what exactly this pressing issue was? Because in my opinion, unless it was life or death, *you stood me up.*"

His face took on an odd expression, a mix of sadness, resolve, and even a hint of rage, all quickly smothered. He quietly said, "And if I told you that it was life or death, would you believe me?"

They stared at one another in silence while the fire snapped in the hearth, sending orange sparks up the chimney, filling the room with a lovely pine-scented glow.

"I don't know. Probably not. But just for shits and grins—was it?"

A muscle flexed in his jaw. He didn't look away from her face when he said, "Yes."

She tried to fathom his expression, but it was unreadable. There was something in his eyes though, a certain urgent pathos, which told her he was telling the truth.

What on earth could he be doing at seven o'clock on a Sunday evening at home that was life or death?

She sighed, defeated. "Well, it doesn't really matter, anyway. I brought the copy of *Casino Royale*, I'll just leave it with you and—"

"No." His voice was forceful. He took a step nearer.

"No? What do you mean, no? You don't want it?"

He stepped nearer. She was forced to step back until her back was against the glass case and couldn't retreat any farther. He leaned in very close, put his mouth near her ear, and said, "You know what I want, September, and it isn't the goddamn book."

Her blood stopped circulating. Which was because her heart had frozen inside her chest. Then he put both hands on the case beside her head and inhaled against her neck, a slow, soft intake of breath as if he was smelling her. The tip of his nose skimmed her neck. She felt the fleet, electric brush of his lips against her skin, and her heart took off at a thundering gallop.

Ember had heard of this before, the weak knees, the dry mouth, the hair-raising electricity that could pass between two people, but she'd never experienced it. She'd had boyfriends, of course, short-lived relationships of varying degrees of intensity, but her body had never responded like this, every nerve screaming simply because a man had inhaled against her throat.

"Christian." She breathed out in a careful, slow exhalation. "Please."

She didn't know what she was asking for—Stop? Go on?—but he responded by encircling one of her wrists in his hand and bringing it to his chest. He drew away so they were looking at one another and flattened her hand over his heart. He held it there, pressed against his chest, with his own hand pressed atop it, and said, "Close your eyes."

Her lids fluttered closed on their own. She held frozen and breathless, her nerves honed to a million excruciating exclamation points.

He said, "Do you feel that?"

She did. Beneath her palm, his heart was pounding as hard as her own. She nodded.

"And what does that tell you?"

His voice had dropped. This close, the scents of his skin, his hair, and his breath, were heady. Soft and sweet, yet musky and dark, he smelled like the outdoors, like night time in the deepest heart of the woods, like something natural and primitive and indefinable, moonlight and magic and fresh fallen snow.

He smelled—wild.

"It tells me that . . . that it's real. Because I can feel it," she whispered, knowing exactly what he wanted.

"That's right," he said, and with his other hand touched her face.

Unable to look at him, she kept her eyes closed. He held her jaw cupped in the open palm of his hand as if it were something fragile. His thumb was just beneath her left ear. Then he slid his hand forward and his other fingers curled around the back of her neck. He began to stroke his thumb lightly over that sensitive spot behind her earlobe, and it raised a rash of goosebumps on her arms.

"I'm not your type," she whispered, all her anger at him gone. She realized it had really only been acute disappointment, both in him and in herself for getting her hopes up, but that didn't make it any easier to look at him. She finally gathered the courage to open her eyes and found him staring down at her, his eyes shadowed and intense.

In response to her words his brows lifted. Then those green eyes of his, always so penetrating, shifted from stormy and dark to amused. "No. You're not."

That stung. Until he amended, "You're smarter than my usual type."

Thumb stroke. The goosebumps spread to her legs.

"Edgier."

Another thumb stroke. Her heartbeat accelerated.

"More . . . interesting."

His smile deepened as he said that. Her heart began suddenly to pound wildly in her chest as if she'd been injected with adrenaline, a thrum and a throb so wild and violent she thought she might faint. "Trust me, I'm about as interesting as vanilla pudding," she said unsteadily.

How could anyone affect her heart rate like that with such a simple touch? She thought if he ever kissed her, she might pass out on the spot. Then the thought of kissing him sent her heart rate into maximum overdrive, a race car screaming toward the checkered flag.

Somehow, he sensed it. His nostrils flared with an inhalation, his gaze dropped to the pulse beating wildly in her throat. He let his gaze travel slowly up her neck and over her face, and when again their eyes met, his were heated.

"Vanilla is my favorite flavor. And pudding . . . " he leaned in and inhaled again, against her skin. He whispered, "Pudding is delicious. The way it melts on your tongue . . . "

Her mouth and brain both barely working, she blurted, "I'd have guessed chocolate would be more your speed."

Christian pulled away, just far enough so he was still dangerously close. If she wanted to, she could have leaned forward a few short inches and pressed her lips to his.

And if she was being honest with herself, she did want to. She so wanted to.

"People think chocolate is more decadent, but . . . " His gaze drifted to her mouth. "Chocolate comes from a tree. You can get it anywhere, even in a convenience store. It's common. Vanilla, on the other hand, comes from orchids. It's one of the most expensive spices in the world, second only to saffron. It's pure, spicy, and delicate, and its essence is used in the finest perfumes. Vanilla is rare." His gaze lifted back to hers. "And the rarer something is, the more value it has."

Another thumb stroke behind her ear, accompanied by a look of such stark hunger Ember had a wild thought he might lean in and eat her.

"You're different. Tonight, you seem . . . different," she whispered. "What's happened?"

His hand stilled on her face. His brows drew together and he looked at her—looked *into* her—with a gaze so penetrating she felt naked. He murmured, "Definitely smarter than my usual type."

"That's not an answer."

He gave her a lopsided smile, very faint, and even more faintly said, "Life is so short, mystery girl. And people like you so few and far between. Perhaps in another lifetime . . . "

From behind them came the sound of a throat being cleared. Corbin said, "Pardon, sir, but there's a phone call from the Earl of Sommerley. I told him you wouldn't want to be disturbed, but he said it was urgent."

"The . . . the Earl of Sommerley?"

Christian exhaled a breath and closed his eyes. "My brother." He opened his eyes, looked at her lips, and slowly traced his thumb across her mouth. He exhaled again and pulled away.

"I'm sorry. I'm afraid I have to take the call. This won't take but a moment."

He turned to leave, then stopped and pinned her with a burning look. "Don't run away," he commanded, and she wanted to laugh.

As if she could run with these rubber legs he'd left her with.

But she only nodded wordlessly, and watched as he walked swiftly from the room.

TEN

Mystery Man

"Ten more are confirmed missing from the colony in Manaus," said Leander brusquely.

Christian's own, "What is it?" when he picked up had been equally brusque. He and his older brother had never been much for small talk.

"I don't understand—how the hell are they getting out? I thought the entire colony was on lockdown?"

"They *are*. But someone is helping them get out, assisting them with passage, arranging the entire damn thing. Probably someone on the inside. We don't know who yet, but one thing we know for sure: we've got to stop the bleeding."

"If they make it to Barcelona—"

"Not if, Christian. When. The six who deserted the colony in Bhakthapur are already there."

"How do we know?"

"One of them made a phone call to his mother. Said he'd arrived safely. Said they should come, too. It was better there. So much more *freedom*."

"Shit," hissed Christian.

To which Leander wryly responded, "Precisely."

"Can we track the call?"

"It was a pre-paid, disposable cell. Untraceable."

Which meant the deserters were taking precautions. Which meant they'd been coached.

Which meant their insane, murderous, diabolical leader wasn't so stupid after all.

"Are you any closer to finding him?"

"Barcelona is a very big city, Leander," Christian said tightly. "We knew it would take some time."

"Unfortunately time is the one thing we don't have, brother. I can send The Hunt—"

"We've been over this a million times," interrupted Christian. "The Hunt is too busy containing the situation in the colonies. Without them, the bleeding would be exponentially worse. We can't afford to divert their attention now. Besides, if we have too big a presence here we'll be noticed before we can find him and they'll just move again. And this time we won't have a clue where he went." His voice lowered. "And I'm the only one without family. It has to be me."

There was a long silence, then a heavy exhalation from Leander. "I know. I still can't wrap my head around this whole thing. I know you're doing all you can. I'm just worried about you. This entire situation . . . I never imagined it would come to this. You're right. I know you're right. But it doesn't mean I have to like it."

Christian took that in. For his older brother to utter the words *you're right* was nothing short of a miracle. It meant something was very wrong.

His voice carefully neutral, Leander added, "Jenna's worried about you, too."

Oh, minefield. Christian's defenses went up, the automatic response to any mention of his brother's wife.

"How is she?"

"Cranky. This pregnancy . . . I had no idea it would be this bad. Not only is her Gift of Sight gone, but she can't Shift because of the baby, and most days she's so sick she can barely get out of bed. The midwife says it's all perfectly normal, but I hate seeing her sick without being able to do anything for her. It makes me feel so . . . helpless."

Helpless. Yes, that's precisely how Jenna made Christian feel, too.

His brother's wife was painfully beautiful, and there had been a time, before she married Leander, when Christian had imagined himself half in love with her. Well, maybe three quarters. She was an American, with that American forthrightness and independence, and had upset the balance of their carefully controlled world in a million different ways.

Jenna was the most powerful of his kind in centuries, which was all the more astonishing because she was half human.

Human . . . like September Jones.

He closed his eyes at the thought of the fragile, feisty human girl awaiting him in his library, the disaster waiting to happen that he was finding himself more and more unable to resist, and remembered the intoxicating smell of her. The soft, sweet scent of vanilla and orange blossom that rose from her skin.

Ember didn't make him feel helpless. Ember made him feel electrocuted. On fire. Alive.

Controlling his voice, he said to his brother, "Send her my regards. And tell her . . . tell her not to worry. Tell her there's an angel looking out for me."

This was met with another silence. Christian knew Leander imagined a different sort of meaning behind his words, a meaning that hinted at his mission and its outcome. But he was really thinking of another angel, an angel with a bad temper and eyes like dark chocolate and a smile like a sunrise, who could look at a man and make him feel like the center of the entire universe or the most irritating creature that had ever lived.

"I'll call you as soon as I've got anything, all right?"

Leander murmured his assent, and they ended the call.

Staring down at the phone, Christian ran a hand through his hair. He'd been so sure he'd caught the scent of this traitor he was looking for earlier in the day, when he was out searching the forest. He'd been doing it in grids since he'd arrived in Barcelona four weeks ago, a concentrated effort that typically took all night and left him exhausted and sleeping through the next day. He doubted his target would be in the city; their kind preferred remote or inaccessible areas, far away from the prying eyes of humanity. So far his search had yielded nothing, but today there had been a trace of something on the wind. It was a faint rumor of exotic spice and heated earthiness, the signature of an adult predator in his prime—fur and blood and appetite. He'd followed it as far as he could, but the trail went cold over the crest of a ridge with a view straight out to the sea, and he'd been forced to abandon the search.

But not in time to be prompt for his date with Ember.

He smiled, thinking of her anger, of her face when she scolded him for being rude. He wasn't sure anyone had ever spoken to him that way in his life.

He wondered that he liked it.

Christian hurried back to the library, half hoping for another scolding. And very much hoping he'd get a chance to finish what he started and see if September's lips were as velvety soft as they looked.

The ride to the restaurant was completed in near silence, and after the intensity of the library Ember felt awkward sitting next to Christian in the back of the car as Corbin drove them into town.

She glanced at him and asked, "Do you ever drive yourself anywhere?"

Looking out the window, he smiled. He turned to gaze at her and said, "Well, I wouldn't want to break the law."

At her quizzical look, he explained, "I don't have a driver's license."

She immediately thought the worst. Had it been taken away? Had he been involved in accidents? Car chases? Was he a bank robber? A criminal on the run? A master jewel thief?

It would explain a lot.

"What kind of a person doesn't have a driver's license?"

He sent her a lazy smile. "The same kind of person that doesn't own a television."

"Okay. Touché. But they're still not the same thing."

His smile slightly faded. "Where I grew up, there weren't any cars. I just never learned to drive."

This intrigued her. She turned her body in the seat and faced him. "No cars? In England? Were you Amish or something?"

He chuckled. "Amish? That's where you go first, really?"

"You have to admit it's weird."

Now he studied her, all humor gone. "There are a great many things about my upbringing that I'm sure you would consider weird."

She waited for more, but when it didn't come, cocked an eyebrow at him. "You can't just dangle that out there and not follow up, that's totally bogus."

"Bogus?" he repeated slowly, the laughter coming back into his eyes.

"Yes. Bogus. Wack. Lame. Wrong to the most high."

He shook his head. "I had no idea your vocabulary was so extensive."

Ember tapped her temple. "I read a lot, big boy. My vocabulary is multifarious."

Christian leaned forward so their faces were very close and murmured, "Did you just call me *big boy*?"

Ember swallowed, her stomach suddenly alight with the dreaded butterflies that refused to die, which had multiplied a thousandfold since the day they met, breeding like frenzied rabbits with every touch, with every glance and shared smile. She was enveloped in his scent again, masculine and exotic, a foreign spice of night and smoke and secrets. The way he was looking at her made her flush straight down to her toes.

"Um. Yes?"

He studied her for a moment in silence, his gaze roving over her hot face, her mouth, her eyes. Finally he lifted a hand and brushed his knuckles over her face with the faintest pressure, following the curve of her cheek down to her jaw. He whispered, "I love this."

Like an elevator plummeting from snapped cables, Ember's stomach hit the floor. She managed to gather her wits enough to respond with a stuttered, "W-what?"

"When you blush for me. It's the best compliment you could give me."

Ember managed a choked, "It's embarrassing."

He spread his hand over her cheek, cupped her face in his palm. "It's beautiful."

His eyes had gone dark, and the crackle was there between them again, electrifying the air. Ember said, very faintly, "I think you need to get your eyes checked. Nothing about me is beautiful."

That brought a look to his face she would have described as anger, had it not been for the softness in his eyes. He said with quiet vehemence, "*Everything* is."

Because she couldn't bear that look, that softness and intensity and naked desire, she closed her eyes. She pressed her lips together and withdrew from his hand, settling herself back into her seat, a much safer distance. "That's very flattering, especially coming from you—"

"The distractingly pretty idiot?" he teased softly, and reached out for her left hand.

She let him take it, let him stroke the scars on her wrist with his thumb, let him follow the scars up her arm, his fingers gentle and faintly questioning. It took everything she had to sit still and let him do that, when all her nerves screamed for her to pull away. Like a photo album of living flesh, those scars were full of Technicolor memories. They made her feel ugly, small, and—on really bad days—cursed. She hated those scars with every cell of her body.

No one had ever touched them except her, the doctor who removed the stitches . . . and now him.

Still without looking at him, she said, "But you've got it all wrong. I told you before, you don't know me. You'll just have to trust me when I say you're wrong."

There was a silence that felt hot and uncomfortable. Then Christian said, "What happened to you to make you hate yourself so much?" and it felt like a punch in the gut.

Grief is a funny thing. Time can temper it, smooth the rough edges that so clawed and gouged in the first raw aftermath of loss, but like Lazarus it can be resurrected, again and again, sometimes with the smallest of invocations. Ember knew all about the soul-eating demon called grief. She knew about the shallowness of sanity, and about how people do and do not deal with the cold reality that life ends.

And she knew that talking about pain did nothing to heal it. Talking only gave it more room to breathe.

She pulled her hand out of Christian's grasp and covered her face. "Nothing. Please. Nothing."

His voice gentle, he said, "I wish you'd tell me."

The heat in her cheeks spread to her ears. Still hiding behind her hands, she whispered, "I'm broken, okay? Is that what you want to hear? I'm broken and there's no fixing me. There's no way to fit all the ugly pieces of my puzzle back together. Please, let it go."

There was a beat of silence, then Christian reached over and pulled her onto his lap.

Before she could even gasp in shock he had her face cradled between both of his hands.

"I won't ask again," he said urgently, his eyes searching hers, "but only because you don't want me to, not because I don't want to know, or because I think you're right about being broken. I don't think you're broken, I think you're wounded, and those are two very different things."

She stared at him, speechless, acutely aware of the heat and hardness of his body and Corbin in the front seat and the fact that her dress had bunched up and her bare legs were exposed to her upper thighs.

He went on, still with that urgency, "We don't have to share our sad stories—I told you before, secrets are okay. And I'm not—I'm not even sure how long I'm going to be around, but I do know for sure I want to spend as much time with you as I can. I want to make you happy. I want to see you smile. I can't explain it in a way you'll understand and it's probably crazy, and it's definitely not in either of our best interests, but . . . "

He faltered. His breathing had become irregular and so had her own. The way he was looking at her now had her heart climbing up into her throat, threatening to choke her.

"But I want you, September Jones. Broken or wounded or whatever it is that you are, I want you. And I know you want me, too."

The city passed by the windows in a sideways smear of color, dark and light and completely unnoticed by either one of them. His hands on her face were hot, so hot, and he was radiating heat, too. Along with his scent, his heat washed over her in waves, and for the first time in a very long time, Ember was gripped with the exquisite ache of desire.

"You sure know how to make pretty speeches, Fancy-pants," she breathed.

J.T. GEISSINGER

He exhaled, and she realized he'd been holding his breath, waiting for her reaction. He moved his hands from her face to her shoulders, then pulled her against his chest and held her there tightly, his arms encircling her, his cheek resting on the top of her head, his lips on her hair. Through his shirt she felt his heartbeat against her cheek, and she closed her eyes, hearing it throb and pulse, loving the sound of it.

Feeling as if her heart might strangle her, she said into his shirt, "I can't believe you didn't end that speech with a kiss."

She felt his chuckle against her cheek too. It reverberated through his chest, pitched deep and low like a bass drum. He took her chin in his hand and tilted her face up to his.

"There will be kisses, little firecracker, many, many kisses—but you're going to have to ask for the first one."

In response to her look of mortification, he added, "Nicely."

"You want me to *ask* you to kiss me," she said flatly.

He nodded, a grin spreading across his face. "It'll be easy, it's just three words. 'Please kiss me.' How hard is that?"

"How about, 'please tell me you're joking,' instead?"

His grin grew dangerous. "I never joke about kissing, Ember." He released her chin, reached out, and lightly touched her bare leg just above her ankle. She sucked in a startled breath and froze, ridiculously grateful she'd decided to shave her legs after all.

He said, "There are several things, in fact, that I never joke about, and all of them have to do with pleasuring a woman."

Holding her gaze, he slid his fingers slowly up her leg, and Ember felt it like a trail of fire on her skin. She was sure if she looked there would be burn marks. A little involuntary shiver went through her.

"Ask me," he whispered, stroking her leg. "Three little words and I'll make you shiver a lot more than that."

"Remember before, when I was telling you what an egotistical something-or-other you are?" She whispered it back to him, her fingers wrapped around the lapels of his suit, her back stiff, their eyes locked together. He nodded, his fingers slowly moving past her kneecap, up her thigh. As his hand spread open over her skin, her voice grew even fainter. "I was right about the egotistical part."

He lowered his head, just far enough so his lips hovered above hers. Against her mouth, he whispered, "Ask me," so that his words brushed her lips, feather-light and fleeting.

Instead of speaking her 'no' aloud, she shook her head back and forth, skimming her lips against his in the touching-but-not-touching way he had done, slow and careful. He made a low, masculine sound in his throat. His hand tightened on her leg and the electricity running between them felt alive, magnetic and hair-raising, a wild animal about to be unleashed.

Then the car slid to a stop and Corbin announced, "We're here, sir."

Ember stifled a groan. "He has the most unbelievable timing."

Christian closed his eyes. "Yes," he said through gritted teeth. "He certainly does."

He inhaled, gave her thigh a squeeze, and released her, setting her back to her side of the seat. She made sure her dress was safely back over her knees and tried not to think about the hardness of his body, his lips and scent and gaze, how it felt to have his arms wrapped around her. Because if she focused on any one of those things, she didn't think they'd make it through dinner.

She thought she'd tell him to take her home to bed, right now.

And she needed more time to figure this out—it was all happening much too fast. She wasn't that girl, the one who had sex on the first date or threw herself at men, hoping for attention. No matter how gorgeous, rich, and swoon-inducing they were.

Christian helped her from the car and kept her hand clasped tightly in his as they entered the restaurant and were led to their table. As her brain began to come back online and her thought processes cleared, Ember was struck by something she'd missed in the emotion of the moment with Christian's arms wrapped around her, his fierce intensity muddling her mind. It was something he'd said, something that seemed more and more ominous with every replay.

I'm not even sure how much longer I'm going to be around.

It made her wonder again about the life or death reason he'd been late for their date. And why he thought spending time together wasn't in either of their best interests.

What exactly was he hiding?

ELEVEN

Sonata

The dinner was extravagant, and quiet.

There was caviar and oysters, silky foie gras and filet mignon, a Bordeaux—which she politely declined—so dark and decadent it looked more like dessert. The menu was French, as was the waiter with the aquiline nose and slicked back hair who bowed and scraped so obsequiously to Christian when he ordered.

In French.

It was an uncomfortable experience for Ember, in part because the electric tension from the car had not dissipated, and in part because it reminded her too much of the early days of her father's marriage to Marguerite. The three of them, along with the Tweedies, would visit expensive restaurants like this one and Ember and her father would suffer through endless commentaries about everything from the quality of the food to the quality of Ember's wardrobe. Both of which were always found to be lacking. Also, she loathed oysters and foie gras, but didn't want to seem rude or ungrateful when Christian ordered them, especially since she'd already turned down the wine.

She longed for a hamburger. And a quick escape route. Or maybe a bullet to the head.

By the time dinner was over, her nerves were frayed. She and Christian had exchanged a total of perhaps two dozen words.

"Well," said Christian as he settled back into the plush confines of his silk-covered chair. Toying with his dessert spoon, he sent her a penetrating look from beneath his lashes. "That was one of the more memorable dining experiences I've ever had. In spite of the fact that I didn't taste a bite of it."

Her lips twisted. She exhaled a slow, ragged breath and tried on a tentative smile. "You live well," she said quietly, looking down at the untouched dessert on her plate, a sugar-dusted hazelnut merengue the waiter had called "dacquoise." It appeared diabetes-inducing.

"Thank you," he murmured. Ember glanced over at him and he was looking back at her with unblinking intensity. Horribly, because of course it would happen, she blushed.

"Okay. How about if we skip dessert and go for a walk instead?" Christian suggested. Ember looked at him and he sent her a wry smile. "I could use some fresh air. You?"

"Yes," she agreed, profoundly grateful. Walking beside him—not having to look right at him—would be much easier than sitting across a table from him trying to ignore all the unresolved sexual tension in the air, or getting back in the car and . . . what? Christian called the waiter over and paid the check. She'd never been so relieved to skip a dessert in her entire life.

Or so conflicted about it.

Once out on the sidewalk, Christian informed Corbin they'd be walking and they set off at a meandering pace down the boulevard. Corbin followed slowly behind in the Audi. She tightened the cashmere wrap around her shoulders to ward off the chill of the night air. Christian, seeing it, asked, "Are you cold? Would you like my coat?"

"No, but thanks for offering." She wrapped her arms across her chest because she was exquisitely aware he might take her hand again if she didn't, and she wasn't quite sure if she wanted him to or not. "Is he your bodyguard or something?" Ember asked curiously as she glanced over her shoulder and saw Corbin's worried face through the windshield. He had a death grip on the steering wheel and was staring at the two of them as if he thought something terrible was about to happen.

The question made Christian chuckle. "That would be a no." After a brief pause, he said, "Why, do you think I seem like I can't take care of myself?"

She laughed out loud. "That would also be a no. But he does seem very . . . protective of you."

Christian's silence seemed fraught. After several moments, he said, "Corbin's a good man. He's known me a long time, since I was a boy, actually. He worked for my father—"

He cut off abruptly and Ember turned to him, remembering with a pang the story Christian had told her about how his parents had died. "Oh no. He wasn't your parents' driver, was he?"

Christian shook his head. "My father's valet. Then my brother's, then, after my brother married, mine."

"All in the family, huh?"

Christian glanced at her, his expression giving nothing away. "Precisely. When I moved here, he insisted on coming. I have a feeling even if I'd said no and left without him, he'd have shown up at my door within a week." His voice grew dark. "That kind of loyalty means everything to me. Especially now."

They were in Gràcia, a colorful, artsy part of the city known for its nightlife, exotic restaurants and trendy bars. In spite of the chill in the air and the thunderclouds looming ominously overhead, the streets were crowded with pedestrians. Artists with easels were clustered under awnings on one side of the palm-lined boulevard, hawking oil and charcoal portraits to tourists. They were flanked by kiosks selling food, fruit, and T-shirts, interrupted constantly by tiny cafés with patios and upscale clothing boutiques and coffee shops. On their side of the street, there were people painted as statuary who would move in infinitesimal increments if they received money in the can at their feet, and street musicians who would play whatever you asked for the same.

With the Carnaval atmosphere infecting everyone, the streets held a buzz of excitement that warmed the cold air. It was a cacophony of noise and color and motion, and Ember was glad for the distraction from the man walking silently at her side.

She was just about to ask Christian what he meant by "especially now," when she saw the woman with the cello.

Seated on a chair in front of a jewelry boutique, the woman had her eyes closed, her fingers poised on the strings. Before Ember could turn away or scream the "No!" that automatically rose in her throat with the hot, gagging acidity of bile, the woman lowered the bow to the strings and began to play.

As the first swell of notes rose into the night air and Ember recognized the piece she used to play so perfectly—Kodaly's *Sonata for Solo Cello*, the piece that had won her scholarship to Juilliard—she felt a crushing sense of claustrophobia, along with an anguish so fierce and burning, so encompassing and incandescent, it was as if she was standing on the surface of the sun.

A cellist had to have the right combination of passion and steel to meet the extreme demands of Kodaly's masterpiece. In live performance, when done well, the ear is fooled into thinking multiple players and instruments are at work. There is an orchestral timbre to the double-stop trills and *pizzicati*, to the haunting and brilliant *czardas*.

When played well, it is like hearing the voice of God.

The cellist in front of the jewelry boutique was playing it well.

With a choked sob, Ember turned and ran blindly away, shoving though the crowds, her left hand shaking so badly it felt palsied. She heard Christian behind her, calling her name, but she didn't look back because she didn't want him to see her face. She didn't want him to see what she knew was looking out of her eyes, the thing like a hunted animal that would be staring back at him. She'd seen it for too many years in her own face in the mirror; she knew how wretched, how ugly a thing it was.

She ducked into a side street, and then into an alley, hoping she'd lost him in the crowd, and collapsed against the rear wall of a restaurant, trembling and gulping air. But he was on her in an instant, his voice as worried as his eyes.

"What is it? What happened? Are you all right?"

Not all right not all right dying dying dying dying. Trembling, feeling panic and pain wrapped around her with the clammy dark finality of a shroud, Ember squeezed her eyes shut and gasped for air.

He took her in his arms and rocked her gently back and forth, murmuring into her ear. "It's okay. Whatever it is, it's okay. Just breathe, Ember. Just breathe."

She curled her hands around his jacket and buried her face in his shirt. Inhaling deeply, she fought the panic, willing her heartbeat to slow and her body to stop shaking, drawing his smell into her nose, that wild, night-scented spice so unique to Christian.

"Easy, little firecracker," he whispered, sliding one hand beneath her hair to cup the nape of her neck. "I'm right here. I'm not going to let you fall apart on me."

Too late, she thought, tears slipping from beneath her closed lids.

Still with one strong arm wrapped around her, Christian took his hand from the back of her neck and tipped her face up to his with his fingers under her chin. "Hey," he said softly when he saw the tears on her cheeks. "I know you didn't like the foie gras, but you don't have to cry about it. My feelings weren't *that* hurt."

His gently teasing tone brought a weak smile to her face. "You could tell, huh?" she whispered.

He wiped her wet cheeks with his thumb then threaded his fingers into her hair. "You're not exactly what I would call poker-faced, Miss Jones." He lowered his forehead to hers. "Prime example: the woman with the cello."

She bit down hard on her lower lip and squeezed her eyes shut again.

"I meant what I said before; we don't have to talk about anything you don't want to talk about. But I'm here if you change your mind. Okay?"

She nodded silently and put her face against his chest again. He held her like that for a while, the night music of the city sparkling bright in the air all around them. A bark of faint laughter, the bickering of car horns in traffic, a covey of crooning pigeons sent into shrieking flight by a child, squealing in glee. In her nose the scent of the man who held her and the sweet, pungent bite of caramelized onions from the restaurant kitchen, on her face, cool air that soothed the flushed skin like a balm.

In her heart of hearts, Ember was quaking apart. She was very good at smothering her feelings, even better at keeping anything resembling happiness away, because she didn't deserve it. Day after week after month after year, she had chosen to stay alive when she knew it would be the right thing to do to kill herself, to take a knife to her wrists or swallow a bottle of Asher's prescription anxiety medication.

It was an abomination she should be alive after what had happened, after all the carnage she'd left in her wake.

The one thing that stopped her, over and over again, was the belief that to go on living was a far greater punishment than death, which would have relieved the relentless guilt eating away at her soul like acid. Life had become an opus of pain, silent and unacknowledged by anyone but her, pain that was lessened a little bit every time she'd thought of Christian. It lessened even more as she stood trembling and stripped emotionally bare in his arms.

No one had held her in years.

How alive do you want to be?

After all this time—especially after meeting Dante's granddaughter Clare, so brave, so unafraid of anything— Ember realized she very much wanted to be alive, even if she didn't deserve to be. She wanted to feel something other than guilt and pain, even if only for a moment.

Into Christian's shirt, she whispered, "Christian?"

"Hmmm?" He stroked a hand over her hair.

"Can I ask you a question?"

"Of course."

She tipped her head back and looked up at him. In a raw, shaking voice she said, "Will you please kiss me?"

Even in the dark alleyway she saw it, the way his eyes flared, the way his expression changed from soft to ardent, faster than she could blink. Tender, Gentle Christian was gone, replaced in an instant with Hungry, Dangerous Christian, the Bedroom Eyes Assassin she'd first seen when he walked into the bookstore, and into her life.

She thought he would devour her, so rapacious was that look, but he merely took her face in his hands, pressed his body against hers and pressed them both back against the wall.

She leaned into him, her heart pummeling her breastbone, her blood racing like wildfire through her veins. He slowly lowered his face to hers, his lips parted, his lids lowered halfway, eyes shining with heat.

When his mouth touched hers she gasped a little, shocked by the current of static that passed over her lips, stunned by how soft, warm, and gently demanding his tongue was, gliding against hers. She arched against him, pulling his head down with both hands around the back of his neck, and he made a sound deep in his throat, a quiet groan of need or pleasure.

It was incredible, his heat, and strength, and maleness, the way he took his time exploring her mouth while every nerve and cell in her body was screaming for him. For *more*. His body was pressed so close against hers she couldn't help but notice the new straining hardness that sprang up between his legs as they kissed; it twitched against her belly when she twisted her fingers into his hair and rubbed her breasts against his chest, suddenly more desperately hungry than she'd ever been in her life.

He dropped a hand from her face and cupped it around her bottom, squeezing and pulling her harder against him. A little animal mewl escaped her, and she squirmed against him, greedy, quickly losing all sense of restraint. And oh, God, the way he tasted—it was addictive. Like sunshine, clean air, and cool water, there was an earthy, elemental taste to his mouth that was at once savory and sweet and completely delicious, and she felt as if she'd been drugged. As if someone had injected a mind-numbing chemical straight into her veins that set her body aflame and squelched the little voice of reason in her head that should have been screaming *Slow down!*

She didn't want to slow down. She wanted to drown in him. She wanted to forget the past and all her terrible memories. With his lips on hers and his body against hers and his delicious taste on her tongue, she *was* forgetting. If he asked her at this moment if he could take her against the brick wall, she would have said an unequivocal yes.

Beneath her expensive, elaborate panties, she was soaking wet.

The kiss went on and on, deep, electric, and fevered, until Christian pulled back and panted a quietly strained, "Fuck."

Ember moaned at the loss of his mouth. She felt hot, so hot and strangely uninhibited she had a wild notion to tear off all her clothes. She didn't know what was happening to her, and honestly, she didn't care.

"Don't stop, Christian. Please don't stop," she whispered, her own breathing as irregular as his. Her hands on the back of his neck trembled.

"You want more of me?" he whispered back, his fingers tightening in her hair.

"Yes. Please. More." It came out in three separate panted breaths as she strained against him, rising up on her toes when he wouldn't lean in far enough for their lips to touch again.

"How much more, September? Tell me exactly how much you want."

He held her back with that hand in her hair, still holding her tight against him with the other hand around her bottom, his gaze fierce on her face, almost ferocious. She shivered, alight with desire and a dark, burning need.

"I want *all of you*," she whispered, staring straight into his eyes. His lids closed for a moment, he inhaled a ragged breath, then he opened his eyes and lowered his head to hers.

Just as his mouth was about to touch hers, he stiffened and let out a sharp, preternatural hiss. A deep, low, animalistic growl rumbled through his chest and lifted all the hair on the back of her neck and arms. He turned his head and stared down the alley.

Shocked out of her haze of lust by the unnatural sound, Ember followed his gaze.

Three men stood at the far end of the alley. Their bodies were facing away but their heads were turned in Ember and

Christian's direction, frozen mid-step as if they'd been walking past on the street beyond and had been arrested by the sight or sound of something. All three of them were tall and dark-haired, vaguely familiar looking, handsome in a predatory sort of way, all eyes and appetite. Pedestrians flowed by on the sidewalk unheeded, as the men stared down the alley with expressions ranging from hostile to flat-out murderous.

That frightening, sinister growl rose in Christian's chest again, but this time it was louder, closer to a snarl. His lips peeled back over his teeth. His body went completely rigid.

"Christian?" Ember said it very quietly, now frozen in fright.

"Get back to the car, September," he answered without looking away from the men. "Go find Corbin and tell him to take you straight home. Now."

Very slowly, he stepped away, pushing her behind him with one arm so he was between her and the men at the end of the alley. As Ember peeked around Christian's shoulder, the men turned, in unison, to face them. They took a step into the alley, very slowly, then another, and Christian's hands curled to fists.

Ember whispered, "Christian, who are those—"

"Get back to the car! *Now!*"

He'd whipped his head around and snarled it out before she could finish her question. But it wasn't his snarl that had her shrinking back in terror. It wasn't because his voice had turned different, deeper and whiskey rough. It wasn't even the look of cold, monstrous violence on his face.

It was his eyes. They'd changed. Something about the pupils.

She realized the change just as Christian turned away and pushed her back, growling another warning to go find Corbin. She stumbled back one step, then two, then finally turned and fled the alley in a flat-out run. Ember didn't even bother to look behind her when the growling turned to a horrifying, unearthly roar of pure, animalistic rage that echoed off the stone walls, reverberating into silence.

She couldn't look back because all she could see as she ran was Christian's brilliant green eyes, the rounded dark pupils in the center that had elongated and narrowed to slits.

TWELVE
Life or Death

The three men at the other end of the alley—who weren't really men at all—began advancing with the slow, measured gait of experienced predators honed in on their prey.

Christian stood his ground as they came, that low growl that had so frightened Ember still rumbling through his chest, the electric charge that gathered just before the Shift surging up to sting his skin.

He crouched to a defensive stance, ready to spring. One of the men held up a hand bringing the other two up short with the motion. They stopped, staring at Christian in silence, until the one with his hand up said something to the other two, in a language that sounded like Latin.

Christian knew they were trying to determine if he were friend or foe. He decided to give them an unmistakable hint.

The electric charge surged to a crackling, snapping peak, and Christian Shifted to panther.

It was the same every time; the flood of feral power, the ache of sudden release. There was fleeting pain as his muscles and tendons and bones transformed—fleeting but terrible—and the sound of his bespoke suit being shredded into ragged pieces was minor compared to the sound of his bones grinding into other, stronger shapes, his skin and muscles ripping apart along ragged seams. The process took all of a few seconds, and when it was done, he was standing on four massive paws instead of two feet, his muzzle curled back over sharp canines, his long, powerful tail snaking back and forth behind him like a whip, his clothes littering the street around him like confetti.

Judging by the shocked expression on the men's faces, Christian had the satisfying realization they'd been expecting anything but that.

He knew he was huge in his animal form, much larger than the big cats he'd seen on those wildlife shows, even larger than many of his kin. Pitch black and heavily muscled, he stood shoulder-high to a human man. If he reared up on his hind legs, he'd tower over any human, big as a bear. All his senses, so sharp even in human form, were exponentially stronger, and he could smell, hear, and even taste the world around him, in all its myriad richness and life.

This was who he really was. This was his heritage, and his Gift. His human disguise was just that, a disguise, but in his natural form Christian had so many advantages over a human it was practically laughable.

For instance . . . speed.

In one lightning-fast motion, he sprang forward and bounded down the dark alley, a roar of pure rage ripping from his throat. *Kill kill kill kill kill kill!* It was all he could think or feel, bloodlust bright as sunlight surging through his veins.

The three men/not-men reacted instantaneously. One of them turned and fled, one of them Shifted to panther, and the third—unfortunately—pulled out a gun.

The first shot missed him completely, ricocheting off the brick wall behind his head with a shrill, echoing *twang.* Behind the man who'd fired, the crowd of people strolling by on the sidewalk broke apart screaming and began to stampede in all directions like a herd of frightened deer. At the same time, the other panther leapt forward with outstretched claws and snapping jaws, snarling as viciously as Christian. Then everything happened at once.

He and the other animal collided in mid-leap, their bodies slamming together with such force it sounded like a small explosion. There was howling, hissing, and the twisting huge bodies, the sharp scrape of claws across his muzzle. They landed on the ground and began fighting in earnest, rolling over and over, slamming against the side of a Dumpster with a hollow *boom*, both of them aiming for a killing strike to the throat. Christian's teeth fastened around his opponent's neck before he could twist away, and he heard a shrill scream as his fangs sank deep into his carotid artery.

He bit down hard and twisted his head sideways, ripping out a huge chunk of furred flesh. Blood spurted, wet and hot and copper-tangy, all over his face and into his mouth.

Then another shot rang out in the alley and Christian realized he'd been hit as agony flared up his spine. In the right rear leg, which buckled beneath him.

His first thought was entirely irrational. It was only a name.

Ember.

It gave him enough strength to turn on the gunman and propel himself forward on his one good leg. He hit his target with both paws spread open over his chest and the gun went flying from his hands. Eight pinpoints of blood flowered out beneath the man's white shirt where Christian's claws had pierced his skin. Then more blood spurted out in a high, arcing spray when Christian leaned in, crushed the sternum between his jaws and tore the man's heart, still beating, right out of his chest.

He gurgled and twitched, clutching his chest as if he could fill the bloody hole with his hands. Then he sagged to his knees, listed sideways, and silently slumped to the pavement. His head hit the ground with a flat *smack.* He jerked once, then fell still. Blood began to pool in a swiftly widening, erratic circle around his body.

Christian looked up just in time to see three blue and white police cruisers screech to a stop at the end of the street, lights flashing. He released the heart—dripping blood and steaming in the night air—from his jaws, turned, and limped away.

As instructed, Ember ran straight to find Corbin, pushing through the crowd that at first was strolling casually, then, when two shots rang out in the night, screaming and fleeing in panic.

She was fleeing in panic, too.

It can't be it can't be it can't be! Over and over in her mind it repeated like a record stuck in a groove.

There were images flashing behind her eyes, voices spinning in her head, things she'd seen on the news and heard on the radio—the few times she'd allowed herself to listen to the radio, which was rarely, as it was too painful to hear music—and a terrible picture was coming together in her mind. A picture of chaos.

A picture of carnage.

She concentrated on pushing it back for the moment, because if she allowed it to break free and flood her with the full horror of it, all the details that were lurking just there behind her wide-open eyes, she wasn't sure if she could put one foot in front of the other, not even to run for her life.

If I told you it was a matter of life or death, would you believe me?

Was it?

Yes.

In light of what she'd just seen, the strange transformation in Christian, his eyes and voice and posture, the vicious, animal hiss resounding in his chest, the conversation took on an entirely new meaning.

She found the Audi idling at the curb two blocks away, Corbin's face white and strained through the windshield as he watched people flood the streets, running, stumbling, shouting. She slammed into the side of the car, clawed at the driver's door handle. She tore it open.

"Christian!" Ember panted it, bent over, staring at a horrified Corbin. "He's—three men—the alley two blocks over—"

She pointed, then froze in horror. Then she turned and ran away, as fast and as far as she could.

Because at her words, Corbin's eyes began to change just as Christian's had.

THIRTEEN
Elsething

Caesar Cardinalis was a man used to getting his own way.

The son of a king, he was now a king himself, his brilliant, devious father having been killed by one of his own personal guard more than three years ago. Caesar had often fantasized about killing his father—patricide had marred the perfection of his lineage on more than one occasion—but lacked the necessary courage to complete the task, not understanding while the old bastard was alive that he was, in fact, risking nothing at all.

Because Caesar was Gifted with something the *Ikati* had never seen, in all their glorious history: immortality.

Oh, they had the Gift of transformation—human to panther, panther to Vapor, some of them could even walk through solid walls—and they had other Gifts, too, powerful Gifts particular to each, like Suggestion and Invisibility and Foresight. Nature having the sense of humor she does, Caesar had none of those Gifts, so common to his people. He couldn't even Shift to panther, their most elemental form, and so was considered by most—okay, all—of his kin a *dedecus.*

Disgrace.

He *used* to be considered a disgrace, that is. It wasn't until he was betrayed by one of his closest council, just as his father had been, until he'd been killed and instantly resurrected, that he realized the full truth of what he'd been given. Then his star had risen like a sign in the East.

For those who have no fear of death, life becomes an extraordinary banquet.

Since he and his small cadre of trusted associates had arrived in Barcelona months ago, Caesar had used the beautiful city the way a child uses a playground. Nothing was off-limits, nothing was left untried or untasted, especially the voluptuous, sloe-eyed Flamenco dancers he so loved.

They screamed *so* enchantingly.

He was enjoying the shrill, choking screams of one of the lovely dancers—stripped bare, chained to the wall, bloody, bruised, and fabulous—just as Nico burst into the room.

"Sire! We're under attack! They know we're here! You're in grave danger!"

Caesar turned away from the girl and gave the panting, sweating Nico a sour once-over. He lowered the cat-o'-nine-tails to his side and sighed. The man was always so dramatic.

"My dear Nico," he drawled, "I'm incredibly busy at the moment, as you can surely see." He gestured to the girl, now moaning and begging in broken Spanish for God to save her. A busty, voluptuous brunette, she writhed against the wall. The iron shackles around her wrists clanged so loudly that the Bach concerto playing softly in the background was momentarily drowned out. "Whatever this danger is, I'm sure it can wait until I'm finished."

Because in reality, there *was* no danger to him. What should he be afraid of? A bullet? A knife? An army of a thousand screaming warriors? No, none of that would make any difference at all. Caesar would go on forever just as he was now, shot or stabbed or attacked by a mob, or torn limb from limb in the streets.

He'd tested it himself. He really couldn't die. Or if he could, he'd failed to find the way.

"But—but sire, we were attacked in the street—there was a stranger—he Shifted—"

"Shifted?"

This got Caesar's attention. The intelligence fed to him by his spies indicated the strict, archaic Law the five *Ikati* colonies hidden around the world operated under was still very much in effect. Especially now. Even though the Queen who led them had allowed them more freedoms of late— including women on their formerly all-male Assemblies, allowing all of them to choose their own mates—the rules that had kept them secret from humanity for thousands of years still stood, iron-clad and unbendable.

For the rest of them, that is. Not for Caesar's little band of rebels. And not for the fed up, disgruntled deserters from the other colonies who were flooding to him day after day after day.

"Tell me what happened," he commanded, turning to Nico, abandoning for a moment the girl shackled to the wall.

Nico—tall and well-formed like all the *Ikati*, black-eyed like only the *Ikati* of the Roman colony were—ran a hand through his thick, disheveled dark hair. He huffed out a long, low breath. "Gian and Armond and I were in Gràcia—near the bordello you like—when we felt him, right there on the street. He's amazingly powerful. I don't think I've felt a male so powerful since your father . . . "

Nico trailed off, realizing his mistake when he caught sight of Caesar's thinned lips, his narrowed eyes. He had the good sense to blanch. "Forgive me, sire—I—I meant no disrespect."

"Of course you didn't," Caesar purred in a menacing tone. "You would never be so stupid, now would you, Nico?"

Nico went a shade paler than before. "No, sire," he whispered, frozen still.

Momentarily mollified by this show of deference and fear, Caesar waved a hand, indicating Nico should continue with his story.

Nico took a shaky breath and continued. "We knew he wasn't a deserter from the other colonies right away because he was aggressive immediately. He Shifted and attacked practically before we could react and charged us. Gian Shifted, too, and Armond pulled out his gun. After that . . . " He trailed off again, an expression of shame creeping over his face.

"What?" Caesar prompted, stepping closer. "After that, what happened?"

Nico's gaze dropped to the floor. "After that I don't know what happened because I . . . I ran away."

Caesar tilted back his head and laughed out loud. It bounced off the cold stone walls of the bunker with an eerie, sinister echo. Upon hearing it, the girl in chains began to sob.

"You *ran away?*" he repeated incredulously, though without anger. Caesar understood the instinct for self-preservation all too well; he'd been running away from things all his life. Well, before he knew he was immortal, that is.

Nico nodded, miserable, still staring at the floor. Caesar clapped him on the shoulder, startling Nico, who looked up at him with unmitigated terror in his eyes. "Not to worry, old boy, we can't all be heroes."

The look of profound relief that crossed Nico's face was priceless, and made Caesar smile. How he loved his people to fear him! The feeling of power he experienced when he scared someone was almost as heady as the feeling of power he had when he whipped a girl bloody.

Terror and violence were such exquisite aphrodisiacs.

Heat rushed to his groin and he shot a glance at the girl on the wall, needing suddenly to get back to his unfinished business with her. "We have to assume this isn't a coincidence, though why this Shifter was alone, I can't fathom—the Council of Alphas would have sent a contingent if they knew we were here—"

"He wasn't alone, sire," said Nico. "He was with a girl. A human girl."

Arrested by this new bit of information, Caesar turned back to Nico. He knew for a fact the other colonies did not allow Shifters to mix with humans, on pain of death. Especially after what he'd done at Christmas. The massive killing spree he'd orchestrated at the Vatican had ended the lives of the pope and many others, ensuring the world would never forget exactly who they were dealing with. In response to his act of terrorism, so many were hunting the *Ikati* it wasn't safe for them anywhere anymore, not even in their heavily fortified colonies. It was all part of his ultimate plan, of course, but for a Shifter to be in Barcelona, alone, and hostile—clearly not wanting to be part of his growing colony as so many others were—what could it mean?

Perhaps he was some kind of outcast? A lone wolf? Or, perhaps . . . an assassin, sent alone so as not to attract attention?

But if he was an assassin, he'd still be bound by colony Law. Why would he be with a human on the street?

Caesar asked, "What was he doing with the human girl?"

Nico made a small motion with his shoulders, the barest of shrugs. "Kissing her, sire. The two of them were kissing in an alley when we passed by on the street. He shoved her away as soon as he saw us and she ran, but before that . . . they were just kissing."

Openly kissing a human. Hostile to other Shifters. Willing to Shift in full view of anyone who cared to look. Mulling over these facts, Caesar's mind began slowly to churn.

"Nico," he said thoughtfully, "would you recognize this girl if you saw her again?"

Nico nodded, a definitive yes. Of course his vision would be keen enough to see over distances and in low light; the *Ikati* could even see in the pitch dark.

"Do you think you would be able to describe her to Marcell?"

Marcell was his second-in-command, fiercely intelligent, with a gift for drawing. Caesar had once seen him draw—Michelangelo's *David* in charcoal—from memory. It was perfect.

Nico nodded again.

"Good," Caesar said, a smile spreading slowly over his face. "That's very good. Get it done." Dismissing Nico with a waved hand, he turned back to the girl. A violent surge of lust rose in him, hot as flame, and his fingers tightened on the corded leather handle of the whip.

Just as the sharp *crack* sounded, in unison with a scream of pain from the cowering girl, Nico whispered, "Yes, sire," and quickly backed out of the room.

The next seven days were some of the longest of Ember's life.

She had no memory of how she'd made it home Sunday evening after running in terror from Corbin. She had no memory of how she'd spent the rest of the long, black hours before the early rays of dawn had lightened the sky, creeping stealthily over the jagged black peaks of the mountains until finally Barcelona was bathed in a shimmering, lovely pink radiance perfectly unsuited to her mood. The first thing she remembered was a feeling of freezing cold, because she was sitting outside on the terrace of her apartment in the pretty apricot dress with no other barrier to ward off the chill of the February morning.

She had been shivering violently, sitting stiff in a chair with her arms wrapped around her drawn-up legs, gazing out toward the sea. Her hair was misted with dew. There were blisters on the soles of her bare feet. Even a week later, she couldn't find the shoes she'd been wearing that night. She assumed she'd somehow lost them along the way as she ran.

Just as she'd lost a few other things in the days since.

Ignorance, for one. Using the Internet she'd done a bit of searching and it was surprisingly easy to find what she was looking for. Newspaper articles, talk show discussions, online forums and eyewitness video, the horrible recording of the massacre on Christmas Day, along with the taped manifesto of the madman who'd devised it. For the last three years, she'd been insulated in her little television-free world. Swaddled as she was in the numbing cocoon of her own pain, her mental state as fragile as that old vellum manuscript in Christian's library, she'd grown accustomed to ignoring most everything else. It wasn't an excuse for her ignorance, but it was a reason—a reason that was now defunct.

Now she could no longer avoid the truth.

Christian was not human.

He was, as her mother would have said, part of the world invisible to humans, elves and fairies and demons and monsters, vampires and goblins and ghosts. Her mother had a word for these kinds of supernatural beings, a word Ember had heard a thousand times as a child and dismissed as a figment of her mother's fertile imagination:

Elsething.

Christian was Elsething, and Ember had feelings for him.

It.

The conversation they'd had in the bookstore came back to haunt her with unwelcome regularity. *Whatever goes upon two feet is an enemy. Whatever goes upon four feet, or has wings, is a friend.*

His eyes and face and voice haunted her, too, and she didn't know what to do with herself, much less what to do about the situation. Because there *was* a situation, a very bad, dangerous situation, in which she was unfortunately caught in the middle, whether she liked it or not.

The authorities were on the hunt for the large, black animal that had escaped the night of the shooting in Gràcia. They'd found one enormous dead panther, its throat torn out—and an unidentifiable man whose heart had been eaten right out of his chest. Curiously, the man had no fingerprints. Which, a local newscaster had explained, was because he wasn't actually a man at all.

Elsething. Apparently they were everywhere these days.

She'd heard them called *Ikati*, an ancient Zulu word that meant "cat warrior." As exotic as the creatures it described, the word also held a sinister undertone when spoken aloud. It sounded supernatural because it was; it sounded dangerous because they were.

They were killers. They were murderers. They were animals, to a one.

All animals are created equal . . .

She wondered if her father had some weird premonition when reading his beloved *Animal Farm* to her when she was a child. She wondered if he somehow guessed one day she would come face to face with a creature that seemed for all intents and purposes the same kind of animal she was— the human kind—but who in actuality was not.

She wondered what her father would do in her shoes, knowing as she did exactly where that animal lived. Knowing there was a substantial reward for his capture, or the capture of any of his kind.

One million euro might have tempted someone of greater greed, but to Ember the money meant only one thing: Christian had a very, very big target on his back.

And he had not contacted her since that night.

Feigning illness, Ember had taken the week off, which forced Marguerite to work behind the counter of Antiquarian Books, an undertaking she loathed and would undoubtedly take revenge on Ember for, one way or another. She'd hidden in her apartment with the door locked and the shades drawn, terrified Christian would call or come over. She was strangely disappointed when he didn't, wracked with the desire to see him and the desire to run for the hills.

The irony that the one person who'd made her feel alive in years was the one person who was more dangerous to her than any other person on Earth—and who wasn't even a *person*, per se—made her wish for the first time in her life that she drank.

And speaking of drinking, she wasn't even seeing Asher, which was worrying him sick.

"Ember," he'd said sternly into her voicemail this morning, his tone just short of angry, "you can't keep avoiding me like this. What's happened? Are you sick? Are you dead? Actually I know you're not dead because I went into the store and that hemorrhoidal stepmother of yours told me you had the flu. Not that I believe her; she's probably poisoned you. If you don't call me back, I'm coming over. Do *not* make me use my key."

She'd texted him back, a mere six words:

Not dead. Don't worry. Everything OK.

Even in type, it looked like a lie.

But she wasn't ready to see him yet. She wasn't ready to see anyone, if truth be told. Because how could she pretend everything was normal and life was just as it had been before, when everything had been turned upside down?

When everything she had believed about the "real" world had turned out to be false?

She hadn't even gone to the animal shelter to volunteer as she usually did on Sundays. When she called in, the man who ran the place—a grizzled, dour, bear of a man by the name of Parker—told her she'd be missed, as they were full to overflowing.

People were abandoning their cats—beloved house pets turned suspected killers—by the hundreds.

Especially the black ones.

It was worse on the news; cats were being burned, tortured, thrown from buildings. Since Christmas, when an *Ikati* had murdered the head of the Catholic church along with dozens of innocent bystanders, zoos all over the world had closed due to fear of retribution on their big cat enclosures from an angry, frightened public. The panic was widespread, and showed no signs of slowing.

Not only black panthers but cats of all kinds were now at the top of the public enemy list.

And what, Ember wondered, was Christian's place in all of this? Was he a murderer, too?

The first clue to an eventual answer came one night in the form of a note slipped under her front door. In Christian's lilting, perfect handwriting, it read, *Why haven't you shared my secret with the world? What are you waiting for?*

You, she decided, the note gripped so tightly between her fingers it began to tear on one side. *I've been waiting for you.*

She burned the note, rinsed the ashes down the kitchen sink, showered, and got dressed for the first time in days. As she locked her apartment door behind her and headed down the stairs, she gripped the gold rings that hung on her necklace with one hand.

In the other hand, hidden inside the pocket of her coat, she gripped the slender metal handle of a switchblade.

FOURTEEN
Quid Pro Quo

"Give me fifteen minutes. If I don't come back by then, you can leave."

The taxi driver looked at her dubiously, then looked out the windshield. It was pitch dark, a cloudy, starless night, threatening rain, and the temperature was dropping rapidly.

"*Estas seguro?*" he asked. He didn't want to leave her alone in the forest in the middle of the night, that much was clear.

She replied in Spanish, "Yes, I'm sure. Fifteen minutes, okay?"

He shrugged—*suit yourself*—and Ember paid him and climbed out of the cab.

The gate to Christian's house was just around a bend in the road; as she began to walk, the sky overhead opened and it began to rain.

She started to run.

By the time she reached the massive iron gates, she was soaked through, her shoes squeaking, her jeans sopping, her hair plastered to her cheeks. Panting from the run, shivering with cold and the adrenaline mercilessly lashing through her veins, Ember lifted a shaking hand to the little electronic box beside the gate.

Before she could push the speaker button, the gates creaked open with a metallic, bone-jarring screech of metal against metal. Ember looked into the small black camera mounted high on the stone column beside the gate and stared into its unblinking red eye for a long moment, then turned and made her way toward the mansion. Silent and unlit, it appeared like a slumbering giant among the trees, the rain-slicked windows black as hollowed eyes.

She wondered if the moat that surrounded it was stocked with crocodiles.

Her "Hello?" was barely a whisper, spoken as she pushed open the massive front door which stood slightly ajar.

Silence answered her.

There was no Corbin to greet her, no lights in the foyer. Most of the house was plunged in darkness as far as she could tell. But from down the corridor she saw the wavering orange glow of a fire reflecting off the polished floor, and heard the spare crackle of burning wood.

Someone was in the library.

Her heart like a wild thing in her chest, Ember eased the door closed and made her way down the hall toward the library. She paused just outside the door, looking in.

Standing with his arms braced against the stone hearth of the massive fireplace, staring down into the flames, Christian didn't acknowledge her presence, or turn to look at her as she slowly entered the room.

Though the light in the room was low, the only illumination the glow of the fire and the tapered candles in a silver candelabra on the desk, everything felt too bright and sharp, the edges of things hurting her eyes. The urge to turn and run away was powerful, and so was the urge to cross to Christian and touch him. He wore loose clothing, ivory linen drawstring pants and a matching, untucked shirt rolled up to his elbows. Against the glossy parquet floor, his feet were tanned and bare.

Now that she was here, ambivalence was a noose around her neck, a noose tightening in degrees with every second Christian stayed silent.

What could she say? What could he? Why, in fact, had she even come?

Finally, he said into the hush in a tone devoid of emotion, "Are you here to kill me?"

That startled her. A little breathlessly, she asked, "What kind of question is that?"

Without turning away from the fire, he lifted his head and turned it slightly so she saw him in profile: tight jaw and stern mouth, the perfect line of his nose, the serious, black slash of his brows. "A logical one. Unless you're planning on playing darts with that blade in your pocket."

Her fingers tightened around the switchblade. Her heart jumped into her throat. "How could you possibly know that?"

Now he did turn, slowly, straightening and lowering his arms to his sides. With the firelight behind him flared into nimbus around his head, his features were cast in shadow. His eyes, however, those preternatural green eyes, flashed silver against the light, like a cat's.

"I can smell it," he said very softly, his gaze locked onto hers. "Just like I can smell the metal in your arm, the fear you have of me now, your ambivalence, and your confusion. I could smell you as soon as you got out of that cab, Ember, which incidentally I also could hear coming, all the way up the mountain." He stepped forward slowly, soundlessly, his gaze still trained on hers. "Why are you soaking wet?"

"Stay where you are," she insisted. The cold and her wet hair and clothes were beginning to have their way with her, and she was shivering uncontrollably. The hand she held out—in vain, she knew—to stop him from advancing, shook.

He'd stopped in place when he saw her outstretched hand, but this little concession did nothing to quell her sudden anxiety. What a fool she'd been, coming here to confront him. Alone. Alone in a house with a supernatural creature who had a predilection for chewing things to shreds. And not a soul on earth knew where she was right now.

Screw it, she thought, straightening her shoulders. *I'm not going to be intimidated by a . . . by a—*

"And when you're angry or irritated," Christian said softly, "it feels like fingernails scraped over my skin."

"Stop that," Ember hissed, a flush of heat rising in her face.

He examined her expression, her flaming cheeks, her stiff back, and shaking hands, and exhaled a slow, controlled breath. Watching her face carefully, he said, "I thought I might never see you again."

Ember's teeth began to chatter. She had to clench her jaws together to keep them from clattering right out of her skull. "I know . . . I know what you are."

His left brow lifted, but that was all.

"You're not human?" She'd meant it as a statement but it was still so unbelievable to her, standing with him so close, looking so normal, that it came out with a lift at the end like a question.

It brought a grim smile to his face. "I assume you already know the answer to that, or you wouldn't have brought a knife. Not that it will help you." He took another step toward her.

She blurted, "So you are dangerous . . . to me."

"You already know the answer to that, too. Yes to the first part, no to the second. And I'm not answering any more questions unless you answer some of mine in return. Quid pro quo, September."

His eyes were fierce and intent, burning with some unknown emotion that had her nerves singing. The term "quid pro quo" always reminded her of Hannibal Lecter and Agent Starling sharing information in *Silence of the Lambs*, something she really didn't want to think about at the moment. Next he'd be telling her about eating someone's fried liver with some fava beans and a nice Chianti.

Hysteria began to take hold of her body, sinking sharp teeth into her throbbing heart.

"Did you kill those—those men? In the alley?"

He nodded, and it took her breath away. She'd seen the pictures on the Internet, she'd read all about the mangled bodies, but it was still stunning. This beautiful man was a murderer.

A murderer. He'd *eaten out* someone's heart.

She managed a horrified, "Why?" but he shook his head.

"My turn. What are those?" His gaze dropped to the chain around her neck and the two gold rings that hung from it.

She whispered, "My parents' wedding rings. Why did you kill those men . . . people . . . creatures?"

He lifted his gaze to hers. Very composed, he said, "Because if I hadn't, they would have killed us both."

Ember opened her mouth, but no sound came out. *They would have killed us both.*

Christian asked, "Why did you come to Spain?" and took another careful step toward her.

She realized dimly that she was dripping rainwater in a widening pool onto the floor around her feet. "To forget," she whispered, feeling her legs solidify to something like cement as he eased ever nearer, very carefully, watching her for any sign she was going to bolt.

"To forget what?" he insisted, but Ember shook her head; her turn.

"Is that what you do for a living? You kill things? That's what your 'work' is?" Her voice was faint, tinged with disbelief and horror, until she had another chilling realization and her voice actually cracked. "Is that what you were doing that night—when you were late for our date?"

"That's four questions. And the answer to all of them is no. Now, answer me this and I'll answer all the rest of your questions, as many as you want: why did you come to Spain? And don't tell me 'to forget.' I want a real answer, Ember. Tell me the truth."

He was close now, within reaching distance, but he'd stopped an arm's length away and wasn't making any moves to come closer. Ember's entire body was shaking now, her knees and hands and even her lower lip were trembling. The bravado she'd felt moments before had drained away, leaving only the cold, cold residue of fear. Water dripped into her eyes but she was too frozen to wipe it away.

"I-I came to Spain to forget . . . to forget . . . " she stopped abruptly when he stepped closer.

"I'm not going to hurt you," Christian said gently. "You should know that by now. Hurting you would only be hurting myself, September."

Hearing him say her full name reminded her of something. She swallowed around the lump in her throat and asked, "How did you know my real name that first day we met?"

"I saw it." When her brow furrowed in confusion, he explained, "There's a framed newspaper article on the wall behind the register, with a picture of your father and you. 'American artist opens rare bookstore in Gothic quarter.' Both your names were beneath."

For some reason, this was the little fact that finally embedded itself into her consciousness as incontrovertible evidence of his un-humanness. The wall behind the register was ten feet back from the counter; the framed newspaper article printed in—as newspaper articles are—tiny, six-point type. Her father had complained when the article came out that he could barely even read it with his glasses on, the paper held close to his nose.

Unnatural speed, immense strength and heightened senses, combined with the ability to turn into some other, animal form . . . Elsething.

But God, this Elsething was exquisite. Was that another of his gifts? Symmetry of features so perfect it would stun his prey into submission, like cobra hypnosis? He was so painfully beautiful it was next to impossible to believe this man standing before her had wreaked the kind of havoc she'd seen in the crime scene photos on the internet, the kind of things only a monster would do. The blood—so much *blood*.

And how could she ever trust he wouldn't do the same thing to her, even by accident? Maybe his bloodlust was affected by the tide or the weather or even the full moon—

In one swift motion, Christian tore open his shirt, exposing his bare, muscular chest. Buttons popped and went flying, clattering and bouncing against the floor. Suddenly imposing and large and angry, he closed the final space between them and growled, "Do it then! If you really think I would ever lift a finger to hurt you, you might as well go ahead and kill me! I won't try to stop you."

The hysteria rose to a peak inside her, burning bright, razor sharp. She sucked in a breath, every nerve and muscle poised to flee—

Then he reached out and gripped her arm. Ember twisted away with a high-pitched shriek that sounded like a mouse when it sees the cat in mid-pounce.

But he was too fast and too strong, and she was too human. She was no match for him.

His arms came around her in a crushing tight band. She struggled against him to absolutely no avail, twisting and bucking, trying to gain release, but he only held her as she struggled, silently, patiently, until she wore herself out and sagged to the floor, her legs folding beneath her. Christian slid down behind her and continued to hold her as she gulped in lungfuls of cedar-scented air, her body wracked with tremors, her ragged breaths echoing throughout the quiet room.

"Breathe for me, little firecracker. Just breathe," he whispered near her ear.

And she did. Shaking and hyperventilating in his arms, she did.

After a few minutes, Christian tentatively loosened his arms. Seeing she wasn't going to make a move—she couldn't, her muscles were frozen stiff—he peeled her soggy coat off her back and tossed it to a nearby chair. On his knees, he slid around in front of her and brushed her wet hair off her face.

"Look at me," he said, when she didn't lift her gaze to his. Childishly, she squeezed her eyes shut tight. "Look at me or I'm going to kiss you," he warned.

Her lids flew open and she stared at him, wide-eyed and shivering with shock.

"You told me you wanted all of me," he murmured, stroking a finger along her cheek. "Tell me that hasn't changed."

She groaned, hid her face in her hands. He pried her hands apart and forced her to look at him. "We'll let that one go for the moment. But tell me this: why didn't you turn me in to the police? Why didn't you collect that big reward and end all your money troubles? You know where I live; you could have led them straight to me. But you didn't. Why?"

His eyes searched hers, searing, haunted. She couldn't have lied to him even if she'd wanted to. "The money?" she whispered hoarsely, shaking her head. "Christian, how could you think the *money* would mean anything to me? It's *you*. But you didn't even call me! All this week I had no idea what happened to you—"

"I wanted to call you, I wanted to see you—God you have no idea—but I can't Shift when I'm injured," he explained quietly, that finger still making slow tracings across her cheek. "I've been stuck in my animal form until today. I can usually heal very quickly, but this gunshot wound was nasty, my entire kneecap—"

"Gunshot!" Ember sat up stiffly, her eyes raking him for signs of injury. "Those bastards *shot* you?"

Amusement flickered over his face. "In the leg, yes. One of them Shifted and tried to eat me and the other one shot me. Does that make you feel better about it?"

For killing them, he was asking. Perversely, it did, and she nodded to let him know, her teeth sunk into her lower lip.

He seemed relieved at her answer. His eyes closed briefly, and when they opened again, he said, very softly, "What are you in Spain to forget?"

It was a long while before she answered him, and his eyes never wavered from her face. "Everything," she said truthfully. Then she realized with sudden, swift horror the two of them were more alike than she'd realized.

They were both killers.

The thought made her sick to her stomach.

She staggered to her feet, a hand cupped over her mouth, nausea rising in her throat. This was too much, it was all too much, and she couldn't think with him so close, with his scent and his dark, molten gaze—she had to get away.

"Ember, wait—stop—"

Now.

She stumbled toward the door, barely seeing anything because her eyes were filling with tears. All those horrible memories she'd been so careful to repress came flooding back and mingled with the Internet images of the massacre on Christmas Day at the Vatican and the two corpses on the street last week, all of them mutilated and covered in blood.

Her footsteps sounded loud as cannon fire in her ears as she ran blindly toward the front door, a sob caught in her throat. Just as she lifted a hand to reach for the massive bronze ring that would unlatch the door and release her to freedom, something pulled her up short and had her scrambling back in shock.

Sinuous as smoke, a pale gray plume of mist snaked down in front of her, coiling and ruffling in the air. It gathered and shimmered for a moment, suspended, an odd cloud blocking the door, then coalesced, quickly gathering mass and taking shape as a form she knew all too well. Feet and legs, arms and chest, sculpted body, and breathtaking face, complete with a pair of green eyes so vivid they glowed.

Christian. He materialized in front of her eyes from nothing more than a thin cloud of fog.

He was naked.

The scream that clawed its way out of her throat was equal parts horror and disbelief.

"Wait," he snapped with a hand outstretched. "Ember, just wait—"

"Let me go, Christian!" she sobbed. "If you care about me at all, just let me go!"

Without waiting for an answer, she ran past him, yanked open the front door, and ran out into the rain swept night.

FIFTEEN
Ten Minutes

The pounding on her apartment door was loud and unrelenting. So was the shouting.

"Ember! Open this door right now, honey! *September!* What the *hell!*"

It was Asher, roused most likely from a Xanax-induced sleep by the sound of her footsteps pounding up the stairs, the door to her apartment slamming shut and her hysterical sobbing, the last of which hadn't let up since she'd collapsed back into the waiting taxi outside Christian's house.

The ride home had been interminable. She kept expecting a cloud of smoke to filter in through the air vents and coalesce in the passenger seat into the naked form of Christian, which would terrify the driver—for so many different reasons—and they'd wind up in a fiery crash.

Ember didn't think Fate would grant her the luck to survive not one but *two* fiery crashes in a lifetime.

Still in her soaked clothes and shoes, she'd flung herself face down on the bed as soon as she got home, buried her face into her pillow, and pulled the covers over her head. Then she tried not to think about how a supernatural cloud of mist—ethereal, insubstantial—would not be hindered by silly little human things like doors and locks.

The pounding on the front door ceased. Thinking he'd given up, Ember enjoyed a brief moment of relief until the sound of it being unlocked and swung open intruded through her sobs. When Asher burst through her bedroom door and started shouting up close, she wished with all her heart she'd never given him that extra key.

"Jesus Christ, honey, what's going on? Are you hurt? I've never heard you cry! And I've never heard anyone cry like *that*. It sounds like someone's skinning a cat! Tell me what's happening, I'm about to blow an O ring!"

Obscure car engine references from a hysterical gay man who'd broken into her house in the middle of the night after she'd discovered her sort-of boyfriend was something right out of a Steven King novel; the world had officially ended.

From under the covers Ember moaned, "Nothing's wrong, Ash. Leave me alone."

She heard his disbelieving "Puh!" just before she felt the bed wobble under his weight as he sat down on the edge of the mattress. A hand began to rub slow, relaxing circles on her back through the comforter. It reminded her of something her mother would do when she was sick as a little girl and brought on a fresh wave of tears.

"Please—you have to tell me you're okay. You've refused to see me all week and I've been worried sick and now you come home like *this*. I haven't talked to you since right before your date last Sunday—what the hell is going on?"

She blubbered, "It's . . . it's Christian. H-he—" She paused, then wailed, "Oh God!"

"That son of a bitch!" Asher shouted at the top of his lungs, scaring the wits out of her. "Did he touch you? Did he hurt you? I swear to God, Em, just say the word and I'll get out my gun and go find that bastard and blow off his di—"

"No!" she groaned, cutting him off. "It's not like that! He didn't hurt me . . . " She trailed off, realizing she'd put just enough emphasis on that last word that Asher, if he was paying attention, would have picked up on it.

Fortunately, Asher was too busy having his own meltdown to notice.

He leapt from the bed and began stalking around the room, punctuating every third word with a foot stomp. "I should have *known* he was too good to be true! That face! That body! That wardrobe! That *accent!* I bet it's all a ruse, isn't it? He doesn't really even have any money. He's some kind of con artist, isn't he? He's a grifter! He lures innocent young women into his trap and then has his way with them—or their bank accounts!"

Ember thought it prudent not to mention she was neither innocent nor in possession of an enticing bank account.

Then Asher pulled up short and with a gasp said, "I bet he's not even British . . . he's probably from somewhere completely horrific . . . somewhere like . . . somewhere like *Utah!*"

Ember threw the covers from her head and shouted, "Asher, please! You're only making me feel *worse!*"

"Oh, sweetie, I'm so sorry." He wrung his hands together, chagrined. Wearing fuchsia pajamas with a pattern of gold and scarlet peonies and a pair of mauve tufted slippers, he hurried to the side of the bed, sat down again, and took her hand. "But you have to tell me what happened or my imagination will get the better of me! What did he *do?* Or what *didn't* he do? Tell me!"

Looking into his worried, beseeching eyes brought a fresh onslaught of tears. She hid her face into the covers again and blurted a muffled, "He's not the person I thought he was."

Her inner voice amended that to a derisive, *He's not a person at all.*

Because life has a cruel and capricious sense of humor, her cell phone rang at exactly that moment. Before she could stop him, Asher had flung himself across the room, retrieved it from where she'd left it atop the dresser, picked it up, and shouted, "Hello?" He listened for approximately two seconds, then screeched into it, "What the hell did you do to her, you bastard?"

Ember moaned into the pillow and put her hands over her ears.

"No, you absolutely will *not!* I don't know what you did but I've never seen her like this and so help me God if you come over here I'll—" He cut off abruptly, listened for another moment, then with a muttered oath that included the words "roasted balls" he slammed the phone down.

Ember sat up in bed. "What? What did he say?"

Furious, Asher looked at her, his face a mottled shade of red. "He says he's coming up."

"What—now?" She looked wildly around the room as if he was lurking behind the curtains or beside the bookcase. "He's *here?*"

In answer, there was a violent pounding on the apartment's front door.

Seeing the look of pure panic on her face, Asher pronounced with venom, "*I'll* take care of this jerkoff," and marched out of the bedroom.

He slammed her bedroom door behind him so she couldn't see what was going on in the living room, but within two seconds there was the muffled sound of shouting, another door being slammed, more shouting, this time louder, then a few unidentifiable thumps and bumps that had her cowering on the bed in terror, imagining the worst. Then her bedroom door burst wide open, disgorging an apoplectic Asher, wielding one of the set of carving knives from the block on the kitchen counter, and a snarling Christian, dressed only in the pair of linen trousers he'd been wearing when she saw him standing in front of the fireplace.

Ember shrieked, "Asher! Put the knife down!"

Then commenced the loudest, most convoluted shouting match Ember had ever heard. Asher screamed something, Christian shouted something back, the two of them volleyed threats and insults and ignored anything the other one was saying until Ember, exhausted and so strung out she thought her head might actually explode, yelled, "STOP!"

They froze. Both their heads whipped around in her direction.

Asher—athletic and muscular, but easily outsized by Christian—was in Badass mode. She'd seen this a few other times when he'd had occasion to divest some bigot of a misconception that gay men were nothing but effeminate, promiscuous, Streisand-loving sissies who'd been molested in childhood, triggering some kind of sexual Stockholm syndrome whereby the victim would forevermore "choose" to be attracted to other men in an effort to heal their painful past.

Despite the pretty pajamas and fluffy footwear, Asher was scary as hell. Color stained his cheeks, his face was hard as granite, his chest rose and fell in sharp, staccato bursts. The hand that held the knife shook. His fingers were curled so hard around the hilt his knuckles showed white. He was Italian, with that Mediterranean passion and volatility, and it showed.

In contrast, Christian seemed relatively composed. Until she looked into his eyes.

What she saw there made her mouth go dry.

He was furious, too, but it was cold and feral and utterly deadly, a savage blackness unfurling even as she started at him, a violence so thick and profound it actually had *heft*. It was nothing like Asher's hot, blustering outrage, and though he was the one holding the very wicked-looking knife, Ember felt a thrill of fear slice through her, straight to the bone.

Her friend could take down the best of the best . . . humans.

Now, he was in mortal danger.

She whispered, "Ash. Put the knife on the dresser. Please."

"I'm not doing anything until you give me a very good reason why I shouldn't relieve this prick of an important body part." Asher's angry gaze flickered to the general vicinity of Christian's crotch.

"Please," she reiterated, keeping her voice as calm as she could. "Christian hasn't done anything to hurt me, physically . . . " She swallowed and began anew, hoping her voice wouldn't crack. "Or emotionally. We're just having a-a fight. It's nothing fatal, there's no need for any amputations."

After a long, murderous glare in Christian's direction, he finally complied. Then he folded his arms across his silk-clad chest, tossed his head and said to her, "That was probably the worst lie you've ever told me, honey. And I'm pretty sure you've told me a lot." He huffed a breath through his nostrils and shot another glare at Christian. "You're lucky she's not PMSing, or you'd be missing your baby-maker, Romeo."

Christian smiled at him, and Ember would have sworn under oath she'd never seen anything so frightening in her entire life.

In a voice low and infinitely dark, his gaze never once wavering from Asher's face, Christian said, "No one has ever threatened me like that and lived to tell about it, but considering you're acting as a guard dog on behalf of someone I care about, I'm going to let that go. A word of advice, however: never do it again. Or *you'll* be missing much more than your baby-maker, friend. Now piss off. Ember and I need to talk."

Before the jumping muscle in Asher's jaw translated into another round of hurled threats, Ember broke in. "Please, Ash. Please, it's okay."

Asher looked back and forth between her and Christian, his gaze clearly disbelieving, anger still evident in every feature on his face. Finally he said, "Since no one will tell me exactly what's going on here, this is what I'm going to do."

He pointed to the door. "I'm going to sit on the sofa in the living room for ten minutes; that's enough time for you to say whatever it is you have to say, and for my girl to listen. During that time, I will be listening for any noise or indication whatsoever that she is afraid, angry, or even the slightest bit *miffed*. If I hear anything out of the ordinary, I'll call the police, and then I'll be back in this room with the entire set of kitchen knives, whether she likes it or not. *Capisce?*"

One corner of Christian's mouth twitched. He stared at Asher for just longer than was comfortable, then said, "*Capisce*, Pacino."

Asher looked at Ember, then looked at the knife on the dresser he'd just put down. He picked it up again, gave the two of them a tight smile. He said, "You kids won't be needing this," turned, and sailed from the room.

Christian shut the door behind him. It closed with what seemed a deadly soft scrape of wood on wood.

She couldn't look at him. She looked at her feet instead, still clad in her wet shoes, hanging over the edge of the bed.

"Well. That was a first. I've never been threatened with bodily injury by a drag queen before."

He hadn't moved from the door. His voice was less frightening than when he'd spoken to Asher, but there was still a hard edge to it, though she sensed he was trying to control himself for her sake.

"He's not a drag queen, he's gay," she said, feeling miserable and confused and exhausted. "And he used to be in the Marines. Gay Marines are the toughest people on earth."

"He's wearing fluffy slippers, September. And women's pajamas."

Faintly, Ember protested, "Those are Gaultier."

Ignoring that, Christian said, "You're still wet." He sounded mad about it.

Following his tactic, she sidestepped his comment. "Say what you have to say, Christian. Then leave. Please. I can't digest all this in the span of one night. Especially with you here—like that."

She made a vague gesture with her hand to indicate his lack of a shirt, which up until now she had been doing a very good job of not focusing on. He hovered enticingly in her peripheral vision, however—bare chest and golden skin and sculpted muscles—so she turned her eyes to the opposite wall, letting them rest on an oil painting in a hideous gilt frame her father had bought for her on a whim at the same flea market where he'd bought her divan. It depicted a litter of sleeping kittens curled together on a knitted blanket in a basket, which at the moment seemed incredibly sinister.

"Oh? Do you find the sight of my body distracting?"

His voice sent a shiver through her. It had changed from dangerous to soft, a liquid sensuality like warmed honey sliding over her skin. She closed her eyes against it and said, "Just say what you came here to say."

There was silence, then a sigh. Then, without warning, his arms wrapped around her.

"Ten minutes," he whispered when she tried to push him away. "Ten minutes and then if you still want me to, I'll walk out that door and I swear you'll never see me again."

He was on his knees at the bedside and she was curled into his chest, her face in her hands, shaking. She tried to swallow around the fist in her throat, but couldn't, and her breath caught.

"I can't . . . I can't . . . "

He pushed her weak protests aside, lifted her in his arms, and deposited them both back onto the bed. He pulled her up against his body and buried his face into her neck. "Ten minutes. Ember. Just ten minutes."

His voice now was barely audible, but she didn't miss the pleading tone. It was dizzying, his switch from deadly predator to sweet suitor, and maddening, too.

How on earth was she supposed to deal with this? With *him?*

"Don't get mad," he warned. Which, naturally, made her mad.

"I can't help being upset! Put yourself in my shoes for a second!"

His arms tightened around her back. "I'm only saying that so I won't get sliced to ribbons by a knife-wielding drag queen—" when she stiffened, he quickly amended that to, "Gay ex-Marine. If he hears you getting mad, I'll be neutered, remember?"

Ember pressed her lips together to stifle the hysterical laugh that threatened to bubble up from her throat. The thought of Asher getting the drop on Christian was impossibly funny. She figured he'd just turn to a raincloud or a wisp of smoke to avoid Asher's lunge.

Because she wasn't in a rational state of mind, Ember relented. "Fine," she whispered. "Ten minutes."

He pressed a fleeting kiss to her throat, warm and soft, and before she could protest he'd sat up, bringing her along with him. "Good answer. Now, let's get you out of these wet clothes. Where do you keep your nightgowns?"

Ember wrinkled her nose. "What am I, ninety? I don't own nightgowns."

"Okay, then. What do you wear to bed?"

She pressed her lips together, but he'd already guessed. His lips curved to a smile.

"Really? In the buff? What an enticing thought." His smile grew larger as her face reddened.

"Can we not make this any harder for me? Please?" She stood and marched over to her dresser, pulled out a pair of cotton pajamas Asher had bought her for Christmas two years ago, crossed the room to the attached bathroom, and shut the door. Christian watched her every move as if expecting her to bolt at any moment.

Safe behind the closed bathroom door, Ember sagged against the sink. She looked at herself in the mirror—damp and bedraggled, wild-eyed as a cornered animal—and dragged her hands over her face.

All animals are created equal, she thought. Remembering how Christian's eyes had changed, how he'd appeared from thin air, she added, *Yeah, but some are more equal than others.*

Once dried and dressed, her hair combed, her face washed, her teeth brushed, she re-emerged from the bathroom and stood looking at him. Even though she was clothed, she felt naked, almost unbearably shy. And yet, she couldn't look away from him.

He was propped up against the pillows on the bed, one leg stretched out, one bent at the knee, barefoot and barechested, looking tense and so beautiful she wished she had the talent of drawing. He lifted a hand and held it out in a silent invitation, and because her body was a traitor where he was concerned, her feet automatically moved her to him as if summoned by a spell.

He didn't give her a decision about where she was going; he pulled her gently down onto the bed with him, curled one arm around her chest, slid one beneath her head, then nestled himself against her back so they were spooned together with his legs drawn up behind hers and their heads resting on a shared pillow.

"Your sense of humor is questionable, little firecracker," Christian murmured into her hair.

The pajamas Asher had given her were decorated with tiny pictures of cats chasing dogs. On the front of the shirt was a big picture of a terrified Chihuahua standing frozen while a nasty-looking black cat with slitted eyes slunk up on it from behind. The caption read, "It's behind me . . . isn't it?"

She closed her eyes and muttered, "It seemed apropos."

They lay like that in silence for several moments, until the tension in her body relaxed and it began to feel a little more natural having him there. So close she smelled the heady, exotic musk of his skin, felt the heat of his body warming hers. Naturally he sensed her easing tension, and a sigh of what might have been relief slipped from his lips.

"I hate it that you're afraid of me," he whispered.

"I'm not . . . at the moment. But you have to admit, Christian, it's a lot to take in."

"I know. Believe me, I know." He paused, thinking, then said, "Thank you for letting me be here."

That struck her as incredibly sweet. "You're welcome."

"Okay," he said, "ten minutes." Then there was another pause as if he were gathering his thoughts. Finally he said, "Do you know the story behind the Sphinx?"

"You mean the statue in Egypt?"

"Yes."

"Well . . . not really, no."

"It's one of the world's largest and oldest statues, its origins lost in the mists of time. Popular theory has it the Sphinx was built in approximately 2500 BC by the pharaoh Khafra as part of the funerary complex of the great pyramids at Giza. The commonly used name 'Sphinx' was given to it in antiquity—long after it was built—in reference to the Greek mythological beast with a lion's body, a woman's head and the wings of an eagle. Its real name has never been discovered because it was built so long ago, but the modern Egyptian Arabic name for the statue is The Terrifying One."

Though she didn't know why, that struck Ember as important: The Terrifying One. A little shiver went up her spine.

As Christian continued, his voice dropped to a spare, lilting murmur. "But that statue wasn't built by Khafra in 2500 BC. And though it was named the Sphinx, it doesn't have the body of a lion."

The air seemed suddenly to crackle with static. "No?" Ember whispered.

"No. It was built a thousand years before, by worshippers of a queen the humans at that time considered a divinity who lived among them. And like the divinity they worshipped, the statue is part human . . . and part panther."

The breath left Ember's body in a small, soundless rush. He went on, and all the tiny hairs on her body began, one by one, to stand on end.

"My kind has been here since the beginning of everything. Native to the darkest heart of the African rainforest, we were predators who excelled at that most necessary of animal survival techniques: camouflage. We could change form to match any environment or mimic any prey, we could even dissolve completely into the mist that was a constant of the rainforest. We lived in a perfect, peaceful bubble for thousands upon thousands of years, co-existing with all the other creatures of the land."

His voice darkened. "Until one day a different sort of creature appeared. It crawled from the mud, gasping air into amphibious lungs. That little muddy fish would change our fates forever."

Ember had a moment of confusion, then in a flash of clarity realized he was talking about *people*. "Fish?" she repeated, disgusted. "You're telling me I'm descended from a *fish?*"

"You'd rather it was a monkey?" he asked, his voice dry. "And if it makes you feel better, *you're* not descended from a fish—your ancient ancestors were."

Neither of those answers seemed satisfactory, so Ember remained silent. Christian's arm tightened around her, and he began to speak again.

"The new arrivals evolved quickly. Once they'd advanced to the point where they had fire, stone tools, and the first, raw grasp of language, we made ourselves known to them. Which turned out to be a colossal mistake."

Ember whispered, "Why?"

"Think about it. Even now the human world is a hard place to live if you're different. Too dark, ugly, or nearsighted, too skinny, fat, or tall, too different from whatever the 'norm' happens to be, you get crucified. Think about your friend Asher. What do you think life has been like for him?"

Hard. His life—until he learned to accept himself and found a soulmate in Sebastian—had been hard. And then after Sebastian had died—harder. Ember knew it was part of the reason the two of them got along so well; they had both suffered for years.

Misery loves company.

"So we were hunted. Because humans bred like rabbits, there were many, many more of them than there were of us, and we were almost driven extinct. That's when we learned our most clever disguise of all."

Ember turned her head and looked at him over her shoulder. Christian smiled down at her, dazzling in all his perfection. He touched a finger to her nose. "We learned how to look like you."

Her mouth dropped open.

"We built human homes, raised human crops, hunted with human spears, and kept very quietly to ourselves. Eventually, after lifetimes of hiding and pretending, there was a truce. And lifetimes after that, we were once again living in the open with humans. So successfully it looked as if we might actually be able to live in the open, forever." His voice grew dry. "Until Cleopatra, of course."

Ember blinked, confused. "What—*the* Cleopatra?"

"The very same. She was one of us, one of the most powerful Queens our kind has ever seen. Cunning, too, that one. And, unfortunately, ambitious."

He sighed, and Ember waited breathlessly.

"Well, you probably know the story. When Cleopatra seduced Mark Antony, she eventually managed to turn him against Caesar Augustus, the ruler of Rome, which was, at that time, the epicenter of the civilized world. She wanted to rule the entire planet, you see. She wanted the *Ikati* back on top of the food chain, so to speak. But the coup failed.

The Queen and her lover died. And her *Ikati* kin—who by that time were being outright worshipped all over Egypt as gods—were hunted once again. We were declared witches, enemies of Caesar, and enemies of the state. We were driven from our homeland, nearly all of us were killed.

"The few who remained formed small, hidden colonies in wooded places around the world, places cloaked in silence and secrecy. We retreated to the old ways of pretending and lying, of keeping to ourselves. And that's how it has remained . . . " His voice grew bitter. "Until one of us decided it was time to return to being worshipped by humans, instead of hiding from them."

With that, Ember remembered in startling detail the video she'd seen, the scary, black-eyed man/not-man who'd killed all those people at the Vatican. Who'd killed the pope himself.

"Caesar," she whispered.

"Ironic, isn't it, that's what he should be named?"

"Ironic," Ember echoed quietly. She lay very still in his arms. Christian, probably sensing the tumult inside her, was still and silent as well. Waiting.

She mulled it over, assuming hysteria would take over again any moment. But the thing she kept returning to again and again—in spite of the logical side of her brain insisting she should really be focusing on what he'd done in that alley—was how truly incredible he was. She hated when people used the word "magical" to describe things they couldn't or didn't understand, but in this circumstance it seemed exactly the right word.

He—and the rest of his kind—were nothing short of magical. Beautiful, magical, and, without a doubt, deadly.

That's when we learned our most clever disguise of all . . .

Curiosity getting the better of her anxiety and ambivalence, Ember tentatively asked, "So you can change to any shape you want?"

"No. We can't, not anymore. We don't know exactly why, but it might be because we've spent so many generations pretending to be human, living in human form. All of us can Shift into our animal form, but now only some of us can Shift to Vapor, as you saw me do. Although," he chuckled, "you're the only person who's ever seen me do that. Even my family doesn't know I have that particular Gift."

"Why not?"

He sighed. "It's complicated. Our Laws, well, let's just say power has to be proven. And as I'm the younger brother of the leader—if the colony knew I had Vapor, like he does, his dominance would be called into question unless—"

"Unless you fought each other," guessed Ember.

She guessed right because Christian's voice darkened and he said, "Leander has already had to do enough terrible things to stay in control. It would kill him if he had to fight me—if he had to hurt me to keep his position. So I keep my secret to myself and everyone's better off."

"I wonder how many others are doing that, too?"

He murmured, "I can't tell you how often I've wondered the exact same thing."

They were silent for a while, then Ember asked, "So you can change to animal or mist, you have amazing speed, and heightened senses, you're strong, and you heal fast . . . anything else?"

"There are as many different Gifts as there are grains of sand on a beach, some as unique as the pattern on a snowflake. There's Suggestion, Sight, Passage, Elemental Control, Telepathy, Shielding, Invisibility—"

Ember gasped. "Invisibility!"

"And every once in a great while, a Skinwalker comes along—"

"*Skinwalker*? That sounds disgusting," Ember interrupted again, now grimacing.

From behind her he laughed silently, shaking the bed. Once under control, he said, "It's just a term we borrowed from the Navajo lexicon. A Skinwalker has all the Shifting abilities of the original *Ikati*. He can change to anything he wants: wind, fire, a dragon, a falcon. There's only one of us now who can do that now."

Astonished, Ember whispered, "A *dragon*?"

In a soft, oddly melancholy voice, Christian said, "Yes. Shimmering white and sinuous, with silver-tipped wings, spiked barbs along her powerful tail, and a silken ruff like a horse's mane down her long neck." His voice grew even softer, and he murmured, "She's one of the most beautiful things I've ever seen."

Sharp as scissors cutting through her heart, jealousy flared inside her.

Who was this beautiful creature that he—such a beautiful creature himself—sounded so enamored with? And why did it hurt so much?

From the living room, Asher shouted, "Five minutes!"

Ember blew out a heavy breath. She muttered, "I should probably go do something about that."

Christian propped himself up on his elbow and stared down at her, his green gaze penetrating. "Does that mean I'm staying?"

She tried to slip out of his arms to stand up, but he held her there, too strong to bother fighting, and grasped her chin. "Does it?" he murmured.

In a barely audible voice she asked, "Do you want to stay?"

His brows drew together, and for a moment he looked almost angry. "Why do you ask me questions you already know the answer to, little firecracker?"

Pinned in the intensity of his gaze, Ember bit her lip and stayed silent.

He shook his head slowly, back and forth, his eyes scorching hers. "Tell me what *you* want."

"I want . . . I want . . . " She swallowed, trying to buy time. Ultimately, she chickened out entirely and buried her face in the pillow, hiding from him. "I don't know what I want."

He lowered his head next to hers, brushed his lips across the exposed skin of her throat. Whispering into her ear, he said, "Let me give you a piece of advice, Ember. Never, *never* lie to yourself. It's the most self-destructive thing you can do. Be brutally honest about who you are and what you want, even if you never reveal it to another soul. If you're not, if you pretend things are different than they really are, if you try to sweep your true feelings under the rug, you will be miserable, and you won't even know why. You will be powerless. Lie to everyone else if you have to, do whatever it takes to protect yourself from all those bastards who will tell you what to do, how to be, what you *should* think or feel. But own your truth. Own it. And never be ashamed."

He grasped her jaw firmly in his hand and turned her face back to his. Looking deeply into her eyes, he said, "Do you want me to stay?"

Haltingly, she said, "Yes. And no. And that's the truth. It's so much to take in . . . I need to think—and I can't when you're so close . . . " She trailed into silence because his gaze had drifted to her mouth, and his eyes had begun to smolder.

"Don't think, then," he said. In one swift move, he'd turned her over so they were chest to chest, thighs to thighs, their bodies pressed close. He took her hand, placed it flat against his bare chest, and whispered, "Just feel."

Beneath her palm, his heartbeat was as fast and erratic as hers. As it did whenever he looked at her as he was looking at her now, heat exploded in her body.

Looking straight into her eyes, he murmured, "Shall I tell you what *I* want?"

Her head made the slightest of up and down motions.

He bent his head, lowered his lips to hers, and gave her the softest of kisses, raising goose bumps on her arms and legs. "I can't tell you all of it because we're not there yet and it will scare you, but right now . . . " His tongue traced her lower lip, the faintest, gliding pressure, and she made a small, involuntary sound of pleasure. "Right now I want your mouth. I want this beautiful mouth all over my body. I want your beautiful body naked under mine, and I want to spread your legs, and bury myself inside you, and hear you scream my name."

Ember's heart had seized, but he wasn't finished. He curled a hand into her hair and pressed them both back against the mattress, one of his legs thrown over both of hers so she felt his erection, hard as steel, at her hip. His voice grew darker, more gruff.

"I want you to learn what pleases me, and I want to learn what pleases you, and I want to watch you come apart at the seams for me, over and over again. I want all of that and I want it so fucking badly it's taking everything I've got not to rip all your clothes off right now because I know you want all of that just as much as I do, only you're scared, which kills me, because I'd rather tear out my own heart than do anything to hurt you."

He lowered his lips to hers and kissed her again, this one longer, harder, more demanding than the first. Ember moaned into his mouth, already coming apart at the seams with just the taste of him.

Trembling, her hands drifted up his back, skimming his heated skin, exploring the hard, sculpted muscles. She reveled in the little shivering tremor that went through him when she lightly scored his back with her nails. She parted her legs and he settled his weight between them with a growl in his throat, pressing his pelvis into hers as she rocked up to meet him better.

She was spinning. She was falling. It felt like gravity had ceased to exist and she was flying through space at a thousand miles an hour, with no oxygen, and nothing to grab onto but him.

He broke the kiss and lowered his mouth to her throat. She groaned as she felt the warm wetness of his mouth against her skin, his teeth pressing down just hard enough to sting. He sucked hard enough she was sure it would leave a mark, but it didn't matter because she didn't care about anything other than the feeling of his body against hers. She encircled his shoulders with her arms, threaded her fingers into his hair—thick and even softer than it looked—and arched against him, his name a whispered entreaty on her lips.

His hand slid up under her pajama top. His fingers brushed the underside of her breast, and Ember couldn't help it. She ground her pelvis against his and moaned, "Yes, *please.*"

He cupped her breast in his hand, pinched her hard nipple, and chuckled when she jerked and whispered it again.

"My little firecracker has a short fuse, hmmm?" He stroked her nipple, his laughter dying when she dug her fingers into his scalp and pushed up into his hand, whimpering.

He whispered, "You're so responsive, Ember. God, that's hot."

Then he pushed her top up and lowered his mouth to her nipple, and she gasped as he drew hard against it with a hint of teeth. The stinging pain relieved almost instantly when he gentled and stroked his tongue back and forth, around and around, hot and wet and wonderful—then pain again with another fierce tug, his other hand pinching her other nipple.

She writhed against him, teetering on a knife-edge precipice of surrender.

Beyond the door came a shouted, "Nine minutes!"

They broke apart, panting, and stared into one another's eyes. Through gritted teeth, Christian muttered, "I am going to kill him."

"No . . . it's . . . he's . . . " Ember couldn't get her mouth to cooperate with her brain. Realizing she was about to do something her body very much wanted to do but her brain was not entirely on board with, she took a deep breath, put her hands against the hard muscles of Christian's chest, and gave a little push.

He looked at her with a look that said, *Please tell me you're not telling me what I think you're telling me.*

She only nodded and gave him another little push.

His eyes closed briefly. He drew in an unsteady breath, then opened his eyes and said, "Okay. But I've still got one minute. And there's something I've been wanting to do."

Unable to answer, Ember just blinked at him.

Keeping his gaze on hers, he rolled off her so his weight was balanced on one elbow, then he slowly ran his hand down her ribcage, over her belly, and beneath the elastic waistband of her cotton pajamas. When his fingers slipped beneath the edge of her panties she gasped, but he softly ordered, "Stay still. And keep quiet."

With her heart hammering against her breastbone, she pressed her lips together and nodded.

When his fingers stroked over that little swollen nub between her legs, she was glad he'd told her to be quiet, because the groan that rose in her throat would have been loud enough to wake the neighbors and send Asher crashing back into the room. She jerked against his hand.

"Shh," he whispered, when her breath caught in her throat and a little noise escaped her as his fingers slid farther down, then slowly penetrated her. Her eyes slid shut, her back arched, and she had to bite her lip to keep quiet.

"You're soaking wet, baby," he whispered into her ear, his breath hot and his breathing irregular, two fingers sunk deep inside her and his thumb making slow circles over her clit. "You're so wet for me."

She whispered his name, rocking against his hand, pleasure gathering to an exquisite bright peak inside her body. She never knew it could be anything like this, so fast, hard, and total, the sensation overwhelming. Every nerve and cell strained, focused on such a small, wonderful area. Her face and chest were flushed with heat, her breath was uneven, her fingers twisted into his hair, and all she could think was *more, more, please, yes, more.*

"I want to watch you come," he whispered, his voice a rough heat at her ear, a blues singer's mix of silk and sandpaper. His tongue flicked out and stroked her earlobe and she shuddered, arching higher into him, her breasts crushed against his chest. He lowered his head, suckled her nipple into his mouth, and she gasped as his fingers probed deeper.

He kept stroking and suckling, his body hot and hard against hers, his breath just as ragged as her own, his fingers and tongue demanding and relentless, until she moaned as the first convulsion rocked her. Then he kissed her, sucking hard on her tongue, stifling her moans with his mouth as every part of her trembled and thrummed. Lightning crackled through her blood, breaking her apart, and she felt as if she were drowning in him, in his scent and taste, in the sweetest, darkest, most powerful pleasure she'd ever known.

Finally she was spent and collapsed back against the mattress, panting, delirious.

Her eyes drifted open. Christian was staring down at her in fierce intensity. "Beautiful," he whispered, pressing the softest of kisses to her lips. "You are so beautiful, Ember."

The he withdrew his hand from between her legs, lifted it to his face, put two fingers in his mouth and sucked them, licking off her arousal.

He did it slowly, with his gaze locked on hers, and it was the sexiest, most carnal thing she'd ever seen.

Then he took those same two fingers and pressed them against her lips. She opened her mouth and took them in, tasting herself—salt and tangy wetness—sucking just as he'd done, their eyes still locked together. There was heat and animal passion in his eyes, a dangerous light. When he withdrew his fingers he replaced them with his tongue, and the kiss they shared was wild, hungry, and desperate, a promise of things to come.

He broke away first. He sat up and set her on her shaking legs, gave her a little push toward the door.

"Go on," he said, his voice husky. "Go on and talk to your friend before I lose complete control of myself."

Stunned and breathless, barely functioning, Ember nodded, smoothed her hands over her hair, inhaled and exhaled carefully, and went to the door. Without looking back at Christian, she turned the knob and walked through the door, closing it firmly behind her. Still trembling, she leaned against it.

On the sofa in the living room, Asher sat with his arms crossed over his chest. When he caught sight of her face, he rolled his eyes and drawled, "Well, I guess that fight's been won."

But Ember, heart pounding, body aflame, had a feeling the real fight was just about to begin.

Whether she liked it or not, she was falling in love with this man who was not a man, and she had to decide what she was going to do about it.

SIXTEEN

Secrets Have a Cost

Christian sat on the edge of the bed looking down at his hands, surprised to see them trembling.

Her response to him had been totally unexpected, natural and abandoned, a sensual reaction that had the animal inside him roaring in pleasure. It took every ounce of willpower he'd had to set her away from him, but he did it because he knew she wasn't ready yet.

Her body was, but her mind was another matter.

He wondered where her heart weighed in on all this.

He blew out a hard breath and stood, ignoring the sound of the words Ember and Asher were exchanging behind the closed bedroom door. He'd practiced for years to master the ability to block things out at will, a necessary skill without which his acute senses would overload his brain to drowning. His brain was already overloaded enough, thank you very much—and he suspected it would only take the tiniest bit of coaxing to push him right over the edge into madness.

For example, if she came back through the door and kissed him again.

Her mouth was so sweet, her scent and small, restless moans even sweeter, the way she looked at him . . . the way she tasted. Christ, the way she tasted. He'd been dreaming about it for weeks, and the reality was so much better than even his best fantasies it didn't seem possible.

He put his head in his hands, thought for a moment, then did the only thing he could do:

He left.

He wrote her a short note that he left on the pillow they'd shared, crossed to the window, and cracked open the panes. Looking up at the winking stars, feeling the cold salt air bracing his face, he closed his eyes and let the magic of the Shift rise to a glittering peak within him.

Then, silently and all at once, he turned to Vapor.

His linen trousers slid to the floor and lay in an ivory pile, leaking air while he rose in a slinking thin plume and pushed through the crack of the window, out into the night.

Asher didn't look entirely convinced by Ember's explanation of what was going on with her and Christian.

She'd had to leave out the most important parts of the last week, of course, because she wasn't going to reveal to another soul what exactly Christian was. Even if she ultimately decided she couldn't be with him, his secret was safe with her.

"Secret?" said Asher sharply.

Ember realized she'd drifted off into her own little world for a moment and had been muttering aloud. His voice brought her back to reality with an unpleasant thud.

"What? Oh, sorry . . . nothing . . . my brain . . . I'm just so *tired*."

Asher's twisted lips and cocked eyebrow indicated he thought about as much as this lame excuse as she did. He made a noncommittal, "Mmm hmm."

She blew out a shaky breath and shook her head. "You know, Ash, I love you for worrying about me, but this is just something I've got to get through myself."

Asher's gaze flickered to the door behind her. His look soured.

"He's not going to do anything to hurt me." Ember realized as she said it she wasn't just saying it to convince Asher not to hurl the cleaver he still had in his hand at the back of the door; she actually believed it. Which was both a surprising revelation, and a huge relief.

Asher considered her in silence. Then he stood from the couch, crossed to the kitchen and laid the knife on the countertop. Looking down at it gleaming wickedly in the light, he said quietly, "There are a million ways someone can hurt another person, Ember, many of them unintentional." He lifted his gaze to hers. "But something tells me this guy knows a lot of very nasty ways to hurt someone, *all* of them intentional."

"Ash—"

"He's beautiful, I'll give you that. He might even be the most beautiful man I've ever seen, and honey, that's saying something. But he's dangerous, too. All I had to do is look into his eyes when he was standing there in your bedroom and I could see it. I could *feel* it. He was ready to tear me limb from limb. All that beauty is worth diddly-squat when you're dealing with someone dangerous. In fact, it makes him even more dangerous because you're too busy ogling all the pretty to notice the poison he's slipping in your drink."

"Ash—"

"You're a big girl and I'm not your father, but I am your friend, and I'm worried about you. I'll let it go because I know you want me to, but remember I told you this, Ember; this guy has secrets. Secrets have a cost, they're not for free. And whatever you do, don't let him give you any shit just because he looks like a supermodel. To paraphrase the great Violet Weingarten, life is too short to take shit, or to be minding it. So be smart. Keep your eyes open. Keep your eyes wide open, you hear? And if you need me, you know where to find me." He tipped his jaw to the front door. "I'm only a phone call away."

Then he turned, made his way silently to the front door and disappeared through it, leaving her alone in the empty living room wondering exactly when everything had gone so insane.

Oh yeah: the night Christian walked out of the rain and into my life.

She sighed and scraped her hair off her heated face, holding her hands against her head for a moment while she mentally prepared herself to walk back into the bedroom.

But when she did, Christian was nowhere to be found. Only a small pile of ivory linen crumpled below the cracked open window was evidence he was ever there at all.

That and the note he'd left on the pillow. The note read, *I'll wait as long as you need. But time is precious. And so are you. Please hurry.*

Time is precious. Again, that reference to time running out.

When Ember turned on her computer and began to do more research on this character Caesar, she got the first, faint inklings of what he might mean.

SEVENTEEN
Gift Horse

Caesar was thoroughly unimpressed with the drawing Marcell presented him with.

It wasn't the quality of the work he found lacking, it was the subject itself. Shoulder-length brown hair, brown eyes, heart-shaped face, symmetrical but average features, the woman staring back at him from the drawing could have been one of a billion different women, all of them boring. A crust of white bread had more interesting things to offer.

"That's her?" he asked, sorely disappointed. "She looks so ordinary." He'd have thought a male of his kind would have better taste in human women, especially considering they were off-limits, on pain of death. Why risk his hide for *that?*

He shifted his gaze to Nico, who stood humbly beside Marcell with his eyes lowered, his hands clasped behind his back. "Does she have big breasts, at least?"

"No, sire," replied Nico regretfully.

Caesar gave an exasperated sigh. "Great ass, great legs, statuesque as a runway model—anything?"

"She was just . . . normal, sire. About five foot four, average weight, average everything."

Average. How depressing. Who was this rogue who'd killed two of his best men and had average taste in women?

He handed the drawing back to Marcell. "Well. Just one more reason to kill the son of a bitch." He dusted off his hands as if the paper had soiled them and instructed, "Get copies of that to everyone. I want to know who this girl is. If we can find her, we can find him. And she'll undoubtedly be much easier to find than our rogue friend." He smiled. "And might make him a little more inclined to comply with our demands."

He sat back in his chair—really, it was more of a throne, high-backed and elaborately carved, cushioned in red velvet—and looked around the room in satisfaction. In spite of the problem with the rogue male, everything was going so well.

The place he'd settled after leaving Rome was a stroke of pure genius, if he did say so himself. With unobstructed views of the sprawling city below and the forested mountain range behind, the abandoned bunkers, remnants of the Spanish Civil War, were situated at the crest of a jutting outcropping of rock. The steel-reinforced concrete structures were crumbling in many places, graffitied by long-ago vandals as well, but afforded an excellent point of ingress and egress, easily defended.

But the above-ground portions of the bunkers were not the most valuable aspects of his new colony. The most valuable aspects were *below.*

A labyrinth of hand-dug tunnels connected larger, open spaces that served as barracks, training facilities, and storage for food, weapons, water, and other supplies. And, of course, his playroom. Also, at a constant chilly 55 degrees, the caves provided the perfect temperature to store their most precious commodity: the serum.

The single thing Caesar admired about his dead father Dominus was the thing that would ultimately allow him to rule the world. A brilliant scientist and evolutionary biologist, his father had invented a serum that would allow human and *Ikati* blood to be compatible. Half-Bloods could live for a while, but eventually were faced with the Transition, a do-or-die event that occurred at twenty-five years of age, exactly at the minute of birth.

Fewer than one percent of half-Bloods survived the Transition, a problem that had defied solution for all of their recorded history. No one knew why, but, just like a clock ticking down to zero hour, there was a definitive expiration date for those of mixed Blood.

Only now, due to the invention of the serum, there wasn't. The serum allowed the delayed first Shift to occur, and a half-Blood survived it without problem. Even better, he was going to use mankind's prolific fertility against them. If all went according to plan, humans had only a few generations left on the planet.

After that—bye, bye, birdie!

In the meantime, terror and anarchy—two of his favorite things—would reign supreme.

He needed to find a trustworthy lab to produce the quantities he needed because he had neither the medical facilities or the mind for science his father had, but the supplies they'd stockpiled would suffice very well to set the plan in motion. As a matter of fact, the first part of the plan was already well underway; they'd already impregnated dozens of women, willing and otherwise. Hundreds more would be similarly situated soon.

The harem and nursery were another wonderful addition to the barren underground caves.

But they needed more offspring, enough to build an army, and it would take time. Considering he was immortal, time was really of no consequence at all. He'd be able to see this plan to its ultimate fruition.

He turned to his second-in-command, a hulking male with a cool, soulless beauty, and those obsidian eyes they all shared. "What's the current count, Marcell?"

Marcell inclined his head respectfully as he always did when speaking to Caesar—a habit Caesar absolutely delighted in—and said, "Two hundred six, sire."

Caesar was pleased. He'd arrived in Spain with only a handful, but now the disgruntled members of the other colonies, ruled as they were by their Draconian Law, were flocking to him in droves. It seemed there were many who believed, as he did, that the *Ikati* should no longer hide in the shadows.

They'd had thousands of years of that. Time to flourish in the light.

Also, time to dig more tunnels.

Caesar sat back in his throne and steepled his fingers beneath his chin. With calm deliberation, he instructed

Marcell, "Go and find me this Plain Jane Nico saw the male with. And then we're going to finalize the plans for The Hammer. I want everything in place and ready by the middle of March; this year Easter is on the thirty-first."

Marcell bowed, he and Nico backed quickly from the room, and Caesar was left alone with his thoughts, all of which brought a deeply satisfied smile to his face.

Just like last Christmas, this Easter would be one humans would never forget.

The telephone ringing shrilly next to her ear awoke Ember with a jolt the following morning.

She looked in confusion around her bedroom, wondering why she wasn't in the bed, when she remembered she'd been doing research far into the early hours of the morning, and must have fallen asleep at the desk.

She stretched her neck, which responded with an ominous series of cracks, reached over, and picked up the phone. Into it she mumbled something resembling a greeting.

"September!" her stepmother brayed into the earpiece. With a wince of pain, Ember jerked it away from her ear. She glanced at the clock; just before eight. What on earth could she be calling about at this hour? The woman never rose before ten.

Then panic hit her, cold as a pail of water splashed in her face. Picturing the bookstore burned to the ground, she bolted upright in the chair. "What's wrong, Marguerite? What's happened?"

"I've had the most wonderful news!" she crowed in response. Ember frowned, confused, because her stepmother was never happy, and she was definitely never happy when she called *her*.

"I don't understand—is everything all right?"

"Breakfast, my dear, breakfast. We'll meet you at Ovando at ten!"

Ovando was Marguerite's favorite restaurant, a swanky affair full of celebrities, posh socialites and prominent businessmen, perfect trolling grounds for finding her next exhusband. Though Ember knew her well enough to find her repulsive, she couldn't deny the woman had a certain way with men. She had long ago perfected the art of discerning men's deepest, darkest desires with a few well-timed questions and a shark-like ability to scent weakness. She found out what they needed and gave it to them. Then when they were emotionally dependent on her, she took it all back and left them clamoring for more.

Genius in her own way, she was also perverted in the truest sense of the word; she was so distorted, her heart so corrupted by the desire for money and power, she could never truly love.

It would have been funny if it wasn't so sad.

Judging by the way Marguerite had said "we," Ember knew her stepsisters would be tagging along. The Tweedies never missed an opportunity to eat.

"Marguerite, it's Monday. I have to work—"

A truly frightening cackle came over the line. "Work! Oh, dear, that's rich! That's too, too rich!"

Ember removed the phone from her ear and stared at it as if it had sprouted horns. Too rich? Who talked like that? And what had this woman on the other end of the line done with her evil stepmother?

"Ten o'clock, September, don't be late. And try to look presentable, will you, dear?"

Marguerite disconnected, the dial tone sounded, and Ember's mind went over every possible explanation for what had just happened. Since when was she "dear?"

In the end she decided there was really only one way to find out.

By the time she reached the restaurant exactly two hours later, Marguerite and the Tweedies had already begun to eat.

"I thought you said ten," Ember muttered, disgruntled as she always was by the sight of her stepsisters. Sitting side by side in the plush leather booth, wearing matching lavender dresses despite being about twenty years past the point when it was either cute or acceptable, Analia and Allegra ignored her appearance and continued eating their breakfasts. Even the food was identical; poached eggs with shaved black truffles, crepes Suzette, Belgian waffles with fresh cream, double sides of sausage, and coffee, black.

Because one just had to spare the calories somewhere.

"Anyone with an ounce of good sense knows you have to arrive early to get the best seating at Ovando," sniffed Analia to her eggs. Allegra agreed with an imperious toss of her head, saying, "And anyone with an ounce of good breeding knows you should always arrive ten minutes before *that.*"

Ember felt a violent urge to stuff one of their sausages into each of their mouths.

"Sit down, September," directed Marguerite with a wave of her hand without looking up. She had some paperwork spread out on the table beside her plate and was fingering it with what appeared to be almost religious reverence.

Ember's brows drew together; whatever this was, it wasn't good.

She took a seat opposite the Tweedies, and ordered coffee from the waiter who appeared then disappeared, silent as smoke.

"You really should eat more," observed Marguerite, looking down her nose at Ember. She shot a proud glance at Analia and Allegra, plump as fatted calves. "That heroin chic look went out in the Eighties, my dear."

There is was again—"dear." The word crawled over her like a cluster of tarantulas.

"What's going on, Marguerite? What's with the paperwork?"

The Tweedies rolled their eyes at one another. "Surly," said Analia.

"American," said Allegra, and both of them burst into a fit of snorting giggles.

The twins had disliked her on sight when they'd first been introduced. Dislike had taken a turn toward hate when it was discovered Ember's father—a relatively famous artist who Marguerite had mistaken for a *rich* artist and married within months of meeting him—would not be able to cure the debts or the bad name their own father had left with the family when he disappeared. General consensus was that the Tweedies' natural father done some bad business with the mob and had most likely been disposed of, leaving his wife—his third wife—and twin daughters in the lurch.

But that wasn't Ember's fault. As far as she was concerned, they were just spoiled jerks.

She looked at them now and said, "Laugh it up, asshats. Once mommy dearest dies, you two vultures will be alone with each other forever. Who do you think will eat the other one first?"

Allegra spit out a half-chewed chunk of Belgian waffle, Analia gagged over her eggs, and Ember enjoyed a profound moment of satisfaction, until Marguerite ruined the entire thing when she spoke.

"Antiquarian Books has been bought."

Ember's head snapped around. She stared at a coldly smiling Marguerite, her brain unable to process what had just been said. "Bought? When? By who?"

"Last week. I didn't want to say anything because the paperwork wasn't completed, but it's done now, everything is in order, all I need you to do is sign over your shares to the new buyer, and it's finished."

Marguerite slid the papers over the pristine white tablecloth to Ember, who stared at them as if they might suddenly burst into flame. "But . . . who . . . why would anyone *want* it? You said it yourself, it's upside down, the creditors alone—"

"It was all arranged through Señor Alvarez," Marguerite responded dismissively, leaning back against the leather. She smoothed a hand over her hair—scraped back off her face as always and pinned to a severe chignon—and took a sip of her coffee. "There was an anonymous buyer, some rich book collector who'd apparently been interested in the store for quite some time. The deal was all cash, if you can believe it! He's paid for the entire catalogue, including all those mid-century cookbooks your father insisted on and I *knew* would never sell. At any rate, it's an incredible stroke of luck. And the offer was ludicrous!" She actually laughed, which made Ember cringe in horror, it was so grotesque. "We'll both be *set*, my dear! *Set!*"

Ember sat there staring at Marguerite in disbelief. Her money problems were over?

Over?

"Exactly how much are we talking here?"

Marguerite leaned over and pointed to a line near the bottom of the top page of the sheaf of documents. Ember squinted at it, sure she wasn't reading it right. She leaned closer, peering, her mouth half open, until the numbers wavering on the page cleared and even upside down made sense.

With an audible *humph*, Ember collapsed back into her chair.

"That can't be right," she said weakly, disbelieving. "That's ten times what it's worth. Twenty! And in this economy . . . who in their right mind . . . "

She trailed off, her brain suddenly blank.

"Well, my dear," Marguerite said brightly, "like I always say, never look a gift horse in the mouth!"

As if squeezed out by a giant, invisible hand that had clamped around her chest, all the air left Ember's lungs.

Never look a gift horse in the mouth. Asher had said those exact words to her—when Dante had told her not to worry about the rent.

Marguerite produced a pen from her handbag and held it out. "Just sign it, September, and let's all be done with it. You and I both know what a mistake it was for your father to open that store—he was as much a businessman as I am a kangaroo. The two of us have equal share in it and I've already signed, so all you have to do is—"

Ember shoved back her chair so abruptly it toppled over behind her, startling the waiter who had come to check if they needed anything else, and the Tweedies, who had gone back to ignoring her but once again choked on their food.

"No."

Marguerite's face went white. Turtle-like, her head stretched forward on her neck as if she didn't quite hear it, or couldn't quite believe it. She quietly repeated, "No?"

There was a fault line running under Ember's life, an almost invisible crack slowly and surely gaining pressure year after year. The mounting friction had recently risen to a dangerously high level. One tiny thing could trigger a seismic event that would topple everything in her world, and for the first time she realized what a tightrope she'd been walking—how close she was to losing the only thing she had left, control—in the blink of an eye.

Never look a gift horse in the mouth.

Ember knew with crystalline clarity who her gift horse was.

She turned and ran from the restaurant, leaving a gaping Marguerite and the Tweedies behind.

EIGHTEEN
From the Mouths of Babes

"Dante?" Ember called through his apartment door as she knocked. "Are you home?"

He was; the sound of shuffling feet alerted her first, then he appeared wearing a plaid robe, black socks and a smile. "Ah, *la hermosa Americana! Buenos dias, como estas?*"

"*Bien, gracias.* But English, remember?"

"Oh!" His hand flew to cover his mouth. "*Si!* I mean yes!" He straightened his toupee, adopted a strange pose with his hands on his hips and one leg stuck out like it was broken, then in the most terrible John Wayne impersonation she had ever heard, drawled, "How's it hangin', pilgrim?"

That stunned her into silence for a moment. When she recovered enough to speak, she asked, "Dante, why haven't you asked for my rent again yet?"

His smile died a quick death. "Er, I, ah . . . I told you . . . don't worry about it—"

"Don't worry about it because it's already been paid, you mean?"

He sucked his lips between his teeth like someone had just stuck a lemon in his mouth.

"Dante," she warned, "don't lie to me."

His nose wrinkled. He blew out a lip-flapping breath, then made a very Gallic shrug, which looked as if it translated to, *you got me.*

Already knowing the answer, Ember asked, "Who paid my rent, Dante?"

He looked left. He looked right. He looked back at her and said, "I can't tell you, *hermosa.* That was part of the deal."

Ember passed a hand over her face. So—it was true. "We're changing the deal, Dante. I'm going to pay you for this month and you're going to give the money back to whoever paid it."

Christian, of course.

But Dante was already shaking his head no. "*Lo siento,* but . . . that is not possible."

She could tell by the look on his face that Dante was very serious. He would not be taking her money this month. Well, fine, she'd just repay Christian directly then, after telling him in no uncertain terms to butt out of her financial problems.

"All right, Dante, forget it. But don't do anything like this again. The rent is *my* obligation, okay? Don't ever take money from anyone but *me* for my rent."

He began to look worried. Hesitantly, he said, "Ah . . . *si* . . . "

Ember crossed her arms over her chest. "Out with it."

There was some fidgeting, some lip-chewing, a little toupee adjustment, then Dante said with regret, "That might present *un pequeño problema.*"

Ember's left eyebrow slid up. "And why would me paying my own rent be a problem?"

He debated silently for a moment, looking at her with a hesitant expression, as if undecided if he were allowed to tell her something or not. Finally he sighed. "Because technically—that is the correct word, yes?—technically you don't *have* any more rent."

Oh no. No, no, no, no, no.

No.

Ember said carefully, "Dante, please tell me you're not saying my rent has been paid for the year?"

Immediately, he brightened. "No! Your rent has not been paid for the year!"

She heaved a sigh of relief. "Oh thank God. You really scared me for a minute—"

"Your rent has been paid *forever!*"

He was smiling brightly as he said this, and flung his arms out in a "ta da!" gesture. Ember just stared at him, uncomprehending.

"What does that mean, exactly?" she said through numb lips.

His smile faded. His arms dropped to his sides. "No more rent for you, *hermosa.* As long as you live in this building, you never pay rent again. This is very good, yes?"

Ember's face had gone red, she knew it by the heat spreading over her cheeks and ears. "No, Dante this is *not* very good! How could you take money from someone else when the rental contract is between you and me?"

He stared at her as if she were insane. "This doesn't change your contract—and there's nothing in the contract that says I can't take money from anyone else for payment of your rent."

"You have to return all the money, Dante."

He laughed at that, a big, belly-clutching laugh that had the heat in her cheeks spreading to the roots of her hair. "Ha ha! I love this American sense of humor! *Muy divertido!*"

"Dante! I'm not kidding! *No es broma!* You have to return all the money, I don't accept!"

It took a while for Dante to stop laughing, but when he finally did, he said, "Ah, *hermosa*. So proud. He said you'd be too proud to like this."

"And who is this *he?*" Ember asked, knowing exactly who he was, but wanting to hear Dante admit it out loud.

He shrugged again. "I cannot say. But I don't think it would be breaking my contract with him to say that I think he knows you very well."

Ember sputtered, "Your *contract?* With *him?*"

He peered at her. "This was a substantial amount of money, *hermosa*. Do you think there would not be a contract for so much money?" He began to tick off a list on his fingers. "It covers what happens if you move out, if the building burns down, if it's bought by someone else, if you die—"

Ember gasped. "If I die! Jesus Christ, Dante!"

Dante was unfazed by her outburst. "It is no good cursing at me—I just sign the thing and take the money. This friend of yours is a very good business man, *hermosa*. He asked me what I wanted to do in case you ever moved out— where the rest of the money should go, because the rent is paid up for a very, very long time. Longer than you would ever live, *hermosa*. And I told him: to the charity for the cystic fibrosis. So it can help other little girls like my grand-daughter Clare. So, you live here as long as you want—your whole life if you want—and if anything happens in the meantime the rest of the money gets put to good use." His brow furrowed. "This is correct—put to good use?"

Ember sat down on the stairs outside Dante's door, put her head into her hands, and groaned. From between her fingers, she saw Dante's sock-covered feet shuffle forward until he was standing right over her. He said in Spanish, "Let me tell you something."

She uncovered her face and looked at him. He said sternly, "Do not look a gift horse in the mouth."

Ember felt like groaning again. Instead she put her head back into her hands and sighed.

Dante went on, "This is not something you give back. This isn't a pair of earrings, Ember. This gift is big—very big—something most people would weep with joy over. You . . . " She felt his disapproving look. "You act like somebody just died. This is wrong thinking. I know you're a smart girl and I know your father was a good man—he brought you up right, God bless his soul. So what you should do is tell this man—and I have not told you who it is, under-stand?—tell this man that you are very happy and grateful, and see if there is something you can do to make him happy and grateful in return."

Ember lifted her head and peered at him with narrowed eyes. He grinned down at her, wiggling his eyebrows. Switching to English, he pronounced, "He is rich, smart, gener-ous, and well-mannered. And I am no Asher, but even I will admit this friend of yours is *muy masculino*—any woman should be glad to have a man like this."

Then he folded his arms across his chest and nodded in satisfaction, as if he'd just finished a commencement speech. Ember wanted to shout, "Yes, he's amazing, except for one little thing: HE'S NOT HUMAN!"

Instead she put her head back into her hands.

"Ember?"

She looked up at the sound of Clare's voice to find her standing in the doorway of Dante's apartment, looking wan and tired in a flowered nightgown. A plastic tube was hooked over her ears and fitted beneath her nose, delivering oxygen from a small metal tank on wheels she dragged behind her. In one arm she clutched the largest teddy bear Ember had ever seen; it was almost as big as she was.

"Hi, honey," Ember said gently. She knew instinctively Clare had gotten worse since they'd met. She glanced at Dante and a look passed between them: *act normal.* "It's nice to see you, Clare."

Clare smiled at her, a true smile, wide and happy, and Ember felt a squeeze inside her chest.

"I have to go back to the hospital tomorrow," Clare said, matter-of-factly. "My bugs are getting bad again."

The squeeze tightened. Bugs—she meant the infection in her lungs. Ember and Dante shared another look.

"I'm sorry, honey."

"I'm not," said Clare, resting her head against the fluffy bear's. "I get to see all my friends there again. Nurse Montoya is really nice, and so is my doctor. She's a lady doctor—if I ever become a lady I want to be a doctor, too. She helps a lot of people. That would be cool."

If I ever become a lady. Translated: if I live long enough to grow up.

Oh God.

Swallowing her horror, Ember asked, "Can you take your bear to the hospital with you?"

Clare brightened. "Yes! Isn't he cool? His name is Peter Parker!"

"She likes the Spider-Man," said Dante, stroking her hair. She looked up at him and smiled wider, and Ember had to look away for a moment because she thought she might start to cry.

Why was life so cruel and unfair? Why would God inflict something like this on such a beautiful, innocent little girl?

Because there is no God, Ember. There is only chaos, and suffering. You of all people should know that.

Ember shoved that terrible thought aside and smiled at Clare and Peter Parker. "He's beautiful. I've never seen such a big teddy bear before."

"Christian gave him to me," Clare announced, and Dante stiffened. His hand on her head stilled. He shot a fraught glance at Ember, but she ignored it, concentrating on what Clare had said.

"Christian?" she repeated slowly.

Clare nodded. "My *abuelito*'s new friend. He's my friend, too. He said little girls should always have a best friend they can tell all their secrets to, and since I spend so much time in the hospital I don't really get to have so many friends. So he gave me Peter Parker so I could talk to him if I ever got lonely." She cocked her head and looked at Ember, her expression now very serious. "I don't ever get lonely, though. I have Roberto and my *abuelito* and Bieber my dog. And God. I talk to Him, too."

There was a winch slowly tightening around Ember's chest, closing her throat and causing her stomach to flatten. Behind her eyes she felt the hot prick of tears but she gritted her teeth and forced herself to smile.

"Does God talk back?"

Clare said, "All the time."

"And what does He say?"

Clare smiled a smile then of such loveliness and innocence it literally stole Ember's breath. She said, "He says I shouldn't be afraid. So I'm not, because God can't lie."

She couldn't look at Dante. If she did, Ember knew she would burst into tears. She simply whispered, "That's good, honey. I'm glad you're not afraid."

In a gentle voice cracking with emotion, Dante said to Clare, "Inside now, *gordita*, back to bed. You should be resting."

"Okay," replied Clare, turning away. Then she turned back, slowly walked to Ember and hugged her. Into her ear, Clare said softly, "You shouldn't be afraid either. I asked God to watch out for you because you seem really sad, and He said He would."

That did it. Tears welled in Ember's eyes and she squeezed them shut, and squeezed Clare tight, her arms wrapped around her frail little body. "Thank you, Clare."

Clare gave her a motherly pat on the back, then broke away and walked back into the apartment, Peter Parker clutched tightly to her side.

Feeling a thousand years old, Ember stood and looked at Dante. A lone tear slipped down her cheek, which she didn't bother to wipe away. They stared silently at one another until Dante finally rested a hand on her shoulder.

"Life is full of pain, but also many gifts, *hermosa*. We accept the pain because we have no choice . . . " His gaze grew penetrating. "Or maybe because we feel we deserve it, but we have to know how to accept the gifts, too. You have been given a great gift by this friend of yours; accept it. But you also have another gift, an even greater one, that you are taking for granted."

He paused, staring at her, eyes misted with sorrow. Ember shook her head. He said, "Time. Don't waste it. You never know when it's going to run out."

Then he turned and went into his apartment, and slowly swung shut the door.

NINETEEN
Mad Euphoria

Ember didn't know how long she'd been walking.

She didn't know how many miles had passed by unnoticed, or when she'd first decided on her destination, her feet on an automatic path, drawn forward as if pulled. She didn't feel the sun on her face or the chilled breeze that came later when the clouds rolled in, blocking out the bright morning sky. She only came to herself when she once again stood shivering and drenched in front of the gate at Christian's house, rain pouring down with what seemed like a personal vendetta, cold and stinging and hard.

She was still in the dress she'd worn to breakfast with her stepmother that morning. Her shoes had rubbed blisters on the soles of her feet.

She pressed the button on the black call box. There was a crackle of static, then a voice came over the line. "Miss Jones."

It was Corbin. He sounded surprised, and concerned.

"C-Corbin," she stammered, shaking with cold. "I'm here . . . I'm here . . . "

She didn't know why she was here. Her brain wasn't working properly. She could hardly speak.

But it didn't matter because the huge iron gate swung open with its metallic groan, and Ember stumbled through.

Off in the distance, the front door of the house opened, and Christian appeared in it. He took one look at her and began to run.

Just seeing him caused the storm inside her to break free with as much force as the sky had opened over her. She sank to her knees in the middle of the gravel road and began to shake uncontrollably. Tears blurred her vision and streamed down her face. He was beside her in an instant, that impossible speed of his bringing him there in a streak of painted color against the gray of the rain, his clothes and hair soaked as he bent down and lifted her into his arms.

She wrapped her arms around his neck, buried her face into his chest, and whispered, "I don't want to waste any more time. I don't want to waste any more time, Christian."

He didn't bother asking her what had happened. He didn't bother with words at all. He simply turned and ran back in the direction he came, holding her firmly against his chest, his feet swift and silent over the ground.

His bedroom was larger than the vast lobby of the hotel she and her parents had stayed in on their trip to New York, when she auditioned at Juilliard all those lifetimes ago.

Designed with an eye for luxury, in a masculine palette of earth tones accented with pops of crimson in a few tasteful accessories—throw pillows on a leather sofa, an abstract oil painting above the fireplace, a sculpted Murano vase on a side table—it was warm because of the fire crackling in the hearth but dark in the far corners. Heavy velvet drapes were drawn across the windows, and dancing shadows played along the ceiling and walls. The firelight and shadows conspired to create an atmosphere of intimacy that perfectly complemented the fever pounding through her veins.

Outside, rain pattered against the windows in a melody that rose and fell, haunting and ineffably sad.

Christian eased her down onto the bed, shucked off her shoes, and pulled the wet dress off over her head. She sat shivering violently on the bronze silk duvet in only her bra and panties, staring up at him with wide eyes, full of a nameless need and the realization that the man standing in front of her now—the man who was not a man—had the ability to make her forget everything. At least for a little while.

Another gift. She was determined to make the most of that one.

She flung her arms around his neck and kissed him.

He was caught off guard, she knew by his fleeting hesitation and the telling catch in his throat, but soon enough *he* was the one kissing *her*, bending her back as he held her face in both of his hands, fierce and intent, his body a hard heated form against hers. She pressed herself against him, feeling the fever in her blood burn even brighter when his hands moved from her face to her body, and began stroking over her skin.

"You're freezing," he said angrily, breaking away for a moment when he felt her goose bumps.

She protested the loss of his mouth with a small moan and tried to kiss him again, but suddenly he lifted her back into his arms and carried her across the room, toward the fire. In seconds she was on her back on the soft rug in front of it, with Christian on top of her, his hands and mouth and body warming hers.

"I'm not complaining, but you have to stop walking here in the rain," he scolded between frantic kisses, reaching around her back to unhook her bra. Desperate to be rid of it, she wriggled out of it and flung it away, then kissed him again.

"No more talking," she breathed, looking into his eyes as she fumbled with the top button of the jeans he wore. She found the way of it, pulling all the buttons open with one hard yank, and then found him, hard and hot in her hand, already fully erect. She stroked him base to tip and back again, and he shuddered. She whispered, "Not another word."

His lips parted and his eyes flared, molten green and glittering in the firelight. His expression changed—tender to ravenous—and a low rumble of noise went through his chest. Large and masculine above her, he was imposing, but instead of feeling fear, she felt a wild sort of freedom, dark and almost as dangerous as he was.

What lay on the other side of this moment, Ember didn't know.

She didn't care.

With one hand, he slid her panties down over her hips. She lifted her bottom and he pulled them off, watching her face. His lips tipped up at the corners in a sly, scant smile that set her nerves alight. He licked his lips and kept watching her as he skimmed his fingers up the inside of one thigh, his smile growing wicked when he pressed his palm between her legs and held it there while she fought to keep her breathing even.

He kept watching her as he waited. She knew what he wanted; she parted her legs and was rewarded with that dark smile again as his finger slid inside her and a small gasp slipped from her lips. She arched her back and her eyes slid closed, a second gasp escaped her as he added another finger to the first and began to stroke the pad of his thumb over her clit.

She felt his mouth close over a nipple. She moaned when he tugged on it with his teeth. Her hands found his hair, she twisted her fingers into it as his fingers found a perfect rhythm. When she began to tremble and writhe against him, he removed his fingers, slid swiftly down her body and replaced them with his mouth.

Ember moaned again, and this one was broken.

Everything became a jumbled blur of sensation: his lips and mouth and tongue; his fingers digging into her bottom; the rough scrape of his unshaven cheeks against her thighs; the sound of the muttering fire and the murmuring rain; her heartbeat loud as thunder in her ears. She was dimly aware of the noises she was making but was unable to stop herself and didn't care in any case—all that mattered was him.

Christian. Beautiful, inhuman Christian.

As he said he'd wanted, and so easily it should have scared her but thrilled her instead, he was making her come apart at the seams.

When the pleasure became an almost unbearable pain, sharp and hot beneath her skin like a thousand heated knifepoints, his mouth was suddenly gone and he was hovering above her, his arms braced beside her head, his stomach pressed against hers.

Wordlessly, his gaze ferocious and dark, he pushed himself inside her.

It was shallow and slow, but his next thrust was deep and hard and buried him to the hilt. Her head thrown back against the rug, Ember cried out and shuddered. She felt his mouth on her throat, on the muscle between her neck and shoulder, tongue and teeth and savage kisses. He thrust again and bit down at the same time and when she sobbed his name he made a noise like a wild animal's.

His hands slid into her hair and he grabbed fistfuls of it, thrusting hard now, his breath hot and ragged at her ear. She wrapped her arms around his back and gave herself over to him, abandoning any remaining shyness or hesitation, her kisses now just as savage as his own.

So male, so big, so deep inside her, he was as tender as he was wild. He told her in broken whispers how good she felt, how much he'd wanted her, from the very beginning, how beautiful he thought she was.

He kept saying that, "Beautiful . . . you're so beautiful," and it moved her in some deep part of her that she'd put away long ago. It made her feel cherished and worthwhile and . . . loved.

For the first time in years, she felt loved. She felt *worthy*. And it was because of him, because of his words and his need and the glowing dark burn of his eyes.

It was all because of him.

In one swift move, he rolled flat onto his back and took her with him. Straddling him, she took him deep as he flexed his pelvis and reached up to caress her breasts. She began to move, small, circular twists that made him groan and growl, his fingers greedy against her flesh, her hair tumbling down her back. She rode him until they were both breathless and mindless, their bodies bathed in sweat and firelight. When she leaned down to kiss him, he took her tongue into his mouth and wrapped his hands around her hips, coaxing her to move faster, harder, to take him as deep as he would go.

She moaned, feeling her orgasm bearing down. She was almost there—almost—

He flipped her onto her back again, leaned down over her and put his hands on both sides of her face. His eyes were wide and dark, staring into hers, searching, burning, his look almost anguished.

Everything honed to a bright, crystalline clarity. Just before she broke apart in his arms, Christian whispered, "Ember—Ember—God—"

His eyes slid shut, he arched back and his entire body shuddered.

She felt him throb and pulse deep inside her, and it pushed her right over the edge with him. Violent, gorgeous, emanating from her core and spreading outward in surging waves, the contractions stole her breath along with the final shred of resistance. Everything in the room, all the furnishings, the fire, and the very air itself, ceased to exist. There was only the two of them fused together, their need and greed and the raw, exquisite pleasure that spun on and on, encompassing.

He dropped his head and moaned into her neck, low and hoarse. Like a struck bell, it reverberated all the way through her.

Still panting and entangled, they collapsed against the rug. Christian hugged her to him, hard, and they lay there in front of the fire for what felt like forever, not speaking, their heartbeats and respiration gradually slowing, sweat cooling over their skin.

Finally he exhaled—a slow, deep breath—and adjusted them both, tucking her into his side with his arm under her neck and one of his legs over both of hers. She felt sated and loose-jointed, utterly relaxed, completely peaceful. He began slowly to caress her arms, stomach, and breasts, her neck and face, his touch soft and reverent. She closed her eyes, nuzzled her face into the space beneath his chin and found it the most comfortable spot in the world.

Just as she was about to drift off, Christian whispered, "Did my heart love till now? Forswear it, sight! For I ne'er saw true beauty till this night . . . "

Shakespeare. He was quoting *Romeo and Juliet*.

She opened her eyes, listening with her ears and every other organ. Just above her eye level, his throat worked. He was staring into the fire, watching the flames with an expression of amazement. His arms tightened possessively around her. He pressed a soft kiss to her hair.

"I've waited so long for you. I've been waiting my entire life. I can't believe I finally found you. I can't believe something so perfect can actually be real."

His voice was so soft, so awed, so *grateful*, it broke something inside her wide open.

Ember understood with perfect lucidity at that moment why people call it "falling" in love. The feeling was the same as jumping off a cliff, or cresting the high curve on a rollercoaster, and beginning the downward plunge. Fierce and magnificent and immediate, it was like nothing she'd ever experienced. Every cell in her body was flushed with a heady sort of mad euphoria, the kind she imagined only lovers, skydivers, and the insane could ever understand.

Love. So this is what all the songs were about, all the art and plays and movies.

Jesus. It was amazing.

She didn't have words for what she was feeling—not the right words, anyway. So she simply kissed him and put everything she felt into it, hoping he would understand.

Ember awoke sometime later in the semi-dark with her head on Christian's chest, her arms wrapped around him. The two of them were still lying together on the rug in front of the hearth, but now there was a pillow under her head and something thick and soft covering them both; a cashmere blanket. She must have been asleep when he'd draped it over them.

The fire had burned down to a burnished orange glow of hot coals and ashes. Outside, the gloomy, wet day had turned to even gloomier twilight. The wind had picked up and was groaning through the trees.

"You're awake," he whispered. She tipped her head up and looked at him. He smiled down at her—gorgeous, black hair in disarray, green eyes shining—and brushed an errant strand of hair gently from her face.

"How long have I been asleep?" she whispered back, not wanting to break the spell.

His smile grew larger. "A few hours."

"That long?"

"I didn't want to disturb you. You looked so peaceful." His lips quirked. "Though I was a little worried all the noise would frighten Corbin."

Yawning, she frowned at him. "Noise? What noise?"

He said innocently, "Your snoring. Loud as a buzzsaw, little firecracker—"

Ember gave him a horrified shove in the chest. "I do *not* snore!"

"That's what you think. It sounded like I had a houseful of lumberjacks—"

"Christian!"

His laugh shook them both. He wrapped his arms tighter around her and kissed her forehead. "Found a sore spot, did I? That was much too easy."

Suddenly she was stricken with a pang of regret. Much too easy—had she been?

"What?" he asked, tensing.

She sighed. "Are you always going to be able to read my mind like that? It's really annoying."

His body relaxed. "I *wish* I could read your mind," he murmured thoughtfully. "It would solve an awful lot of problems." He skimmed his fingers over her shoulder and down her arm to the crook of her elbow. "It's not your mind, though. It's your body. Your body is an open book for me."

"Yes," she said sourly. "Among other things."

He chuckled, but the sound faded as he trailed his fingers past her elbow and hesitated over the vein on the inside of her arm. Slowly his fingers drifter farther and he began to trace the outline of her scars. One by one, silently and with an almost religious reverence, he learned the length and width of them, where they puckered and pulled, where they were smooth and nearly unnoticeable, all the way from elbow to wrist. She allowed it because she knew he wanted to do it.

And because she was certain he wouldn't ask her about them again, she was suddenly gripped with the urge to tell him. She began, hesitantly, to speak.

"I was eighteen," she whispered.

His fingers stilled on her arm. He glanced up at her face, but she dropped her gaze to his chest, hiding, and drew a ragged breath before she continued.

"It was the day I graduated high school. My dad bought me a new car for my graduation present, though it was really for my mom because I would be going away to school in New York in the fall. I'd won a scholarship to Juilliard that spring and I was going to spend the summer performing with the Taos School of Music."

"The cello," he whispered, his body utterly still.

Ember nodded. "I was good. I was really good. Better than that, actually, my teachers all thought I'd be the next Yo-Yo Ma. But . . . you know . . . " Her voice wavered. She took another breath and said, "Life is what happens when you're busy making other plans."

Christian waited, just holding her, watchful and silent. A chunk of wood fell through the grate in the fireplace and sent an orange feather of hot ash floating up into the chimney with a sigh.

"It was a little red Honda, nothing expensive, but I thought it was the most beautiful thing in the world." She closed her eyes and remembered with vivid detail her excitement when her father had driven it into the driveway and honked the horn so they would all come outside to see it. The glossy paint, the new car smell, the black tassel from her graduation cap, with the little gold plastic numbers that commemorated the year, which she hung over the rearview mirror.

"I drove it around to all my friends to show off, then picked up my mom and my little brother Auggie. My parents had a special dinner planned for me at my favorite restaurant."

The name of the restaurant was La Fiesta. Ember would remember that detail for the rest of her life.

"My dad was going to meet us there. He just wanted to finish a painting he'd been commissioned for; it was due the next day. So the three of us went ahead." She paused, swallowing, feeling an old, familiar weight begin to press down on her chest. Quieter than before, she said, "There used to be these really nasty electrical storms on the mesa during the summer monsoons—they came on sometimes without much warning. So it was raining when it happened . . . just after sunset . . . like it is now."

Christian whispered, "Baby."

The pressure in her chest increased. She moistened her lips, ignoring the water gathering beneath her closed eyelids. "The car hydroplaned. There weren't guardrails on the main highway then, between the oncoming traffic or on the shoulder. So when I lost control of the car, we spun right into oncoming traffic, and then went over the edge into a ravine."

Christian's fingers were digging into her arm. He'd stopped breathing.

"They put in guardrails after," she whispered. "So it could never happen again."

It was the second worst car crash in New Mexico history. There were eleven vehicles involved by the time it was over, and thirteen fatalities.

Thirteen dead.

Ember was the only one who survived.

When she hit the first car, a Chevy truck that crushed the entire right side of her Honda, her sliding spin instantly and violently changed to a flying tumble that rolled them over and over, shattering every window as it went. She remembered nothing of that roll but the screaming, which seemed to go on and on and come from everywhere. There was the sensation of motion and gravity pulling in the wrong direction, then a horrible sound like a bomb detonation, then blackness.

When she blinked her eyes open, she was upside down, still strapped into the driver's seat, and her mother was dead in the passenger seat beside her.

In the back seat, her little brother was screaming.

There was a lot of smoke and water, along with the acrid stench of burned electrical wire and scorched rubber. Ember's left arm had been crushed between the seat and the driver's door, which was now a crumpled hunk of metal. She couldn't turn her head to look at Auggie because there was something wrong with her neck, but she could see his face in the cracked rearview mirror. She saw him lying there, his face contorted in pain, his legs mangled beneath him. He hadn't been wearing his seat belt.

She found out later it was almost twenty minutes before the paramedics and police came; there was no one left alive but her. The closest cell tower had gone down in the storm, so the cars that arrived on the scene immediately after the accident had no mobile phone service. Someone had to drive all the way back into town to the police station to report it.

Ember hung upside down in the car in the smoke and the rain for twenty minutes, with her dead mother beside her, while her little brother slowly bled to death in the back seat.

And all the while he cried. Through her agony and shock, she tried her best to comfort him, telling him it would be okay, they were going to be all right, someone was going to come. But over and over, he just kept crying and pleading, "The Broken Man is coming to get me, Ember. Don't let him get me. Don't let him get me," until finally his cries turned to silence and the only sound was the rain.

The Broken Man.

Those three words forever after haunted her, like a trinity of demons sent from the blackest bowels of hell by the devil himself.

She whispered, "My father couldn't bear to stay in New Mexico after that. We moved to Florida, but that wasn't far enough, so a few months later we moved to Spain. He thought the only way we could start over was in a new country, but it didn't help."

Unnoticed and unfettered, tears streamed down her cheeks. "He never finished a painting again. He would start one, then abandon it for another. And I never played the cello again; even after the surgeries, my fingers didn't work right. There was too much nerve damage."

She drew in a long, shuddering breath. "Neither one of us ever moved past that day. We went through the motions, but everything was hollow. Nothing meant anything anymore. It was as if we'd both died, too—we were the walking dead. The day I graduated high school was really the last day of my life."

Christian's arms around her were crushing. Against her cheek, his heart beat furiously, keeping time with her own.

He whispered her name and she had to squeeze her lips together to keep from sobbing because his voice was so full of compassion.

She didn't deserve his compassion. She deserved only his disgust.

Because there was one other little detail she'd left out. The one detail that mattered the most.

Christian cupped her face in his hands. "I know you blame yourself because you were driving, Ember," he said urgently, gazing at her with his brows drawn together and his eyes shining with empathy. "But you can't. It was an accident. It was raining, it could have happened to anyone—"

Ember whispered, "I don't blame myself because I was driving, Christian. I blame myself because I was *drinking* and driving."

Suddenly it was as if all the air had been sucked out of the room. Christian made the smallest little sound of horror, a sound that was reflected in the new look in his eyes, the look that replaced the compassion from seconds before. All the color drained from his face.

As swift and hard as two fingers snapping, he recoiled from her and sat up.

TWENTY
Hard Lessons

"You have to go," he said in a hoarse, flat voice, his back turned to her. To Ember it felt like a shotgun blast to the stomach.

Shaking, she whispered, "Christian—"

He stood abruptly, ignoring his nudity, letting the cashmere blanket fall, and strode away. He disappeared into an open door on the far side of the room and reappeared mere seconds later, dressed in a new pair of jeans, carrying a small pile of clothing. Without looking at her, he dropped another pair of jeans and a sweatshirt at her feet, pulled on a white T-shirt over his own head, and said, "Put those on. They won't fit. You'll have to roll them up."

His voice was still flat and empty, his head turned slightly away as if he couldn't stand to look at her. Ember sat up and pulled the cashmere blanket tightly around her body. The shaking was getting worse, and her throat didn't seem to be working right; no words would form around the fist-sized lump that blocked it.

Christian strode to the door of the bedroom, pausing just before passing over the threshold. Over his shoulder he said, "Corbin will take you home," then he walked out.

Without ever once meeting her eyes.

In cold shock, she dressed quickly, rolling up the legs of the jeans to her ankles, the too-long sleeves of the sweatshirt to her wrists. She stood unsteadily, looking around the room but not really seeing anything because there was too much water in her eyes, making her vision waver and swim.

She deserved it—but she hadn't been expecting it. That's what really hurt. Shame had kept her secret well-hidden for six years, and with good reason; this moment was proof. No one in their right mind would forgive someone who'd done something so heinous. No one should.

And, most of all, no one as bad as she was deserved to find happiness—or love.

Another lesson learned the very hardest way of all.

With her arms wrapped around her waist, wincing and hunched into herself as if expecting a blow, Ember fled Christian's bedroom. When she stumbled out the front door, barefoot and crying, Corbin was already waiting in the drive with the car. He stood beside it, holding the door open for her, and tipped his hat in his hand.

She fell into the car, drew herself into a ball on the back seat, and began to quietly sob into her hands.

They drove that way for a while, Corbin silent, Ember's choked sobs occasionally drowned out by the rain pummeling the roof, by the rhythmic *swish swish* of the wipers.

Finally as they neared her apartment building, Corbin spoke. "It's not my place to say this, miss, but he's always been a hothead. And he's used to getting his own way. I'm sure he didn't mean whatever he said that's made you so upset. But just as quickly as he gets mad, he gets over it. He's going to call you and apologize tomorrow, you'll see."

It made her heart ache that he thought this was in any way Christian's fault.

"It's not him, Corbin," she whispered, wiping her eyes and sniffling. "He didn't do anything wrong; he just finally got to see the real me, that's all. And he"—she hiccupped— "didn't like it. Not that I blame him. Not that I blame him at all."

She saw his frown in the rearview mirror. "I find it hard to believe there could be anything about you that he doesn't like, miss. Or that anyone wouldn't like, for that matter. I've never seen him so happy. I know you're to thank for that."

The car slid to a stop at the curb on the street where he'd stopped that first night he'd brought her here, when she was in the cat costume and Christian had come up to her apartment. A thought occurred to her, something Christian had said that night in her kitchen, and Ember sat up, wiping her nose and face.

In a hoarse whisper, she asked, "Corbin, would it be all right if I asked you a question? A personal question . . . about Christian?"

He turned in the seat and looked at her, then nodded once.

"It's just, something Christian told me about . . . about where he grew up."

Corbin's brows lifted. He peered at her in silence, waiting.

"He said there were no cars."

Corbin nodded, still waiting.

"Well, he told me his parents had been killed in a car accident, and I wondered . . . I wondered . . . "

"They were away—on a trip," he said quietly, and Ember sensed by the tone of his words and the expression on his face there was a lot more to it than that. She didn't ask for details.

"Oh. I guess . . . I guess it doesn't matter. I just wondered what happened. Because my . . . " She swallowed, and her throat tightened all over again. "Because my mother and brother were killed in a car accident, too."

A fleeting look of sympathy crossed his face. "I'm very sorry, Miss Jones." He stared at her thoughtfully for a moment. "It's terrible to have something so painful in common, but perhaps in a way it could be a blessing, too."

He saw her look of shock.

"Forgive me. It might be indelicate to say and I may be entirely wrong. But it seems to me that only someone who's lost someone they love in such a violent way can relate to the pain of another in the same circumstances. You're kindred spirits, so to speak."

Kindred spirits. Clearly he didn't know the circumstances under which she'd left. The pull of morbid curiosity prompted her next question.

"Was it a storm or something? What happened—to his parents?"

Corbin turned back around in his seat. With his hands gripping the steering wheel, staring straight out into the rainy night, he said darkly, "No, not a storm, miss. That would have been merely tragic. It was murder."

Their eyes met in the rearview mirror, and Ember knew with sudden, freezing surety what he was going to say before he even said it.

Because of course it would be. Of course it would.

"It was a drunk driver. Christian's parents were instantly killed." He made a sound of disgust. "The man who hit them survived though, sorry bastard."

Dying all over again, Ember whispered, "They always do, don't they?"

Before Corbin could agree with her, Ember opened the door, leapt from the car as if it was on fire, and ran away through the pouring rain.

TWENTY-ONE
Soul Sick

The next few weeks were neither good nor easy, a reality Ember resigned herself to with a certain amount of gratitude. Nothing should ever be easy or good for her, a fact she'd forgotten in her state of temporary insanity brought on by falling in love.

Love. Her mind flinched from the word like an abused dog, expecting a kick.

Things had returned to "normal." She was back working at the bookstore and volunteering at the shelter on Sundays and three evenings a week as they continued to be overloaded with unwanted house cats who were being euthanized by the hundreds. Had she not been quite so numb, it would have sickened her, but she accepted this too with the resignation of someone for whom horror was a daily part of life.

Marguerite was furious with her for not signing over her shares in the bookstore and had threatened to never speak to her again if she continued to refuse. This suited Ember just fine. She didn't know why Christian hadn't withdrawn the offer, but he hadn't. It stood as further testament to his character, which was so much finer than hers she felt like an insect in comparison, like something that should be smashed underfoot.

But she wouldn't sell. She knew the reasons behind his offer to Marguerite were motivated by misplaced affection for her. And even if he were too much a gentleman to withdraw the offer the way he'd withdrawn his affections, she wouldn't take advantage of it.

Now if she could only figure out a way to return all the money for her rent.

It came to her one night as she was cleaning out a cage at the shelter. Holding a filthy litterbox in one gloved hand and a pooper scooper in the other, she froze.

She had to move out of her apartment.

It was so simple she was surprised she hadn't thought of it sooner. If she moved out, all the money would go to the cystic fibrosis foundation Dante had designated in his contract with Christian. She could help other children like Clare. It would be, in some small way, a payment toward an unrepayable debt.

It wouldn't be recompense, but it would be something.

That very day, Ember found an apartment on the other side of town near the docks, in a rundown building with thin walls, bad plumbing, and questionable locks. As she signed the paperwork with her new landlady—a sour-faced old woman with a mouth like a prune and a withering stare that shot laughter from the air like a clay pigeon—she wondered briefly if the group of surly young men lounging around the entrance giving her hostile, assessing looks would murder in her in her sleep or merely beat her unconscious before they rifled through her handbag for drug money.

Either way, she didn't care.

Asher, however, was not quite so laissez-faire about the situation.

"You've got to be fucking kidding me," he said as he stood in the kitchen the day she moved in, gazing around her new apartment with his hands on his hips and his face blanched in disgust.

She imagined the word "kitchen" with air quotes around it, because it was little more than a gouged stainless steel sink, a dwarf refrigerator the color of a rancid avocado that rattled and wheezed, and a hot plate crusted with the remains of what looked like a cooked squirrel. Or maybe the fur was just growing from the layer of black mold that lurked beneath the heating element.

"Home sweet home," Ember replied flatly to Asher's cry of horror as he gingerly lifted the corner of an ancient placemat on the scarred wood dining table and a roach scurried out. Asher swept it to the floor and crushed it with one stomp of his Prada-shod foot.

"Ember, there is no way you're living here!" he snapped. He swept an arm around in an angry, jerky motion. "Look at this place! You're going to catch the plague from the rats living in that couch"—he jerked his chin toward the sagging, faded, plaid sofa in the "living room,"—which, judging by the frayed holes in the cushions and the small black piles of droppings on the floor around it, did indeed appear to be home to a large family of rodents—"or you're going to fall through that hole by the window and wind up in the apartment below. Which is probably occupied by a gang of meth-addicted parolees, if the crew hanging around outside this place is any indication of the quality of the tenants!"

To be fair, the hole in the floor near the "window" wasn't large enough for her to fall through. A large cat, perhaps. Maybe a small dog.

"It's perfect, Ash." Ember's voice was as hollow as her heart.

Asher gave her a sharp look, his eyes narrowed behind his glasses. He crossed his arms over his chest and cocked his head. "Why don't you tell me what this is *really* all about?"

Ember avoided his penetrating gaze and moved to the small, dirty piece of leaded glass that passed for a window. It overlooked a narrow, dark alley. The abandoned building on the other side was surrounded by chain link and barbed wire. There were little patches of grass growing on the roof, which in some places was caved in; the wood structural beams showed through like bones.

"Nothing," she lied.

"Okay, I call bullshit on that."

She turned back to find Asher staring at her, the look on his face clearly telegraphing his disbelief—and more than a little anger.

"I couldn't afford to live in Dante's building anymore, that's all. This is what I can afford." She looked around the dirty, dreary room and added, "Believe me, it's perfect."

The "for me" she left unsaid.

There was a long silence, broken only by the sound of a dog barking furiously a block or two over and the sporadic metallic clanging of the empty soup can a rag-draped homeless man was kicking down the alley below.

Then Asher lowered his arms to his sides and accused in a low, shocked voice, "You're running away from him."

"What? Who?" she replied, in a futile attempt at avoidance.

"Supermodel Asshole, *that's* who!" he shot back. In three long strides he was in her face. His own was turning red. "What the hell did he do this time?"

She sighed, closed her eyes, and pinched the bridge of her nose between her fingers. "Oh, Ash. He didn't do anything. This isn't about him. I just couldn't afford my old apartment anymore. I swear." She let her hand fall and looked into his eyes, trying with all her considerable acting skills to keep her face entirely devoid of emotion. She'd practiced this look for years, and had perfected it on the endless rounds of therapists her father had insisted she visit, before they all gave up on her for good.

He studied her face carefully, then said softly, "Yeah, I'm going to have to call bullshit on that, too, honey."

Ember lowered her forehead to his chest; he wrapped his arms around her and rested his chin on the crown of her head. After a moment, she said tiredly, "I know you won't believe me, but Christian didn't do anything wrong. He was the best thing that happened to me in a long time, Ash, and *I* screwed it up, not him. If you only knew how generous he really is, how thoughtful . . . "

How right he is to hate me.

She shivered and pulled out of his arms. She went back to the window, wrapped her arms around herself and stared up at a fat, glossy crow circling lazily in the slate gray sky above. Asher stood where she'd left him, and though she wasn't looking at him she felt his eyes like two hot pokers boring into her back.

"This isn't on him. So let it go, okay? Don't pick on him anymore. Let's just pretend the whole thing never happened."

She hadn't told him what happened between them; she'd barely mentioned Christian's name at all over the past few weeks, and only when Ash had asked for updates. The only update she ever gave him was this: we're not together.

End of story.

"I don't like this, Ember. I don't like this one bit. You're holding something back from me, and you're obviously lying to me about your reasons for wanting to live in this dump. And, if I may say so, your face looks like a thousand miles of bad road."

Ember's lips twisted to a wry pucker, but she didn't have the energy to be really offended. "Gee, thanks."

"Thank me when I'm done," he shot back. "You're dropping weight like it's going out of style, you've got spooky haunted house eyes and those bags you're incubating beneath them look like they're going to hatch something evil. So please be straight with me: what the *hell* is going on with you?"

His voice grew softer, and definitely more worried. "Are you sick?"

Lovesick. Heartsick. *Soul*sick. Sick with grief, and regret, and an ocean of self-hatred, cold, black, and infinite. Yes, she was very, very sick indeed.

She was all of those things and much more, but aloud she only offered him a weak, "No, I'm not sick, Ash. And there's nothing wrong. I'm just . . . I just needed a new apartment, that's all. Everything's fine."

There was another long silence. Suddenly the sound of Asher's footsteps pounding toward the front door made her turn in surprise. He yanked open the door and paused on the threshold, staring back at her with an expression that fluctuated between rage and disappointment.

"You know something, Ember? I always knew you had things you didn't want to talk about and I was okay with that—I accepted you just like you accepted me; the Full Monty, no questions asked. But I never thought you were a coward. Until now."

Her mouth dropped open as pain lanced straight through her chest. Through the hand that flew up to cover her mouth, she whispered a choked, "Ash!"

"You don't want to tell me something, that's your prerogative. But we've been friends—good friends, I thought—for years, and you have the nerve to lie right to my face—multiple times now—when I want to help you. Which in my book is a big 'fuck you, Asher.' So I get the hint; you don't want my help. But I'm sorry, I'm not going to hang around and watch you waste away and wallow in this depression like a pig in shit, without any kind of inkling of what the hell is happening, or without being allowed to help in some way. Do you have any idea how . . . how *impotent* that makes me feel? How frustrating that might be for me? Or are you too busy feeling sorry for yourself that you can't see past the end of your own nose?"

She stood there in shock with her mouth open, heat burning her cheeks.

But he wasn't quite done yet.

He said, "I am so tired of people feeling sorry for themselves. Sorry for their shitty parents, sorry for their shitty friends, and their shitty jobs, and all the shitty things that happen every day in life to everyone, but somehow everyone seems to think their particular brand of shitty is the shittiest of them all. But you know what? There's *always* someone else who's got it a thousand times shittier than you. So suck it up and quit your bellyaching and try focusing on someone *else.* It might make your problems seem a little bit better in comparison. Or if not, at least it will make you less of an asshole!"

Breath left her lungs as if she'd been punched in the chest. Her eyes filled with tears. She began to stammer an apology, but Asher held his hand to his ear and snapped, "What's that? I'm sorry, I couldn't hear you over your tragic past!"

Ember cried, "What the *hell,* Asher?"

He stared at her long and hard. Behind his glasses, his dark eyes burned. "You didn't invent suffering, Ember, no matter what happened to you. And just because you're suffering doesn't give you the right to lie to your friends and make them feel useless and unwanted. People who care about each other help each other out when they're hurting, they don't *shut* each other out. That's what you do to people you don't really give a shit about. Which, coincidentally, is how you've made me feel. Congratulations on losing your only friend."

He turned to walk out the door, and she crumbled.

Sobbing his name, she ran across the room and flung herself at him, catching him off guard so he stumbled against the wall. With her arms wrapped around his neck, she sagged against him and cried like a baby into his shirt, blathering apologies and a long, incoherent description of what had happened between her and Christian, interspersed with background story of what had happened that fateful day in New Mexico.

By the end of it, he was crying, too, and her troll of a landlady shouted at them from the end of the hall to shut up or take it inside.

They went inside.

He held her tightly, leaning against the back of the closed door, until her crying stopped and she hung limp in his arms.

"I'm so sorry," he said in a broken voice. "I didn't know . . . I had no idea—"

"Please don't apologize, that will only make me feel worse," she whispered. "I don't deserve any sympathy. I should have been locked up for what I did. They should have locked me up and thrown away the key."

Or worse.

"Did the police . . . why didn't the police . . . "

He hesitated, and she lifted her head and looked at him through swollen eyes. He couldn't say it, but she knew what he meant: Why didn't they arrest you?

"Technically they couldn't. There wasn't enough . . . my blood alcohol level . . . something went wrong with their test and it came back negative. I kept telling them—I told them as soon as they got there and the paramedics took my blood but it didn't work."

They'd taken blood at the hospital, too, with the same result: nothing.

No one would listen to her when she tried to tell them what she'd done. They all looked at her as if something had broken inside her head. All the therapists afterward had looked at her the same way, so she finally learned to arrange her face into an emotionless mask and tell them what they wanted to hear, which was that accidents happen and it wasn't her fault.

It was almost worse than the accident itself, the sympathy she was shown by the police, social workers, and therapists. By her friends and her friends' parents. Even by her father, who should have hated her most of all, but never did.

She wanted them to scream at her. She wanted them to kill her. But what she got was as excruciating as having her skin peeled off and made her want to die: pity.

To be denied righteous guilt about something horrible you've done, to feel true remorse and have no one accept it, or believe you, or even think you have a reason to feel guilty in the first place, is soul-killing. To move forward, to heal, you must first be allowed to say you're sorry. You must be allowed to express your regret. If you can't or you won't or your regret is mistaken for something else—like arrogance or bullshit or mental illness—you will never move forward.

You will be trapped inside your body like a fly in liquid amber, dead and buried but perfectly preserved on the outside, so everyone who looks at you sees only a tomb.

So she stopped talking to the therapists. She stopped talking to her friends, she stopped talking to anyone about anything. And when she and her father moved to Florida, and then to Spain, she found she'd lost the ability to be open with people, like a muscle that atrophies from disuse.

Which worked perfectly well. Until Christian. Until now.

"And you told Christian all this . . . and he walked out on you." Asher's voice was harder than before.

"No, you don't understand, Ash. I didn't tell you the worst of it yet."

His brows lifted: *what could be worse than what you've already told me?*

Ember whispered, "His parents were killed in a car crash. By a drunk driver."

Asher closed his eyes. "Oh, honey. Jesus. Fuck."

Yes. Exactly.

"So now . . . now you know why he . . . why we can't be together. And why I'm such a mess." She rested her cheek against his chest and hugged him tighter.

He hugged her back. Her head lifted and fell with his deep inhalation, his slow exhale. He wound a lock of her hair between his fingers and gave it a gentle tug, and she looked up at him through wet lashes.

"Okay," he said softly. "So what's our plan?"

"Plan? Well . . . I'm going to clean this place up a little, then maybe do a little food shopping—"

"No, dummy," he interrupted with a gentle smile. "What's our plan to get him back?"

Ember looked away and swallowed. Outside, a cloud had passed over the sun, and the room was suddenly darker and even more depressing than before. "There's no getting him back, Ash. You don't get over something like this. This is a deal-breaker. And rightly so."

He took another breath, then set her away from him with his hands wrapped around her shoulders. "Honey, that man was willing to kill me if I didn't let him talk to you, do you remember that? *Kill. Me.* Whatever kind of a shock this was, you telling him about—you know—he still has feelings for you. There's no man on earth who can flip off that switch once it's been flipped on, understand?"

"Ash—"

"So it's been a few weeks, he's probably had time to think it over and cool down—"

"Asher—"

"He's probably hurting just as bad as you are, honey—"

"I don't want him back, Ash!"

Asher stared at her, inspecting the expression on her face. "Why not?"

Ember took a breath and said quietly, "Because I don't deserve him." She glanced around the apartment. "This is what I deserve; that's why I'm here. And it's not feeling sorry for myself, it's really just . . . it's more like . . . " she floundered for a moment, then found the perfect word and whispered it. "Penance."

A muscle twitched in Asher's jaw. He was getting angry again. "You don't think you've done enough of that over the last six years?" Before she could open her mouth and respond, he added, "Who do you think you're helping by living like this? Do you think you're honoring their memory, all those people? Do you think hurting yourself makes a damn bit of difference in the end?"

Her eyes pooled with tears again. "No. But it's only right that I suffer as much as possible, after everything I took away from so many people. It's the only way I can think to make amends."

His head dropped. He didn't let go of her arms, he just stood there holding her like that for a moment until he looked up at her again. "You are seriously fucked up, you know that?"

This, she knew, was a rhetorical question. She bit the inside of her lip and didn't answer.

"Okay." He was thinking, staring at her with the wheels turning behind his keen brown eyes. "Here's what we're going to do. We're going to clean up this shithole and get some better locks installed so you don't get murdered in your sleep. Then we're going to go through the phone book and find you a good therapist, because you really need to get your head screwed back on straight, sweetheart."

"I've already had dozens of therapists, Ash. They don't help—"

He gave her a hard little shake that snapped her jaw shut. "Then you just haven't found the right one yet. A therapist is *non-negotiable*, Em, if you want to keep my beautiful ass in your life."

She stared at him in horror. "You're blackmailing me!"

He shrugged, unfazed. "Take it or leave it. And when I say that, I mean *take* it."

She hung her head and stared down at their feet, toe to toe against the faded linoleum kitchen floor. Something scurried past on buggy legs in her peripheral vision and she sighed, envying how simple its little buggy life must be. Around the lump in her throat she whispered, "Okay."

Asher gathered her to his chest in a fierce hug. "Good girl."

Into his chest, after a moment of silence, she accused, "You called me an asshole."

He chuckled. "I know. But you're a tough nut to crack, honey, so I had to play my trump card. I should have called you names years ago. Chicks hate that."

"Jerk," she whispered, and hugged him as tight as she could, as if she were drowning, and he was the only thing keeping her afloat.

Because he was. Right now, he really was.

TWENTY-TWO
Struggle

"Are you listening to me *at all?*"

Leander's curt question jerked Christian back from the memory of Ember's face. The depth of anguish he'd seen in her eyes when he'd recoiled from her had been seared into his memory with the excruciating, scarring permanence of a red-hot brand. It hovered around the edges of his vision like a malicious specter, a poltergeist always ready to torture him with some fresh misery when he was least expecting it.

"Yes," he answered flatly into the phone. "I'm listening."

A blatant lie. He couldn't get himself to concentrate long enough to focus; she invaded his every waking thought, and even his dreams. He'd never had nightmares before, even after his parents had died, but now they were a nightly occurrence. Flames and screams, squealing tires and pounding rain—and always her face, her eyes, her look of wretched torment. Then everything would spin to black and he'd jerk awake in bed, sweating and panting as if he'd run a marathon. It had been this way every moment for the past two weeks.

He'd never, ever experienced such relentless hell.

There was a long, heavy silence. Then Leander said, "Why don't you tell me what's on your mind so we can get back to business."

Damn. His brother knew him too well. Avoidance was useless; Leander was a pit bull when it came to getting answers. Christian passed a hand over his face and sighed. "Have you ever tried to reconcile two totally opposing viewpoints about something?"

He used the word "viewpoints" instead of feelings. He and his brother didn't talk about feelings.

"You mean like, on the one hand, I know there's a genocidal megalomaniac who needs to be taken down or thousands of people will die—and my brother is the best man for the job—and on the other hand, I'd do anything to ensure my brother never gets hurt, but giving him said job pretty much guarantees that he will?"

Christian's lips twisted to a wry smile. "I'll take that as a yes."

"You're damn right that's a yes."

There was another long silence, and Christian felt Leander's frustration and worry even though he was a thousand miles away. They'd always been close; somehow they'd grown even closer over the past few months, the way people do when they know time is scarce.

"So how did you reconcile it?"

"I didn't. I can't. But being conflicted about something doesn't mean you put logic aside. You have to weigh all the pros and cons and make a decision. In my case, that decision has to be best for the majority, which means even though I'd rather cut off my own arm than see you get hurt . . . " He left the rest unsaid, but his silence filled in the blanks. "In your case, that decision has to be whatever your conscience can accept without the guilt killing you."

Guilt. He'd hit the bullseye with that one. Because even though logic told Christian that he and Ember were possibly the worst mismatch in history, and even though part of him was horrified by her admission, and even more horrified by the ways in which fate could be cruel—dangling such a tantalizing carrot of happiness in front of him only to rip it away with a few whispered sentences, by even putting her in his path *now*, of all goddamn times in his life—he still felt a tremendous sense of guilt about turning away from her.

Like it had been the wrong thing to do.

Like he had let her down when she needed him most.

So his mind and his heart were in total conflict about what she'd done, what he'd done, and what he should do next, all of which made it very hard to concentrate on anything else. The sleepless nights alone had taken their toll; he was about as animated as a zombie, all day, every day.

"One other thing, too, helps in making a hard decision," said Leander.

"Which is?"

"Information. If you have to choose between the lesser of two evils, you need as much information as possible in order to decide which way to go. It might not make you less conflicted, but at least you'll get some comfort knowing you did all you could to inform yourself beforehand."

Christian looked up from his desk and looked through the library windows to the day outside, sunny and bright. "Thanks, brother," he murmured, watching a tiny white butterfly hover over a blooming bush of rosemary outside, then fly out of sight with bumpy grace.

"Don't mention it. Can we get on with the conversation now?"

Christian smiled. Leander hated discussing things over which he had no control. "Aye, aye, captain."

"Good. I'm emailing you all the information I have about this character Jahad who's now running the *Expurgari*—"

"How'd you get it?" Christian asked, surprised. The *Expurgari*—a group of religious zealots affiliated with the Catholic church since the time of the Inquisition who'd made it their mission to eradicate the *Ikati*—were notoriously secretive, their ranks impenetrable. If the Council of Alphas, of which Leander was leader, had obtained any information on their enemy, it almost certainly involved a great deal of danger or bloodshed or both. This was confirmed with Leander's next, darkly spoken, words.

"The old-fashioned way."

Christian understood in an instant: interrogation. Torture.

"You caught one of them."

Leander made a noise of assent. "Near the Quebec colony. We think he was doing recon."

"For?"

"We don't know. Unfortunately he expired before we could find out. Xander is a little too good at his job."

"Xander's back?" This, too, was a surprise to Christian. Xander was the tribe's most feared assassin from the Brazilian colony who'd retired a few years ago.

"So is the rest of The Syndicate," Leander said, respect evident in his voice. Then his voice turned lighter, filled with amusement. "And so is Morgan. Apparently retirement didn't suit them."

Morgan Montgomery. At the mention of her name, Christian had to smile.

Xander's wife, the first woman ever to serve on an Assembly, the first person to remind you she'd rather kick your ass than say hello, was a force of nature and fierce with a capital F. They'd grown up together, and he suddenly felt a pang of homesickness when he thought of her and all the trouble they'd gotten into when they were young.

Then he felt a second pang—darker, more twisted—when he thought of another woman who could be described by a word with a capital F: his little firecracker.

An ache unfurled in his chest like a snake unwinding its coils.

He'd fallen for her fast, hard, and completely, in spite of his attempts to keep away, to keep his head. And now that she wasn't around, he felt like one of those people who'd had a limb cut off but still felt it itch and throb, a phantom presence that wouldn't fade no matter how he tried to distract himself. No matter how hard he wished it away.

There was just something about her. Something that stuck. He realized she'd gotten under his skin in a way he'd never expected . . . and couldn't appreciate fully until she wasn't there anymore.

He'd stared at her number on his cell phone for so many hours over the past few weeks the image was probably burned into his retinas.

He tuned back into the conversation just as Leander was saying, " . . . we did find out however, that they still don't know about the colony in Brazil. Which is damn good luck, since most of the other colonies have been moved there. It's just a matter of time, though. If they're watching us and we're leaking deserters like a sieve, they're going to catch one of them before we can. And our goose will be cooked."

Which meant it was even more important Caesar be dealt with—immediately.

"They're keeping a very low profile, wherever they are," said Christian. "They're being careful. I've been back to Gràcia nearly every day since . . . "

He didn't say "since the murders," because that would have been a little too obvious—and he'd already taken such a shitstorm of criticism over the debacle that he didn't want to bring it up again. If he were anyone else, at any other time, that kind of display in public would have signed and sealed his death warrant. The *Ikati* had lasted in the human world as long as they had because of only one thing: secrecy. Not that it mattered anymore.

"But they're nowhere. They're ghosts."

"Well, even ghosts can leave trails. Just keep your eyes and ears open. And listen—there's one other thing."

Christian waited, his attention now caught by the edge in Leander's voice, the new undertone of warning.

"Xander got a lot of useful information from his mark, but the most interesting piece of information was that this Jahad is headed your way."

Christian knew instantly this meant two things. One, the incident in Gràcia had drawn the leader of the *Expurgari* to Spain—more unanticipated fallout of his decision to attack in public—and two, this was a perfect opportunity to kill two birds with one stone. So to speak.

Leander knew exactly what he was thinking. "It's too dangerous. Caesar is the primary target, we can deal with the *Expurgari* later—"

"This Jahad won't travel alone—there will be at least half a dozen of his top men with him, maybe more. It couldn't be more perfect if we'd orchestrated it ourselves. We can cut off the head of the snake—"

"It would be quite a coup, I admit, but if Caesar finds out Jahad is closing in, he might run. And since Jenna won't be able to See where he's gone until after the pregnancy, we can't take the risk of losing him—"

"Unless I can get Caesar and Jahad in one room together," Christian said abruptly.

"And how exactly do you intend to do that? Send out engraved invitations?"

Christian knew if he could see his own face in a mirror, something ugly and dark would be looking back at him. Something violent and vicious and altogether wild. He said, "Let me figure that out, brother. If there's a way to do it, I will."

He disconnected the call before Leander could ask any more questions, opened his laptop, clicked through his email until he found Leander's message, and began to read.

His parentage was unknown, as were the exact date of his birth and his real name. He was known only as Jahad, an Anglicized version of jihad, a word which in Arabic means "struggle," to go from imperfection to perfection, to establish the truth over wrongdoings, to achieve the Kingdom of Heaven while tempted by the myriad pleasures and sin on Earth.

Born with the melanin defect that produces albinism, he was found swaddled in blankets on the steps of an orphanage in Rome, abandoned at only a few weeks old. Little was known of his early life except that he was relentlessly bullied and tormented by the other boys in the orphanage, taunted for his marble skin and gray-violet eyes so pale they were nearly tintless. As it inevitably does when unchecked, the bullying turned violent. One Christmas Eve when he was approximately fourteen years old, the albino boy was set on fire and left to writhe and scream in agony on the basement floor of the orphanage while the others watched, laughing.

It was only the intervention of a visiting priest that saved his life. The priest arrived in time to douse him in a bucket of water drawn from the well, but by then almost all the skin on the right side of his body had been eaten away by the flames.

He refused to name the perpetrators. It took him nearly a year of excruciating physical therapy to regain the use of his right hand and leg. To celebrate the milestone, he burned the orphanage to the ground—with all the boys in it.

It was at that point he was recruited by the *Expurgari*.

With no earthly ties, a pathological thirst for revenge against wrongdoers, and a psyche as scarred as his body, Jahad was a perfect addition to their cause. In possession of a near-genius IQ, the new recruit demonstrated an exceptional ability to strategize and lead others. He quickly rose through the ranks, making a name for himself with his total devotion to *Expurgari* canon, unquestioning loyalty, and unflinching application of violence in the advancement of the holy war against evil.

Expurgari means "purifiers" in Latin, and Jahad, a man who'd been transformed by pain, believed pain was the only true path to purity.

Every day except Sunday he wore a spiked metal cilice cinched tight into the flesh of his thigh, which pricked holes that bled and scabbed and bled again. He flagellated himself with a corded leather whip while naked on his knees, until his back was bloody and raw and his vision was dim. He practiced celibacy, fasting, and self-denial in many forms, yet still was not satisfied with all he did to check the needs of the flesh. One day a month he allowed the basest desires of his nature to reign and he visited one of the specialty establishments in the city that catered to men of his particular tastes.

Afterward, he strangled the animal while reciting the Lord's Prayer and dumped its body in the Tiber River.

"Jesus Christ," Christian muttered as he read that little detail in the dossier Leander had sent. To which his subconscious wryly replied, *Not even close.*

He clicked on a link and opened a file that held four verified pictures of Jahad, taken from various angles. Two were too blurry to be of much use, but showed the substantial bulk of his figure striding away from the camera, his face in profile, features obscured in the shadows thrown by the brim of a hat. A third picture was clearer, taken from the front as Jahad was looking right, again in a hat, this time in mirrored sunglasses, with the bright sun overhead winking off the corner of one lens.

But the fourth picture was arresting. Taken head-on at what seemed an arm's length distance but was probably through a powerful high-resolution lens, it depicted a shirtless Jahad on the balcony of a hotel staring straight into the camera. No hat this time, nothing to cover his head or hide his features. Christian felt an odd sort of fascinated disgust, as one might when driving by the scene of a fatal accident, repulsed by the carnage but unable to look away.

His eyes, which read pale silver in the photograph, held the flat, killer gaze of an assassin. His head was snow white and entirely bald—satin smooth, without the telltale stubble of a man who shaves it—and it became clear as Christian studied the photo that Jahad had no eyebrows or eyelashes to speak of. He was, in fact, entirely devoid of any hair at all. The right side of his body from his jaw to his waist was covered in hideous scar tissue, puckered and shiny, and his right hand was little more than a claw that hung at an odd angle by his hip.

But beneath the ruined skin was the impressive, well-developed musculature of a dedicated athlete.

Christian checked Jahad's stats: six-foot-two, two hundred and thirty pounds.

Big. Almost exactly as big as he was.

A notation farther down caught his eye—*alopecia areata universalis.* Autoimmune disorder that caused a total loss of all body hair.

Wonderful. A bald albino bodybuilding religious zealot with a near-genius IQ and a predilection for sadomasochism, pyromania, and bestiality. He felt a twinge of nostalgia for the old leader of the *Expurgari,* who was just your garden-variety nut job with a God complex.

He closed the files and logged out of his email, then sat staring at the computer screen, trying to concentrate on the job at hand and all that needed to be done. But his conversation with Leander about deciding between the lesser of two evils kept circling his brain, one word nettling him like a burr.

Information.

That was Leander: controlled, calculated, dispassionate. It was the price of leadership, this careful, logical approach to decision making. He couldn't afford to make mistakes because too many lives were at risk. Too many people counted on him.

Christian, on the other hand, was the second son. Relieved of the burden of power that came with being the Alpha heir, he'd always been the wilder of the two, relaxed and indifferent where Leander was disciplined and reserved. His wild streak had gotten him into plenty of trouble on many occasions, but possibly never as much as the trouble he knew he was in now.

September Jones, whether he liked it or not, had brought him to his knees.

With her sweetness and her smile, with her pride and her passion, with her sharp, scathing wit. Her vulnerability was incredibly alluring, as was her strength. So were all the shadows in her eyes, which drew him like a moth to the flame. A moth that knew it would be burned, but didn't care.

It came over him then the way the day breaks—slowly, and then all at once.

He didn't care.

He didn't care about her past. He didn't care about his own past. He didn't care about what he should be thinking or feeling or doing, or all the ways in which they were both broken, or the tragedies that had broken them, or the colossal stupidity of trying to make something work between two people so different.

He just cared about *her*.

He wanted her and he'd walked away.

And damn it all to hell, he knew, even as she was telling him the story, she'd punished herself every second of every day over the past six years for what she'd done—that she was not only remorseful, but *self-loathing*—and still he'd walked away.

"You're a bloody wanker, you know that, McLoughlin?" he muttered, running a hand through his hair. Abruptly, he stood from the desk, fished his cell phone from his shirt pocket, and began to dial, doing his best to ignore the shaking in his hands.

When he heard the automated message informing him the number was no longer in service, the shaking got just that much worse.

TWENTY-THREE

A Troubling Pause

"Tell me again why I agreed to this?"

"Because you love me, that's why."

Ember sent Asher a sour sidelong glare and muttered, "Debatable."

They stood looking at a modest walk-up with a brick façade the color of cinnamon on a quiet, tree-lined street in the Clot district, a mainly residential suburb bordering the Sagrada Família. There was a quaint café next door with a spotted dog sunning itself in an arched doorway, and two old men playing chess beneath a striped umbrella. It was tranquil and idyllic, but to Ember it might as well have been the entrance to hell.

It had taken Asher all of twenty-four hours to find her a

psychiatrist, one he claimed was the best in the city. He really wasn't kidding around.

Standing beside her now beneath the spreading arms of a blooming acacia across the street from the cinnamon walk-up, he gave her a friendly nudge with his elbow. "Go on, chicken. I'll pick you up after and we can go for *suspiros de monja*."

Suspiros de monja—literally translated as "nun's sighs"—were a golden, crispy, cream-filled dessert made famous by the nuns of the Catalan convents. They were also a potent incentive for Ember, as they were her favorite sweet.

"If I haven't slit my wrists by then," she threw over her shoulder as she stepped off the curb and crossed the street. She heard Asher's low chuckle behind her and kept walking.

The waiting room was tasteful and far more homey than the others she'd haunted. There were no thumbed-through magazines littering a crappy coffee table, no cheap chairs crowded too close together, no hideous pastel prints on the wall. And no aquarium, thank God. Aquariums always made her feel claustrophobic; she couldn't help but imagine herself as one of the brightly colored, frantically darting fish, trapped forever inside.

The one item ubiquitous to a therapist's office in any part of the world was there, however: the round call button on the wall. She pushed it and it illuminated, alerting whoever lurked behind the waiting room walls to her presence.

Before she could plop down onto the comfortable-looking armchair, a door on the opposite side of the room opened and a woman appeared. Dark-haired, dark-eyed, chic and sleek in a navy suit and low nude heels, she was of an indeterminate age somewhere between thirty and fifty. She wore a double strand of pearls around her neck, and Ember knew they were real by the dull, luxe sheen. So were the pearl and diamond studs in her ears, and the very large sapphire and diamond ring on her manicured hand.

Marguerite would be eating her heart out right about now.

"Señorita Jones?"

Ember nodded and the woman stepped forward with an outstretched hand and introduced herself.

"*Estoy* Katharine Flores. *Encantado de conocerte.*"

"*Un placer,*" said Ember as she took her hand, surprised she hadn't introduced herself as "Doctor" Flores. In her experience, anyone with an MD wore it like a badge of honor. Or a war wound.

"You're American?" Katharine said in English, sounding equally surprised.

Ember smiled. "And here I thought my Spanish was pretty good."

"It is," replied Katharine, still in English. She spoke without a trace of an accent. "It's excellent, in fact. Where'd you learn?"

"School, mostly, but both my parents spoke Spanish, too. We had a large Hispanic population where I grew up. What gave me away?"

Katharine glanced briefly down at their hands, which were still joined. She met Ember's gaze again and her brown eyes were sparkling with amusement. "No one shakes hands like an American. It always feels like you're sealing a blood pact."

"Is that good or bad?"

Katharine smiled at her. "Does it have to be one or the other?"

Ember released her hand and shrugged. "Everything is."

Katharine cocked her head and made a very doctorly, "Hmm," and Ember realized the session had already begun.

"Okay, doc, time to shrink my head. You sure you're up for this? It's pretty ugly in there."

With a Mona Lisa smile and a hand held toward the door she'd just come through, Katharine said, "After you, September."

Feeling like she was going off to face a firing squad, Ember walked through the door.

An hour later, after her interesting new patient had been escorted out and she sat alone behind her polished mahogany desk, the yellow pad of scribbled session notes beside her and a blank patient file open on her computer, the good doctor pressed the rewind button on the small cassette recorder she used to tape her conversations.

Most new patients had an extreme aversion to being taped at first, eventually learning to ignore the recorder as their trust in the process and in their therapist grew, but Ember hadn't even flinched when Katharine had asked her permission to use it. This, in itself, was telling. She'd admitted to seeing "a few" psychiatrists in the States, but judging by the practiced way she articulated her responses, Katharine suspected the number was probably in the double digits.

She clearly had extensive experience telling professionals what they wanted to hear.

Surprisingly forthright—especially for a first session—September Jones had spoken openly about the crash that had killed her mother and little brother. She was composed, almost clinical, and there was a slightly faraway look in her eyes as she spoke, as if she were telling a sad story about someone else.

Katharine had seen this before. A well-prepared patient with very strong mental barriers could quite easily disassociate themselves emotionally when speaking about a trauma they'd suffered, especially if it were years in the past. If there were no immediate emotional triggers, she could safely share, as if from a comforting distance.

But the devil was in the details. And after nearly twenty years of practice, Katharine knew with canny precision where the real skeletons lay.

She checked a notation on her yellow pad and rewound the tape to the number she'd written. She pressed play and Ember's steady voice filled the quiet room.

" . . . and after that I drove home and picked up my mother and brother, and we headed to the restaurant."

Katharine heard her own follow-up question. "Do you remember how much you had to drink before getting in the car?"

Here was the troubling pause. It wasn't long, but it had a sense of fraught heaviness, as if something very important hinged on whatever she said next.

"A lot. Too much. Probably . . . " Another pregnant pause, and she fumbled her next words. "Um, a whole bottle of . . . scotch. One of the big ones. The biggest."

Katharine paused the tape.

There were several things that troubled her about this. The majority of people who were in alcohol-related automobile crashes had little to no memory of the actual crash or the hours leading up to it, especially if they'd ingested the quantity of alcohol September had described. After consuming a large bottle of hard liquor, at her height and body weight, she would have been, as they say, "blind drunk," yet she'd chronicled in minute detail exactly what had happened before, during, and after the accident.

Also, her mother certainly would have noticed her daughter's impairment—aside from the slurred speech and affected motor skills, the smell of whiskey on the breath is very distinctive—and protested she shouldn't drive, especially with August in the car. Indeed Ember most probably would have been unable to operate a vehicle at all, especially to drive twenty minutes out of town toward their destination as she'd later said.

And there were the pauses. Katharine's intuition was a finely honed organ, something she often referred to as a sixth sense, and those pauses felt all wrong. They didn't feel like guilty or embarrassed hesitations, or the courage-gathering spaces before a confessional that they should have been.

They felt calculated.

As if September was deciding something.

Or hiding something.

Or lying.

Katharine flipped through the consent and information forms she'd had September fill out prior to leaving and noted the name of her last—admitted—psychiatrist, a Dr. Kensington in New Mexico.

Then she logged onto the Internet to see if she could find a telephone number.

Christian stood outside Ember's apartment building, gazing up at her fifth-story window. No lights were on inside, which meant she wasn't home, which—considering she hadn't been home all day yesterday, either—he found very worrying.

Just as worrying as her disconnected phone had been.

He'd lasted all of two minutes after hearing the recorded message before barking an order at Corbin to get the car. He'd come here first to find no one home, then he'd gone to the bookstore and seen an older brunette, attractive in a severe, femme fatale kind of way, standing behind the counter. He guessed from his conversations with Señor Alvarez this was her stepmother, Marguerite.

He watched through the windows from across the street, but Ember never appeared. Corbin drove him back to Ember's apartment building, but she never showed up there, either.

He went home. He paced. He spent the night in a fitful, nightmare-riddled sleep.

Now, empty-handed more than twenty-four hours later, he was determined to find out what was happening, even if it meant breaking into her apartment to do it.

He took the stairs three at a time. As soon as he hit the fourth floor landing, he stopped dead.

It sizzled through him with the electrifying intensity of a lightning strike. First it was a ripple of power, still palpable though it was hours old. Then he caught the scent—a complex bouquet of forest floor, masculine musk, and spices—and an involuntary growl rose in the back of his throat.

Ikati. Male. More than one. They'd been here, and recently.

Hackles raised, ears straining for any hint of danger, he eased silently up the next flight of stairs. At the top of the landing he paused, listening, testing the air, but only that slight pulse of power and the fading aroma of hot-blooded predator in the air belied their recent presence. Whoever it was had been here since he'd last been here. And might, even now, be on their way back.

He looked at Ember's apartment door and a flash of pure rage crackled through him.

What did they want with her? How the hell had they found her? And where the hell *was* she?

A noise from inside the apartment across the hall snapped his head around. His eyes narrowed and his muscles tensed, but he relaxed a fraction when he heard whistling, then a muffled thump and a low curse as someone behind the door bumped into something. A chair, judging by the way it skittered across the floor. Then a man's voice, chastising himself for his clumsiness in an aggravated mutter.

"Good job, knucklehead, walk right into the kitchen chair! Is it time for new glasses?"

Asher. Of course, he lived right across the hall.

Christian didn't waste any time applying his knuckles to Asher's door.

"Jesus Christ, what's the emergency? Is the building on fire?" came Asher's annoyed voice as he approached.

Apparently he'd knocked a little harder than he realized.

He heard the sound of a chain being unlatched and a lock being turned. Then the door swung open and Asher said, "This better be good, Dante, I'm right in the middle of—"

He froze when he caught sight of Christian. His mouth snapped shut, his eyes narrowed, and his jaw went tight.

"It's not Dante."

Asher gave him a slow, assessing once over, taking in his livid face, the tension in his muscles, his stance, which undoubtedly telegraphed his readiness to break something.

"Clearly," he said. His expression hovered somewhere between wariness and irritation. "You look in a lovely mood. Did the beauty salon run out of your favorite conditioner?"

Christian growled, "Where is she?"

Asher crossed his arms over his chest and drawled, "*She?*"

He hissed a slow breath through his teeth, realizing this wasn't going to be easy. He'd forgotten how viciously Ember's guard dog protected her. "You know who I'm talking about. Where. Is. She?"

They stared at one another for a moment—fleeting but arctic—until Asher snapped, "She moved! And don't bother asking me where, because I'm pretty sure she doesn't want to see you."

Moved. Okay—she was safe. For the moment. Something loosened in Christian's chest, but tightened again when he absorbed the last part of the sentence. It became slightly harder to breathe.

"You're pretty sure she doesn't want to see me, or you're sure?"

Asher pursed his lips. "She didn't say those exact words, but it was implied."

There was another frigid pause as the two of them stared at one another in a jaw-clenching stalemate. Then Christian huffed out a hard breath, ran a hand through his hair and looked at the floor. He briefly closed his eyes, gathering his frayed patience and the ragged edges of his anger with a surprisingly difficult exertion of will, then looked back up at Asher, meeting him eye to eye. When he spoke, his voice came very low.

"You're her friend; I respect that. I respect your loyalty. But I have to see her. I *have* to. You can help me or not, but I'll find out where she is one way or another. Believe me when I say it's in her best interests if I find her sooner rather than later."

Asher remained stone-faced. Christian realized this could go on all night, so he tried another tactic.

"And . . . I need to apologize to her."

Slowly, millimeter by millimeter, Asher's brows lifted.

Christian bit the inside of his cheek—hard—to hold back the snarl that wanted to rip from his throat. He wasn't used to being in the position of explaining himself. And he did *not* like it.

"You heard me. Don't make me say it again."

Asher cocked his head and narrowed his eyes at him. He examined his face for long, silent moments, then said, "All right. I actually believe you, miracle of all miracles. So I'll tell you what—I'll give her a call and ask her what she thinks. But if she doesn't want to see you, you can forget about it."

Blood spread in a heated wave over Christian's face. "You have her new number?"

Asher had the audacity to smirk. "Oh, did she not give that to you? Ouch." Then he instructed curtly, "Stay here," and shut the door in Christian's face.

Christian exhaled, uncurled his fists and braced his arms against either side of the doorframe. He bowed his head, closed his eyes, opened his ears, and let the world and its cacophony rise over him like a wave.

Traffic, from miles around. Dogs barking. Voices. Wind slipping through leaves. Birds rustling in the hollows of tree branches and the hum of insects and the low, throbbing drone of a thousand different appliances. The electrical buzzing of the streetlamps. Breathing. Heartbeats. The slow, grinding pulse of the earth.

And then the musical tones of the push buttons on a phone from inside Asher's apartment. Christian focused on that and let all the other sounds fade to background noise.

"Em, Christian showed up at my apartment looking for you."

A long, silent pause. Her voice came fainter than Asher's, but still clear. "What did he want?"

"I'll give you one guess," said Asher with quiet sarcasm.

"What did you tell him?"

"I told him you didn't want to see him."

Another long pause and Christian strained his ears so hard he thought something inside his head might burst. His heart began to pound in his chest.

In a voice so soft and aching it nearly broke him in two, Ember asked softly, "How did he seem? Is he okay? I've been worried about him."

He let out a soft, disbelieving groan. She was worried about him. He'd thrown her out of his bed and out of his house after she'd confessed the worst thing she'd ever done, and *she* was worried about *him*.

His hands curled around the wood doorframe so hard it began to splinter.

"He seems like he always seems—pretty and pissed off. What do you want me to tell him?"

At the top of his lungs, Christian shouted through the door, "I need to see you, Ember!"

"Oh my God," said Ember into the phone. "Is that him? He's there now?"

"Well it's not the fucking Easter bunny, sweetheart. Tell me what you want me to tell him before he breaks down my door."

"Just tell him . . . tell him I said whatever goes on four legs will always be a friend"—her voice cracked over "friend"—"and we just should leave it at that."

"Okaaay," drawled Asher. "And what do I tell him when he asks for a translation?"

"He'll know what it means. Just tell him that."

Christian shouted her name through the door again, so loudly and for so long the cords in his neck stood out and lights blinked on in apartments all over the building.

Asher muttered, "Yeah, I have this funny feeling he's not going to give up so easily, Em."

"It doesn't matter. It's not like he's going to accidentally stumble across my new address. Nobody ever comes to this end of El Raval but junkies."

Asher's answer was full of disapproval. "Don't forget the *rats*; they love the docks almost as much as the junkies. But he could just go to your work . . . "

Christian turned and flew down the stairs, not bothering to listen to the rest of the conversation.

He had all he needed to go on. Now he just had to trust his nose.

TWENTY-FOUR
Oil and Water

"Well, smack my ass and call me a cab. He *did* give up that easily. He's gone, honey."

"What do you mean, *gone?*" Ember had been pacing the floor of her apartment as she spoke with Asher, chewing her thumbnail and hyperventilating, but now she froze in place.

"I'm telling you, I just went to the door to tell him to piss off and he wasn't there. I guess he wasn't really as determined as he seemed."

But she knew with sudden, chilling certainty that wasn't what had happened. She replayed the last few moments of her conversation with Asher in her head, then slumped against the kitchen counter and muttered, "Shit."

"I'm sorry, honey."

And so was she. But not for the reason Asher thought she should be. "I have to go."

"Okay, but I'll see you Wednesday, right? Three o'clock?"

He was picking her up for her next appointment with Dr. Flores; there was no way he was letting her get out of missing a single session, so he'd insisted on driving her to and from the therapist's office like a den mother on carpool duty. Ember murmured her assent and disconnected the call.

Then she went to the window and yanked down the shade.

She turned off all the lights in the apartment, made sure the deadbolts Asher had installed were securely locked on the front door, then slowly retreated to the darkest corner of the living room.

To wait.

Twenty-three minutes later, as she was both dreading and hoping it would, the knock came. Two short raps, then Christian's voice through the wood, infinitely dark, supple as silk.

"September. I know you're in there, little firecracker. I can smell you. Open the door."

Knowing he could hear her as easily as if she shouted, she whispered, "Go away."

"We can do this the hard way or the easy way. It's up to you. *Open*. The *door*."

Beyond the howling chaos inside her head, she wondered briefly what the "hard way" would look like. Trying to ignore the shaking in her hands and knees she said, "There's nothing to talk about, Christian. Please go away."

She actually *felt* the intensity of his focus on her voice. There was a short pause in which the booming of her heart was a near deafening racket in her ears, then an ominous sound came through the door: a slow, light scratching, like fingernails dragged down the wood.

"Do you think I can't get through it? Do you think you can hide from me?"

"Christian. Please. Listen to me. Go. Away."

His answer to that was a low, menacing chuckle.

A three-quarters moon shone brightly overhead, spilling ghostly pale light through the gaps in the window shade, so it wasn't particularly difficult to see the first, sinuous curl of mist billow beneath the door.

The gap between the floor and bottom of the door was hair-thin, but it was enough.

He came in a sleek, unfurling coil of gray Vapor and rose swiftly from the floor to gather in a glittering plume, hovering silently just inside the doorway. The Vapor shimmered, a thousand sparkling pinpricks of light, then coalesced into the form of a man. Feet first, then legs, then torso and arms and chest, strong and muscled, then Christian's face and eyes, those vivid green eyes, lucent as emeralds in the shadows.

He was naked.

"You changed your phone number. You moved," he said, sounding outraged in spite of the softness of his tone. His gaze swept over her, and he blinked, startled. His expression darkened and he growled, "And you've lost weight. Christ, Ember—haven't you been eating?"

Keeping her gaze carefully above his waist-level, she snapped, "Oh, hi, it's nice to see you, too, Christian! How've you been for the last two weeks? Good? Me, too! Everything's just peachy keen as a matter of fact! So glad you broke in—glided . . . whatever—so we could catch up, but now if you'll excuse me, I have to go back to living my life. Which doesn't include you!"

Ember wasn't sure exactly why she was being such a bitch, but it probably had to do with the fact that if she wasn't yelling at him she would dissolve into tears at how much it hurt to have him standing there naked in her living room looking so beautiful and so impossibly out of reach. Because he was a gentleman at his core, if she were crying it might lead to him trying to comfort her, which might lead to her doing something pathetic and desperate like trying kiss him. Which would obviously just lead to further tragedy and heartbreak.

So going the bitch route was actually perfectly logical. Satisfied with that, she crossed her arms over her chest and glared daggers at him.

"Funny," he drawled, "you don't seem very happy to see me."

"Ah, irony," she replied in exactly the same lightly sarcastic tone. "I've recently become very familiar with the concept. For instance, the tragic irony of falling in love with the one person in the world guaranteed to be unable to love me back."

The instant the words were out, she regretted them. She mashed her lips together in horror and slapped a hand over her mouth.

He tensed. His eyes flashed. Then very, very quietly, he said, "Did you just tell me you're in love with me?"

Ember understood in that moment the true definition of the word "mortified." Her face flamed red, and even though the room was full of shadows, she knew he saw it.

She gave a little sideways jerk of her head—*no*—because she was too humiliated to speak, and her lips were still mashed together.

He nodded slowly, his gaze scorching the air between them. "Yes you did."

"I want you to leave now." Her voice was no longer steady.

"I don't think you do. And anyway, I'm not going anywhere."

He took a step forward. She took a step back.

Still in that deadly soft tone he asked, "Let me ask you a question, Ember. Why do you think I made the offer to buy your failing bookstore?"

Ha! I knew it! Ember said, "Because you're a control freak who likes to butt into other people's business?"

He shook his head. "Wrong. Guess again."

"Because you have more money than sense?"

A corner of his mouth lifted, a dark, lopsided smile with an edge of danger that made her heart hammer against her breastbone. "Wrong again. Next question: why do you think I paid your rent?"

"So you admit that, too!"

He lifted a shoulder, unapologetic. "I knew you'd figure it out eventually. And even though it was written into the contract, Dante doesn't exactly strike me as the type who can keep secrets."

"Well, see my previous two answers."

"Yet again, wrong. It's the same reason I'm here now. Because I want to take care of you—"

"Stop. Just stop. I can't listen to this."

Why the hell was he even here? He'd made his feelings perfectly clear, they both knew it was a disaster, he hadn't tried to contact her at all—

"I panicked," he said abruptly, reading her face as clearly as he was obviously reading her body language. "I didn't know what to do and so I did exactly the wrong thing. I should have talked to you. I should have done . . . anything other than what I did. I'm sorry. I can't stand to be without you. I didn't know what alone really was until I was stupid enough to walk away from you. The last two weeks have been a living hell."

She breathed in and out in shallow, rapid breaths, trying to regain her equilibrium. His words had kindled a fire in her that was spreading liquid heat throughout her limbs, but she could think about them later, she could savor this moment later—right now she had to get him out of her apartment before she did something very, very stupid.

"No. You were right to walk away. We both know it was a mistake."

He advanced another slow, calculated step, his eyes burning, his jaw hard. "Do we?"

"Corbin told me, Christian. I know about your parents, about what happened to them. So *yes*, we know. People like us—we're oil and water. We don't mix."

He came another step closer but Ember held her ground. He wasn't going to push her around, not in her own apartment, not anywhere. Still, it felt like there was a rabid hummingbird trying to escape from inside her chest.

With fierce intensity, he asked, "Is that how you felt that night, before I was such an ass? Is that how you felt when I had you in my arms? When I was inside you? Like we didn't mix?"

When I was inside you. A tremor of longing ran through her, but she pushed it aside, concentrating on the important thing: getting him to leave before her willpower crumbled, along with her pride.

"You think there's going to be a happy ending to this, Christian? You think this can go any direction but south? Because I think you're lying to yourself if you do."

"Like you're lying to yourself about wanting me to leave?"

I'm not lying to myself, I'm lying to you, she silently corrected him. She knew she wanted him to stay, which is precisely why he shouldn't. She dropped her head into her hands and pressed her knuckles into her eye sockets, blocking out the sight of him. Softly, she begged, "Please, please, Christian don't make this any harder for me—"

But she never got the rest of the sentence out of her mouth because suddenly he was right in front of her. Before she could jerk away, his arms had encircled her, one of his hands had fisted into her hair. He pinned her against him. His heat and strength burned her, straight through her clothes.

He pulled her head back and said roughly into her ear, "You think this is easy for me? None of this is easy, but that doesn't make it wrong. You and I have something that I've never had with anyone else before, and even though it's messed up and we can't change the past, I'm not letting you go. We are going to work this shit out, right here, right now."

"And I don't get a say in any of this?" she cried, trying to push him away. It was like trying to move a mountain, and equally effective. "You just get to decide what's going to happen and what I want doesn't matter?"

"If you think for one second I'm going to believe that you don't want me, you can forget it. You can fight me all you want but your body doesn't lie." He inhaled deeply against her neck. When he spoke again, his voice had dropped an octave. "And like it or not, you already admitted how you feel. You're in love with me, little firecracker. Selfish bastard that I am, I'm not giving that up. That's mine. You're mine. So stop fighting it."

Suddenly furious, wanting to hit something, Ember gasped. "You arrogant, cocky, vain, overbearing—"

"Dick?" he supplied, lifting his head to gaze at her. He wasn't smiling, but there was a hint of laughter in his eyes that made her even angrier.

"Yes! Dick! Thank you!"

"You're welcome."

She hissed, "I don't want to be with you, understand? My body might want to, but *I* don't want to, and I don't want your money or your charity or your help—"

He stiffened. The laughter in his eyes died. "Charity? What the hell—"

"Yes, charity, that's what it's called when you donate money to the helpless and the needy! I might not be the best businesswoman in the world, but that store is mine and it's the only thing left I have of my father and I'm not ever going to sell it, you understand?"

He stared at her for a moment with a quizzical look on his face while she huffed and glared back at him. Her hands were pressed flat against his bare chest and she felt his heartbeat, fast and hard, beneath her palms.

"Ember, I wasn't going to take the store from you. I wanted you to have the money for it, yes, but I was going to turn the ownership back over to you as soon as the purchase agreement was signed. I don't want a bookstore, I just wanted you not to have to worry about money anymore. That store is always going to be yours, no matter what."

Oh. Wow. The sharp edges of her fury fizzled. "Well . . . you still paid my rent—forever. I'm not a child, Christian. And I'm not in the market for a sugar daddy."

He cocked an eyebrow at her. "Is *that* why you moved?"

She looked away and bit her lip.

He sighed and the fist in her hair loosened. He cupped her face in his hand and turned it toward his. With his thumb, he gently pried her lower lip from between her teeth. "I'm going to take care of you because I want to and I need to and I can, not because I think you're a charity case or a child, or a woman who can be bought—"

"I don't need to be taken care of—"

"I wasn't finished!" he said, hard, and her mouth snapped shut. He inhaled and exhaled slowly, then began again in a measured tone that belied how hard he was trying to maintain his patience. "This thing between us is real. Messy, yes, but real. I'm going to make mistakes and you're *definitely* going to make mistakes"—her mouth opened to protest, but he forged on—"and it might get ugly sometimes, but it's going to be worth it. Every messy, ugly, amazing minute is going to be worth it because things like this don't happen every day. People live their whole lives hoping to feel something like this"—he gave her a swift, hard squeeze on that last word—"and most of them never do, Ember.

"I made a mistake in walking away from you like I did. What happened in your past and what happened in mine are two separate things. You're only responsible for your end of it, not mine. And I know how you've punished yourself; I've seen it. But no one should be defined by the lowest point in their lives."

His voice dropped and he murmured, "Please give me a second chance. Please let me show you how much I need you. Please, Ember. Please be mine."

God how she wanted to cry. But she'd done enough crying and it didn't help anything anyway, so she just swallowed hard and tried her best to keep her breathing under control. Lashes lowered, she whispered, "I knew the money would go to the cystic fibrosis foundation. That's the real reason I moved."

He made a masculine sound low in his throat, grasped both her wrists and brought them up around his shoulders. He took her face in his hands. Looking deep into her eyes he said, "Tell me again, what you said before."

Her brows drew together in confusion.

He lowered his head and brushed his lips across hers, raising the hair on her arms. He whispered, "That you're in love with me."

"I-I didn't . . . really . . . say . . . that." She was having a hard time concentrating on anything she might have said over the last five minutes.

His tongue skimmed the corner of her mouth. His teeth grazed her lower lip. "Tell me."

Crumbling, crumbling, the footing beneath her feet, as if she stood on the edge of a very high cliff and piece by piece, inch by inch, the ground was giving way beneath her.

She breathed his name. Her hands around the back of his neck trembled, and she felt his smile against her mouth, a gentle curve of his lips she wanted to trace with her fingers. With her tongue.

"All right. I'll let you off the hook for the moment. But you have to go and pack a bag now. Just bring the essentials,

I'll get you anything else you need—clothes and whatever else—tomorrow."

Blinking out of her daze, Ember asked, "What?"

Christian raised his head and gave her a wide, dazzling smile. "Oh, didn't I mention? You're moving in with me."

When her mouth dropped open in shock, he added firmly, "Tonight."

TWENTY-FIVE
Bloodlust and
Holy Missions

Caesar decided that aside from the sounds of a whip cracking, a woman screaming and a stronger man than he whispering a deferential, "Yes, sire," the most beautiful noise in the world was the wet crunch a finger made when smashed beneath the heavy steel head of a hammer.

Well, the howl of pain that accompanied it was pretty good, too.

"Oh, don't be such a whiner, Nico, you know it'll heal in a few days!" he said cheerfully to the man writhing in agony in a chair opposite him. He was being held with his arm stretched across a wood table by four others, trusted males who'd proven their appetites for pain nearly matched his own. A fifth was vigorously applying the hammer to Nico's fingers, one by one.

They were still on his left hand. Caesar wanted to prolong this little show as long as possible.

He held up a knife, ran a finger along its serrated blade, and watched all the blood drain from Nico's face. "The wounds from this blade, however, might take a bit longer to heal."

There would be scars, however. Lovely, lovely scars.

Nico begged, "Sire, the girl was already gone. There was nothing I could do. She moved—"

"Nothing you could do?" repeated Caesar with lifted brows. "Well if there's nothing you can do, why on Earth am I keeping you around?" He smiled at Nico and watched with gleeful satisfaction as he cringed in terror. There was snickering from the other four. The male holding the hammer was silent, watching Caesar with avid, unblinking eyes for a sign to continue.

Caesar gave a tiny nod, and he lifted the hammer.

"Her landlord!" Nico screamed, seeing the sinister motion. "I can find out where she went from her landlord!"

Caesar held up his hand. The hammer paused.

"Why didn't you do that in the first place, Nico? We could have avoided all this if you'd just done your job correctly."

Not that Caesar wished he had. This was far too much fun.

Caesar liked to watch things bleed. In fact, "liked" was too soft a word, much too tepid to describe the surge of lust and hot excitement that gripped him when he saw blood. Any blood—even his own. He'd gotten into many fights as a younger man simply to watch himself bleed. It didn't matter that he inevitably lost. Just the sight of that lush, crimson liquid dripping down his face gave him such a raging hard-on he'd explode as soon as he touched himself.

This bloodlust ran in his family. His father had it, and his grandfather, and if the whispered rumors he'd caught snatches of all his life were true, his great-grandfather had it, too.

But as far as he knew, none of them shared his particular attraction to dead things.

His particular *sexual* attraction to dead things. The females he chained up and whipped until they expired were of use to him long after they grew cold.

Well, no matter. Those men were all six feet under and he wasn't—he never would be—so what he shared in common with long-dead ancestors was of no consequence. What was of consequence: finding the bland-as-white-bread brunette who would lead him to the male who'd killed two of his men and most probably wanted to kill him, too. They'd almost had her; one of his men had chanced upon a newspaper article featuring a picture of her staring with big, haunted eyes into the camera at the opening of a bookstore a few years ago. Once they knew her name, it was simple enough to find out where she lived.

But then the idiot Nico had botched it.

Caesar made a motion indicating Nico should be released. He slumped in his chair, cradling his mangled hand to his chest, sweating and white and bleeding from a small cut beneath one eye where Marcell had punched him to keep him from Shifting to avoid his punishment. If the skin was broken, Shifting was impossible, so Marcell had surprised Nico with the unleashed strength of his fist as he came around a corner in the dark tunnels of the bunkers, and then dragged him here to face his king.

His peeved, perverted king.

"Nico," that king said now, drawing the blade lovingly across the flesh of his palm, "I want you to understand something." He glanced up to find Nico staring at him through a haze of agony. His voice dropped to a low, menacing murmur. "Failure will not be tolerated. Failure is for losers, and fools, and the weak. And we are none of those things. Are we?"

"N-no, sire," whispered Nico, swallowing around the words.

"I take care of my friends, Nico. You know this. You also know what I do to my enemies."

Caesar waited for an acknowledgement. It came in the form of a jerking head shake.

"So. My advice to you is this: *do not fail again.*"

And then Caesar received the pitiful, whispered, "Yes, sire," he so loved to hear. He smiled at Nico, told him to go, and watched in warm satisfaction as he stumbled from the room, clutching his ruined hand to his chest.

At precisely the same moment, a tall, muscular, bone pale man stepped off a private plane that had just landed at the El Prat airport in Barcelona.

Followed by a silent line of men clad in simple, funereal black garb who spread out behind him over the tarmac in a V like a flock of geese as he progressed toward the sliding glass doors of the gate, he moved quickly and with purpose. He didn't pause to speak with the bowing man who appeared by his side inside the gate to take his bags, nor glance in either direction as he made his way through the crowded terminal to the line of black SUVs that awaited them at the curb.

Jahad was on a holy mission. He did not have time to stop, or look, or speak.

The SUVs took them to a budget hotel near the Sagrada Família cathedral. Jahad had never been to Barcelona before, and he'd never seen Gaudi's fabulist cathedral, the enormous bulk of which, awash in a riot of colorful lights, dominated the skyline. Gazing at the extraordinary, soaring spires, he felt gripped by a fervor of kinship for the dead architect, a profoundly religious man whose ascetic lifestyle and devotion to God mirrored his own.

He lifted his gaze to the heavens. In Latin, he recited a line from Psalms.

"Let them be as chaff before the wind; and let the angel of the Lord chase them."

A prayer against the enemy, one of many he knew by heart. In fact he knew both Testaments, Old and New, by heart. He'd had many years to study, many years to contemplate, many years to think on the moment when all his study and contemplation would come to its ultimate fruition and he would hold the beating heart of his enemy—ripped from his chest, fresh and throbbing—in his hand.

Jahad smiled up at the dark sky. Yes, the angel of the Lord *would* chase them. And he would find them. And he would smite them from the Earth, one by one, until their abomination was only a distant memory, never to rise again.

Followed by his cadre of silent, watchful men, he turned and went into the hotel.

Once the lodging had been paid, the men had dispersed, and he was alone in the shadowed confines of his room, he slowly removed all his clothing. He folded it into a small, neat pile on the bed, removed the braided length of leather from his satchel, and sank to his knees on the bare wood floor.

The first lash raised an angry red welt on his back, but didn't break the skin.

He whipped himself harder.

After one hundred lashes his back was properly shredded. Rivulets of blood ran down his naked buttocks and thighs and pooled in spreading circles beneath his knees. Though his breathing was irregular and his pupils had dilated, his hands did not shake. He did not allow himself to utter a single noise.

He dressed, not bothering to wipe away the blood or tend to his wounds, and called his second-in-command. To the man's deferential, "How may I serve you, *electus?*" Jahad responded with only four words.

"Find me a goat."

Then he disconnected the call, lowered his bulk to an uncomfortable chair in the corner of the room, and settled in to wait.

TWENTY-SIX
Casting Lots

"I'm sorry, *what* did you just say?"

Ember had frozen stiff in Christian's arms. Gazing up at him, with her arms still wrapped around his shoulders, her unblinking eyes grew so wide he saw the whites all around her dark irises.

"You're moving in with me tonight," he repeated. His voice was low but the tone indicated there was no room for discussion, which, of course, made Ember's face flush with anger. The woman just hated being told what to do.

How inconvenient.

"Not only is that not your decision, it's totally crazy," she replied bitingly. She tried to extricate herself from his embrace but he held her against his body, pinning her arms to her sides when she tried to wriggle free.

He ignored her cries of protest.

"I'm not asking you, Ember, I'm telling you. You're moving in with me, and it's happening tonight—"

"Just like that? We're not going to talk about what happened? You're not going to even ask me if I *want* to?"

"—so go and pack a bag." He paused a moment. "And I dare you to tell me you don't want to while keeping a straight face."

Her mouth opened—outrage or alarm, he couldn't tell—but he could tell the thought of moving in with him excited her. Her blood had begun to pound through her veins and a sweet bloom of heat rose from her skin, tinged with the scent of delicious hot readiness.

God, what that scent did to him. His body reacted on a molecular level and an erection charged to life between his legs.

Seeing how he was naked and pressed tight against her, she didn't miss it. Her face flushed a deeper shade of red. She bit her lip and gazed up at him, the expression on her face alternating between a furious scowl and something else. Something a little more ambivalent.

"Why?" she whispered. "Why now?"

Fighting the urge to kiss her, tear her clothes off, or otherwise get her into a compromising position, he hesitated, deciding whether to tell her the truth. But no—he had to tell her. She deserved to know what was happening.

Watching her face carefully, he said, "Those men in the alley, that night in Gràcia."

Her breath hitched. She stared at him, silent and apprehensive, waiting for him to continue.

"Their group knows where you live. Or at least they did—they were at your old apartment earlier today. It's only a matter of time before they find you here."

Judging by her reaction, it might have been wiser not to tell her the truth.

At the top of her lungs, she shrieked, "What?" then spun wildly out of his arms, frantically looking around the apartment as if expecting them to leap from behind the furniture. Her eyes grew even more huge than before, her face paled to white. "The ones you said would kill us both?"

He felt a little awkward standing naked in the middle of her living room, aroused, but he only said, "Yes."

"Oh, my God. Oh, my God! What are we going to do?"

"I told you. You're moving in with me."

"I can't—I can't—this is insane! What am I supposed to do, hide for the rest of my life?"

"No," he said, very calmly. "Just until I kill them."

She gaped at him. Several seconds ticked by and then slow, spreading recognition transformed her face from panic to understanding.

"That's why you're here. That's why you're in Spain. You're an . . . an . . . " she trailed off then swallowed. "Assassin," she finished in horror.

"No," he protested instantly, then paused to think about it. "Well, yes, but not really. That's not what I normally do, this is a special circumstance—an emergency, really—I can't exactly explain it."

She was still gaping at him. Outside, the sound of two cars colliding in a traffic accident on a street a few blocks away underscored the lunacy of the situation with a thunderous, metallic bang.

"I knew it," she whispered. "I knew it the first time I saw you."

His brows raised. "That's very interesting. You can tell me all about it in the car." He was by her side in two long strides and pulled her up against him. Gazing intently down into her eyes he said, "Don't be afraid. I'm not going to let anything hurt you; you have my word. You'll be perfectly safe in my home—"

She sputtered a horrified laugh. "Safe in the home of an assassin?"

"I just told you, I'm not really an assassin—"

"*Not really* an assassin is pretty much the same thing as being not really dead, or not really pregnant! You either are or you're not!"

His face hardened. "Ember, this is no time to split hairs—"

"No," she declared with a hardness to her voice that brought him up short.

He glowered at her, but she only shook her head and crossed her arms over her chest, edging out of his grip.

"No, Christian. No way. Absolutely not. I'm not moving in with you. And I'm sure not moving in with you under these circumstances, especially with all the baggage we have to sort through. We'll just have to figure something else out."

He felt anger begin to thread a burning path through his nerve endings. Very quietly, doing his best to keep his anger and frustration in check, he said, "They will kill you, Ember. If they find you, they will kill you. But not before they've had a bit of fun with you, if you get my meaning."

Her nostrils flared. A little muscle beneath her eye twitched.

He said, "Yes. Use your imagination. Think of the worst thing that a sadistic, genocidal madman might do to you, and then multiply that by a hundred. Maybe a thousand.

Then think about how I would feel, knowing I put you in harm's way, knowing I failed to keep you safe. What do you think that would do to me?"

His voice, the dark, menacing tone of it, the weighted way it emerged from between his gritted teeth, made her hesitate. She actually did appear to think about it. Then she haltingly said, "You would . . . you would be . . . "

"Devastated," he finished roughly, closing what little distance there still was between them. She dropped her arms to her sides but didn't move away, and he got right up in her face and looked down at her, letting her see the truth of his words. Letting her see the emotion in his eyes.

"It would kill me, Ember. It would be the end of me. If anything happened to you . . . " he stopped himself because his voice had grown unsteady, his tone a little unhinged. He breathed in a deep, lung-clearing breath and started anew. "I wouldn't be able to live with it. Do you understand what I'm saying to you?"

She stared at him in silence, her brown eyes burning his. Her gaze flickered to his mouth, drifted back up to his, and then a tiny, tiny smile lifted the corners of her lips. "I think you're saying you're in love with me."

He breathed out, closed his eyes, and reached for her. She allowed him to gather her into his arms.

"Which is only fair," she continued with her cheek pressed against his bare chest, "seeing as how I kind of told you the same thing."

Feeling as if his heart would claw its way out of his chest, he murmured into her hair, "Kind of?"

"This is no time to split hairs," she said, throwing his earlier words back at him. "But yeah, kind of. It's not official yet because we haven't actually said *the* words, but . . . " She looked up at him, and something in her expression brought a smile to his face: mischief.

"It'll do for now."

Christian exhaled slowly, shaking his head. "Will you please just go and pack a goddamn bag?" he said, his voice low and rough. "And stop trying to give me a stroke?"

She pursed her lips, considering. "I want my own room," she pronounced, and he made a sound that was both a groan of disbelief and a growl of frustration.

"I'm not going to hop into your bed and set up camp there. We have shit to work out, Christian. A lot of it. We're going to actually have to *talk*."

He lifted his gaze to the ceiling and slowly counted to ten.

More softly, she said, "Maybe I'll *visit* your bed, however."

He looked down at her.

Her smile was both shy and beautiful. "Maybe."

"You have five minutes before I throw you over my shoulder and forcibly remove you from this apartment," he said gruffly, feeling not anger but almost a fierce sort of glee that he'd soon have her in his home, near him, able to touch her and kiss her whenever he wanted. He tried his best not to show how happy he was, how eager, because the situation was still dire and dangerous, but God—he was so happy he could sing.

Sometimes terrible situations had a silver lining more precious than sterling. You just had to look at them the right way.

He turned her around, smacked her on the ass—which elicited a startled, outraged cry—then gave her a little shove toward the bedroom. "Five minutes," he repeated firmly. "Only the necessities. Hurry."

As she threw him a sour look over her shoulder and disappeared into the bedroom, he crossed to the front door and opened it.

The clothes he left on the floor in the hallway when he'd Shifted to Vapor had disappeared. With a hissed curse under his breath, he slammed the door and startled Ember when he barged into her bedroom.

"One of your very fine neighbors has stolen my clothing. Do you have anything I can wear?"

She pretended to think. "Um, I have those kitty pajamas Asher gave me—"

Christian said her name on a growl and she had the audacity to smirk.

"Actually, I do have something you can wear."

She went to a tiny door in one corner of the tiny bedroom and pulled it open. From it she produced the pair of jeans and sweatshirt he'd given her that fateful day two weeks ago, when he'd thrown her out of his house. She'd washed them and kept them among her things—the thought of it made his heart do a funny little flip inside his chest. She handed them to him with a pointed look, then turned back to the dresser and began to fill a small bag with clothes.

She was ready in less than five minutes. He hurried her downstairs to the Audi and Corbin, awaiting them in the back alley. She and Corbin exchanged muted hellos, and the car pulled silently away.

"This is only temporary," she said quietly, staring out the window, deep in thought. "I can't hide forever. This is just temporary, until you . . . until . . . ."

Gripped by the sudden, awful realization that temporary could mean anything from one day to one week to one month, depending on how long it took him to find Caesar and his colony, Christian murmured his assent. He reached across the seat and took her hand. He gave it a squeeze and she glanced over at him. All traces of humor and anger and confidence were gone, and now she looked at him with only deep worry and more than a little fear on her face.

"What about work?"

Christian slowly shook his head.

Her brows rose. "Volunteering at the shelter?"

Another head shake and her voice climbed an octave. "Asher?"

"Not until I find them. You can't go anywhere you usually go. Your normal routine is off-limits, it's too dangerous. In fact . . . I think it's best if you don't leave the house at all."

She pulled her fingers from his and dropped her head into her hands. "This is unbelievable," she whispered, and Christian had the sinking feeling she was beginning to rue the day she ever met him.

Just as they turned the corner onto the main street, he saw through the window a trio of rangy, unkempt young men, fighting beneath the flickering fluorescent glow of a street lamp over a small pile of clothing. A suit jacket, trousers, a shirt, and a pair of polished, gleaming shoes. When he recognized the items as his own, his skin crawled with the sudden memory of a reading an archbishop had given at the pope's funeral just months before. It had been an international event, televised all over the world, full of pomp and somber regalia, but the reading had stuck with him more than the pageantry. As the pope had died a martyr, that theme permeated the proceedings, and the line that stuck like a burr was from the gospel of Matthew, about the death of the most famous martyr of them all.

"And after they had crucified him, they divided up his clothes by casting lots."

Because Christian believed every little thing had some kind of meaning, that all the seemingly inconsequential details and coincidences of life are quite the opposite, the sight of those young men dividing up his stolen clothes on the street sent a shiver of cold, black premonition straight down into the darkest corners of his soul.

"Everything is going to be fine," he murmured to Ember. "Don't worry. Everything is going to be just fine."

But even to his own ears, it sounded like a lie.

TWENTY-SEVEN
Thirteen

Doctor Maximilian Reiniger—also known as the Doctor, Agent Doe or simply Thirteen—was a man with a plan.

A former German Special Forces soldier who'd lost his mother in a gruesome animal attack when he was a small child, he'd developed a hatred for cats that was the very definition of pathological. It had been a cat, after all, that had taken his beloved *mutter*, a Bengal tiger that had suddenly decided during a traveling circus act that it was finished with jumping through hoops—and was also in the mood for a snack.

Under the yellow and white striped big top, little Maximilian and his mother had been sitting in the front row of the bleachers. He'd seen up close what those long, sharp fangs could do when applied with vigor to vulnerable human flesh.

By the time the tiger had sated its hunger, there was nothing recognizable left of his poor mother but a few bloodied shreds of floral print dress, and a single patent leather shoe.

After witnessing such a horrific mauling at such a young, impressionable age, little Maximilian's mind warped like wood exposed to water, and he became obsessed with only two things:

Killing cats. And saving people.

So after he was grown and finished with his secondary education, he entered medical school, where he excelled. Not satisfied to merely go into private practice or work for one of the government-run hospitals where he would spend his life tending to the sick, but doing nothing to protect people from the multitude of threats they faced from enemies human and otherwise, the newly minted doctor decided to round out his medical education with a stint in the army. There he learned to shoot, blow things up, operate with a clear mind while under extreme physical duress, and obey commands from higher-ups without question.

That last one would prove his most valuable asset of all.

He rose through the ranks and was recruited by the Special Forces Command. Only forty percent of new recruits are able to pass the initial three-week-long psychological training regimen, and only about eight percent of those pass the subsequent physical endurance phase. Reiniger passed all with flying colors and was sent to El Paso, Texas for his three-year special instruction cycle in desert and bush training. With more than twenty jungle, desert, urban and counter-terrorism courses at seventeen schools worldwide, it was pure chance he was sent to the one where he would be introduced to the man who would eventually change his life.

He still did not know this man's real name. No one did. He was known simply as the Chairman, or One.

To Reiniger—who would later be named Thirteen when he was recruited to the Chairman's organization and advanced near the top—the Chairman was only ever a voice on the other end of a telephone line. There were no face-to-face meetings, no videoconferences, no emails, or even a physical address that could be traced to him by any one of the thousands of people who worked under his umbrella of multi-national companies, most of them in the bioengineering industry. The Chairman was a shadowy figure who, according to legend, had learned on a trip to Africa of an old, old local myth about the *Ikati*, creatures with superhuman powers that could manipulate their shape.

Who could turn into, of all things, cats.

Panthers, to be specific. Big, black ones.

The Chairman, whose wife had died of a rare neurological disease that his daughter had inherited, had made it his life's mission to find a cure. He believed the answer lay only partly in medicine and science . . . the other part lay in capitalizing on the abilities of the nonhuman life forms he wholeheartedly believed lived alongside man, hidden in plain view.

Like the *Ikati*. Creatures he knew were not just the stuff of local legend, but real.

He'd found enough proof over the years to convince him of their existence.

So he funneled the considerable resources available to him into his ultimate goal—capturing one of these supernatural creatures and learning exactly what made them tick. He had his very personal reason for his goal, of course, but the Chairman was also a businessman, so naturally there was another reason: money.

The profits that might be made from the medical and scientific breakthroughs garnered from the study of such creatures would undoubtedly be huge.

But the Chairman needed a certain type of hunter to pull off such a feat. A hunter who was not only smart, dedicated, trained in medicine, unsqueamish about conducting experiments on live, sentient subjects, but most importantly . . . loyal.

Money can buy a whole lot of loyalty, but it can't buy the best kind. The strongest kind of loyalty is only found in those who have dedicated themselves, heart and soul, to a cause.

A cause like killing cats. And saving people.

So Maximilian Reiniger was an ideal recruit for the Chairman, and a man he met in a dusty El Paso bar one sultry summer evening didn't hesitate to tell him so. He'd overheard the story a half-drunk Reiniger was telling his friend: the story about what made him go into medicine and the army.

The story about his mother, mauled to death by a tiger under the big top, in front of his very eyes.

"Join us," said the man, whose name was Doe, "and get your revenge."

Reiniger had never heard six more beautiful words in his life.

So he quit the Special Forces Command and joined the Chairman's organization as the head of Section Thirty, in charge of investigating supernatural phenomenon in Western Europe. He and each of the leaders of the other twenty-nine sections around the world—all called Doe, as in John—were fanatics to the cause and unquestioningly loyal, but only he had actually caught one of the creatures they'd all been searching for.

He'd experimented on her, too.

That had surprised him a little—that the creature was female. Also that it looked so . . . well, human. Probably because he had such tender memories of his mother, he'd imagined these vile creatures would be male, or even non-gendered, like some kind of alien life forms that procreated through osmosis or mind-melding. Either way, he'd been laughably wrong. For all intents and purposes, when these creatures were in their human form, they *were* human.

That was probably what angered him the most. Filthy copycats.

The creature he'd caught had managed to escape, but not before Reiniger had sustained a few injuries in the process. He'd lost his left eye, and now wore a patch. His left leg didn't work well, either—there'd been an explosion, and unfortunately he hadn't gotten away unscathed.

His devotion was unscathed, however. So when the news came that these creatures had been sighted again, this time in Barcelona, he was tagged to go.

He had the cooperation of the local police because the Chairman had greased many, many palms. Unfortunately, the Chairman didn't waste money on things like luxurious lodging, so he'd been ensconced in a budget motel not far from the Sagrada Família. It was late by the time he arrived, so he didn't bother to begin that first night. He would wait until morning, after he'd had a good sleep.

And then Reiniger—aka Thirteen, Agent Doe and the Doctor—would begin the hunt once again.

He knew just where to start.

TWENTY-EIGHT
Marked

The bedroom Ember had chosen in Christian's mansion in the woods was on the second floor, with a view over the rambling, unkempt rose garden in the back of the property that led right up to the thick, dark line of the trees.

The trees were tall and old, the forest very dense. When she looked out the window on a night like tonight, awoken as she had been by some strange noise she couldn't identify, even the moon that hung like a great shining pearl in the black dome of the sky didn't cast enough light to penetrate the thick canopy of branches. All she could see as she gazed into the dark line of trees was . . . the dark line of trees, opaque as obsidian.

She *could* see, however, the naked figure striding slowly through the rose garden.

"Christian."

She whispered his name. Her hand rose to rest against the cold panes of beveled glass.

For the last three days since she'd arrived, he'd been careful and courteous, almost solicitous, inquiring how she'd slept—poorly, though she didn't admit it—what she wanted to eat—nothing, but he insisted—and what he could do to make her more comfortable. She wasn't *un*comfortable, exactly, but she still hadn't quite gotten her head around the situation.

She was here—in Christian's house—because someone wanted to kill her.

Or him. Or, in all likelihood, both of them.

They'd skirted around that terrible fact during the long conversations they'd had during what was becoming their habitual morning walk. Ember arose early, almost always by six. Christian, due to the nightly excursions that took hours and hours, and sometimes longer than that, arose much later, groggy and handsome with a shadow of beard on his jaw, and a tired, dull look in his eye.

A look that transformed whenever he saw her.

She was beginning to get used to it—to look forward to it, the way his eyes lit up when they rested on her. She thought more than once that just the memory of the heat and tenderness in his eyes would be enough to sustain her through whatever darkness the future might hold.

She wasn't spending too much time thinking about the future, however. She was taking this whole mess one day at a time.

On their walks, they talked of books, music, and family, of food they hated, of movies they loved. He told her about his brother, Leander, and sister, Daria, and the place where he grew up in England, a place he said was not so unlike this little slice of heaven in the woods. She told him of the sprawling adobe pueblo in the middle of Taos that was built a thousand years ago, and the palomino horse she'd had when she was ten, and how she and her parents would go up to the roof of the old La Fonda hotel and watch the electrical storms far off in the distant hills while they ate albondigas soup and homemade tortillas slathered in mole sauce. How the color of the sky there was the bluest blue she'd ever seen.

And how much she missed it.

She also told him about Dr. Flores, and his eyes grew so soft they shone. He was glad she was talking to someone, glad Asher had forced her to go.

There were only two things they never discussed. The accidents, and what was going to happen after he found what he was looking for in the woods.

And somehow, though they talked about almost everything, they'd become physically shy around each another. It was as if by being in such close proximity, an invisible wall had been erected that they both felt but were pointedly trying to ignore. Or maybe not a wall, exactly, but an electrical fence. Because all the crackling, dangerous energy was still there, the tension and awareness of heat and intensity and how easy it would be to simply slip into his bed in the middle of the night, or he into hers.

But neither one did. They barely even touched. He gave her a chaste kiss on the forehead each night before walking away from her bedroom door to his own room, far at the other end of the mansion.

She wondered if, in the few hours he had to sleep, he stared up at the ceiling just as she did, wretched with longing.

It was actually worse than mere longing. It was an ache, a vast, pounding emptiness, a hole that grew larger and harder to fill every day they were so close, yet so far apart.

As she watched him stride off through the rose garden now, nude and breathtaking in the moonlight, the ache grew just that much stronger. He melted into the trees, disappearing as quickly as a stone dropped into dark water, and Ember sighed, not realizing she'd been holding her breath.

He'd probably be gone until morning. Her stomach growled; she decided to go downstairs to the kitchen and forage for food.

Corbin had his own quarters on the ground floor, as did the housekeeper, the groundskeeper, and the cook, but they were far off in another wing and it was half past one, so she doubted very much she'd run into anyone. Only Corbin had given Christian an odd look when he'd been informed Ember would be staying with them; the others didn't seem to have an opinion either way.

They were human, Christian had explained. Hired help who came with the house.

It had been rented, but the astonishing collection of books in the library were his own. He said he'd had most of it shipped over on a whim when he'd first arrived, when the thought of sitting alone in the house with nothing to read became so depressing he couldn't stand it.

Before he'd met her, and forgotten about books altogether.

It brought a faint smile to her face, remembering the way he'd said that. The way he'd looked at her when he said it, a sideways, penetrating glance from beneath sooty lashes as he walked beside her on the stone path in the garden, his hands clasped behind his back. She'd bitten her lip and looked away, and he'd changed the subject.

Ember padded down the curved staircase from the second floor and reached the foyer landing. Passing the drawing room on the right, she came upon that lovely library and paused at the entrance, looking around.

It was truly magnificent. Not only the glass cases with row after row of leather-bound books, but the marble fireplace, the huge potted palms, and the grand piano. All was quiet and cool, the outlines of the room sketched in pale moonlight.

She stood arrested for a moment, staring at the enormous Steinway. She didn't know how to play the piano—her lessons had always only been cello—but it had been so long since she'd even touched a musical instrument that just looking at it struck a chord of yearning somewhere deep inside her.

She crossed the room, sat down on the glossy black bench, flipped open the cover, and lightly set her hands on the keys. Unexpected anguish rose up in her throat, and she yanked her hands away and curled them to fists in her lap.

She closed the cover and leaned over, resting her head on her arms on the dark wood. She was suddenly tired, so tired, and she closed her eyes for a moment, allowing her heartbeat to slow and her breathing to follow. She drifted into sleep.

And when she opened her eyes again sometime later, she wasn't alone.

She felt him first. He was a dark presence behind her, a tangible, burning heat. She sat upright with a gasp and whirled around, her hand at her throat.

Christian stood over her, staring down at her face with eyes incandescent as stars.

"What are you doing?" His voice was low and throaty, a whiskey-deep growl, as if he'd been swallowing rocks.

"I'm-I-I couldn't sleep—I was hungry—I was—"

"Are you all right?" His gaze raked over her, hungry and hot, and she noticed he was breathing deeply, his nostrils flared, his hands just slightly trembling by his sides. He looked to be barely holding himself in check.

He wore a half-buttoned white cotton shirt rolled up to the elbows and a pair of faded jeans. His feet were bare. His hair was mussed. There was a vein throbbing at the base of his throat.

Beyond her surprise at his sudden appearance, her brain registered danger. Her mouth went dry.

She swallowed and said, "Yes. Are you?"

It took him several moments to answer, in which his throat worked and a muscle flexed, over and over, in his jaw. His hot, unblinking gaze never left hers.

"It takes a while after I Shift back . . . I'm not . . . I didn't expect to see you."

Her brows lifted. She waited, blood pumping hard through her veins.

"The animal," he whispered, his teeth gritted. "It's not . . . completely . . . " His gaze drifted over her, lingering on her mouth, her breasts beneath the T-shirt she'd worn to bed. His eyes flared hotter.

"Oh," she breathed, understanding in a heartbeat. "Ah, should I . . . " she glanced at the doorway.

"No," he said immediately, a little too loud, then closed his eyes and moistened his lips. After a few deep inhalations, he said, "Yes. Probably. It's not entirely . . . safe. The way you *smell*—it's difficult to—argh! Fuck!"

He broke off and turned away from her in one swift pivot, his hands clenched in his hair, and stood there with his head bowed, silent, his entire body tensed.

The adrenaline that surged through her body was electrifying. She knew what was happening, her body knew what was happening, and it was responding in every way it could.

He wanted her. And he didn't want her in a roses, poetry, and violins kind of way. He wanted her in a violent, animal, starving way. A possessive way.

An owning way.

Instantly, she wanted him that way, too.

As if he sensed it, he let out a soft, agonized groan. "Go back to your room," he whispered. His broad shoulders rolled forward in a way that accentuated their breadth, and as she watched, fascinated, pinned in place, as a tremor ran through them. He said her name on a growl when she stayed where she was, and when she still didn't move he spun around, advanced, and towered over her, glowering and shaking, molten hot.

"Go back to your goddamn room!"

His voice had dropped even lower than the register it held before, and Ember heard the unraveling edge of restraint in it as clear as if someone had struck a bell. But it didn't frighten her. It excited her. It turned her inside out.

Slowly, with trembling hands, keeping her gaze locked on his, she reached out and touched him, flattening her hands over his chest. At the same time, she whispered, "No."

He stiffened and made a sound that was part snarl, part hiss, and utterly primal. His nostrils flared again, and his eyes grew flatly dangerous.

Slowly, slowly, Ember slid her hands down his chest, over his abdomen, to the waist of his jeans, feeling his muscles twitch and flex beneath her fingers. As softly as she could, she said, "You're not going to hurt me. I know you're not going to hurt me." Then she slid her hands up and under his shirt.

His skin was on fire.

The moment her hands touched the exposed flesh of his stomach, his eyes flared with such pure, primitive lust she felt as if cocaine had been injected straight into her bloodstream. He gripped her around the waist, set her up on the edge of the piano, kicked the bench aside so hard it went flying away and hit a stone urn with such force the bench split apart with a crack. He yanked her against his body.

"I can't be gentle!" hc snarled, his lips peeled back over his teeth. "I can't go slow! I'm still too strong—I *will* hurt you!"

He was trying to warn her. But she didn't want his warnings. She wanted him.

So she kissed him.

And just like that, the fever that always simmered between them ignited and engulfed them both in flames.

His mouth was devouring, his hands, ravenous, the sound he made in his throat purely animal. His fingers sank into the soft flesh of her hips and he bent her back, kissing her so savagely it stole her breath. Her took her lower lip between his teeth and bit it; suddenly she tasted blood, coppery sweet, and it sharpened her lust to a pagan fury.

Starvation and need thrummed through her. She pressed herself against his chest, tangled her fingers in his hair and pulled him in. Harder. Closer.

Panting, he broke away and took hold of the neck of her cotton T-shirt with both hands. He ripped it straight down the middle, tearing it in two with one hard pull. She gasped, shocked at the violence of it, but he only pushed her down against the cool, hard surface of the piano with one hand flat on her chest and his eyes locked on hers, curled a hand around her pajama bottoms, and tore those off, too, in one swift yank, so she was lying there, fully exposed, with only her panties.

They were torn off next. His gleaming, ferocious gaze never left hers.

He freed himself from his jeans, leaned over and gathered both her wrists in one of his hands, pressed her arms back over her head so they were pinned against the piano, wrapped an arm beneath and around her waist, and, without preliminaries or a single word, shoved deep inside her.

She arched and cried out. He was hard and hot inside her—so *hot*—

He growled something unintelligible next to her ear, a curse or a garbled plea. It almost sounded like *mine.*

He thrust into her again, and again, and again. His face was pressed against her neck, his heated breath brushed over her skin, his body burned with that unnatural heat. He filled her, stretched her, held her locked in place against him with his arm like an iron band around her waist. She moaned his name and he stilled for a moment, breathing raggedly, trying, it seemed, to slow himself, or contain himself, but she didn't want that—so she flexed her hips and took him deeper.

"Don't stop," she begged. "Don't slow down. Please, Christian, don't stop."

He released her wrists and wrapped his hands around her waist. He reared up and pulled her right to the edge of the piano so her bottom hung off.

"Say it again," he demanded, his voice still that strange, gravelly whisper. "Say my name."

He slid one of her legs up and hooked her ankle over his shoulder, and simultaneously pressed forward, deeper inside her, so deep it made her shudder. Her eyes slid shut.

"Christian!"

He slid almost all the way out, then slammed back inside her. A shockwave of pleasure tore through her; she shivered and groaned.

"Again."

Now his hands were on her breasts, roughly pinching her nipples, sending spikes of pleasure straight down between her legs. His mouth quickly followed his fingers and she felt his tongue, hot and wet, sucking, incredibly wonderful, then pain as his teeth fastened around one sensitive nipple. She cried out and he gentled a bit, sucking again, still greedy and hungry.

"Say it again, Ember!"

His words were a rough command, muffled against her breast. She dug her fingers into his hair, whimpering. When she felt the sting of his teeth again, she gasped his name and he snarled his approval.

"Fuck, I love that—I *love* my name on your lips."

His hands against her skin were strong and sure, roaming everywhere as he pumped into her. She felt as if she were being consumed, devoured—possessed.

She opened her eyes and saw him there above her, drenched in moonlight, his eyes shining clear and lucid green past the shadows over his face. His shirt was still on and she wanted it off; she wanted to see all of him.

"Take it off," she panted, tugging at the material. He complied with swift, brutal precision, tearing it off exactly how he'd torn her own shirt off. Buttons popped and went flying as he yanked it apart and tossed it to the floor; she had a moment to admire him, hard, muscular, and beautiful, before he leaned over and took her mouth. He kissed her with vicious intensity, his tongue thrusting in time with his hips, the heat of his body burning her chest and stomach.

Then his mouth was gone, he withdrew, and he flipped her over so quickly she gasped in shock. Her belly and breasts were pressed flat against the cool, slick surface of the piano.

"On your toes," he hissed, and fisted a hand into her hair. He pulled her hips back with his other hand so her back was arched and her bottom stuck out. She complied without thought, eager to have him inside her again, and was rewarded instantly as he slid between her legs and buried himself as deep as he could go.

Ember made a sound that was part groan, part whimper, part *Thank you, Jesus!*

His thrusts came harder, faster. He reached around and slipped his fingers between her legs. When he touched her slick, swollen nub she jerked and cried out. Pleasure sizzled through her limbs, making her knees shake, her breath falter, and her heart throb in her chest.

She was close, so close. Her nipples were hard and aching, rubbing against the piano with each of his thrusts, sending more waves of pleasure through her as he wound her higher and higher with his body inside hers and those clever, demanding fingers stroking between her legs.

"Christian—please—hurry—together!" It was a gasped, stuttering plea, which he answered in a tone so urgent and rough it was nearly incoherent.

"Can't—ovulating—mouth."

How he knew she was ovulating was a question she would ask later, but what she gathered from those three disjointed words was he wanted to come in her mouth so she didn't get pregnant. She lifted her head and looked at him over her shoulder. "No—it's okay—the accident—I can't—you can't get me pregnant."

He froze for a millisecond. His eyes took on a haunting, uncanny glow, vivid green in the shadows, as if they were lit from behind.

Then he pulled them both down to the rug beneath their feet.

He only withdrew to turn her around again, then she was flat on her back and he was between her legs, his hands on either side of his face, his face contorted in something like agony.

She reached down between their bodies and grasped him, stroked him base to tip as he groaned and shuddered. He kissed her savagely as she guided him inside.

White fire and aching, breathlessness, heartbeats pounding against chests. She ran her hands down his back, loving the flex of his muscles, the softness of and heat of his skin, and cupped his hard ass, pulling him deeper inside as he thrust into her. He dug his fingers into her hair and held her head in place, staring down at her as his breath came harder and more uneven, little groans working from his throat.

The world shrunk to the few short inches between their faces. Christian whispered her name.

It was the way he said it that finally pushed her over the edge. The urgent, desperate plea was both tender and rough; it made her feel wild and delirious. Combined with the expression on his face—astonishment, rapture, stark worship beyond the primal pleasure—it made her feel beautiful.

It made her feel loved.

The orgasm that ripped through her was so hard she couldn't even make a noise. She arched against him, mouth open in a silent scream, eyes clenched shut, the pulsing throb in her core so glorious and encompassing she could only cling to him wordlessly as he continued to pump inside her. He lowered his head and took her nipple in his mouth, sucking hard, and she jerked against him, her throat finally opening to let out a sob.

"Yes, baby." His teeth and hot, wet mouth drove another cry from her throat as he suckled her. "Make noise for me. Let me hear you come."

She moaned, loud and wanton, clawing at his back.

He shuddered, his entire body tensed. "Oh God," he said in a gasped whisper. "Ember—I'm coming, too—angel—"

She opened her eyes, locked her gaze to his and panted, "Yes, Christian . . . now . . . give it to me. Give it all to me *now!*"

Her words drove him wild. Hard and uncontrolled, he crashed into her, pounding deep, groaning, all his muscles in his body flexed and rippling. She clenched her thighs around him harder, digging her fingers into his back, moaning louder with every furious thrust of his hips.

Then, with a strangled groan, he faltered. He pumped deep. Once, twice. He gasped her name and came inside her. She felt it—throbbing, twitching, a spreading heat—

then he collapsed on top of her with a gusted exhalation and crushed her against his chest.

They lay fused together for long, silent minutes, letting their heartbeats slow, catching their breath, both of them wracked by the occasional spasm, sated and flushed.

Christian inhaled a slow, deep breath against her throat. Then he roused and slowly nuzzled her neck, rubbing his face into her skin, her hair, the space between her throat and shoulder.

Without withdrawing from her body, he shifted and moved slightly lower to rub his face against her breasts.

He did it slowly, with an almost reverent solemnity, dragging his face one way and then the other across her chest, down her ribs, back up to her neck and shoulders, caressing her with his lips and hands, the slight stubble on his jaw tickling her over-sensitive skin. All his wild tension and that edge of raw danger seemed to be gone, replaced by sweet, possessive tenderness.

"What are you doing?" she whispered, stroking her fingers through his hair as he lifted one of her arms and rubbed his face against her bicep, burrowing into her armpit with his nose.

"Marking you." She thought for a moment she'd misheard him, but he lifted his head and gazed at her, his eyes heavy-lidded and warm. "With my scent."

Her lips parted, but there didn't seem to be a correct response to that.

"Because you're mine," he softly explained, seeing her bewilderment. "And I'm yours. And the animal inside me is yours. No matter what happens from now on, Ember, that will never change—I want you to remember that." His eyes grew soft, and he almost looked haunted. "Come what may."

For a blind, breathless second, she was consumed by panic. "Why does that sound like a good-bye?" she whispered, searching his face.

He smiled, a charming, lopsided quirk of his lips. "I just told you I'm bonded to you, and you take it as a goodbye?"

His smile loosened the knot in her chest and she breathed a little easier. She lifted her hand to stroke his cheek. "Bonded?"

Still buried inside her, his weight heavy and wonderful on top of her, he cradled her face in his hands and said, "It's the way of my kind. Like swallows and swans, we mate for life. For us, love creates a mark. A fingerprint, if you will, except on the soul. Something is changed inside of us. The bond between two mates is sacred; even attempting to interfere with it is a crime punishable by death. There's no divorce, no affairs, nothing at all that can separate a bonded *Ikati* from his mate. Not even death."

The knot in her chest reappeared. Another one formed in her stomach. Her eyes filled with tears and she whispered his name.

His voice both soft and firm, he said, "I'm going to take care of you for the rest of your life, I want you to be very clear about that. You are the most precious thing I've ever known. And you've given me the most amazing gift, one I'll always treasure."

She stared at him, her heart clenched inside her chest, the hand on his face trembling.

Eyes shining, he murmured, "You make me feel free."

This time she couldn't even whisper his name, the emotion was so intense. So overwhelming.

"My entire life I've been constrained, restricted, forced to follow rules I didn't create and never wanted to obey. But

I did. I had no choice. Until I met you, and you made me realize I *do* have a choice. There was always a choice. I just never had anything valuable enough to risk my neck for. And because you've given me all that you have, I'm going to ensure that you never again have to worry about money, or the future, or anything at all."

When he saw the look on her face, his voice hardened. "This is not a discussion. I'm informing you of the facts. You're going to sign that agreement for the bookstore, and you're going to let your wicked stepmother have her share so she'll leave you alone, and then you can go right back to working there if you want. But you're going to sign it."

Dizzy with his declaration and still glowing from pleasure, she decided to argue about the store later. "Wicked stepmother?"

A wry smile crossed his face. "Señor Alvarez had a few choice things to say about our friend Marguerite. A few very *unflattering* things." He leaned down and kissed her shoulder. "You're trembling," he noted, running his hand up her arm.

"Your fault, Mr. Sex God. I probably won't be able to walk for days."

He tensed. "Did I hurt you?" he whispered, his fingers caressing her upper arm.

With her heart aching and tears burning her eyes, Ember wrapped her arms around him, and buried her face in his neck. "Never," she whispered. "I'm just trembling from happiness. You make me so happy, Christian. Thank you."

He exhaled a relieved breath and chuckled, brushing the hair off her face. "I like this side of you, little firecracker. I certainly hope you're going to be this defenseless and tender every time we make love."

"Only one way to find out."

He chuckled again. Then he swiftly sat up, gathered her in his arms and stood. "Yes, let's go find out right now. Only I think I'd like to be in a bed this time; rug burn isn't really my thing."

He walked swiftly through the dark house and up the stairs, and carried her to his bedroom. They made love again in his huge, soft bed, and this time it was tender and slow and even more beautiful. Afterward, Christian fell asleep wrapped around her, one heavy leg thrown over both of hers, his breathing deep and steady at her ear.

But Ember couldn't sleep. Even when dawn showed faintly pink and gold over the horizon, she was still staring up at the ceiling, trying to put her finger on the sense of dread that had overtaken her at Christian's words, his promises she would be taken care of.

I'm going to ensure that you never again have to worry about money, or the future, or anything at all.

She couldn't shake the feeling that three words were missing from that sentence. Three words that would have been equally at home at the beginning or the end.

After. I'm. Gone.

TWENTY-NINE
Eye for an Eye

Dante had a very bad feeling about the man who'd knocked on his door, rousing him from sleep in the middle of the night.

It wasn't the look in the man's dark, dark eyes—a look so wild it was nearly unhinged—or his size, which was substantial, or the charcoal drawing he held in one crooked, bandaged hand, or the way he'd demanded to know where the girl in the drawing now lived.

It was the gun he pointed in Dante's face.

Slowly, with his hands held up in submission, the night air swirling around his bare shins beneath his robe, Dante repeated in a shaking voice what he'd just said, a lie he was hoping wouldn't get him killed.

"She moved out. I-I don't know where she went."

He said it in English this time, because the man with the gun clearly didn't speak Spanish. Dante had a fleeting, deranged thought that maybe the man spoke Martian. He had an unnervingly alien look about him, all eyes, teeth, and appetite.

Keeping his wild black gaze trained on his, the man silently stepped over the threshold into Dante's apartment. He kicked the door shut behind him, and Dante retreated, terrified but saying a silent prayer of thanks that Clare was in the hospital, and not in her bed in the second bedroom.

The man lowered the gun to the general level of Dante's crotch. "I'll give you three seconds. And then I'm going to start shooting things. Things that won't kill you right away, but will hurt. A lot." He paused as Dante gaped at him in horror, then said, "One."

"I told you! She moved out! I don't keep records of where the tenants go when they leave. She didn't tell me where she was moving—"

"Two." The man grew an ugly smile, a malicious specimen that bared his teeth in a truly horrific, animalistic display.

Dante was sweating. His heart raced, his hands trembled, his bowels threatened to spill their contents onto the tile floor. "I swear!" he shouted, backing away. "I don't know!"

"*Three.*"

The man's finger moved to the trigger and every thought except surviving blew out of Dante's head. "The docks! The docks at El Raval! The building is called *La Brisa Marina!*" He screamed it at the top of his lungs, then sucked back in a breath of dismay, instantly realizing what he'd done.

Ember would be getting a visit from this crazy man next.

Before he had time to contemplate that, the man smiled another of his feral smiles, darted forward in two short steps, and smashed the butt of his gun directly into Dante's temple.

Fireworks exploded behind his eyes. He staggered, and the ground came up hard to catch him.

Then there was only blackness, and the sound of satisfied laughter, quickly fading to silence as Dante was swallowed by the dark.

The sound of a ringing phone dragged Ember from the restless sleep she'd finally fallen into just after sunrise.

She lifted her head, blinking against the bright sunlight that spilled through the tall windows along the east wall, and yawned, looking around. She was in Christian's vast, sumptuous bed, alone; he was nowhere to be seen.

The phone rang and rang and rang. She finally spied it, an old-fashioned black rotary model on a desk across the room. She called out Christian's name and waited, but heard only the shrill ringing of the phone in answer.

She was nude—her pajamas were probably still shredded on the floor of the library—so she pulled the sheet from the bed and wrapped it around her as she crossed the room. Feeling a combination of anxiety, dread, and ambivalence, she laid her hand on the receiver and stood there debating with herself as the phone continued to ring.

Should she answer it? Should she go back to bed? Should she pretend to be the maid to whoever was calling?

Her mind seized on that idea and curiosity got the better of her. She decided that yes, she would be the maid and take a message for whoever was on the line.

She picked up the phone. Just as she was about to say hello, Christian's curt voice came on the other end.

"Yes."

He'd answered it from somewhere else in the house. They'd picked up at the same time. She was just about to hang up when she heard a masculine, accented voice, very similar to Christian's, but darker, much more tense.

"A goddamn answering machine wouldn't be too much to ask!"

"I was outside in the garden. Watching the sunrise. It took me a minute to come in."

Christian's voice was calm and unapologetic, and for some bizarre reason, Ember was proud of him, standing up to whoever this arrogant caller was without even getting ruffled.

The arrogant caller made a disgruntled sound that also managed to sound full of fondness. "Watching the sunrise? How terribly romantic. Going soft in your old age, brother?"

So this was Christian's older brother, Leander. Ember's fingers tightened around the phone. She had the sense to press the mute button, so no sound could be heard on her end. There was no way she was hanging up now.

"You have no idea," replied Christian.

There was a pause as Leander absorbed that. Then he said, "I got your message. So you found the son of a bitch."

Ember's heart screeched to a stop inside her chest.

Christian softly exhaled and made a noise of agreement.

"Tell me everything."

There was a command in Leander's voice, gentle but absolute, with a note of assumed compliance. Clearly, this was a man used to being obeyed.

"I caught the scent purely by accident. I've been near the spot before, but the wind was right last night, and I got lucky. They're in an abandoned bunker complex in the hills above the city."

"Bunker?" Leander sounded surprised.

"A remnant from the Spanish Civil War." Christian's voice turned grudgingly admiring. "It's perfect, actually. Good visibility from within, well-concealed from the outside, easy to protect. There are probably hidden exits all over the place, too. And, from what I was able to gather from the Internet, the network of tunnels and chambers beneath those bunkers are extensive. There's plenty of room for them to grow."

"But how are they keeping out of sight? A place like that seems like it would be crawling with tourists, history buffs—"

"The government cordoned off the whole area with barbed wire decades ago. Apparently there are unexploded land mines all over the place, left over from the war. They don't have enough money to do the necessary clearance and cleanup, so they just blocked it from public access."

"Jesus," said Leander. "How long can a land mine stay live?"

"Not sure. The government's plan is just to leave the area untouched until all the mines are defunct, but in the meantime—"

"It's a perfect hiding place for a nest of rats," Leander finished, his voice hard.

"Exactly. And since they can smell where any live munitions are and avoid them, there's no danger for their colony, but anyone else who might venture near—*kaboom!*"

There followed a long, tense silence. Ember held her breath, hoping neither of them could hear her thundering heartbeat through the phone line.

"Are you . . . taking care of it tonight, then?"

Leander sounded brusque, but beneath his businesslike tone, Ember heard the raw current of anguish. *Taking care of it* . . . she assumed that meant killing Caesar. Ember's hands shook so badly it was difficult to hold the phone to her ear.

Christian made another soft exhalation. "No, tomorrow night. Everything is ready, but I can't . . . I need one last day."

Leander's swallow was loud enough to be heard clear as if he'd uttered something. His voice very low, he said, "I understand."

"No, actually you don't."

"Christian—"

"I've met someone."

Those three words were blurted out, throbbing with emotion, and they took both Ember and Leander equally by surprise. There was a long, cavernous silence.

"A woman," Christian began to explain, but Leander cut him off.

"Dear, sweet God in heaven, are you *insane?*"

He was obviously horrified—horrified and furious. The words were shouted, reverberating with condemnation.

But Christian was having none of his brother's anger. He snapped, "Yes, I'm insane! Because sane people don't frequently volunteer for suicide missions!"

And with that, the bottom fell out of Ember's world.

She sank silently to her knees with the sheet clutched in her fist, frozen, blind, deaf except for those two words, repeating themselves over and over inside her mind.

Suicide mission.

Suicide mission.

Like the pieces of a dark, twisted puzzle, it all clicked into place. All the little things he'd said, hints of his plan and purpose, the research she'd done on the Internet, the look on his face, the look in his eyes when he told her she'd be taken care of for the rest of her life. Now it all made perfect, terrible sense.

He was here to kill the man who'd killed the pope, she knew that. But—according to eyewitness accounts from the Swiss Guard who'd attempted to gun Caesar down—he couldn't be killed. He'd been riddled with dozens upon dozens of bullets and had simply revived within seconds with a smile.

So how did you kill a man who couldn't be killed? Incinerate him in a super-heated fire? Melt him in molten steel? Blow him to smithereens in a huge explosion?

She didn't know. But if a gun wouldn't work, it had to be something far more violent, something that would obliterate all traces of a form that could simply regenerate itself when damaged.

"Anything that can be made can be *un*made; it's a natural law. Unfortunately, sometimes Nature needs a helping hand . . . and someone willing to get those helping hands dirty."

Christian had given her this terse explanation when she'd broached the subject on one of their walks. By his dark tone and even darker glower she'd understood that was the end of the conversation, but then he'd sighed and stared off into the distant horizon. He took her hand and an expression of quiet melancholy settled over his features, replacing the glower. Then in a soft, haunting voice, he'd added, "Sometimes sacrifices have to be made for the greater good."

"Sacrifices? Like what?" she'd asked sharply, hearing something in his tone. He'd looked at her and smiled, shaking his head as if dispelling an unpleasant thought.

"Like being away from you when all I want to do is spend every minute by your side."

He kissed her then, a soft press of his lips against hers before he pulled away, but it was enough to distract her. And his words were enough to flatter her into dropping the subject.

But now she realized the sacrifice Christian had been talking about . . . was *him*.

Whatever he had planned for Caesar, whatever mechanism he'd decided could kill an unkillable man, it would also take his own life in the process.

And he was going to do it tomorrow.

Tomorrow.

A hot whirlwind of panic descended on her. Shaking uncontrollably in shock, she sagged against the desk, unable to support her own weight.

Leander exploded. "Jesus, Christian! You're involved with a human woman? Of all the stupid things to do! How much does she know—"

"She's trustworthy!" Christian shouted back. "She'd never do anything to put me in danger—"

"It's not just you—it's the rest of us, too! How do you know she isn't some kind of spy, trying to get information about the rest of the colonies—"

"For fuck's sake, Leander! Give me some credit!"

"There's a huge bounty on all our heads, Christian! You think some *human* is going to pass up the opportunity to cash in—"

"*You're talking about the woman I love!*"

It was a primal thing, those seven screamed words, and Ember's body reacted to them on a purely primal level. She went cold then hot. Sweat broke out over her entire body. Her heart hammered against her breastbone and her chest constricted so tight she had to fight to breathe. It was only when she felt hot wetness dripping onto her bare leg that she realized she was crying.

Leander and Christian were both breathing hard, silent, the tension between them thick and sharp as knives. Finally Leander's voice, deadly soft, cut the silence.

"And this woman who you *love*—does she know why you're there? Does she know there's a ticking bomb over your head?"

Christian didn't answer.

"Right. So what's going to happen to her once you're gone?" His voice turned caustic. "Let's assume for an idiotic moment that you're right; she's trustworthy. She won't tell anyone anything, all our secrets are safe with her. Have you given any thought to what your death might do to *her*?"

His voice cracking, Christian said, "She'll be taken care of. I've made all the arrangements. This house is going to be hers—my inheritance will go to her—"

"So she's a gold digger, then? All she cares about is your money?"

Leander was being an ass, but Ember knew the point he was trying to make. And so did Christian, evidenced by his anguished, hollered answer.

"I KNOW IT'S WRONG, ALL RIGHT? I know it's fucked up and she'll get hurt and I'm the biggest, most selfish asshole in the world, but I didn't mean for it to happen! What the hell do you want me to say, Leander? I didn't mean for it to happen, but I fell in love with her! She makes me feel alive! She makes me feel like my life wasn't a complete waste! She makes me happy—you can understand that, can't you? She makes me happy the way Jenna makes you happy—was there ever any choice for you that you *wouldn't* fall in love with her? Did you have any control over that? Did you tell your heart, 'No, not going to go there, it's stupid and dangerous?' Because believe me, I tried! And it didn't fucking work!"

After Christian's outburst, Leander's silence felt deadly. He quietly asked, "And she feels the same way about you?"

There was a pause filled by the sound of Christian's labored breathing. He whispered, "Yes."

"Then I feel sorry for her."

Leander's tone had entirely changed. Vanished was the sarcasm, the anger and outrage, and in its place: weariness, and a bitter kind of disappointment. "Because I'd rather cut off my own arm than do anything to hurt my woman. But you were willing to let her fall in love with you, knowing there was no future for the two of you, knowing being with you would put her in danger, knowing full well there was nothing in it for her but pain. You, brother, are a *prick*."

"I know." Christian's voice broke. He sounded on the verge of tears. "And I hate myself, believe me. But I just couldn't stay away. I can't . . . I can't breathe without her, Leander. I tried, I tried *so hard* to let her go. But I couldn't. My heart didn't give me a choice."

There was a low, muttered curse, a long, aggravated sigh, then more silence. Finally, sounding resigned, Leander asked, "How can I help?"

Christian drew a few ragged breaths and Ember imagined him standing there with his jaw tight and his beautiful face flushed, running his hand through his thick dark hair. He said hoarsely, "Afterwards—when it's done—she'll need support. She doesn't have family . . . she'll need—"

"We'll be there," was his brother's instant reply.

"God . . . thank you Leander." The relief in Christian's voice was palpable, but Ember barely heard it over the howling ice storm inside her skull.

Christian was going to die.

Tomorrow.

Impossible! her mind screamed, reeling and recoiling from the horror of it. And then, as Christian and Leander continued to talk, their conversation fading from her hearing as if a dial had been turned down, Ember was gripped but the sudden, fierce conviction Christian was *not* going to die.

Because she was going to save him.

An eye for an eye. A tooth for a tooth. Her own life in trade for his. Then maybe, finally, her soul would be free.

She would find out what his plan was, and do it herself.

Ember waited until Christian and Leander disconnected their call, then with shaking hands she slowly returned the phone to its cradle. She knew if he found her like this, he would immediately be able to tell something was wrong, so she forced herself up, climbing to her feet by dragging herself up the desk with arms like rubber, and walked unsteadily into the bathroom. She shed the sheet on the floor,

turned on the water, and stood under the spray, not knowing whether it was hot or cold, if she was burning or freezing, because all her limbs had gone strangely numb under
the crushing weight of her new resolve.

Save him.

Yes, that's exactly what she was going to do.

THIRTY

The Woodshed

Disappointment was not something Thirteen was accustomed to, but as he stood in the slanting, sun-dappled light of the unfinished Sagrada Família cathedral's central nave, and stared up at the soaring columns, designed to look like a forest of trees rising from the floor to the vast, vaulted ceiling above, he felt its ugly sting, and was not pleased.

Today had not gone well.

First he'd been delayed at the hotel by a group of odd men who silently milled around the lobby like a swarm of restless sharks. He'd barely pressed through their sinister, black-clad bulk and made it to the street where he'd hoped to catch a taxi, when they'd exited the hotel en masse and shoved roughly past him into a cavalcade of black SUVs with dark tinted windows that pulled around the corner in a coordinated line and screeched to a stop at the curb. The line of bulky cars idled for a few more minutes, effectively blocking traffic on the narrow street, until another man appeared through the revolving glass doors of the hotel.

Thirteen narrowed his eyes at this new arrival. Big, bald, blinding white as snow on sunlight, he had burn scars on one side of his grim face and walked with a determined, rigid gait, as though in pain but trying not to show it.

Intrigued, Thirteen watched as the big albino climbed into the first SUV and drove away with the cavalcade following behind like ducklings following their mother, all in a row. He went back into the hotel and discreetly inquired at the front desk about the men who'd just left.

"*Sacerdotes*," came the response from the clerk. "*Desde el Vaticano.*"

If those were priests from the Vatican, he was Mickey Mouse.

But he decided to investigate that later, and finally hailed a taxi to take him to his first stop of the day: the catacombs beneath the *Església de Sant Just*, one of the city's oldest Christian churches, dating from the fourth century. Much smaller than those beneath Paris where the creatures he hunted once lived, these catacombs were darker and narrower and ultimately a bust.

That was just his first stop. There were many, many underground hiding spots on his list.

Over the past few days he'd explored the parts of the subway that had collapsed into a sinkhole and been abandoned. He explored the sewer system, the stone quarry, the archeological digs that exposed an ancient, subterranean Visigoth town. He'd searched three more churches, two cathedrals, and a castle, all rumored to have catacombs or large underground fortifications, but none of which did.

And now it was just before sunset and he stood empty-handed in the half constructed Sagrada Família with a knot of tourists chattering in a dozen different languages, and he was not happy.

He sighed and reached into his coat pocket. From it he withdrew a typed list, sent to him from the Chairman. There were half a dozen locations beneath those he'd crossed out so far, and the last one on the list looked interesting. *Spanish Civil War bunkers*, it read, with map coordinates beside it. He decided to try that one first tomorrow.

When he arrived back at the hotel, he was surprised to find the desk clerk he'd spoken to in the morning conferring quietly with two uniformed officers of the municipal police. Turning to another guest who had stopped near the door to stare at the pair of officers, Thirteen asked, "What's going on?"

To which the guest replied with his upper lip curled in distaste, "Some sicko strangled an animal and dumped it in the pool out back. Apparently it had been floating there for days before the gardener found it, bloated as hell." Thirteen knew the pool had been closed for the winter; the little sign on the front desk attested to that. The guest—a man in his early fifties, with short gray hair and the doughy paunch of someone who enjoys too much food and too little exercise—added, "Can you believe it?"

In fact, Thirteen had no problem believing it. People did all kinds of strange things. His curiosity piqued, he asked, "What kind of animal?"

With a quizzical look in his direction, the man replied, "A goat."

Then he walked away, while Thirteen mused over the kind of person who would strangle a goat and dump it into a public pool. A sick person no doubt—but a goat seemed an odd choice. Why not a cat, or a dog, something a little easier to come by in the middle of a city, and definitely more discreet than a large, ornery farm animal?

He watched two animal control personnel in khaki coats transport a dripping lump covered in a white sheet through the lobby on a stretcher. The dark shine of a cloven hoof peeked out from beneath one edge, and it occurred to him that a goat was far more symbolic than a house pet. Dogs weren't historically used as sin offerings, whereas goats . . . well, there was a reason behind the term "scapegoat."

A biblical reason.

Two and two clicked together in his mind like a plug into a socket, and Thirteen smiled to himself, wondering when the "priests" would be arriving back at the hotel.

He'd love to have a nice chat with the albino.

A survivor of the Majdanek death camp in Poland during World War II, Ursula Adamowicz was a woman who had long ago been stripped of fear.

By the age of ten, she'd seen both her parents murdered before her eyes, had survived rape, beatings, starvation, and torture, and been forced to watch as thousands of her countrymen were systematically eliminated by such wonderful means as firing squad and burning alive. Once the camp was liberated in 1944, she went to live with a distant relative in Spain, but they were poor, and life was hard. Life had never been anything but hard for Ursula, and she didn't expect it to be.

So the man standing before her with a gun pointed in her face was not much of a surprise. Or much of threat, for that matter.

"Which apartment?" the dark-haired man growled, holding up a drawing of a young woman.

Ursula inspected the drawing. Quite good, she thought. The artist had talent.

"Two-oh-four," she replied calmly, pointing to the end of the hall. "But she's not home. Hasn't been in a few days."

The man stepped forward in a menacing way, taut and wild-eyed, but Ursula merely raised her brows at him, refusing to step back and let him in her apartment. Clearly he didn't expect that, as he blinked at her, confused.

"I don't know what your business is with her, and I don't care," she said bluntly, staring down the barrel of the ominous silver gun. "But I do care if you get blood on the carpet. Bloodstains don't come out." Ursula knew from firsthand experience exactly which fabrics and materials bloodstains could be removed from. "So don't get any blood on the carpet, got it?"

The man blinked at her again, and Ursula shut the door in his face.

Then, with a better idea, she reopened the door. "She works at the little bookstore on Baixada Viladecols— Antiquarian, something like that. Six days a week. You'll find her there."

Then she shut the door in his face once again.

She waited a few minutes, until the sound of his receding footsteps had faded off into the evening, then picked up the phone and dialed a number she had written down a month ago and stuck to her refrigerator with a magnet. The number had been broadly advertised on television and radio, in all the papers internationally and locally, even in the gossip rags Ursula liked to read. It was a reward hotline for any information leading to the capture of the notorious terrorist who'd killed the pope, the man known only by the name Caesar.

Ursula knew the man at her door wasn't Caesar. But with those midnight black eyes, that dark hair, high cheekbones, and sharp, shiny teeth, he sure looked damn close. He was one of those creatures, she was sure of it.

And she knew where he was headed. That kind of information could be very, very lucrative indeed.

"I have to go out for a little while."

Obviously startled, Ember looked up at Christian from her chair on the back patio, and covered her eyes to shade them from the setting sun. He'd found her here, staring past the rose garden into the dark line of the forest beyond, with her legs pulled up under her chin, pensive and silent.

"Oh. Okay. See you later."

Christian frowned at this response. No "Where are you going?" No "Can I come with you?" It didn't seem like her.

Then again, she'd been acting strange all day. He'd gone to the bedroom after his call with Leander in the morning to find her already showered and dressed, standing at the windows with her arms hanging loosely at her sides, breathing deeply and staring off into space. Much like she was doing now. Senses prickling with the certainty something was wrong, he opened his nose, sniffing for the cool, bittersweet tang of sadness, the sour acidity of fear, the telltale heat and spice of anger.

What he smelled was only the natural perfume of her skin; warmed vanilla and orange blossom. He breathed a sigh of relief, crossed to her and pressed a kiss to the top of her head.

"Are you hungry? I can have some food brought out—"

She startled him by looking up into his eyes and blurting in a low, terse voice, "I'm only hungry for you, Christian. Always, only you."

She reached up, grasped his face, and pulled him down for a fevered and demanding kiss. He broke away with a groan when he felt the all-too-familiar flash of heat to his groin, and chuckled, pulling her out of her chair and wrapping his arms around her. He nuzzled his face into her neck, inhaling the clean, woodsy scent of her hair.

"I'm glad to hear it. But I'll never get anything done if you keep kissing me like that," he said, smiling.

"How long will you be gone?" she asked into his shirt, her voice still low.

He stroked his hands over her hair and down her back, trailing his nose down her throat to the warm, steady pulse at the base of her neck. "Just an hour or two."

He'd arranged a late meeting with the manager at his local bank; he was going to finalize the paperwork that would transfer all his liquid assets to a trust in Ember's name. He meant what he'd told her: she'd be well taken care of, for the rest of her life. That was the one thing of which he was determined to make sure.

She tipped her head back and looked at him, really *looked* at him, her eyes shadowed and intense, her gaze lingering over his face as if trying to memorize his features. Slanting sunlight caught in her lashes and tipped them fairy dust gold.

Somewhere in the garden, a bird began to trill a song, notes that rose and fell and rose again, haunting and sweet.

"I'll be waiting for you," she whispered, staring deep into his eyes. "Don't take too long."

Christian frowned at her, certain there was something he was missing, some hidden meaning beneath those words that her tone and the haunting birdsong hinted at, but then she broke into one of her brilliant, heartbreaking smiles, and his heart melted like a pat of butter on a hot scone.

She kissed him again and then pushed him away, still smiling. "Go on, then. Go get your work done. And when you get back . . . " she cocked a seductive eyebrow, "we'll have dinner in bed."

"Oh, you evil temptress," he said, smiling back at his love, "you have no idea."

She blew him a kiss and he turned and left, eager to get the errand over with, eager to get back into her waiting arms.

Eager to make every last second together they had really count.

Ember watched him go and felt all her false bravado, and the tenuous calm it had taken her all day to perfect, unravel.

A sob rose in her throat; she smothered it with the back of a hand to her mouth. She couldn't cry now—not while he was still so close, not when she still had so much left to do.

There would be time enough for crying later.

Knowing he'd be able to sense her moods, she'd done her absolute damndest to quell any stray emotions with the deep breathing and visualization exercises she'd learned all those years ago when she first went into therapy. Calm was a state relatively easy to achieve if one knew how . . . but extraordinarily difficult to maintain over hours, with adrenaline flooding the central nervous system. She done it with a strength of will she didn't even realize she had, because she had to fool Christian before she could save him.

She made her way to the front drawing room and watched Christian's Audi slowly pull away from the circular driveway and disappear up the long gravel road. Then she turned and ran up the curved staircase, her heart pounding like a drum, every nerve on fire.

She checked the master bedroom first. Closets, desks, beneath the bed, in the bathroom. Nothing. She rifled through drawers in the library, she upended boxes that turned out to contain only files, she peered into cupboards and cabinets and the dark, dusty niches of the attic.

Nothing.

Room by room she swept the mansion, looking for anything deadly, any poison or bombs or strange-looking devices, anything that screamed *I can kill you!*

But she found nothing. She even searched Corbin's room because he'd left with Christian, the housekeeper's room because she was out shopping, and the groundskeeper's room because he was off on the east side of the front of the property, mowing the emerald lawn. There wasn't a single thing in the entire mansion that hinted at danger, at least nothing she was able to find.

The frantic search took over two hours. The sun had dipped below the horizon. At any moment, Christian would come back, and her window of opportunity would vanish.

Panicked, shaking with tension and about to burst into hysterical tears, she ran out the back door and looked wildly around the elegant patio, the rambling garden, the burbling fountain surrounded by a circle of uneven stones.

That's when she saw the woodshed.

Dreary and decrepit, it stood off to her left, partially obscured by a thicket of pines. The moment she saw it she knew it was where she needed to go.

The hinges made an eerie groan when she opened the door. It was dark and dusty, filled with cobwebs, and smelled of damp wood and mold. There was no light so she stayed still a moment, allowing her eyes to adjust, and just looked around.

A cord of wood, stacked teetering along one wall. A bare dirt floor, a small rack of saws and tools, a large plastic chest near the back.

The chest sported a large, shiny padlock, obviously new. Unlike everything else in the shed, the chest was not covered in a thick layer of dust.

Ember's heart began to pound even harder.

Big enough to fit a body in, she thought in mounting dread as she ran her hands over the smooth plastic lid. The realization that Christian might keep the key somewhere in the house, or even on him at all times, didn't deter her from looking for it anyway. She felt under the edge of the lid, all around the bottom, strained her eyes for any small nook or cranny in the walls where one could hide a key. She looked everywhere, until the dirt floor finally revealed a clue.

In the dust were two sets of footprints. Her own, and one much larger pair. They crisscrossed and obliterated each other in some places, but there was one place her own prints did not go but the others did: to the rack of tools on the opposite wall.

Ember stood in front of the rack and just stared at it, every cell in her body screaming for her to hurry. On the very back of the lowest shelf, past the handsaw, ball-peen hammer, and a rusted, bitless drill, there was a rock. A rock without a speck of dust that sported a perfectly flat bottom.

A bottom that opened when twisted, revealing a tiny silver key.

Ember tossed the plastic hide-a-key to the floor and fit the key into the padlock on the chest. She opened the lid, peered down at its contents, and felt all the blood drain away from her face. Her mouth went dry and her pounding heart stuttered to a dead stop inside her chest.

She had found what she was looking for.

THIRTY-ONE
Beautiful Monster

In retrospect, Ember's plan wasn't much of a plan at all. In fact, it could quite accurately be called a classic example of delusional thinking.

She wasn't stupid; she realized what a piss-poor operation this was, but on such short notice it was really the only option available. As the cab slid away from the front gate of the mansion, she wished she were religious. Given the circumstances of the moment, prayer seemed apropos.

The cell phone in her jacket pocket rang and she gasped, startled, nerves frayed. She answered it with shaking hands, swallowing the hysterical sob that threatened to burst from her throat.

"Hello?"

"Ember! Oh my God, did you hear what happened to Dante?"

It was Asher, shrieking at her from the other end of the line. She sat forward on the seat, muscles as rigid as the old leather. "What do you mean? What happened?"

"He was attacked by some psycho with a gun—who was looking for *you!*"

At the exact moment the breath left her lungs, Ember spotted Christian's black Audi flying up the opposite side of the mountain road about half a mile away. She threw herself down on the back seat, flattened herself against it, and whispered into the phone, "Oh, God, no! Is he all right? Tell me what happened—is he hurt? Where is he? Where's Clare?"

Terror, dark and encompassing, gripped her. She clutched the phone so hard she thought it would splinter to pieces in her hands.

"They're both at the hospital. Clare wasn't home at the time, thank God! She was getting her treatments for cystic fibrosis. Dante's going to be okay, but Jesus Christ, Ember—a man with a gun is looking for you!"

Ember swallowed, fighting the panic that wanted to claw its way out of her chest. "I know."

Asher gasped, "*What?* How do you know if you didn't know about Dante? Forget that—where are you? I'm coming to get you and we're going to the police—"

"No. No police. I'm taking care of this myself."

Her voice, though shaking, was firm enough to give Asher pause. "What the hell are you talking about?" he demanded. "Does this have to do with Christian?"

She hadn't told him she'd moved in with Christian, because at the time, she'd thought it was temporary and she'd be back at her apartment before he could find out. She also hadn't told him she was the target of a mass murderer, that Christian was on a suicide mission, or that she'd decided to take care of that last thing herself. At this moment, knowing she only had a few hours left, she thought there was really only one important thing Asher should know.

"I love you, Ash," she said, and now her voice went beyond shaking; it broke. Tears began to gather, hot and prickling, in her eyes. "You were the best friend I ever had—the best friend anyone could ever have, and I'm so grateful to have known you."

She felt his shock, his growing horror at the realization that something was very, very wrong. "Ember. Whatever this is about, we can fix it together—"

"I want you to know that no matter what happens, you did everything right by me. I know you; don't second-guess yourself. You're amazing, and I love you, and . . . and . . . "

She had to stop because her throat closed. Tears began to stream down her cheeks and she wiped them angrily away with the back of her hand. "I love you, that's all, okay?"

"Ember! Goddammit! What the hell is going on! Where are—"

"Good-bye," Ember whispered, and pressed "End" on the phone.

The only sound in the cab for a few moments was the flamenco station on the radio. Ember guessed the driver didn't speak English—either that or he was used to having hysterical females lying down on the back seat of his cab, saying teary goodbyes to their best friends.

The phone rang again. Assuming it was Asher, she looked at the screen and was shocked to see it was her stepmother, Marguerite.

She remembered a documentary she'd once seen on television about ancient torture methods. The one that had struck her as somehow the worst was stoning; not the kind where angry townsfolk lobbed rocks at you until you died, but the pressing kind where they strapped you to the ground and placed a big board over your chest, then slowly and methodically added weight in the form of large stones until your ribcage snapped and all your organs were crushed.

Looking at the readout on the phone, she felt exactly that.

She clicked the "send" button and whispered a hello.

"Well, *hello*, September," came an unfamiliar male voice, silken and purring and dark. "I'm so glad you answered your phone. And your stepmother is glad, too."

In the background, Ember heard a long, trembling wail of pain, and all the tiny hairs on her body stood straight on end.

"W-who is this?"

The caller clucked his tongue. "I'll give you three itty bitty guesses. But I'd advise you to make it quick—I'm not sure how much more mileage I can get out of our Marguerite, here. We've had a bit of fun, but the old gray mare is fading fast."

"Caesar," she breathed, choked in horror.

"Bingo!" came the delighted response. There was a pause, then he added, "That is the right use of the word, isn't it? Bingo? I've never actually played the game, but I understand when you get the right answer you shout the word at the top of your—"

"You sick son of a bitch!"

This was screeched as Ember kicked the door, realizing Caesar was, at that moment, doing something very bad to her stepmother. Though she hated the woman and had often wished her ill, falling into Caesar's hands was not something she would wish on anyone. The taxi driver flicked her a disinterested glance in the rearview mirror, then turned his attention back to the road; just another routine drop off.

On the other end of the line, Caesar chuckled in glee. "Oh, dear! Someone sounds a bit *put out*. Well, I know how awful it is when things don't go your way. But surely you must realize I have no interest in you—forgive me, but you really aren't that interesting. You know who I want." His voice hardened, losing all its playful lightness, and like a snake he hissed, "Give him to me and your stepmother lives."

Ember's mind was a sudden tangle of flying goose feathers. This wasn't something she anticipated. She'd have to get Caesar to let Marguerite go before she could get him alone—but how was she going to do that?

"I-I'll need proof that she's okay. You have to let her go first—"

"Plain *and* stupid, hmmm? She's not going anywhere until I have what I want."

Ember swallowed, shaking hard. "I don't know where he is right now," she said, stalling for time to think.

"Let me worry about the details, September. I assume you have a way to contact him?"

She whispered, "Yes."

Caesar made a noise of approval. "Just come to me and I'll take care of the rest. Once I have what I want, you and your stepmother can go. As I said, I have no interest in you. You're just a means to an end. Give me what I want and neither of you will get hurt. Or . . . "

There was a pause, then a scream came over the line, hair-raising, vibrating with agony.

" . . . or I'm going to make you both suffer so badly you'll beg for death, and I won't give it to you." His voice had dropped to a husky, excited whisper, and Ember's skin crawled in horror.

Whatever he was doing to Marguerite, he was enjoying it.

"Where . . . where do I go?"

"Your bookstore." There was a slight pause, another broken scream from Marguerite, then he added darkly, "You better hurry," and disconnected the call.

The cell phone in Christian's pocket rang and he answered it without looking at the screen.

His attention was fully absorbed with thoughts of Ember, of getting back to her and getting her in his arms. He and Corbin were almost home; it wouldn't be long now. And in the two hours since he'd left her, Christian had a revelation.

He couldn't do it.

He couldn't leave her alone.

He'd been sitting there with the banker and the transfer paperwork, staring at the pen in his hand, when that epiphany had stolen his breath.

Ember mattered more to him than anything. His family, his future, even his *honor*.

How could he abandon her? How could he voluntarily die, now that he had something so precious to live for?

Put simply, he couldn't. The thought of leaving her burned like acid in his throat.

So Christian tore up the paperwork and ran out of the bank, thinking he'd just have to make alternate plans to kill that bastard Caesar. Now that Christian knew his whereabouts, he could lay low and determine some other way to wipe him from the face of the earth that didn't include getting himself killed in the process.

Ember. That's all he could think about now. His heart pounded in anticipation.

He was so eager to see her he even imagined he could smell her. A hint of orange blossom teased his nose, and he closed his eyes, inhaled deeply, and relaxed back into the plush leather seat. He must have her scent on his shirt from when they'd said good-bye earlier; it was so luscious a flash of heat tightened his groin. He almost groaned with hunger for her.

Into the phone, he said, "Yes."

"Good evening, Mr. McLoughlin. This is Dr. Katharine Flores," a woman said in response. Christian frowned, not recognizing the name.

"Dr. Flores? I'm sorry, are we acquainted?"

"I'm September's psychiatrist. Is this a good time for us to speak?"

Christian's attention snapped back into the present and honed in on the ominous note in the woman's voice. "How did you get this number?" he asked, instantly, violently on edge.

"September listed you as her emergency contact on her treatment form."

Christian realized several things simultaneously. One: Ember had listed him as her emergency contact during the two weeks they hadn't been speaking and she'd first seen this doctor, which he guessed meant she assumed he'd refuse to hear anything about her and would just hang up. That made his heart ache as if someone had put a hammer to it. Two: this phone call was not going to make him happy.

He growled, "What's this about?"

She began hesitantly, her voice full of professional concern. "Well, this is a delicate situation, but September signed a standard release waiver allowing me to communicate the details of her medical history with other healthcare professionals or immediate family if I felt it necessary to the success of her treatment plan."

"Go on," he insisted, bolting upright in the seat. It became a little harder to breathe.

"And, I must admit, after speaking with a few of her former doctors, I'm very worried for her. For her safety."

Christian felt as if he'd been injected with adrenaline. A cold sweat broke out all over his body and his heart throbbed painfully. He said, "Former doctors?"

Dr. Flores paused for a moment that felt like years. Then she asked in a gently compassionate tone, "If I might ask— are you aware of Ember's history with mental illness?"

"Mental illness?" he repeated in a horrified whisper. Everything beyond the sound of Dr. Flores's voice faded to black.

"I'm guessing by the tone of your voice that's a no." She sighed. "That's very common; many patients are reluctant to share that kind of information with people they care about, fearing it will drive them away."

"I . . . the accident that killed her family. I know she was . . . she's understandably haunted by that—"

"The clinical term is 'survivor guilt.' It's a symptom of posttraumatic stress disorder, and in Ember's case it's quite severe. Sufferers blame themselves for the deaths of others, even though there was nothing they could have done to save them. It's commonly found among survivors of combat or natural disasters, even among friends and family of people who commit suicide. It's extremely debilitating, and, in my clinical experience, sufferers of this particular syndrome are prone to very self-destructive behaviors. Even to the point of taking their own lives."

From Christian's throat came a strangled, incoherent noise.

"Ember believes she is responsible for the automobile accident that killed her mother and brother—"

"She was drinking—she told me all about it!" Christian choked out. His throat was so constricted his voice sounded unnatural. Corbin glanced at him in the rearview mirror, his brows raised.

"That is the script her mind has adopted to cope with the guilt of surviving. It's an adaptive reaction to unbearable stress. You see, Mr. McLoughlin, the truth of the matter is that Ember had a single drink—a light beer—at a friend's house prior to driving home to pick up her mother and brother that night before dinner. She had a blood alcohol level of exactly zero when she was tested at the accident site, and several witnesses testified that the single drink she'd had was hours before she got into the car. There was a comprehensive investigation, as you can imagine, but Ember was cleared of any wrongdoing. The car simply hydroplaned in the rain.

"But for Ember, the accident is entirely her fault. Her mind has created an alternate version of how much she had to drink that night. Put another way, her mind's way of dealing with the terrible reality of being the only survivor of a crash that killed her mother, younger brother and eleven other people was simply to . . . improvise. The human brain is a beautiful monster, Mr. McLoughlin. When it works perfectly, it's a miracle of engineering. But it also possesses the ability to cannibalize itself until there is nothing left of what you and I would call the 'truth.'"

"Oh God," Christian whispered, remembering in excruciating detail the expression on Ember's face when he'd thrown her out of his house that night. The absolute self-loathing, the black, bottomless depth of despair.

It was a lie. She didn't kill anyone. The only thing she was guilty of was surviving when everyone else died.

"The reason I'm telling you this, Mr. McLoughlin, is that I'd like you to be involved in her treatment, if at all possible. The more support she has, the better her chances of recovery. I don't know if she's still cutting herself—"

"Cutting!" Christian hissed, physically sickened at the thought of Ember hurting herself.

"Yes, apparently that was an issue when she lived in the States. Her last doctor prescribed lithium to manage her depression, although I doubt if she's still taking it—if indeed she ever did. The medication would have done too much to dull the pain. Pain she very much feels she deserves."

Christian fought the urge to scream. To smash something with his bare fists. To beat something bloody.

"I'd like you to watch her very carefully for the next few months for any signs that she may be hurting herself physically, and let me know. Also . . . please keep this call between the two of us. At this point in her treatment, it will do more harm than good if she feels cornered. I'll suggest to her during our next session that she start bringing you along, perhaps once a month, and we can go from there. Does that sound all right with you?"

Christian was speechless. He felt as if someone had just cut his legs off at the knee.

"I know it's a lot to process. Please call me if you have any questions; once you've had a chance to absorb this, we can talk further."

As if from the bottom of a deep, black well, Christian heard his voice thanking her and saying good-bye.

When he arrived home, he felt Ember's absence in the house as a solid coldness inside his chest as soon as he crossed the threshold of the front door. He ran from room to room calling her name, he dialed her cell phone over and over, but there was no answer.

Then he found the letter.

Left on top of the Steinway where they'd made love, it was folded in thirds and enclosed in an envelope that also held the necklace she always wore, the fine chain with her parents' gold wedding rings.

The letter tore his heart out of his chest, ripped it in two, and left it broken and bloody on the floor.

Then, when he found the door to the woodshed open, the plastic chest inside empty, the pain turned to panic, which turned to cold, limb-numbing horror.

Because he realized exactly what Ember was going to do.

THIRTY-TWO
Eternal Flame

Dear Christian,

As I write those words, I'm smiling. People use the word "dear" all the time without really thinking about what it means, but that is exactly what you are to me: dear. Beloved. I never imagined I would feel that for anyone, much less someone as amazing as you. You told me I make you feel free, but you gave me something even better, something I will never be able to adequately express—at least not in words.

You showed me the way out of hell.

For that, I will love you forever.

I want you to know I realize this won't be easy for you. I know how much this will hurt, how you'll blame yourself, how you'll wish you could have done something differently. And I'm sorry. Please believe me when I say that, because it's true. But you are strong and I am so, so weak—you will survive this. Please forgive me. Please live your life and find someone who deserves you, someone kind, and beautiful, and unbroken. Don't let the memory of me ruin even a single day.

Because this is the only thing I can do that will make up for everything bad that came before. I know that now. And because of you—because you loved me—I'm not afraid.

You make me unafraid. Do you have any idea what a gift that is?

It's beyond a gift. It's a blessing.

You found me in the dark, you shone your light on me, and you made me feel beautiful, for the very first time in my life. I want to say thank you for that. I want to say it to your face and then kiss you, but this letter will have to do. Know that if I could, right now I'd be kissing you, because that's one of the best things I ever knew.

Humans can be bonded mates, too—I wasn't sure if you knew that. I suppose it doesn't happen very often, but it can. I'm proof of it. There is nothing in this life or any other I wouldn't do for you. I love you, and all the broken things inside me love you, too. I'm sorry now that I didn't say it out loud, that I didn't tell you how I felt over and over. You are the dream that I didn't deserve, but am so grateful for.

I love you, Christian. I love you.

That is the one thing I got right. Loving you made all the rest of it—the years of darkness and hell—worthwhile.

Even if we'd only had a single day together, it still would have been worth it.

If I believed in heaven, I'd say I hope to see you there one day. But I know there are no angels on clouds, no cherubs, or singing choirs waiting for me. I don't know what will come once

I've left this life behind, but in my heart of hearts I hope it's just . . . peace. Quiet. An end to all the pain and madness.

Only one thing will never end: my love for you. No matter where I go after I'm dead, you will be with me. You will be the flame in my soul that never burns out.

Always. Forever. Until the end of time.

Ember

THIRTY-THREE
Operation

Sitting across from him at a small wooden table in the quiet, shadowed courtyard in the back of the budget motel, the albino was hulking and silent, staring at Thirteen with a narrowed gaze that held all the geniality of a dragon about to spew fire on a group of screaming villagers.

He'd caught the albino's attention with a few well-chosen words. He'd walked right up to him in the lobby when he and his black-clad minions had arrived a few moments ago, looked into his scarred, ghost-pale face and said in a placid voice, "I understand you're a priest. I'd like to make a confession. Involving a dead goat."

Then Thirteen had smiled at the albino, a mild curve of his lips that was non-threatening and sincere, but also managed to convey he knew that they both knew exactly who should really be making confessions involving dead goats, and perhaps they should have a chat about that.

The albino hadn't said a word to him, or to his minions. He'd simply looked at him a moment—looked *into* him, as if trying to slip inside his body using only his colorless eyes—then jerked his chin at his head minion—*leave us.* The head minion and the others immediately and silently had. Then the albino had jerked his chin toward the opposite side of the lobby at the swinging glass doors that led to the back courtyard, where they now sat across from each other in semi-darkness under the spreading branches of a ficus tree festooned with drooping strands of tiny white lights.

Because the albino didn't seem like the chatty type, Thirteen decided to break the ice by getting directly to the point. "I'm called Doc. I'm a hunter. Like you."

If the albino had eyebrows, they would have risen at those words, but since he appeared to be totally hairless—lacking even eyelashes—Thirteen only knew the albino was surprised when three sharp creases appeared in his white, unlined forehead.

Thirteen shrugged. "I can tell by looking at people. You're either one of two things: a meat-eater or the meat."

The albino absorbed that in silence.

"I received a phone call a few minutes ago—just before you arrived, in fact—that the . . . creatures . . . I'm hunting have been found. At least, I know exactly where *one* of them is now, or will be shortly."

This was both carefully worded bait and the unvarnished truth, as Thirteen had been informed by an email from the Chairman that the tip line he'd set up had yielded credible information from a woman named Ursula

Adamowicz. A suspected *Ikati* was stalking a girl that worked at a little bookstore on the Baixada Viladecols. The store was closed at this hour, so the creature would either lie in wait inside, or keep surveillance somewhere nearby. Either way, the information was the most interesting they'd had in months.

But even more interesting was the way the albino reacted to what he'd said.

He jerked forward in his chair. One big, white hand shot out, lightning fast, and he curled his fist around Thirteen's shirt collar. The albino yanked him forward so they were nose to nose across the table, and growled, "Tell me where they are or I'll cut off your tongue!"

So—Doc's suspicions were confirmed. This goat murderer was looking for them, too. Considering the city was crawling with mercenaries eager to get their hands on the reward money, it wasn't much of a surprise.

"I know a dozen ways to kill a man with my bare hands, *freund*," replied Thirteen in a soft voice, staring unflinchingly into the albino's eyes. "And a hundred more to kill you with the blade stashed up my sleeve. So I'll give you a second to decide if you'd rather fail at cutting off my tongue and have my knife embedded in your brain, or if you'd like to hear what I propose."

The albino's gaze flickered to Thirteen's hands, spread flat in readiness against the surface of the table. A muscle in his jaw worked as he swiftly calculated his options. Then he opened his hand and slowly relaxed back into his chair, the flush of blood rising in his pale cheeks the only indication of his rage. His glittering gaze settled on Thirteen's face, and he inclined his head.

Thirteen adjusted the collar of his shirt. "Good choice," he said, unruffled. "As I was about to say before I was so rudely interrupted, if we find one of the creatures, we can find them all—"

"How?"

He smirked. "A pair of pliers. A chain saw. An electric drill. Take your pick."

For the first time, the albino smiled. It was a carnivorous, teeth-flashing grin that would have looked at home on a shark.

Thirteen continued as though he hadn't been interrupted by such a naïve question. "The organization I work for has very close ties with the police, so I could avail myself of them and their resources, but in my experience they'll do more harm than good."

He resisted the urge to adjust the patch over his eye, remembering exactly how badly his last experience with the police had ended.

"My own team and supplies are fifteen hours out. Twelve at best. This particular situation requires a much quicker response or we'll probably lose the target, so I'd have to work fast, and alone, neither of which are optimal for my chances of success." Thirteen's mild, knowing smile returned. "Unless I can temporarily partner with someone who's already here."

He watched the albino process it. His sharky smile faded, and that muscle in his jaw began to jump again, making the ruined skin that covered it purse and pucker. "I don't like partners," he pronounced, ominously low.

"Agreed. But I also don't like letting a golden opportunity slip through my fingers. I'm willing to sacrifice my personal preferences in order to gain what I want." He paused dramatically. "And you can have all the reward money. I don't care about that."

Technically, he wasn't even eligible to receive the reward money because it was the Chairman who was offering it, but the albino didn't have to know it. But then the albino hotly snapped, "Neither do I!" and it was Thirteen's turn to raise his brows.

Judging by the rancor in the answer, he'd offended him. He wouldn't have thought it possible to offend a man who got his kicks squeezing the life out of farm animals, but then again, the hypocrisy of someone who posed as a priest from the Vatican while engaging in said squeezing could not be underestimated.

Thirteen drawled, "A fellow purist, eh?"

"Some things are more sacred than money," the huge albino whispered with a lunatic gleam in his eye, and Thirteen couldn't help the chuckle that escaped him.

"You see that? We're in agreement again. This is looking quite positive."

The albino gazed at him in silence for a long, long time, while the voice of the city at night murmured in the cool air around them.

"It's a very simple equation," Thirteen said reasonably, feeling the other man's animosity like an iceberg between them, frozen and hard, the vast bulk of it invisible but far larger and more dangerous than what was out in the open. "I have something you need, and you have something I need. And . . . " he spread his hands open as if presenting evidence, "you already know you can trust me."

"And how do I know that?" came the instant, ferocious reply.

Thirteen sat back in his chair and clasped his hands over his stomach. "If you couldn't, it would be the police who'd be sitting here talking to you right now regarding the matter of one strangled goat."

The albino spat, "I don't know anything about a goat!"

Thirteen smiled indulgently. "Of course you don't. And believe me, I don't judge. But the police are a little less open-minded than I am, which I happen to know because I have quite a few friends in law enforcement. They might like to search your room for any, oh I don't know, animal blood or hair, just in case."

Deadly silence. A black, smoldering glower. Then, finally, the albino's mouth quirked into an odd, pinched sneer of respect, and he nodded.

Thirteen's smile grew wider. Then he leaned forward and began to outline his plan.

As the blade sliced through the tender flesh of her left forearm, Ember abandoned all the courage she'd managed to muster on the cab ride to the bookstore, and screamed.

"Well," said Caesar, her screams rising to an ear-splitting pitch as he dug deeper, "she's not much to look at, but she's got a pair of lungs on her to rival Pavarotti's, doesn't she boys?"

Chuckles from the four others with him, two of whom held her immobile against her father's scarred old desk in the back room of the bookstore while Caesar investigated her arm with the cold, serrated tip of his knife.

He'd smelled metal the instant she'd walked through the door, and, desperate to offer him an explanation that would keep them from locating what was hidden beneath her bulky sweater and coat, she'd shoved up the sleeve of the sweater to reveal her scarred, metal-filled arm.

Had she known it would induce this little game of Operation, she might have tried something else.

Agony throbbed through every cell in her body. The room spun; color, sound, and scent were magnified a thousandfold, hallucinogenic in their pulsating violence.

"Well done, Nico. You're officially off my shit list," Caesar said to one of the tall, black-haired males standing off to the side who was watching the scene with smug pride. He clutched a bandaged hand to his chest, but when he heard those words, he dropped his hand to his side, broke into a huge, exultant smile, and stood straighter.

"Please," sobbed Marguerite. Strapped to a chair several feet away with plastic zip ties cutting into her wrists and ankles, she was barely able to hold her head upright.

Ember had nearly gagged in horror when she'd first spied her stepmother. Blood saturated the bodice of her ripped black dress, dripped into a hideously gleaming red pool beneath the chair with an intermittent, sinister splash. Through the rips in the fabric, her breasts and abdomen showed pale against the lurid sheen of crimson. A series of oozing, irregular wounds gave awful testament to what had occurred inside this room before Ember arrived.

"Please," Marguerite gasped again, her eyelids fluttering as she struggled to keep them open. Her dark hair had come undone from her bun, and hung around her shoulders in a wild, gray-streaked mane. "Please stop. Please let us go."

"Oh—absolutely! All you had to do was say the magic word!"

The others laughed, while Caesar, seeming energized by the agony, by all the blood, turned away from Ember to gaze in amused affection at the blood-splattered, semi-conscious Marguerite.

Suddenly he went rigid, and sniffed the air like a hound scenting a fox. Then he whirled back around and stared at Ember with eyes very wide and black.

Handsome as the devil, tall and well-made and obviously insane, he cocked his head and let his gaze travel up and down her body while she sat there in an agonized haze, blood gushing from the gaping slices in her arm. His lips parted and a look of erotic, exultant fervor shone from his eyes. He whispered, "Oh my. What a wonderful, unexpected surprise you are, my plain little rabbit. You're not only a pair of big lungs, now, are you? No, you're something *much* more valuable than that."

Then he moistened his lips and, as Ember tried to recoil in absolute terror and failed because of the iron clamps of his men's hands around her biceps, wrists, and the back of her neck, Caesar leaned close to her mangled arm and inhaled, slowly and deeply.

After a moment of weighted silence, he straightened, threw back his head, and laughed.

He laughed, and laughed, and laughed—uproariously, with total abandon—while his men exchanged glances, Marguerite sobbed, and Ember's heart shrank to the size of a peanut inside her chest.

"Holy Horus," he gasped between hoots, "I swear I have the best fucking luck!"

"Er, sire?" one of the other men asked uncertainly.

Caesar, swiping happy tears from his eyes, waved a hand, indicating he couldn't yet respond because he was too racked with laughter. As he took a slow turn around the room clutching his stomach, the maniacal laughter eventually faded to a series of long, blissful sighs punctuated by disbelieving chuckles. He dragged another chair across the room and set it right next to Marguerite, sat down in it and began idly playing with her hair while he stared, smiling, at Ember.

He said something to his men in a language Ember didn't recognize, though it might have been Latin. Whatever it was, his men gasped and shared meaningful glances with one another. They looked back at her with something new in her eyes. Then the men holding her released her arms and pushed her back into her chair.

Ember moaned in pain and clamped her right hand over the throbbing wound in her left forearm, trying to put pressure on it to stop the bleeding.

But the bleeding was bad. Blood spurted between her fingers in a pulsating stream. It looked like an artery had been severed.

"Do you have a first aid kit, little rabbit?" Caesar suddenly appeared concerned, with a furrow between his brows, the laughter vanished as he stared at her arm.

"Fuck you," Ember hissed, almost unable to answer through the pain.

"I'll take that as a no. But we can't have you bleeding out on us quite yet."

He pursed his lips, twirling a lock of Marguerite's long hair between his fingers while she leaned as far away from him as she could, sagging sideways over the arm of her chair, sobbing quietly.

Then Caesar brightened, leapt to his feet, and approached Ember with a wicked gleam in his eye. "You know, there's something I've been meaning to try. And you, little rabbit, have just given me the perfect opportunity!"

Ember's hands shook uncontrollably. The smell of blood was overpowering, sharp and penny bright in the air. Her stomach heaved and she tasted the sour bite of bile in the back of her throat. She stared at the advancing Caesar, so like Christian in his effortless grace and beauty, his perfect skin and teeth and hair, and fought desperately to maintain a semblance of control. She needed to keep her wits about her, because as soon as she could get him away from Marguerite, this bastard was toast.

Trying to rise, she lurched forward in the chair, but hands clamped around her shoulders and roughly shoved her back. She gasped as a bolt of agony seared a path up her left arm and straight down her spine. The room narrowed to a small circle of receding light, as if viewed from the end of a very long tunnel.

Then Caesar slapped her hard across the face.

Her head rocked back; all the bones in her neck popped. Reeling, she cried out and jerked upright in shock.

"That's better," said Caesar as she straightened. He sounded satisfied. He leaned down, placed his hands on his thighs and smiled at her. Then he wagged a finger in her face, tutting like a mother scolding an errant child. "No passing out on me. I need you lucid. We haven't even gotten to the good bit yet."

He straightened and gestured to his men, and she was suddenly over the table again, her chest and cheek pressed flat against the wood. One hard, large hand held her head immobile when she struggled to free her arms, similarly pinned. Caesar picked up his knife from the corner of the desk, stroked a finger up its edge and said, "Stop struggling or stepmommy loses an ear."

Panting in panic, Ember fell still. She cut her gaze to Marguerite, who seemed to be praying. Her eyes were squeezed shut tight and her lips were moving rapidly with silent words.

Caesar came and stood over Ember. He gently turned her left palm up, revealing the mangled mess of the inside of her forearm. He put the knife between his teeth, slowly rolled up the sleeve of his white shirt to reveal a tanned, muscular forearm, and held it out directly above Ember's own arm. Then he took the knife from between his teeth and in one hard, slashing motion, cut deep into his own skin, straight across the vein.

Blood sprayed from the wound. Horror dried her tongue to jerky in her mouth.

No one else in the room seemed particularly surprised by this turn of events, however. Caesar's men held her down while he calmly held his outstretched arm over hers and let the torrent of blood rain down over her wounds.

"Oh my," he breathed, his voice trembling with excitement. "Look at all that *blood*."

With her head on the desk, Ember was eye level with Caesar's crotch. Beneath his blood-spattered pants, she saw him grow instantly hard. She squeezed her eyes shut in disgust.

But then . . . burning.

Itching, like a thousand biting fire ants nibbling on her skin. A wave of heat enveloped her body, and she was drenched in sudden sweat. It became very hard to breathe; the earlier nausea returned with a vengeance. She thought she would throw up.

"*Olé!*" cried Caesar, satisfied. "I had a feeling that would work!"

Ember looked at her arm, and knew her eyes weren't working properly. She must be hallucinating from the pain.

Because, as she watched, the gaping, serrated cuts that sliced through the skin and muscle of her arm were swiftly, silently knitting together.

The man holding her head murmured an awed, "Whoa."

Frozen in horrified astonishment, unable to think or move or breathe, Ember glanced at Caesar. He held up his arm, and there was nothing there except a smear of blood. The vicious cut he'd given himself had entirely healed in the space of a few seconds.

When she looked again at his face, he winked.

Then he reached out and gently stroked a finger up and down her arm, smearing his blood into all the healing wounds on her own skin, getting it into every nook and cranny, deep down into the muscle next to the bone where he'd dug out one of the thin metal plates. She watched his progress with disbelieving eyes, watched as the flesh smoothed itself out and grew together.

It hurt but it didn't, still burning, still itching, and Ember couldn't look away.

Caesar leaned down near her ear. "Are you religious, September? Myself, I used to think it all a bunch of mumbo-jumbo jabberwocky, but I have to admit my thoughts are now somewhat . . . in flux about the matter. I mean, immortality has really changed my perception about the state of life on this planet."

She finally tore her gaze away from her arm to stare into his eyes. Black and wild, they burned with devout fire.

He said, "Imagine a world without suffering. A world without sickness, or poverty, or war. A world without death. It's possible, you know. *I* am going to make it possible."

"By murdering the innocent?" Her voice was hoarse, shaking with fury. "Like those people at the Vatican—"

"That was just to get your attention," he scoffed, straightening to gaze imperiously down at her. "Unfortunately you humans don't respond to anything but a show of power, so . . . I gave you one." He smiled, a chilling, rabid smile that made her skin crawl. "I'm afraid more displays of power will be necessary before your species is brought to heel."

He motioned to her arm. Ember followed the direction of his hand and gasped when she saw all her wounds were healed. The only thing left were streaks of blood, glistening red in the overhead fluorescents.

Her arm was whole. Unblemished. Perfect.

Tentatively, she flexed her hand open; there was no pain, not even the old stiffness. She stared down at it in total disbelief.

"You're welcome," said Caesar, and all his men laughed. He motioned for them to release her and she sagged back into the chair, stunned.

Caesar came and stood over her again, and now all his lightness and teasing were gone, all the chipper, chilling playfulness vanished. He was utterly serious, the light shining blue off his black hair, his face wiped clean of emotion. Even his black eyes had gone flat; this seemed more ominous than any of his other moods.

"It's been lovely getting to know you, little rabbit," he said coldly. "But I'm afraid playtime is over. Tell me how to contact your boyfriend or I'll cut off stepmommy's head. And I'm pretty sure that's not something that can be healed with a few drops of my blood."

From behind him, Marguerite let out a low, anguished moan. Ember hesitated, and Caesar added, "Although I'm willing it try it if you are."

"No," Ember whispered. She swallowed and sat up straighter in her chair, a loud buzzing in her ears. "Please, listen. Just let her go and I'll tell you whatever you want to know. I promise you I'll cooperate. But please—let her go. She doesn't have anything to do with this."

One corner of Caesar's mouth curled, the tiniest smile. "*Au contraire*, little rabbit. She has everything to do with this. She's what I like to call *motivation*."

Without taking his gaze from hers, he backed up slowly until he was beside Marguerite's chair. The whole time he'd been holding the knife, and now he raised it to Marguerite's face. She stiffened in horror and let out a choked sob.

"Her left eye first," he said softly, savoring the words. "Then her right. Then her ears. Then her lovely, lovely lips. And then—if she's still alive at the end of all that—her head. *After* I scalp it."

Ember felt the room begin to spin. This was not how this was supposed to happen. She had to get him alone, away from Marguerite . . . she had to think—

She begged, "Please—please Caesar—"

"No negotiating!" He pressed the tip of his knife against Marguerite's cheek, and she froze, a little mewl of terror escaping her lips. Caesar moved the knife up to a millimeter beneath her eye socket, and his question came deadly quiet.

"How do I contact him, September?"

Trembling in rage, Ember looked him in the eye and said, "All right. I'll tell you, but there's something you should know first."

Caesar's brows rose, and Ember screeched, "He is going to tear! You! *Apart!*"

An eye roll, then an aggravated sigh. With a glance at one of his men, Caesar directed, "Search her for a cell phone, will you? This is getting tedious."

Ember's heart seized. Her mind screamed *No!*

It took all of four seconds for her coat to be stripped off, rifled through, and tossed aside. Then she was surrounded, thrown to the desk and pinned once again, her arms yanked roughly back and held aside while a pair of hands shoved up her long, bulky sweater to her waist.

"Here we go," said a satisfied voice as her cell phone was pulled from the back pocket of her jeans. The man tossed it to Caesar who caught it easily in on hand.

For a breathless, heart-stopping moment, Ember thought she was safe. But then she glanced at Caesar and knew she was oh so wrong.

His eyes, wolf bright, had focused on where her sweater bunched up around her waist. His lips parted; he took a slow step toward her, his expression one of outraged disbelief.

Then faster than her eyes could track, he was beside her. He yanked up the sweater, revealing what lay beneath. Then he looked at her with such violence in his eyes she thought he might kill her with his gaze alone.

In the darkest, most threatening voice she'd ever heard, Caesar whispered, "Oh you silly, silly rabbit. Tricks are for *kids.*"

He flipped her onto her back, slammed a hand around

her throat, and tore off the sweater with his other hand, ripping it down the middle as easily as if it were tissue.

And the air in the room went electric.

"Don't touch it!" Caesar screamed when one of his men reached for the black nylon vest strapped around her body. Front and back, the vest sported pockets filled with thin orange bricks of plastic explosives.

Ember kicked out with both her legs, but the big black-haired males grabbed them before she could make another move, and her arms were similarly subdued. Shaking in fear, anger, and desperation, she was stretched out over the desk, utterly helpless.

Across the room, Marguerite stared at her in white-faced, open-mouthed horror.

"Semtex," said one of Caesar's men, looking down at the nylon vest with an expression of grudging admiration. "That's some serious shit, boss."

"Serious shit indeed—and enough of it to blow anything to kingdom come," hissed Caesar. He leaned directly over Ember, staring down at her with hatred and a crazed sort of fury, his teeth peeled back over his lips. "Where's the detonator?"

Ember spat in his face.

He snarled and squeezed his hand harder around her throat, cutting off her air supply.

The lights began to dim. Her heart pounded so hard against her chest it felt as if it would burst. There was a roaring in her ears and a thrum like a thousand wing beats inside her head. Images flashed before her eyes, color and light and movement, but all she could think was a single word.

Christian.

It wasn't over yet. She could still find a way.

Caesar reared back, then slammed his fist into her face.

She heard the crunch of bone as if from very far away, felt the wet warmth spread over her cheek and down her neck. There was still no air, and her lungs burned with the effort to breathe. Caesar screamed his question in her face again, but the room was starting to go black, and everything was fuzzy around the edges.

"This can't have been her idea—the boyfriend must have planned this—we have to assume he knows where we are!" Caesar was furious, shouting at his men, the vise around her throat tightening with every word. "Call Marcell—evacuate the bunkers—institute emergency protocol! And for fuck's sake, *make sure they take the serum!*"

Suddenly the vise was gone and Ember was dragged off the desk, landing with a bone-jarring thud on her knees. She coughed and gagged, gulping air and tasting blood. Her arms were held high over her head as Caesar ran his hands carefully over the vest, and around her waist, legs, and shoulders, searching for the detonator.

He found the short metal cylinder, slender as a pen, taped to her right forearm.

He carefully removed it, unstrapped the vest from her body, and set both aside on the desk.

"Take that with us Nico, we might have a use for it—but be fucking careful!" he barked.

The one with the bandaged hand came forward and took the vest, while another picked up the detonator between two fingers, stared at it for a beat, then slowly left the room, holding it at arm's length in front of him.

The two men holding her released her arms at Caesar's command, and Ember collapsed to the floor, struggling to remain conscious. Pain flared like fireworks through her nerve endings, and everything was fractured and disjointed, like images in a funhouse mirror. Caesar stared down at her, his chest rising and falling rapidly, eyes silvery-black and glittering like coins at the bottom of a wishing well.

"You're so lucky you have something I want. If you didn't, you'd already be gutted like a fish."

He leaned down, grabbed a fistful of her hair, and dragged her to her feet. He held her up while she swayed and struggled to focus her eyes on him, to breathe through her shattered nose. He pulled her closed and hissed into her face, "What should we name him?"

He saw the confusion in her glassy eyes, and smiled with evil glee. "Oh dear, this just keeps getting better! You don't know, do you?"

In the frozen, bottomless moment that followed, Ember's mind struggled to absorb what he was saying while at the same time recognizing the sound of cars pulling into the lot behind the store and braking to a screeching stop. Caesar heard it too, and so did his remaining two men. They all stiffened, on instant high alert.

"Out the front!" he commanded. In one swift movement he lifted Ember off her feet and threw her over his shoulder, headed for the door.

"What do we do with this one, sire?" asked one of Caesar's men, indicating a petrified, panting Marguerite.

Without even looking back, Caesar snapped, "Break that bitch's neck."

Hanging upside down with blood from her nose dripping in her eyes, Ember saw the two men approach Marguerite. She cowered back into her chair, sobbing as they surrounded her.

Even above the sound of her own screams, Ember heard the crunch of bones, then an abrupt, ghastly silence, then nothing at all as Caesar's hand closed hard around her throat, cutting off her air supply, and dragging her down into darkness.

THIRTY-FOUR
Guerrilla Warfare

"I told you we shouldn't have come in so goddamn hot!" shouted Thirteen to Jahad as they raced to catch up with the two black sports cars speeding away from the bookstore through the crooked tangle of Barcelona's streets.

"Shut up or I'll rip out your intestines through your throat!" growled the albino.

Thirteen ignored that and screamed, "They can hear everything—they can hear a pin drop from a mile away! you think they wouldn't be able to hear us pull into the lot like bats out of hell? You just blew the element of surprise, you stupid fucking snowflake!"

Jahad shot him a murderous glare then drove on in glowering silence while Thirteen in the passenger seat pounded his fists on the dashboard of the SUV, red-faced with fury and frustration.

This was not how he'd imagined this moment.

Though Thirteen had the sneaking suspicion his throat would be slit the moment he let his guard down or turned his back, the albino had agreed to work with him. It was clear the other man didn't like being threatened, even clearer he hated having to rely on anyone outside his little cult, but he'd called his men together, gathered his weapons and supplies, and let Thirteen ride shotgun as he directed him to the little bookstore where the tip had indicated the *Ikati* might be.

As it turned out, the tip was 100% spot on.

But instead of sneaking up in a covert fashion, the albino had come in guns blazing and they'd blown the whole thing. Now they were engaged in a high speed car chase through the narrow, cobblestone streets of a city with an excellent police force who were armed with Walther P99 sidearms and known for shooting first and asking questions later.

Fucking brilliant.

"They're separating!" Thirteen watched in dismay as one of the black sedans took a right-hand turn at full speed, squealing off onto a dark side street, while the other zoomed straight ahead toward the entrance to the two-lane highway that led out of the city and up into the hills.

"Which way?" spat the albino, and Thirteen's mind, accustomed to thinking under pressure, offered up a little gem: the Chairman's list.

If they were headed for the hills, they might be headed for the only place on it that lay outside the city limits.

The abandoned Civil War bunkers.

"Follow him!" shouted Thirteen, pointing to the car speeding away in front of them. Jahad punched it and the SUV leapt forward. In the side mirror Thirteen saw the line of SUVs filled with Jahad's men follow. They passed the street the other car had turned down and as he watched, a pair of red taillights disappeared around another corner.

Hoping he'd made the right choice, Thirteen gritted his teeth, sat back, and hung on.

The air this high in the atmosphere was chilled and thin and much easier to maneuver through than the heated, thicker air of the city, which was one of the reasons Christian had decided to approach the bunkers from the forest side.

The earth below gently curved as it bled off into the night horizon. Over the pointed dark tips of the sea of pines, he spied his destination, magnified by his intense concentration like the crystalline lens of a spyglass. Off in the distance, the lights of Barcelona blazed Christmas-tree-bright right up to the dark indigo strip of the Mediterranean; beyond that there were only the tiny, twinkling pinpoints of stars.

He was grateful he couldn't feel emotions as Vapor. Grateful the rage and anguish he'd felt reading Ember's letter at the house had disappeared when he'd shed his human form, like a snake shedding its skin. The short time it took him to travel through the night sky from his home in the forest to the bunkers perched far above the city offered him a reprieve of sorts; without all that emotion short-circuiting his brain, it was much easier to think.

Using a narrow channel of fast-moving air, he descended silently toward the back of an outlying cement structure in the compound, swift as smoke, stretched as thin as possible to avoid detection by any curious eyes that might happen to look up.

He counted six sentries above ground at the complex. Armed with rifles, they prowled the exterior walls and barbed wire fences, silent and watchful.

Not watchful enough, however. Christian materialized right behind a muscular male farthest away from the others and broke his neck before he could whirl around or even make a sound of surprise.

He dragged the body into the opaque shadows beneath an Aleppo pine and stripped it of clothes, weapons, and a small mobile satellite phone.

He stared at the phone for a beat, surprised. Depending on the architecture of the system, the coverage of a sat phone might include the entire Earth—and would also include the GPS coordinates of the other phones on the system. He didn't have time to think more about it though, because his ears picked up the sound of cars driving up the winding road to the bunker.

There were perhaps a dozen, one slightly ahead of the rest—and they were moving fast.

He dressed in the dead man's clothes, slung the rifle over his back, stuffed the sat phone into the zippered pocket of the cargo pants, covered the body with fallen branches and brush, and set off at a silent run toward a gaping hole in the ground about three hundred yards away from the main bunker entrance that he'd spotted on his descent, avoiding four buried landmines in the process. He suspected the hole was one of the hidden exits to the labyrinth underground tunnels, and when he stepped down carefully into its pitch black opening, his suspicions were confirmed.

He smelled hundreds of *Ikati*—males and females both—spread out over several acres, a few dozen human females in close proximity to one another to the east who he assumed were captives, the sour metallic tang of a large cache of weaponry to the north, stores of food and water to the west, the dull organic smells of damp earth, dead rock, and vegetation all around, and underlying everything a cloyingly sweet chemical scent he didn't recognize.

He held still for another moment, stretching his senses, opening his nose and ears to probe the deepest recesses of the tunnels, allowing the night air to waft over his body, bringing with it all the evidence of everything unseen.

Then he began to panic.

No vanilla. No orange blossom.

Ember wasn't here.

Caesar's sat phone rang just as he stepped into the opulent burl wood and butter crème leather cabin of the motor yacht he kept docked in the harbor of Port Vell.

Since he'd killed the captain who'd sailed it south for him when they'd fled France, Caesar had taught himself to operate the hundred-foot luxury craft, and spent quite a bit of time cruising the glistening waters off the golden coast of Barcelona, daydreaming and scheming, imagining in vivid detail the outcome of the operation he'd aptly dubbed "The Hammer."

Depending on how dire this little road bump turned out to be, a serious crimp could be made in his plans.

And he simply couldn't allow that to happen. He'd worked too hard. He'd waited too long. He'd arranged everything, and now all he was waiting for was Easter Sunday when he'd pull the trigger and watch the world implode. He wasn't going to let a little thing like being chased by inferior life forms in SUVs stop him.

So when he looked at the ringing mobile in his hand and saw it was Armond, one of the guards who patrolled the bunker, he experienced a brief thrill of dread.

This couldn't be good.

"Armond!" he barked into the phone. "What's happening?"

There was no answer. Only a brief burst of static crackled through the line, then it went dead.

In the huge, luxurious living area that sprawled in an elongated oval behind the bridge, Nico dumped the semiconscious girl he'd carried from the trunk of the car onto the sofa, and bound her wrists together with plastic zip ties. She was bleeding profusely from the nose and made a soft, choked moan when Nico stuffed a handkerchief in her mouth.

Seeing that, Caesar snapped, "If she suffocates, I'll cut off both your hands!"

Nico removed the handkerchief. Caesar turned back to the bridge and fired up the engines.

Shaking in a fury that felt thermonuclear on the other end of the phone Caesar had just answered, Christian scrolled through the recent calls menu, selected the stored number he'd dialed, brought up the GPS option, and pressed "locate."

Google maps appeared in a browser window, then a red dot followed, along with coordinates.

Port Vell.

He looked up just as a dozen SUVs chasing a lone sports sedan came roaring over the crest of the hill toward the bunkers at top speed.

Then he watched as chaos unfolded.

Thirteen knew it was over the minute he heard the tiny click when he stepped on a small, innocuous-looking mound of dirt. He just had time to look down at his feet in horror before the world exploded into a huge, orange fireball of heated gasses and pain.

That fucking albino. This was all his fault.

Even the dumbest soldier knows you don't stage a direct assault on a highly motivated enemy in a heavily fortified encampment with zero intel about their numbers or weaponry and no offensive strategy of your own. Direct assaults don't work. Guerilla warfare—now *that* works, especially when dealing with non-human creatures far stronger and faster than you are, accustomed to living in hiding and fleeing at a moment's notice when discovered.

But Jahad was like Rambo Jesus: he was on a holy mission to kill. Apparently he didn't have time for pesky little things like plans.

So he'd blown their cover at the bookstore, and he'd blown their cover at the bunker by driving up the dirt road in single file behind the sedan like the biggest bunch of idiots on planet Earth. Then Jahad and all his minions had jumped out of the SUVs, screaming like banshees, when the sedan screeched to a stop at the top of the hill in a billowing plume of dust.

Then came the firefight.

The two males who exited the sedan started firing first, one of them laying down cover for the other, who ran across the dirt expanse between the car and the chain link fence topped with barbed wire in less time than it took Thirteen to blink. Jahad's men returned fire, but not before the man at the fence turned into a huge, snarling animal and leapt clear over the top of the barbed wire in a single bound, then took off toward the main concrete building on the other side in a streak of black, almost imperceptible against the night.

He'd disappeared inside the building, while the other one continued to exchange gunfire with Jahad's men.

Thirteen had a weapon as well, the H&K P8 semi-automatic pistol he'd kept from his time in the Kommando Spezialkräfte, but he didn't bother to engage in the stupidity, and instead crept off behind the line of SUVs, around the back of the bunker where the barbed wire fence disappeared into a stand of trees.

There he cut a five-foot tall opening in the metal links of the fence with a bolt cutter, and stepped through.

From his vantage point behind the main building, he saw a flurry of activity that was hidden from the front. Emerging from a hole in the ground bedside a large boulder that clearly served as hidden access to the bunkers, dark shapes quickly and efficiently loaded small plastic boxes into the back of a pickup truck. There was another narrow dirt road that led off through the trees, and when the back of the pickup was fully loaded with boxes, it set off down the road, the sound of its engine concealed entirely by the loud reports of gunfire from Jahad's men.

The pickup was followed by a silent line of figures, moving fast, who quickly melted into the night.

Shit. They were getting away. He had to capture at least one of them.

He withdrew his gun from the waistband of his pants. He slunk forward in a crouch, scanning the darkness ahead of him, grateful he was upwind of the hole and the bunkers.

Then came the little, horrible *click*. Then the orange fireball of pain.

Then there was nothing at all.

THIRTY-FIVE
Captive

Feeling as if her head had been used for batting practice by an entire team of sluggers, Ember slowly swam up into consciousness.

Gritting her teeth against the shooting pain in her skull, she opened her eyes and found herself lying chest-down on a sofa in an unfamiliar room, hands tied behind her back. Without lifting her head, she glanced around and quickly determined she was on a boat—a yacht, more correctly—in the marina. Through the windows she saw night sky, bobbing masts of adjacent boats, and the graceful, lighted arches of the pedestrian bridge that connected the city to the aquarium and Maremagnum shopping complex. Nearby, voices murmured and the vibrating hum of big engines shivered the walls.

She was alone. The Semtex vest was casually draped over a desk beneath a window across the room, as if deposited there in a hurry and forgotten.

Carefully, holding her breath, she swung her legs over the edge of the sofa, sat upright and tested the binds around her wrists.

Tight. Unbreakable. Shit.

She swallowed, tasting blood, then spat a mouthful of it onto the ivory silk, filled with dark satisfaction when it seeped through the cushions in a splattered cranberry stain.

Of three things she was certain. One: her nose was badly broken. Two: Caesar was on this yacht somewhere and other parts of her body were likely to get broken if she didn't act fast. And three: killing him had become more than her mission.

It had become her religion.

She felt deep horror and anger over what he'd done to Marguerite. She felt responsible, too, because that was her mind's default setting when everything went to hell, even though she knew on some level he would have killed Marguerite no matter what she did or didn't do. That was just Caesar's MO.

But she also felt a profound sense that ridding the world of this murderous, crazy bastard was the *right* thing to do, not only for Marguerite and for Christian, but for everyone else on the planet as well.

He was a rabid dog that needed to be put down.

And she was the one who'd do it.

She stood, then froze as a wave of vertigo hit her and her head began to spin. When it passed in a moment, she kicked off her shoes and stepped over to the desk, careful to keep her feet as silent as possible against the floor. It wasn't too hard; a thick layer of white carpet muffled the sound. She crept up to the desk, frantically scanning the glossy mahogany surface and the vest itself for any sign of the detonator.

It wasn't there. Without the detonator, the vest was useless.

She turned around, slouched down and, looking over her shoulder, opened the top drawer of the desk with one of her bound hands. It wasn't there, either. So she searched for anything else that looked like it could be used as a weapon. It wasn't as good as the vest, but she knew there were several things that, if inserted with enough force into the brain stem, could kill someone.

Something like a knife. Or—her heart stopped—a letter opener. Her gaze fell on the silver letter opener with an elaborately engraved handle and a long, thin blade and Ember nearly laughed aloud in relief.

Or panic. Or hysteria. She wasn't exactly sure which.

She gripped the letter opener in her hand and slid the drawer shut with her hip, then darted back to the couch as the sound of voices grew louder.

" . . . blow it. If we have the serum, that's all that matters."

Caesar entered the room from the bridge, talking into a chunky mobile phone with a long antennae. He saw her sitting up on the couch and his brows raised as his gaze raked over her. He leaned against the wall and sent her a dark, lazy smile.

"Leave them. They're not important. You know where to rendezvous, I'll speak to you when I'm close," he replied to a question posed from the other end of the line. Then he disconnected the call and stood staring at her, with that sinister smile and a heated intensity that filled the room.

"The broken nose is an improvement," he drawled, eyeing her bloody face. "At least now you'll have some character in that boring mug."

That didn't even sting. Feigning fear, wondering how the hell she was going to stab him with her hands tied behind her back, Ember dropped her gaze to the floor.

"Aww, did I hurt your feelings, little rabbit?" He moved toward her with a leisurely stride, and she stiffened as he stopped in front of her and touched the top of her head. He stroked his fingers through her hair and she shuddered, disgusted to feel any kind of intimate touch from such a monster.

Caesar mistook her disgust for terror. "Is that what he liked about you? Your sensitivity? Your small-animal trembling? Because honestly, rabbit, you're so goddamn average, I've been having a hell of a time figuring it out."

He squatted down in front of her. Ember glanced up at him, and they were eye to eye.

It was amazing to her that a creature so purely evil could be so beautiful. Except for a pair of black, glittering eyes that held no empathy or human kindness whatsoever, his face and body were as lovely as an angel's.

A random memory: she and her father watching an old Jacques Cousteau episode about great white sharks, and Cousteau explaining in his French accent as the shark gleefully tore a seal to bloody shreds, "Zee most beautiful creatures are always zee most dangerous."

How right he was.

Swallowing around the urge to spit in Caesar's face, Ember whispered, "Well, you can't judge a book by its cover. We're both proof of that."

This made him smile, which flashed a dimple in his tanned cheek. "Hmm. Maybe it's your sense of humor he likes. Though I've always thought clever women are over-rated." He lifted his hand and trailed the tip of one finger over the blood crusted on her upper lip.

She held immobile because she realized when she appeared to be cooperating, she didn't get hit. Also, she needed to stay conscious—and close—if she was going to kill him.

Still tracing her lips with his finger and staring at her with hooded eyes, Caesar murmured, "We're going to have a lot of fun, you and I. I'm *so* going to enjoy breaking you in." He leaned closer and inhaled against her neck while she clenched her teeth and tried not to vomit. "You do smell rather edible, I'll give you that. And I already know how well you can scream."

Ember stopped breathing as a big, hot hand spread open on her thigh. The single finger on her lips became five cupped firmly around her nape when he slid his other hand around her neck. His voice beside her ear grew husky. "How loudly do you think you'll scream when I fuck you?"

Filled with revulsion, Ember tightened her fingers around the letter opener and decided to rip off this pig's ear with her teeth and worry about the rest later.

Then the phone he'd tucked into the front pocket of his shirt rang.

With an audible sigh of frustration, Caesar pulled away, stood and paced to the windows. "Armond, talk to me," he growled into the phone. "What's happening up there?"

Whatever was said on the other end of the line caused Caesar to spin around and stare at her in sudden, crackling fury. That look made Ember's heart began to stutter in dread; her mouth went dry.

"Well, hello, friend! I've been so *hoping* we could meet," Caesar hissed. An ugly smile spread over his handsome face.

Ember realized who was on the other end of the line, and that's when her heart stopped beating altogether.

THIRTY-SIX
Come What May

Christian mistakenly slammed the SUV into drive instead of reverse, shouted a curse, and wished, for not the first time in his life, but definitely the most fiercely, that he'd learned to drive.

The powerful engine propelled the car forward with a lurch, and he crashed into the SUV parked in front of him.

He'd been able to sneak undetected to the car from his hiding place behind the pines because there was still a gun battle raging at the bunker compound. Though the shooters led by Jahad—he recognized the big albino, but didn't have a clear shot as the man bounded for the main entrance with Kamikaze determination and disappeared inside— had killed the *Ikati* left behind at the sedan they'd been chasing, dozens more had erupted from hidden holes in the ground all around the area like rats from a sinking ship.

Armed, angry rats.

Conveniently, Jahad's men had even left the car running for him. Which was lucky, because Christian wasn't entirely sure he'd be able to locate the key, find the ignition and turn the engine over, on top of figuring out which direction to pull the shifter on the steering wheel column to make the car move forward and back.

Before this moment, he'd thought driving a car was a matter of simple common sense.

Too bad he hadn't tested that theory under better circumstances.

He slammed the shifter in the other direction and stomped his foot on the gas pedal. The car surged backward with surprising force, throwing him into the steering wheel, and tearing off the rear bumper of the other SUV. Quickly righting himself, Christian eased his foot off the pedal, gripped the steering wheel, and executed a squealing 180-degree turn that miraculously managed to point him in the right direction down the hill. The demolished metal bumper went flying off into the darkness beyond the headlights.

This time when he punched the accelerator, he knew what to expect.

He didn't look behind to see if he was followed. He didn't look behind to get a better look at what sounded like a small munitions explosion, possibly one of the buried land mines. He *did* look behind just as he reached the bottom of the hill—a quick glance in the rearview mirror before he made the turn onto the main road—when a much larger explosion rocked the night, lighting it brilliant orange and crimson and blue like a tropical sunset.

Bodies flying in slow motion. A giant fireball of flame and debris. A spectacular flare of color against the sky, then everything fell dark and silent except for a few piles of flaming rubble and the squalling of a half dozen car alarms, oddly alien among the trees and grass and sky.

"Jesus," muttered Christian, flooded with relief that Ember hadn't been in that compound; apparently Caesar had the whole thing wired. With the amount of explosives it must have taken to induce that kind of light show, he doubted if anything identifiable would be left.

Then he smiled in dark satisfaction. *So long, Jahad. I bet the goats in hell have much sharper teeth than all the ones you killed up here, you miserable bastard.*

He pulled the sat phone from his zippered pocket, set it on the seat beside him, and did his best to stay on the right side of the yellow line as he flew down the two-lane highway and into the outskirts of the city.

It took too long. His heart felt like it was eating its way out of his chest. The air had become too thin to breathe.

Narrowly missing oncoming traffic, he blew through three stoplights before he finally had to stop at a busy intersection near the marina. Seconds ticked by like hours as he waited for the light to turn, and as soon as it did, he was flying like a madman over the pavement once again.

Ember was with Caesar. He knew it. He felt it, deep in his bones.

Just as he knew he was going to tear that son of a bitch's head right off his body.

He abandoned the SUV near the aquarium building in the marina parking lot and set off at a dead run with the rifle slung over his back and the phone in his hand, following the direction of the little red dot. The boat slips were at the opposite end of the parking lot with the smaller vessels nearest the lot and the larger yachts at the end of the wood slip decks. Barcelona was loaded with mega-yachts and their rich owners, so the marina was forested with sleek, gleaming ships, but he had the phone, and he knew exactly where he was going.

When finally he stood panting at the end of the dock eight boats removed from a sleek number ironically named *God of Vengeance*, Christian knew without looking at the mobile that Ember was inside.

He smelled her. He was so attuned to her scent now he could find her blindfolded in the middle of a huge crowd.

He expected to smell fear, but strangely she was angry. Angry and repulsed—Christian didn't want to know what Caesar might be doing to her to make her feel that way.

He dialed a stored number. Caesar picked up on the second ring.

"Armond, talk to me. What's happening up there?"

"You have something that's mine," said Christian, his voice deadly soft. A shadow moved across one of the windows inside *God of Vengeance*, and Christian's gaze snapped to the movement.

Top deck. Gotcha.

"Well, hello, friend! I've been so *hoping* we could meet," came the hissed reply. "In fact, your girlfriend and I were just talking about you!"

Christian curled his hand so tightly around the phone the plastic casing cracked. "If she's hurt, you're going to wish you were never born!"

"Oh, she's fine, aren't you, little rabbit? A little bloody, a few broken bits, but she's none the worse for wear."

Christian went hot with rage at the intimate tone in Caesar's voice and the suggestion—he hoped to God it was just a bluff—that Ember was broken and bloody. The world went black for a moment as fury blinded him, but he inhaled slowly and deeply, calming himself, willing his anger to focus.

Wanting Caesar to think him still at the bunkers so he retained the element of surprise as he silently crept nearer, Christian said, "I know it's me you want. So I'll make you a deal. Tell me where you are and I'll trade—"

Caesar laughed. "No deal. At this point, I couldn't care less about you. The cat's out of the bag. My colony is already compromised, so I don't need to kill you to stop you from outing my location to your little coffee klatsch anymore."

He was referring to the Council of Alphas. They'd just love hearing themselves called a "coffee klatsch."

"And now that I have September . . . well, we can just call it even for the two men of mine you killed. You took two, I took two. Tit for tat, so to speak!"

He laughed, a self-congratulatory, maniacal sound that sent something unpleasant crawling down Christian's spine.

Tit for tat? What the hell was he talking about?

Then the yacht's idling engines changed gear, and it began to glide away from the dock.

Christian had two choices. If he approached in human form and jumped on before the gap between the dock and the yacht widened too far, he'd give himself away; they'd hear him *and* scent him. If he Shifted to Vapor, not only would he have to stage a surprise attack totally nude, which was less than appealing, but he'd lose the weapons he'd gained from the guard's clothing—a wicked folding blade, a handgun and the rifle. None of those would take care of Caesar permanently, but they'd certainly take care of who-ever else was with him, and at least Christian would have a chance to snatch Ember and get the hell off the yacht be-fore Caesar could heal from the magazine of ammo that had been unloaded into his brain.

But until then, there really was only one other option: Swim for it.

Like all his kind, he hated getting wet in his animal form, and avoided it at all costs. But as a man, Christian was a strong, fast swimmer. And water had the added benefit of dampening his scent. If he was quick and lucky, he could swim to the stern and climb aboard unnoticed, all while keeping his weapons.

Decision made.

Christian growled into the phone, "We'll *never* be even, you piece of shit. And I'll see you in hell before I let you have her!"

Then without even bothering to disconnect the call he dove into the cold water of the marina with a neat, noiseless splash.

Caesar smiled at the look on Ember's face as he lowered the phone to his side.

"In case you're getting the wrong idea, your boyfriend isn't coming to the rescue. He's looking in the wrong place. Even as we speak, he's probably sifting through dead bodies to find you far, far away. But he's never going to find you, rabbit. You and I will have *plenty* of time to get to know one another properly."

This was spoken in a tone of gleeful delight as he swaggered toward her. Halfway there, he stopped, frowned, and looked down at the phone in his hand. "Though I'll have to jam the locator on this, we don't want him figuring out—"

He cut off abruptly. He punched something into the phone, paused for a beat while he stared intently at the screen, then screamed "*No!*"

Nico darted in from another door behind her. "Sire? What is it?"

"*He's here!*"

The instant he spoke those words, Ember saw a flash of movement in her peripheral vision. With an animal snarl, a dripping wet Christian bolted into the room and dropped Nico with a brutal fist to the face before he could turn. Nico crumpled to the floor at his feet, Christian grabbed the rifle he had slung over his shoulder, and Caesar turned and began to run.

Christian fired a volley of rounds that pierced Ember's ears like cannon fire. A spray of bullets punctured the walls and shattered two windows before the gun jammed and Caesar vanished down a hallway. Blood misted the corner of the doorway he'd just disappeared around.

"Shit. Saltwater," muttered Christian, jerking the magazine out and peering at it. Then, as if he'd just noticed her cowering on the couch, he spun and stared at her.

He dropped the rifle. In a heartbeat he was beside her, vibrating rage and danger, big and brawny with scalding green eyes as he knelt down and grasped her arms, his expression horrified, tender, and furious all at once.

"Are you—Jesus, your face. Baby, *what did he do to you?*"

"I'm fine! It's worse than it looks—my hands—"

He saw her bound wrists, removed a folding knife from a pocket of his cargo pants and, in one quick move, cut the plastic zip tie. She moaned as her hands slipped forward and sensation came flooding back into her numb arms.

He touched her face and growled, "Get off the boat! Jump off the back—swim—we'll talk about your stupid fucking plan later—"

"It was *your* stupid plan first! And I can't swim!"

At his look of disbelief, Ember said, "I grew up in Taos, for God's sake. It's seven thousand feet above sea level! Nobody even had a pool!"

But he didn't respond to that. He'd frozen, and was staring in what looked like horror at her face. At the blood smeared all over her broken nose, mouth, and chin.

"I told you, it's not as bad as it looks—"

He knocked aside the hand Ember covered her nose with, put his face nearer to hers and inhaled. Then he jerked back as if she'd stabbed him. He went pale. His eyes burned with some unidentifiable emotion.

Without another word, he lifted her in his arms and took off through the living area, headed to the stern of the yacht.

Just as they flew through the open glass doors to the rear patio and stepped onto the teak deck out into the cool night air, they were hit by something hard from behind, and they went down.

Christian landed on top of her, but immediately rolled off and started fighting with Nico, who'd jumped on his back. They rolled over and over on the polished teak deck, punching and hissing savagely as they went, until they hit the low deck wall with a muffled boom, and Christian gained the advantage. In one blinding motion, he was atop Nico, pummeling him in the face with his fists.

Across the deck, a slender, silver shape rolled toward Ember and came to rest only inches away.

Her mouth fell open. Her lungs stopped working. Her heart jumped up into her throat.

The detonator. Nico must have been carrying it.

"Jump, Ember, jump! I'm right behind you!" Christian screamed, still punching Nico, who was barely managing to keep his arms in front of his face to ward off Christian's blows.

But then Caesar appeared in the doorway. Ember snatched up the detonator and hid it behind her back.

In his hand Caesar held a gun. Which he pointed directly at Christian.

"Stop!" he shouted.

Christian froze, looked up at him, and his lips peeled back over his teeth. "A dozen bullets won't stop me from taking you down," he growled, murder in his eyes. Nico lay bloody and unmoving beneath him.

"Okay," said Caesar mildly, "but this might." Then he turned the gun to Ember and smiled.

Everything screeched to a halt. Her heartbeat, her thought processes, time itself.

Christian's livid face burned with hatred. "Son of a—"

"Very smart man, as it turns out," Caesar interrupted. He slowly moved closer to Ember, all the while keeping the gun pointed right at her head. "I never really got it when he was alive, but my father was truly a genius. Farsighted in a way I can now respect." His smile turned mocking. "Unlike you."

He'd reached Ember's side. Without looking away from Christian, he said, "On your feet, rabbit," and waved the gun.

Shaking uncontrollably, Ember stood. Caesar reached out and pulled her against him with a hand fisted in her hair. She cried out but he silenced her by shoving the gun against her cheek and growling into her ear, "Another noise and I'll blow your head off. But I'll blow his head off first so you can watch."

By now they were perhaps half a mile away from the docks. Barcelona burned bright against the dark hills that rose up from the sea. Wind whipped Ember's hair into her face and salt spray stung her eyes. The gun was cold and hard against her cheekbone.

"On your feet," Caesar directed Christian. With a grim glance at her face, Christian complied.

And Ember saw what was coming.

"Wait," she whispered, turning her head a fraction to look at Caesar. "I have a proposal for you."

Caesar snorted. "As if you'd have anything to bargain with. And I've already told you, rabbit, no negotiating." He removed the gun from her face and pointed it at Christian's chest, and every cell in Ember's body jumped shrieking to its toes.

"I can take a lot of pain," she whispered, staring with laser-like intensity at Caesar's profile. "You've already seen it—you dug a metal plate out of my arm. It takes much more pain for me to pass out than a regular person. The doctor who put those plates in my arms said I had the highest pain tolerance of any patient he'd ever had."

He hesitated just long enough to let her know he was listening. Remembering the way he'd grown hard at the sight of her blood and his own, remembering the dark excitement in his voice when he'd hurt Marguerite and the flare of lust in his eyes when he'd broken her nose, Ember breathed, "Because I like it."

Caesar slid his gaze to hers, and she slowly nodded, looking deep into his eyes.

"Just like you need to give pain, I need to receive it. I used to cut myself just so I could feel it, just so I could watch myself bleed. We're the same, you and I. We're opposite sides of the same coin."

Caesar's breathing had grown uneven. His pupils had dilated. He moistened his lips.

This was working. This could actually work!

Very throaty, she asked, "Have you ever had a woman beg you to hit her harder?"

"Stop this, Ember!" shouted Christian, but he was ignored by both of them. Caesar's eyes were locked on hers.

She leaned into him, brushing her breasts against his chest. "Have you . . . sire?"

He stared at her, frozen, color rising to ruddy his cheeks, and she pressed her advantage.

"If you let him go, I promise you I will never try to run from you. I will never disobey you. I will serve you in any way you like for as long as you like." She whispered into his ear, "I will bleed for you, and scream for you, and worship you *forever*."

He held still for a moment. Ember felt his heart pounding in his chest. He whispered, "You're lying."

She tilted her head back, exposing her throat. "I know you can smell the difference between a lie and the truth. Go ahead. You decide."

Then she closed her eyes and crossed her fingers that all the things broken inside her were broken enough to convince him this wasn't just a ploy to get Christian to safety . . . and him alone.

Behind her back, gripped in her shaking hand, the detonator was a cool, slender weight.

He bent nearer. She felt the fleet brush of his lips over the pulse in her throat. She heard him inhale against her skin, and then she heard his exhalation, and his next words, spoken in a tense, husky whisper.

"Well, well . . . not such a scared little rabbit after all."

He pulled away and gazed at her with hooded eyes, jaw twitching. The pulse in his neck throbbed.

Then he turned back to Christian and fired a round into the air above his head.

Ember jumped but Christian didn't move at all. He merely stared at her, motionless, taut as a bowstring as he knelt over the unconscious Nico.

"Overboard," directed Caesar, and Ember felt a rush of relief so profound she almost sank to her knees. The hand Caesar still had fisted in her hair helped her to stay on her feet.

When Christian didn't move, Caesar said, "Make me say it again and you'll still go overboard, but it will be with a bullet in your head."

Smoothly and silently, Christian rose from his knees and stepped over Nico's unconscious form. He looked back and forth between her and Caesar, then said to her, "Just stay alive. I'll find you."

Caesar leveled the gun at Christian's face. "One more word, friend—just one, and it's all over."

With his chest heaving, nostrils flared, and fury burning in his eyes, Christian slowly backed up against the low wall of the deck. He leaned against it, calculating, looking for any opportunity, his body tensed for flight.

Ember knew he was stalling. He wasn't going to jump overboard; this was the final calm before the storm broke and he charged.

"And if I don't hear a splash and see you floating behind us, all bets are off," Caesar hissed.

Christian raised his hands and the air around him warped and shimmered. His rage was a palpable thing, washing over her in heated waves, and it brought a smile to Caesar's face.

"Sucks to be you," he mocked.

Then Nico's eyes blinked open. He looked up at Christian standing over him, let out a bellow, leapt to his feet in a whip-crack move and launched himself at him. He hit Christian in the chest full force—

—And they both tumbled over the low deck wall and disappeared into space.

Ember screamed. There was a flat smack and a splash, then nothing. Several seconds later two heads popped up in the frothing white wake behind the boat. There was a quick struggle, then only one head was left bobbing above the dark water.

Christian. He screamed something but the wind stole it, and Ember watched as he grew smaller and smaller as the yacht sailed forward into the night.

I will love you, until the end of time.

Tears pooled in her eyes, then slid down her cheeks as the sight of Christian's face disappeared altogether, swallowed by the dark.

"Now," said Caesar, spinning her around with both hands on her upper arms and pulling her hard against his chest. He leered triumphantly down at her. "Let's see exactly how much pain you can take."

Ember whispered, "Exactly *this* much."

Then she closed her eyes and depressed her thumb on the detonator's trigger.

In the infinitesimal moment before the explosion knocked her off her feet and the world went black, her last thought was, *Come what may.*

THIRTY-SEVEN
Two Words

There were many who saw the huge explosion in the dark waters off Port Vell that night, many who saw the other huge explosion in the hills above the city, many who saw them both. But there was only one person who was close enough to both to see the bodies fly.

Christian.

He was floating in the frigid water when the yacht was torn to pieces in a thunderous eruption that sent a shockwave of heat roaring over him and an orange ball of fire and smoke billowing high into the sky, still screaming what he'd been screaming since he'd gone in the water, the words the wind had stolen from his lips. The words Ember would never hear.

The two most miraculous words in the world, which would now eat at his soul like a cancer until the day he died.

You're pregnant.

Salt water choked him. He was blinded by tears. He didn't even bother to wait until the huge fireball contracted or the debris stopped raining down into the waves.

He just began to swim. Frantically, as fast as he could, he swam.

THIRTY-EIGHT
All I Need

Death wasn't nearly as peaceful and quiet as Ember had hoped it would be.

For one thing, there was too much talking. Granted, the voices weren't loud, but the way they murmured constantly, the cadences rising and falling while the words remained indistinct, was really irritating. She wanted to shout at them to shut up because she was trying to concentrate on being deceased, but her throat wasn't working properly. Her tongue, furry and swollen, felt like a dead animal inside her mouth.

Then there was the incessant beeping. She imagined it might be some kind of mechanical contraption designed to process souls through the underworld, a conveyor belt maybe, crowded with the disembodied spirits of the recently departed on their way to be sorted. Or perhaps it was a waiting room like in the movie *Beetlejuice*, filled with the patient undead, and the sound was the clock of eternity, forever announcing the same, unchanging hour.

Also, there was a hell of a lot of pain involved. She thought this death business was supposed to be the *absence* of pain, especially since she no longer had a body, but somehow agony crackled through her, angry as a nest of spitting snakes. How was that possible, if she no longer had nerves?

The worst thing, though, was the crying.

It was soft and muffled and anguished, its tone of utter misery worse than everything else combined. She caught a few whispered words that reminded her of something, but she couldn't quite remember what.

"Don't leave me, little firecracker. Please, please don't leave me."

This was followed by a low, choked sob, then another.

Ember hated to hear that. The pain in those quiet sobs was . . . it was . . .

Awful. Piercing. Bottomless.

Ember wanted to comfort the crier. She wanted it so badly she finally managed to force her eyes open, though they felt stitched closed, to look around for the source.

And this was confusing, because the afterlife looked a lot like . . . a hospital room. White walls, fabric curtain hanging from the ceiling, the sharp sting of antiseptic in the air.

How disappointing. Why would anyone decorate the afterlife like a hospital room? Honestly, some people had no imagination. Or maybe it was God's sick sense of humor?

Or maybe this was hell?

In any case, whoever this crier was, he was doing it all over her left arm.

A head of glossy black hair, a pair of shaking broad shoulders, two large hands gripping her arm hard enough to turn his knuckles white. A big body bent over in a chair beside her bed. And tears, hot and wet, sliding over her skin.

In a voice that sounded like it emanated from the bottom of a well, Ember whispered, "Hey. I'm trying to be dead here. Could you please cut that out?"

Then the crier lifted his head and stared at her in shock and red-eyed joy. Ember felt electrocuted as memory came flooding back.

Christian. The crier was Christian. And he looked very much alive.

Which meant she wasn't dead after all.

He jolted out of the chair and began to plant frantic kisses her all over her face, chanting her name in a reverent whisper as if reciting the rosary.

"Ember, Ember, oh God Ember—"

The murmuring in the room abruptly ceased, and then she was surrounded by people and everyone was talking at once.

"She's awake!"

"Jesus, you gave us a scare!"

"Don't crowd her, let her breathe!"

"*Dios mio*, call the doctor! Call the doctor!"

"I told you He would look out for you."

This last one was pronounced with quiet satisfaction from Clare, who stood on the right side of Ember's bed next to a smiling Dante with a bandage on one side of his head. Clare wore pink pajamas, clutched Peter Parker and had the plastic oxygen tube, attached to a portable tank, wrapped beneath her nose. Pale and thin with bluish bruises under her eyes, she was nonetheless gazing at Ember with the serenity of a medieval Madonna.

"God," explained Clare, seeing Ember's confused look. "Remember? I told you I asked him to look out for you, and He said he would. So He did."

She shrugged, as if it were preposterous any of them had doubted her, and Ember's eyes welled with tears.

Whoever it was, someone had definitely been looking out for her; she should be dead. Maybe it was time she repaid the favor and started being grateful for life, instead of wishing for the alternative.

She turned her head—the room spun briefly before settling back into lucidity—and there on the other side of her bed, holding hands, were Asher, biting his lower lip and blinking back tears, and a very scared-looking Rafael. Next to him was Christian, still hovering over her, looking as if he was about to have a nervous breakdown.

At the foot of the bed stood Allegra and Analia, pale as powder, dressed identically in black.

"Marguerite," Ember whispered, feeling an immense surge of guilt as those memories came back, too, sharp as knives.

"It wasn't your fault," said Allegra, her round face pinched. "We know . . . " she swallowed and moistened her lips. "We know what a monster he was. That man. We know he was the one who . . . the pope . . . "

She was having trouble getting the words out, and Analia placed a gentle hand on her sister's back. She seemed to take comfort from that, and straightened. "But you killed him. He's dead; that's all that matters now. He can't hurt anyone else."

You killed him. Ember stared up at Christian in shock, searching his face. He nodded, looking haggard with his unshaven face and dark circles under his eyes. She'd never seen him look so . . . human. So vulnerable. Big and beautiful and capable of carnage, at this moment he looked more like a lost little boy.

It was painful to speak, but she managed, "But how did I . . . if he—"

"I think he shielded you from the brunt of the blast. He was standing right in front of you, blocking you. He must have taken the lion's share of the impact because there was just . . . nothing left of him. They've combed the debris, dragged the ocean bed, searched the shoreline where anything might have washed up in the currents. There was plenty of wreckage from the yacht, but . . . "

He trailed off into silence, staring at her with haunted eyes, then he said in a choked whisper, "I thought I watched you die."

His beautiful face crumpled. He sank to his knees next to the bed and buried his face in the blanket over her stomach, gripping her so hard he shook.

Ember was overcome with emotion. She lifted her hand to stroke his hair and blinked when she saw it was wrapped in a gauze bandage. As was her entire right arm.

"You were burned," Asher explained gently. "Flash burns from the explosion, first and second degree, mostly on your right hand and arm and your lower legs. There's bleeding and swelling in your lungs from the pressure of the shockwave, and your intestines, well, they're not going to be working right for a while. The doctors said you were lucky you weren't in an enclosed space, and being in the water helped shield you from a lot of the debris fallout. The worst was the brain swelling, though . . . "

He swallowed, and Rafael glanced at him and squeezed his hand. Asher whispered, "They had to do surgery to relieve it. We thought . . . we didn't know . . . the doctors weren't sure if you'd remember much . . . if you'd be . . . *you* . . . "

She touched her hand to her head and felt skin, a bald patch where the hair had been shaved, a ragged row of stitches. Christ. With her broken nose, shaved head and burns, she probably looked like the bride of Frankenstein.

Christian lifted his head and stared into her eyes. His own were wild and searing. "Do you?" he asked hoarsely. "Do you remember?"

She smiled at him and watched his eyes spark with hope. "As if I could ever forget a single moment with you," she whispered.

And there it was again, that look of transformation she'd come to know so well. His gaze was so intense and burning, so filled with love, she thought he could light them both on fire with it. There was a surge of heat in the atmosphere and he leaned over the bed and kissed her, passionately, his mouth pressed hard and hot against hers.

It hurt.

She winced and protested with a weak, "Ow." Christian instantly pulled away with a whispered apology, and there were relieved chuckles from Dante and Asher and a nervous twitter from Rafael.

"We should let you rest," said Dante, wrapping his arm around Clare's shoulders and drawing her close. As if on cue, a wave of fatigue swept over her, and she felt as if her body weighed a thousand pounds.

"I don't need to rest, I want to talk to everyone," she said, but it came out garbled. Her eyelids drooped.

Asher reached out and squeezed her left hand, whispered, "See you later, knucklehead. Love you," and led Rafael to the door. Analia and Allegra said their good-byes, then so did Dante and Clare, who added a kiss on her cheek and one from Peter Parker.

Then she was alone with Christian.

He lowered the metal bar on the left side of the bed and crawled in next to her, moving the clear tubes that were stuck in her arm and neck carefully out of the way, tucking his arm under her neck and gently cradling her. He began to croon to her and pet her, smoothing her hair off her forehead, lightly trailing his fingers over her face. He seemed proprietary and overly cautious, sober and vigilant, as if at any moment she might disappear in a puff of smoke.

"How long have I been here?" Ember asked, soothed by his ministrations. Her lids closed and she sighed, filled with quiet joy.

She was alive. Christian was alive. Caesar was dead.

Everything was going to be okay.

"Too long," he whispered, brushing a feather-light kiss to her temple. "Five days that felt like five thousand." He chuckled. "And the doctors are getting pretty sick of me. I'm sure they'll be glad to see you're awake so they can send us home."

She cocked an eyebrow at him, and he said, "I haven't exactly been patient with them. The terms 'overbearing' and 'maniac' have been used on more than one occasion."

And why didn't that surprise her?

His stomach rumbled a loud complaint and Ember weakly scolded him, "When was the last time you ate?" Only it came out as, " 'En 'as th' las' time y'ate?"

"Don't know. Doesn't matter. All that matters is right here in my arms, right now." His voice dropped. "And if you ever try anything so stupid again I'll kill you. I can't live without you little firecracker—don't make me."

"Mmpf."

He petted her a while longer in silence until he murmured, "Dr. Flores called me."

Ember's eyes flew wide open. She glanced at him and he was staring at her with stern adoration.

"We're going to work on your issues *together*, you know that right?"

It was useless to argue, she knew that. So she simply nodded and tucked her head beneath his chin, burrowing into the space between his neck and shoulder. She inhaled, smelling his wonderful mix of warm spice and skin, and thought *home.*

Only she must have said it aloud because he chuckled again and whispered, "Wherever we're together, that's home, angel. Though, if you're open to it, I'd like to go back to Sommerley so the three of us can have a real home. Leander and Jenna really want to meet you, and I want you to meet them. And everyone. You're something of a legend with my kind now, the human who risked her life to save us all . . . "

"Not for them," she sighed into his neck. "For you. Did it for you. And England sounds good. Maybe I'll even teach you how to drive."

She felt his chest rise and fall with his deep exhalation. He tightened his arms around her and pressed a kiss to her forehead.

Though her mind was fuzzy, she thought of something and frowned. She lifted her head and focused on Christian's face. "The *three* of us? You want Asher to come, too?"

His smile was beautiful. He swallowed hard, and his eyes were bright with unshed tears. "No, angel. Not Asher. Someone else. Someone you'll love even more."

He moved his hand from where it had been stroking her arm, and spread his big palm gently on her belly.

Ember blinked at him. This brain swelling might turn out to be a problem after all, because she either wasn't hearing him right, or her brain was improperly processing what he was saying. She just shook her head in confusion.

"Our little miracle," he whispered, eyes shining with devotion. "I think he's even more stubborn than you are; he held on against all odds. He's a fighter . . . like his mama."

Something huge was rushing at Ember. Something so vast, bright, and impossible it didn't have a name, but it carried with it every hope, dream, and happy ending in the universe, in all of history. She didn't even dare draw a breath for fear of chasing it away.

Her eyes were wide, wide open, as wide open as they could go.

"No," she whispered as she stared into Christian's eyes. "It's not possible. The accident . . . the doctors told me—"

"Apparently they were wrong," he said with laughter in his eyes.

Pressure in her chest, crushing. Suddenly she couldn't breathe. Her eyes were wet. Her hands began to shake.

"So you're telling me . . . what you're saying is—"

"It's a boy," he gently said when she could no longer go on. "The doctors don't know yet because it's too early, but I do." He tapped his nose, smiling.

The beeping Ember had thought was the clock of eternity began to accelerate, chiming wildly in the silence of the room. It was a heartbeat monitor, and Christian sat up and looked at it, suddenly vibrating tension and worry.

"Are you all right? Are you hurting? Tell me what I can do, tell me what you need—"

"You," Ember sobbed, curling her hand around the front of his shirt and pulling him down beside her. "All I need is you."

He relaxed beside her, stretched out like a lazing lion, and cupped her face in his hand. She looked up at him through a prism of tears and he said, "Then we're both set, because nothing will ever separate me from you. Nothing."

He pressed his lips against hers and murmured, "Come what may."

Epilogue

In the early morning hours of March 31, three very important phone calls were made, by three very different men. All three calls would change the course of the future.

Each of these men was a leader among his kind. Each was driven, each was ambitious, each was heartless and cold.

And each of them was badly injured.

Two of them sustained serious injuries that would mar them forever. One man lost a leg, a hand, and a good portion of his sanity when he stepped on a land mine. Another was trapped by falling rock when a tunnel beneath a bunker collapsed but was saved from death by a pair of steel support beams that buckled but didn't break. He suffered shrapnel wounds from the explosion that triggered the collapse and lung damage from smoke inhalation. He would also develop crippling claustrophobia from being trapped in the blackness below ground for hours before rescue personnel finally dug him out.

The third man—who wasn't really a man at all—was so mangled and mutilated he was unrecognizable, even to the curious fish who swam up to investigate him, floating face down in the sea, just another piece of flotsam on the water.

It would take the first two men many months to heal from their injuries, to move forward with their lives as before, but it took the third man all of a few minutes before he healed and lifted his head, furiously coughing up sea water, physically right as rain.

The first man made his phone call while being transported to the local hospital in the back of an ambulance. Though in shock and suffering from severe blood loss, he still managed to convince the EMT to lend him a cell phone, and he dialed a number he knew by heart. There wasn't a live person on the end of that call—there never was—but a machine took his message, and it would be replayed later by the one it was intended for, who had the means to set the wheels of pursuit in motion.

His message was simply a license plate number, memorized just moments before he stepped on the mine.

The second man's call was made to the Vatican, to a private line only a handful of people in the world knew. When the phone was answered, he recited a verse in Latin from the gospel of Peter. "Be watchful; your adversary the devil prowls like a roaring lion, seeking someone to devour."

To which a voice on the other end replied, "But we shall devour him first."

Made from a payphone in the Port Vell marina, the phone call from the third man was collect, as he was nude and had no money. It was as succinct as the other two calls, and consisted of only three words, spoken as the high, shrieking whine of police sirens grew nearer.

"Drop The Hammer."

It was Easter Sunday in Barcelona, and the world would never be the same again.

ACKNOWLEDGMENTS

As always, I'd like to thank the wonderful team at Montlake Romance, including my editors Eleni Caminis and Maria Gomez, and the author relations, marketing, and proofreading and copyediting teams.

Marlene Stringer of Stringer Literary deserves special thanks for her continued support and sage advice, for taking a chance on an unknown author, and convincing a publisher to do so as well.

A deep bow goes to Melody Guy, who always gives such valuable feedback, and whose ideas make my books better.

To my readers, a warm and heartfelt thank you for purchasing this book, and for the wonderful enthusiasm you've shown for my work. I so appreciate you! I also sincerely thank the many bloggers who have so generously reviewed the Night Prowler books and spread the word about the *Ikati.*

To my very dear gay friends who were generous enough to answer intimate questions about being a gay man and how far we've come since Stonewall, I thank you and give you virtual hugs for your bravery and willingness to let me into the most private part of your lives. The Wednesday Night Book Club "ladies" were, in particular, beautifully open with me, and I love you for it. I'd also like to especially thank Anthony Vigliotta for "Carmen MiRambo," an idea which was originally his own, and he has the pictures to prove it.

Thank you to my parents, Jean and Jim, for staying married for nearly fifty years. You'd be surprised how much that means to me. I'm so grateful for your love, and the commitment you've shown each other.

And finally to my own personal Alpha, Jay, the man who is the bedrock on which the foundation of my life is built . . . thank you for every single thing you do each day to show me how much I am loved. Thirteen years ago, you showed me happily-ever-after isn't the end—it's just the beginning.

ABOUT THE AUTHOR

 J.T. Geissinger's debut novel, *Shadow's Edge*, was published in 2012 and was a #1 Amazon US and UK bestseller in both fantasy romance and romance series, and won the PRISM award for Best First Book. Her second book in the Night Prowler series, *Edge of Oblivion*, was a finalist for the prestigious RITA® award for Best Paranormal Romance from the Romance Writers of America. She lives in Los Angeles with her family and is currently at work on book six in the series. Visit her online at jtgeissinger.com